The *Roci* lay half-dressed in the vacuum. With the outer skin cut away and her inner hull shining fresh in the work lights, she looked small.

The scars of their adventures had, for the most part, been borne by the outer hull. Those scars were gone now, and only the deeper injuries remained. He couldn't see them from here, but he knew what they were. He'd been on the *Rocinante* as long as he'd been on any ship in his career, and he loved her better than any of them. Even than his first.

"I'll be back," he said to the ship, and as if in answer, a welding rig lit up at the curve of her drive cone, brighter for a moment than the unshielded sun in a Martian sky.

Also by James S. A. Corey

THE EXPANSE
Leviathan Wakes
Caliban's War
Abaddon's Gate
Cibola Burn
Nemesis Games
Babylon's Ashes

THE EXPANSE SHORT FICTION
The Butcher of Anderson Station
Gods of Risk
The Churn
Drive

BOOK FIVE OF THE EXPANSE

JAMES S. A. COREY

www.orbitbooks.net

This book is a work of fiction. Names, characters, places, and incidents are the product of the author's imagination or are used fictitiously. Any resemblance to actual events, locales, or persons, living or dead, is coincidental.

Cover design by Kirk Benshoff
Cover illustration by Daniel Dociu

Orbit
Hachette Book Group
1290 Avenue of the Americas
New York, NY 10104
orbitbooks.net

First Edition: June 2015
First Trade Paperback Edition: May 2016

Orbit is an imprint of Hachette Book Group.
The Orbit name and logo are trademarks of Little, Brown Book Group Limited.

The Library of Congress has cataloged the hardcover edition as follows:

Corey, James S. A.
Nemesis games / James S.A. Corey.—First edition.
pages ; cm.—(The expanse ; book five)
ISBN 978-0-316-21758-3 (hardback)—ISBN 978-0-316-21759-0 (ebook)—ISBN 978-1-4789-0395-6 (downloadable audio edition)—ISBN 978-0-316-38729-3 (autographed edition)—ISBN 978-1-4789-3380-9 (audio book CD)
I. Title.
PS3601.B677N46 2015
813'.6—dc23

2015007979

ISBN: 978-0-316-33471-6 (trade paperback)

Printed in the United States of America

LSC-C

10 9 8 7 6 5 4 3 2

To Ben Cook, without whom

NEMESIS
GAMES

Prologue: Filip

The twin shipyards of Callisto stood side by side on the hemisphere of the moon that faced permanently away from Jupiter. The sun was only the brightest star in the endless night, the wide smear of the Milky Way brighter by far. All along the ridges of the craters, harsh white work lights glared down onto buildings, loaders, scaffolds. The ribs of half-built ships arced up over the regolith of stone dust and ice. Two shipyards, one civilian and one military, one Earth-based and one owned by Mars. Both protected by the same anti-meteor rail-gun defenses, both dedicated to building and repairing the vessels that would take humanity out to the new worlds beyond the rings when and if the fight on Ilus got worked out.

Both in a lot more trouble than they guessed.

Filip slid forward, the rest of his team close behind him. The suit LEDs had been gouged out, the ceramic plating scoured until nothing was smooth enough to cast a reflection. Even the heads-up display was dimmed almost to the point of invisibility. The voices in Filip's ears—ship traffic, security feeds, civilian chatter—were picked up on passive. He listened while transmitting nothing in return. The targeting laser strapped to his back was powered down. He and his team were shadows among shadows. The faint countdown timer in the left of his visual field passed the fifteen-minute mark. Filip patted air barely thicker than vacuum with an open palm, the Belters' physical idiom to move forward slowly. Around him, his team followed.

High in the void above them, too distant to see, the Martian naval vessels guarding the shipyard spoke in clipped, professional tones. As thinly as their fleet had been stretched, they had only two ships in orbit. Probably only two. It was possible that there were others hidden in the black, hugging their own waste heat and shielded from radar. Possible but unlikely. And life, as Filip's father said, was risky work.

Fourteen minutes, thirty seconds. Two secondary timers appeared beside it, one with a forty-five second counter, the other with two minutes.

"Transport ship *Frank Aiken*, you are cleared to approach."

"Message received, *Carson Lei*," Cyn's familiar growl came. Filip could hear the old Belter's smile in the words. "Coyos sabe best ai sus bebe come we low?"

Somewhere up there, the *Frank Aiken* was painting the Martian ships with innocuous ranging lasers set at the same frequency as the one strapped to Filip's own back. When the Martian comm officer spoke, there was nothing in his voice that showed fear.

"Don't copy you, *Frank Aiken*. Please repeat."

"Sorry, sorry." Cyn laughed. "You fine upstanding gentlefolk know any good bars a poor Belter crew could get a drink once we get to the surface?"

"Can't help you, *Frank Aiken*," the Martian said. "Maintain course."

"Sabez sa. Solid as a stone, straight as a bullet, us."

Filip's crew topped the crater ridge, looking down at the no-man's-land of the Martian military yard; it was just as he had expected it to be. He picked out the warehouses and supply depots. He pulled off the targeting laser, set the base into the dirty ice, and powered it up. The others, spread along the line wide enough that none of the guards would be out of all their sight lines, did the same. The lasers were old, the tracking platforms strapped to them salvaged from a dozen different sources. Before the tiny red LED on its base turned green, the first of his two secondary timers reached zero.

The security alert tritone sounded on the civilian channel, followed by a woman's anxious voice.

"We've got a runaway loading mech on the field. It's...ah, shit. It's heading for the meteor array."

The panic and alarm cascaded in his ears as Filip moved his team along the rim of the crater. Thin puffs of dust rose around them and didn't fall, widening instead like a mist. The loader mech, failing to respond to overrides, trundled across the no-man's-land and into the wide eyes of the meteor defense cannons, blinding them, if only for a few minutes. Four Martian marines emerged from their bunker, as protocol demanded. Their powered armor let them slide over the surface like they were skating on ice. Any one of them could kill his whole team and suffer nothing worse than a moment's pity. Filip hated them all and each one individually on principle. The repair crews were already scrambling for the damaged array. The whole thing would be back in order within the hour.

Twelve minutes, forty-five seconds.

Filip paused, looking back at his team. Ten volunteer soldiers, the best the Belt had to offer. Apart from himself, none of them knew why the mission to raid the Martian supply depot was important or what it was leading to. All of them ready to die if he told them to, because of who he was. Because of who his father was. Filip felt it in his belly and in his throat. Not fear, pride. It was pride.

Twelve minutes, thirty-five seconds. Thirty-four. Thirty-three. The lasers they'd placed came to life, painting the four marines, the bunker with the backup team, the perimeter fences, the workshops, and the barracks. The Martians turned, their armor so sensitive that even the gentle caress of invisible beams of light was noticed. As they moved they lifted their weapons. Filip saw one recognize the team, gun shifting away from the lasers and toward them. Toward him.

He caught his breath.

Eighteen days before, a ship—Filip didn't even know which one—out in the Jovian system somewhere had made a hard burn, topping out at ten, maybe fifteen gs. At the nanosecond specified by the computers, the ship had released a few dozen lengths of tungsten with four disposable, short-burn rockets at the center of mass and cheap single-frequency sensors tied to them. They were barely complicated enough to be called machines. Six-year-old children built things more sophisticated every day, but accelerated as they were to one hundred and fifty kilometers per second, they didn't need to be complex. Just shown where to go.

In the time it took for the signal to propagate from Filip's eye, down his optic nerve, and into his visual neocortex, it was over. He was aware of the thump, of the ejecta plumes where the marines had been, of the two brief new stars that had been warships overhead, only after the enemy was dead. He changed his suit radio to active.

"Ichiban," he said, proud that his voice was so calm.

Together, they bounced down the crater's side, shuffling their feet. The Martian shipyards were like something from a dream, plumes of flame rising from the shattered workshops as the stored volatile gasses vented as fire. Soft snow billowed from the barracks as the released atmosphere sprayed out and froze. The marines were gone, their bodies ripped apart and scattered. A cloud of dust and ice filled the crater, only the guidance of his HUD showing him where the targets were.

Ten minutes, thirteen seconds.

Filip's team divided. Three went to the middle of the open space, finding a place large enough to begin unfolding the thin black carbon structure of the evacuation scaffold. Two others unstrapped recoilless machine pistols, ready to shoot anyone who emerged from the rubble. Two more ran toward the armory, and three came with him, to the supply sheds. The building loomed up from the dust, stark and forbidding. The access doors were shut. A loading mech lay toppled on its side, the driver dead or dying. His tech specialist went to the door controls, prying the housing open with a powered cutting bar.

Nine minutes, seven seconds.

"Josie," Filip said.

"Trabajan, sa sa?" Josie replied curtly.

"I know you're working," Filip said. "If you can't open it—"

The great access doors shifted, shuddered, and rose. Josie turned back and flicked the suit's helmet lights on so that Filip could see the expression on his craggy face. They went into the warehouse. Towers of curved ceramic and steel made great piles, denser than mountains. Hair-thin wire hundreds of kilometers long stood on plastic spools taller than Filip. Massive printers waited, ready to fashion the plates that would fit together over the emptiness, define a volume and make it a bubble of air and water and complex organics that passed for a human environment. Emergency lights flickered, giving the wide space the eerie glow of disaster. He moved forward. He didn't remember drawing his gun, but it was in his hand. Miral, not Josie, was strapping into a loader.

Seven minutes.

The red-and-white strobe of the first emergency vehicles flickered in the chaos of the shipyard, the light coming from everywhere and nowhere. Filip shuffled down the rows of welding rigs and metal printers. Tubs of steel and ceramic dust finer than talcum. Spiral-core mounts. Layers of Kevlar and foam strike armor piled up like the biggest bed in the solar system. In one open corner of the space, an entire Epstein drive lay disassembled like the universe's most complex jigsaw puzzle. Filip ignored it all.

The air wasn't thick enough to carry the sound of gunfire. His HUD brought up a fast-mover alert in the same moment that a bright patch appeared on the steel beam to his right. Filip dropped, his body seeping down in the microgravity more slowly than it would have under burn. The Martian jumped down the aisle. Not the powered armor of the guards, but a technical exoskeleton. Filip aimed for the center of mass and emptied half his clip. The rounds flared as they left the muzzle, burning their own fuel, tracing lines of fire and red-gray exhaust through the thin Callistan air. Four hit the Martian, and gouts of blood drifted down in a frozen red snowfall. The exoskeleton flipped to emergency alert status, its LEDs turning a grim amber. On some frequency, it was reporting to the yard's emergency services that something terrible had happened. Its mindless devotion to duty was almost funny, in context.

Miral's voice was soft in his ear. "Hoy, Filipito. Sa boîte sa palla?"

It took Filip a moment to find the man. He was in his loader, his blackened vacuum suit becoming one with the huge mech as if they'd been made for each other. Only the dim split circle symbol of the Outer Planets Alliance still just visible beneath the grime marked Miral as anything but an ill-kept Martian mech driver. The canisters he'd been talking about were still lashed to their pallets. A thousand liters each, four of them. On the curving face: High Density Resonance Coating. The energy-absorbent coating helped Martian military ships avoid detection. Stealth tech. He'd found it. A fear he hadn't known he was carrying fell away.

"Yes," Filip said. "That's it."

Four minutes, thirty-seven seconds.

The loading mech's whirring was distant, the sound carried by the vibrations in the structure's flooring more than the thin atmosphere. Filip and Josie moved toward the doors. The flashing lights were brighter, and had taken on a kind of directionality. Filip's suit radio filtered through frequencies crowded with screaming voices and security alerts. The Martian military was ordering back the relief vehicles from the civilian shipyard, concerned that the first responders might be terrorists and enemies in disguise. Which was fair. Under other circumstances, they might have been. Filip's HUD had the outlines of the buildings, the half-built evac scaffold, its best guess on the locations of the vehicles given IR and light trace data too subtle for Filip's eyes. He felt like he was walking through a schematic drawing, everything defined by edges, all surfaces merely implied. As he shuffled onto the regolith, a deep shudder passed through the ground. A detonation, maybe. Or a building finally completing its long, slow collapse. Miral's loading mech appeared in the open door, backlit by the warehouse lights. The canisters in its claws were anonymous and black. Filip moved toward the scaffold, switching to their encrypted channel as he shuffled.

"Status?"

"Small trouble," Aaman said. He was with the scaffold. Filip's mouth flooded with the metal taste of fear.

"No such thing here, coyo," he said, fighting to sound calm. "What is it?"

"Some of the ejecta crap's fouling the scaffold. I've got grit in the joints."

Three minutes, forty seconds. Thirty-nine.

"I'm coming," Filip said.

Andrew's voice cut in. "We're taking fire in the armory, bosslet."

Filip ignored the diminutive. "How much?"

"Plenty some," Andrew said. "Chuchu's down, and I'm pretty pinned. Might need a hand."

"Hang tight," Filip said, his mind racing. His two guards stood by the evac scaffold, ready to shoot anybody that wasn't them. The three builders were struggling with a brace. Filip jumped over to them, catching himself on the black frame. On the line, Andrew grunted.

Once he saw the stuck connector, black grit fouling it, the problem was clear. In atmosphere, it would have just taken a hard breath to clean it. Not an option here. Aaman was digging frantically with a blade, flipping out tiny bit after tiny bit, trying to empty the thin, complex channels where the metal fit together.

Three minutes.

Aaman hauled the brace into place and tried to force the connection. It was close, very close, but when he tugged back, it came apart. Filip saw the man cursing, flecks of spit dotting the inside of his faceplate. If they'd only brought a can of air, Filip thought...

Which, of course, they had.

He plucked the knife from Aaman's hand and shoved the blade into his suit's wrist where the articulation made it thinnest. A bright pain told him he'd gone just a little too far. That was fine. His suit alarm blinked into place, and he ignored it. He leaned forward, pressing the tiny opening in his suit to the clogged connector, the escaping air scattering the dirt and ice. A single drop of blood spat out, freezing into a perfect crimson sphere and bouncing away from the material. He stepped back, and Aaman slid the connection together. When he tugged this time, it held. The injured suit sealed the hole as soon as he pulled the knife out.

Filip turned back. Miral and Josie had cut the canisters free of their pallets and strapped one to the scaffold. The flashing emergency lights had dimmed, the relief vehicles passing them by in the haze and confusion. Heading, likely, for the firefight at the armory. It was where Filip would have seen the greatest threat too, if he hadn't known better.

"Bosslet," Andrew said, his voice thin and anxious. "Cutting close here."

"No preoccupes," Filip said. "Ge gut."

One of the two guards put a hand on his shoulder. "You want me to go fix that?" she asked. *Should I go save them?*

Filip lifted a fist and shook it gently back and forth. No. She stiffened when she understood what he was saying, and for a moment, he thought she'd disobey. Her choice. Mutiny now was its own punishment. Josie slid the last canister into place, tightened down the straps. Aaman and his people fit the last brace in position.

One minute, twenty seconds.

"Bosslet!" Andrew screamed.

"I'm sorry, Andrew," Filip said. There was a moment of stunned silence and then a stream of obscenity and invective. Filip changed frequencies. The emergency services for the military shipyards were shouting less. A woman's voice speaking crisp, calm German was delivering commands with the almost-bored efficiency of someone well accustomed to crisis, and the voices answering her took their professionalism from hers. Filip pointed to the scaffold. Chuchu and Andrew were dead. Even if they weren't dead, they were dead. Filip pulled himself into his position on the scaffold, fitted the straps around his waist and under his crotch, across his chest, then laid his head back against the thick padding.

Fifty-seven seconds.

"Niban," he said.

Nothing happened.

He turned his radio back to the encrypted channel. Andrew was weeping now. Wailing.

"Niban! Andale!" Filip shouted.

The evac scaffold bucked under him, and he suddenly had weight. Four chemical rockets under high burn lit the ground below him, scattering the empty pallets and knocking Miral's abandoned loading mech on its back. Acceleration pushed the blood down into Filip's legs, and his vision narrowed. The sounds of the radio grew thinner, more distant, and his consciousness flickered, stuttered. His suit clamped down on his thighs like being squeezed by a giant, forcing the blood back up out of them. His mind returned a bit.

Below, the crater was an oblong blister of dust on the face of the moon. Lights moved in it. The towers at the crater's edge had gone dark, but flickered now as the systems tried to reboot. The shipyards of Callisto reeled like a drunkard, or a person struck in the head.

The countdown timer slid to two seconds, then one.

At zero, the second strike came. Filip didn't see the rock hit. As with the tungsten slugs, it was going much too fast for mere human sight, but he saw the dust cloud jump like someone had surprised it, and then the vast shock wave, blooming out so powerfully that even in the barely-extant atmosphere it was visible.

"Brace," Filip said, though there was no need. Everyone on the scaffold was already braced. In a thicker atmosphere, it would have been death for all of them. Here, it was little worse than a bad storm. Aaman grunted.

"Problem?" Filip asked.

"Pinché rock holed my foot," Aaman said. "Hurts."

Josie answered. "Gratia sa didn't get your cock, coyo."

"Not complaining," Aaman said. "No complaints."

The scaffold rockets exhausted themselves; the acceleration gravity dropped away. Below them, death had come to the shipyards. There were no lights now. Not even fires burning. Filip turned his gaze to the bright smear of stars, the galactic disk shining on them all. One of those lights wasn't a star, but the exhaust plume of the *Pella*, coming to collect its wayward crew. Except Chuchu. Except Andrew. Filip wondered why he didn't feel bad about the loss of two people under his command. His first command. His proof that he could handle a real mission, with real stakes, and come through clean.

He didn't mean to speak. Maybe he didn't. Maybe it was only a sigh that passed his lips. Miral chuckled.

"No shit, Filipito," the older man said. And then, a moment later, "Feliz cumpleaños, sabez?"

Filip Inaros lifted his hands in thanks. It was his fifteenth birthday.

Chapter One: Holden

A year after the Callisto attacks, almost three years after he and his crew had headed out for Ilus, and about six days after they'd gotten back, James Holden floated next to his ship and watched a demolition mech cut her apart. Eight taut cables anchored the *Rocinante* to the walls of her berth. Only one of many in the Tycho Station repair dock, and the repair section was only one of many in the massive construction sphere. Around them in the kilometer-wide volume of the sphere a thousand other projects were going on, but Holden only had eyes for his ship.

The mech finished cutting and pulled off a large section of the outer hull. Beneath lay the skeleton of the ship, sturdy ribs surrounded by a tangled confusion of cabling and conduit, and under that, the second skin of the inner hull.

"Yeah," Fred Johnson said, floating next to him, "you kind of fucked her up."

Fred's words, flattened and distorted by the comm system of their vacuum suits, were still a punch to the gut. That Fred, the nominal leader of the Outer Planets Alliance and one of the three most powerful people in the solar system, was taking a personal interest in his ship's condition should have been reassuring. Instead, Holden felt like he had a father checking over his homework to make sure he hadn't screwed anything up too badly.

"Interior mount's bent," a third voice said over the comm. A sour-faced man named Sakai, the new chief engineer at Tycho after the death of Samantha Rosenberg at what everyone was now calling the Slow Zone Incident. Sakai was monitoring the repairs from his office nearby through the mech's suite of cameras and x-ray scanners.

"How did you do that?" Fred pointed at the rail-gun housing along the ship's keel. The barrel of the gun ran nearly the entire length of the ship, and the support struts that attached it to the frame were visibly buckling in places.

"So," Holden said, "have I ever told you the one about the time we used the *Roci* to drag a heavy freighter to a higher planetary orbit using our rail gun as a reaction drive?"

"Yeah, that's a good one," Sakai said without humor. "Some of those struts might be fixable, but I'm betting we're going to find enough micro-fracturing in the alloy that replacing them all is the better bet."

Fred whistled. "That won't be cheap."

The OPA leader was the *Rocinante* crew's on-again, off-again patron and sponsor. Holden hoped they were in the on-again phase of the rocky relationship. Without a preferred client discount, the ship's repair was going to get noticeably more expensive. Not that they couldn't afford it.

"Lots of badly patched holes in the outer hull," Sakai continued. "Inner looks okay from here, but we'll go over it with a fine-toothed comb and make sure it's sealed."

Holden started to point out that the trip back from Ilus would have involved a lot more asphyxiation and death if the inner hull hadn't been airtight, but stopped himself. There was no reason to antagonize the man who was now responsible for keeping his ship flying. Holden thought of Sam's impish smile and habit of tempering her criticism with silliness, and felt something clench behind his breastbone. It had been years, but the grief could still sneak up on him.

"Thank you," he said instead.

"This won't be fast," Sakai replied. The mech jetted off to another part of the ship, anchored itself on magnetic feet, and began cutting another section of the outer hull away with a bright flash.

"Let's move to my office," Fred said. "At my age, you can only take an e-suit so long."

Many things about ship repair were made easier by the lack of gravity and atmosphere. The trade-off was forcing technicians to wear environment suits while they worked. Holden took Fred's words to mean the old man needed to pee and hadn't bothered with the condom catheter.

"Okay, let's go."

Fred's office was large for something on a space station, and smelled of old leather and good coffee. The captain's safe on the wall was done in titanium and bruised steel, like a prop from an old movie. The wall screen behind his desk showed a view of three skeletal ships under construction. Their design was large, bulky, and functional. Like sledgehammers. They were the beginnings of a custom built OPA naval fleet. Holden knew why the alliance felt the need to create its own armed defensive force, but given everything that had happened over the past few years, he couldn't help but feel like humanity kept learning the wrong lessons from its traumas.

"Coffee?" Fred asked. At Holden's nod, he began puttering around the coffee station on a side table, fixing two cups. The one he held out to Holden had a faded insignia on it. The split circle of the OPA, worn almost to invisibility.

Holden took it, waved at the screen, and said, "How long?"

"Six months is our current projection," Fred said, then sat in his chair with an old man's grunt. "Might as well be forever. A year and a half from now human social structures in this galaxy will be unrecognizable."

"The diaspora."

"If that's what you want to call it," Fred said with a nod. "I call it the land rush. A whole lot of covered wagons heading for the promised land."

Over a thousand worlds open for the taking. People from every planet and station and rock in the solar system rushing to grab a piece. And back in the home system, three governments racing to build enough warships to control it all.

A welding array flared to life on the skin of one of the ships so brightly that the monitor dimmed in response.

"If Ilus was anything, it was a warning that a lot of people are going to die," Holden said. "Was anyone listening?"

"Not really. You familiar with the land rush in North America?"

"Yeah," Holden said, then took a sip of Fred's coffee. It was delicious. Earth grown, and rich. The privileges of rank. "I got your covered wagon reference. I grew up in Montana, you know. That frontier shit is still the story the people there tell about themselves."

"So you know that the mythology of manifest destiny hides a lot of tragedy. Many of those covered wagons never made it. And more than a few of the people who did wound up as cheap labor for the railroads, mines, and rich farmers."

Holden drank his coffee and watched the ship construction. "Not to mention all the people who were living there before the covered wagons showed up and gave everyone a nifty new plague. At least our version of galactic destiny doesn't displace anything more advanced than a mimic lizard."

Fred nodded. "Maybe. Seems that way so far. But not all thirteen hundred systems have good surveys yet. Who knows what we'll find."

"Killer robot things and continent-sized fusion reactors just waiting for someone to flip the switch so they can blow half the planet into space, if memory serves."

"Based on our sample of one. It could get weirder."

Holden shrugged and finished off his coffee. Fred was right. There was no way to know what might be waiting on all of those worlds. No telling what dangers lay in store for the would-be colonists rushing to claim them.

"Avasarala isn't happy with me," Holden said.

"No, she is not," Fred agreed. "But I am."

"Come again?"

"Look, the old lady wanted you to go out there and show everyone in the solar system how bad it all was. Scare them into waiting for the government to tell them it was okay. Put the control back in her hands."

"It was pretty scary," Holden said. "Was I not clear on that?"

"Sure. But it was also survivable. And now Ilus is getting ready to send freighters full of lithium ore to the markets here. They'll be rich. They may wind up being the exception, but by the time everyone figures that out, people will be on all those worlds looking for the next gold mine."

"Not sure what I could have done differently."

"Nothing," Fred agreed. "But Avasarala and Prime Minister Smith on Mars and the rest of the political wonks want to control this. And you've made sure they can't."

"So why are you happy?"

"Because," Fred said, his grin wide, "I'm not trying to control it. Which is why I'll wind up in control of it. I'm playing the long game."

Holden got up and poured himself another cup of Fred's delicious coffee. "Yeah, you're going to need to parse that for me," he said, leaning against the wall next to the coffee pot.

"I've got Medina Station, a self-sustaining craft that everyone going through the rings has to go past, handing out seed packs and emergency shelters to any ship that needs them. We're selling potting soil and water filters at cost. Any colony that survives is going to do so in part because we helped them. So when it comes time to organize some sort of galactic governing body, who are they going to turn to? The people who want to enforce hegemony at the barrel of a gun? Or the folks who were and are there to help out in a crisis?"

"They turn to you," Holden said. "And that's why you're building ships. You need to look helpful at the beginning when everyone needs help, but when they start looking for a government, you want to look strong."

"Yes," Fred said, leaning back in his chair. "The Outer Planets Alliance has always meant everything past the Belt. That's still true. It's just...expanded a bit."

"It can't be that simple. No way Earth and Mars just sit back and let you run the galaxy because you handed out tents and bag lunches."

"Nothing ever is," Fred admitted. "But that's where we'll start. And as long as I own Medina Station, I control the center of the board."

"Did you actually *read* my report?" Holden asked, not able to keep all the disbelief out of his voice.

"I'm not underestimating the dangers left on those worlds—"

"Forget what got left behind," Holden said. He put down his half-empty coffee cup and stalked across the room to lean across Fred's desk. The old man sat back with a frown. "Forget the robots and railroad systems that still work after being powered down for a billion years or so. The exploding reactors. Forget lethal slugs and microbes that crawl into your eyes and blind you."

"How long is this list?"

Holden ignored him. "The thing you should be remembering is the magic bullet that stopped it all."

"The artifact was a lucky find for you, given what was—"

"No, it wasn't. It was the scariest fucking answer to Fermi's paradox I can think of. Do you know why there aren't any Indians in your Old West analogy? Because they're already dead. The whatever-they-were that built all that got a head start and used their protomolecule gate builder to kill all the rest. And that's not even the scary part. The really frightening part is that something *else* came along, shot the first guys in the back of the head, and left their corpses scattered across the galaxy. The thing we should be asking is, who fired the magic bullet? And are they going to be okay with us taking all of the victims' stuff?"

Fred had given the crew two suites in the management housing level of Tycho Station's habitation ring. Holden and Naomi shared one, while Alex and Amos lived in the other, though in practice that usually just meant they slept there. When the boys weren't partaking of Tycho's many entertainment options, they seemed to spend all their time in Holden and Naomi's apartment.

When Holden came in, Naomi was sitting in the dining area scrolling through something complex on her hand terminal. She smiled at him without looking up. Alex was sitting on the couch in their living room. The wall screen was on, the graphics and talking heads of a newsfeed playing, but the sound was muted and the pilot's head lay back and his eyes were closed. He snored quietly.

"Now they're sleeping here too?" Holden asked, sitting down across the table from Naomi.

"Amos is picking up dinner. How did your thing go?"

"You want the bad news or the worse news?"

Naomi finally looked up from her work. She cocked her head to one side and narrowed her eyes at him. "Did you get us fired again?"

"Not this time. The *Roci*'s pretty beat up. Sakai says—"

"Twenty-eight weeks," Naomi said.

"Yeah. Have you bugged my terminal?"

"I'm looking at the spreadsheets," she said, pointing at her screen. "Got them an hour ago. He's— Sakai's pretty good."

Not as good as Sam hung in the air between them, unspoken. Naomi looked back down at the table, hiding behind her hair.

"So, yeah, that's the bad news," Holden said. "Half a year of downtime, and I'm still waiting for Fred to come out and say that he's paying for it. Or some of it. Any of it, really."

"We're still pretty flush. The UN's payment came through yesterday."

Holden nodded the comment away. "But forgetting money for a minute, I still can't get anyone to listen to me when it comes to the artifact."

Naomi gave him a Belter shrug of her hands. "Because *this* time it would be different? They've never listened before."

"Just once I'd like to be rewarded for my optimistic view of humanity."

"I made coffee," she said, pointing at the kitchen with a tilt of her head.

"Fred gave me some of his, which was good enough that I am ruined for lesser coffees from now on. Yet another way in which my meeting with him was unsatisfying."

The door to the apartment slid open, and Amos stomped in carrying a pair of large sacks. A curry and onion scent filled the air around him.

"Chow," he said, then dumped the bags on the table in front of Holden. "Hey, Cap'n, when do I get my ship back?"

"Is that food?" Alex said in a loud, groggy voice from the living room. Amos didn't answer; he was already taking foam cartons out of the bags and setting them around the table. Holden had thought he was too annoyed to eat, but the spicy smell of Indian food changed his mind.

"Not for a long time," Naomi said to Amos around a mouthful of bean curd. "We bent the mount."

"Shit," Amos said, sitting and grabbing a pair of chopsticks. "I leave you guys alone for a couple weeks and you fuck my girl up."

"Alien superweapons were used," Alex said, walking into the

room, sleep-sweaty hair standing out from his skull in every direction. "The laws of physics were altered, mistakes were made."

"Same shit, different day," Amos replied and handed the pilot a carton of curried rice. "Turn the sound up. That looks like Ilus."

Naomi turned up the sound on the video feed, and the voice of a newscaster filled the apartment. "—partial power restored, but sources on the ground say this setback will—"

"Is that real chicken?" Alex asked, grabbing at one of the cartons. "Splurgin' a bit, are we?"

"Shush," Amos said. "They're talking about the colony."

Alex rolled his eyes, but said nothing as he piled spicy strips of chicken on his plate. "—in other news, a draft report detailing the investigation into last year's attack on the Callisto shipyards was leaked this week. While the text is not finalized, the early reports suggest that a splinter faction of the Outer Planets Alliance was involved, and places blame for the high casualty—"

Amos shut off the sound with an angry stab at the table's controls. "Shit, wanted to hear more about what's going on with Ilus, not some dumbass OPA cowboys getting themselves blown up."

"I wonder if Fred knows who was behind that," Holden said. "The OPA hardliners are having trouble getting over their 'us against the solar system' theology."

"What did they want there anyway?" Alex said. "Callisto didn't have any of the heavy munitions. No nukes. Nothing worth a raid like that."

"Oh, now we're expecting this shit to make sense?" Amos asked. "Gimme that naan."

Holden sighed and leaned back in his chair. "I know it makes me a naïve idiot, but after Ilus I actually thought we might get a moment's peace. No one needing to blow anyone else up."

"This is what that looks like," Naomi said, then stifled a burp and put her chopsticks down. "Earth and Mars are in a prickly detente, the legitimate wing of the OPA is governing instead of fighting. The colonists on Ilus are working with the UN instead of everyone shooting each other. This is as good as it gets. Can't expect everyone to be on the same page. We're still humans after all. Some percentage of us are always going to be assholes."

"Truer words were never spoken, boss," Amos said.

They finished eating and sat in companionable silence for several minutes. Amos pulled beers out of the small refrigerator and handed them around. Alex picked his teeth with his pinky fingernail. Naomi went back to her repair projections.

"So," she said after a few minutes poring over the numbers, "the good news is that even if the UN and the OPA decide that we're responsible for our own repair bills, we'll be able to cover them with just what we have in the ship's emergency fund."

"Lots of work flyin' colonists out through the rings," Alex said. "When we're flyin' again."

"Yeah, because we can stuff so much compost in our tiny cargo hold," Amos said with a snort. "Plus, broke-as-hell-and-desperate is maybe not the customer base we should be chasing."

"Let's face it," Holden said, "if things keep going the way they are, finding work for a private warship may get pretty tough."

Amos laughed. "Let me get a preemptive I-told-you-so in here. Since when that turns out not to be true, like it always does, I might not be there to say it."

Chapter Two: Alex

The thing Alex Kamal liked most about the long haul was how it changed the experience of time. The weeks—sometimes months—spent on the burn were like stepping out of history into some small, separate universe. Everything narrowed down to the ship and the people in it. For long stretches, there would be nothing but the basic maintenance work to do, and so life lost all its urgency. Everything was working according to the plan, and the plan was for nothing critical to happen. Traveling through the vacuum of space gave him an irrational sense of peace and well-being. It was why he could do the job.

He'd known other people, usually young men and women, whose experience was different. Back when he'd been in the Navy there had been a pilot who'd done a lot of work in the inner planets, running between Earth, Luna, and Mars. He'd transferred in for a trip out to the Jovian moons under Alex. Just about the time an inner planet run would have ended, the young man started falling apart: getting angry over trivial slights, eating too much or not at all, passing restlessly through the ship from command center to engine room and back again like a tiger pacing its cage. By the time they'd reached Ganymede, the ship's doctor and Alex agreed to start putting sedatives in the guy's food just to keep things from getting out of hand. At the end of the mission, Alex had recommended the pilot never be assigned a long run again. Some kinds of pilots couldn't be trained as much as tested for.

Not that there weren't stresses and worries that he carried with him. Ever since the death of the *Canterbury*, Alex had carried a certain amount of baseline anxiety. With just the four of them, the *Rocinante* was structurally undercrewed. Amos and Holden were two strong masculine personalities that, if they ever locked horns, could blow the crew dynamic apart. The captain and the XO were lovers, and if they ever broke up, it would mean the end of more than just the job. It was the same sort of thing he'd always worried about, whatever crew he was with. With the *Roci*, it had been the same worries for years now without any of them ever being how it went off the rails, and that in itself was a kind of stability. As it was, Alex always felt relieved to get to the end of a run and he always felt relieved to start the next one. Or if not *always*, at least *usually*.

The arrival at Tycho Station should have been a relief. The *Roci* was as compromised as Alex had ever seen her, and the shipyards at Tycho were some of the best in the system, not to mention the friendliest. The final disposition of their prisoner from New Terra was now soundly someone else's problem, and he was off the ship. The *Edward Israel*, the other half of the New Terran convoy, was burning its way safely sunward. The next six months were nothing but repair work and relaxation. By any rational standard, there should have been less to worry about.

"So what's bugging you?" Amos asked.

Alex shrugged, opened the little food refrigeration unit that the suite provided, closed it, shrugged again.

"Something's sure as shit bugging you."

"I know."

The lights had the yellow-blue clearness that mimicked early morning, but Alex hadn't slept. Or not much. Amos sat at the counter and poured himself a cup of coffee. "We're not doing one of those things where you need me to ask you a bunch of questions so you can get comfortable talking about your feelings, are we?"

Alex laughed. "That never works."

"So let's not do it."

On the burn, Holden and Naomi tended to fold in on each other, not that either of them noticed doing it. It was a natural pattern for lovers to take more comfort in one another than in the rest of the crew. If it had been different, Alex would have been worried about it. But it left him and Amos with mostly one another as company. Alex prided himself on being able to get along with almost anyone on a crew, and Amos was no exception. Amos was a man without subtext. When he said he needed some time alone, it was because he needed some time alone. When Alex asked if he wanted to come watch the newly downloaded neo-noir films out of Earth that he subscribed to, the answer was always and only a response to the question. There was no sense of backbiting, no social punishment or isolation games. It just was what it was, and that was it. Alex wondered sometimes what would have happened if Amos had been the one to die on the *Donnager*, and he'd spent the last few years with their old medic, Shed Garvey.

It probably wouldn't have gone as well. Or maybe Alex would have adjusted. Hard to know.

"I've been having dreams that...bother me," Alex said.

"Nightmares, like?"

"No. Good dreams. Dreams that are better than the real world. Where I feel bad waking up from them."

"Huh," Amos said thoughtfully and drank his coffee.

"Have you ever had dreams like that?"

"Nope."

"The thing is, Tali's in all of them."

"Tali?"

"Talissa."

"Your ex-wife."

"Yeah," Alex said. "She's always there and things are always… good. I mean, not like we're together. Sometimes I'm back on Mars. Sometimes she's on the ship. She's just present, and we're good, and then I wake up and she's not here and we aren't. And…"

Amos' brow lowered and his mouth rose, squeezing his face into something smaller and thoughtful.

"You want to hook back up with your ex?"

"No, I really don't."

"You horny?"

"No, they're not sex dreams."

"You're on your own, then. That's all I got."

"It started back there," Alex said, meaning on the other side of the rings, orbiting above New Terra. "She came up in conversation, and ever since then… I failed her."

"Yup."

"She spent years waiting on me, and I just wasn't the man I wanted to be."

"Nope. You want some coffee?"

"I really do," Alex said.

Amos poured a cup for him. The mechanic didn't add sugar, but knew to leave a third of the cup for cream. One of the little intimacies of crew life.

"I don't like how I left things with her," Alex said. It was a simple statement, and not revelation, but it had the weight of a confession.

"Nope," Amos agreed.

"There's a part of me that thinks this is a chance."

"This?"

"The *Roci* being in dry dock for so long. I could go to Mars, see her. Apologize."

"And then ditch her again in order to get back before the ship drive goes back online?"

Alex looked down into his coffee. "Leave things in a better place."

Amos' shrug was massive. "So go."

A flood of objections crowded his mind. The four of them hadn't been apart since they'd become a crew, and splitting the group now felt like bad luck. The repair crew on Tycho might need him or want him or make some change to the ship that he wouldn't know about until it became a critical point somewhere down the line. Or worse, leaving might mean never coming back. If the universe had proved anything in these last few years, it was that nothing was certain.

The chime of a hand terminal saved him. Amos fished the device out of his pocket, looked at it, tapped the screen, and scowled. "I'm going to need a little privacy now."

"Sure," Alex said. "Not a problem."

Outside their suite, Tycho Station stretched in long gentle curves. It was one of the crown jewels of the Outer Planets Alliance. Ceres was larger, and Medina Station held the weird null-zone between rings, but Tycho Station was what the OPA had taken pride in from the start. The wide sweeping lines, more like a sailing ship than any actual craft that she served, weren't functional. The station's beauty was a boast. Here are the minds that spun up Eros and Ceres; here is the shipyard that built the largest vessel in the history of humanity. The men and women who, not so many generations ago, had braved the abyss beyond Mars for the first time were smart and powerful enough to make this.

Alex made his way down a long promenade. The people who passed him were Belters, their bodies longer than Earth standard, their heads wider. Alex himself had grown up in the relatively low Martian gravity, but even he didn't quite match the physiology that a childhood rich in null g gave.

Plants grew in the empty spaces of the wide corridors, vines crawling up against the spin gravity as they would have against the normal pull on Earth. Children scampered through the halls, ditching school the way he had back in Londres Nova. He drank his coffee and tried to cultivate the peace of being on the burn. Tycho Station was just as artificial as the *Roci.* The vacuum outside its hull was no more forgiving. But the calm wouldn't come. Tycho Station wasn't his ship, wasn't his home. These people walking past him as he went to the common area and looked up through the massive and multilayered clear ceramic at the glittering spectacle of the shipyards weren't his family. And he kept wondering what Tali would have thought of all this. If she could have come to a place that saw the beauty in it the way he hadn't been able to with the life she'd wanted on Mars.

When he hit the bottom of his cup, he turned back. He ambled along with the flow of foot traffic, making way for the electric carts and exchanging the small, civilized courtesies in the polyglot linguistic catastrophe that was the Belter argot. He didn't think too much about where he was going until he got there.

The *Roci* lay half-dressed in the vacuum. With the outer skin cut away and her inner hull shining fresh in the work lights, she looked small. The scars of their adventures had, for the most part, been borne by the outer hull. Those scars were gone now, and only the deeper injuries remained. He couldn't see them from here, but he knew what they were. He'd been on the *Rocinante* as long as he'd been on any ship in his career, and he loved her better than any of them. Even than his first.

"I'll be back," he said to the ship, and as if in answer, a welding rig lit up at the curve of her drive cone, brighter for a moment than the unshielded sun in a Martian sky.

The suite Naomi and Holden shared was just down the corridor from the one where he and Amos slept, its door with the same homey fake wood texturing and the number set into the wall just as bright. Alex let himself in, stepping into the conversation already going on.

"—if you think it's called for," Naomi said, her voice coming from the suite's main room. "But I think the evidence is pretty strong that you cleaned the last of that out. I mean, Miller hasn't been back, has he?"

"No," Holden said, nodding to Alex. "But just the idea that we had some of that goo in the ship for so long and didn't even know it creeps me out. Doesn't it creep you out?"

Alex held out his coffee cup, and Holden took it and filled it automatically. No sugar, room for cream.

"It does," Naomi said, coming to the kitchen. "Just not enough to take the whole damned bulkhead out over it. The replacements are never as strong as the originals. You know that."

Alex had met Naomi Nagata back on the *Canterbury*. He could still see the rawboned, angry girl who Captain McDowell had introduced as their new junior engineer. She'd hidden behind her hair for almost a year. Now, she had the first few threads of white among the black. She stood taller, more at home in her own skin. Surer of herself and stronger than he would have guessed she could be. And Holden, the swaggering, self-impressed executive officer who swept into civilian work wearing his dishonorable discharge like a boast had become this man handing him the cream and cheerfully admitting the irrationality of his fears. Time had changed all of them, he supposed. Only he wasn't sure how he had been affected. Too close to the question, he guessed.

Except Amos. Nothing changed Amos.

"What about you, Alex?"

He grinned and let his Mariner Valley drawl thicken. "Well, shoot, I figure it didn't kill us when it was here, it ain't gonna kill us now it's gone."

"Fine," Holden said with a sigh.

"It'll save us money," Naomi said, "and we'll be better off."

"I know," Holden said. "But I'm still going to feel weird about it."

"Where's Amos?" Naomi asked. "Is he still catting around?"

"No," Alex said. "He hit the brothels hard enough to burn through his petty cash the first few days in port. Since then, we've just been passing the time."

"We'll need to find something to keep him busy while we're on Tycho," Holden said. "Hell, we'll need to find something to keep all of us busy."

"We could look for work on the station," Naomi said. "I don't know what they're hiring for."

"We've got offers from a half-dozen places for paid debriefings on New Terra," Holden said.

"So does every other person that came back through the Ring," Naomi said, laughter in her voice. "And the feed there and back still works."

"You're saying we shouldn't do it?" Holden said, his tone vaguely hurt.

"I'm saying I can find a lot of things I'd rather get paid for than talking about myself."

Holden deflated, just a little. "Fair point. But we're stuck here for a long time. We're going to have to do something."

Alex took a deep breath. Here it was. The moment. His resolve wavered. He poured the cream into the cup, the blackness of the coffee resolving into a gentle tan. The lump in his throat felt as big as an egg.

"So," he said. "I've…ah…I've been thinking about things—"

The suite door opened and Amos stepped in. "Hey, Cap'n. I'm gonna need some time off."

Naomi tilted her head, her brows coming together, but it was Holden who spoke.

"Time off?"

"Yeah, I got to go back to Earth for a little bit."

Naomi sat at the stool by the breakfast bar. "What's the matter?"

"Don't know," Amos said. "Maybe nothing, but I kinda need to go look to find out. Be sure. You know."

"Is anything wrong?" Holden asked. "Because if it's a thing, we can wait for the *Roci* to be fixed up, and we can all go together. I've been looking for an excuse to get Naomi back down to Earth so the family can meet her."

The annoyance that crossed the engineer's face was almost faster than Alex's refresh rate. Moments like that made him nervous. The way Holden could push Naomi past her comfort zone and not even know he was doing it. But she recovered even before Amos could speak.

"May have to keep looking for your excuse, Cap. There's a little time pressure on my thing. Lady I used to spend time with died. I just need to go make sure everything there's on the up-and-up."

"Oh, I'm so sorry," Naomi said at the same moment Holden said, "Taking care of her estate?"

"Sure, something like that," Amos said. "Anyway, I booked transport to Ceres and then down the well, but I need to cash out some of my shares for spending money while I'm there."

The room went still for a moment. "You're coming back, though," Naomi said.

"Plan to," Amos said. It struck Alex that the answer was more honest than a yes. Amos planned to, but things happened. In all the time they'd spent in all their runs on the *Cant* or the *Roci*, Alex had never heard Amos talk about his life back on Earth except in the most general terms. He wondered if it was because the past wasn't worth mentioning or was too painful to talk about. With Amos, it could have been both at the same time.

"Of course," Holden said. "Just tell me how much you need."

The negotiation was brief, the transfer made on their hand terminals. Amos grinned and slapped Alex on the shoulder.

"All right. You got the place to yourself."

"When are you shipping out?" Alex asked.

"'Bout an hour. I should go get in line."

"All right," Alex said. "Take care of yourself, partner."

"You bet," Amos said and was gone.

The three remaining crewmen of the *Roci* stood silently in the kitchen, Holden looking shocked, Naomi amused. Alex felt like he was about halfway between them.

"Well that was weird," Holden said. "You think he's going to be okay?"

"It's Amos," Naomi said. "I'm more worried about whoever he's going to check on."

"Fair point," Holden said, then hitched himself up to sit on the counter and faced Alex. "Anyway. You were saying you'd been thinking about something?"

Alex nodded. *I was thinking about how hard it is to break up family and about the family I broke up before, and that I need to see my ex-wife again and try to find some sort of resolution to who we were to each other and all the things we did.* Seemed kind of anticlimactic now.

"Well, seeing how we're going to be in dock for a good long time, I was thinking I might take a trip to Mars. Check in on the old digs."

"Okay," Holden said. "But you'll come back before the repairs are done, right?"

Alex smiled. "Plan to."

Chapter Three: Naomi

The Golgo table was set for opening throws, the first and second goals untouched and the field still empty. The throbbing bass line from the Blauwe Blome's main room was a vibration in the deck and a murmur that wasn't too loud to talk over. Naomi hefted the steel ball in her hand, feeling the subtle play between mass and weight, different at every gravity. Across from her, Malikah and her teammates from the repair crew waited. One of them was drinking a Blue Meanie, the bright azure fluid staining his mouth like lipstick. It was three years—no, four?—since Naomi had played a game of Golgo, and these people played every Thursday. Naomi hefted the ball again, sighed, and spun it. Instantly, the opposition balls sprang out to hold her short, matching her spin and trying to co-opt her throw.

It was the sort of response you played against a beginner. Naomi was rusty, but she wasn't a beginner. The table registered, ending the throw, and Naomi's marker appeared, well past the field's half mark. Her team cheered, Malikah's groaned. Everyone smiled. It was a friendly game. Not all of them were.

"Next up, next up!" one of Naomi's new teammates shouted, waving his wide, pale hand. His name was Pere or Paar. Something like that. She retrieved the steel ball and tossed it to him. He grinned at her, his eyes only flickering down her body and back. Poor little shit. Naomi stood back, and Malikah moved to stand with her.

"You still got it," Malikah said. She had a beautiful voice, the accents of Ceres Station mellowing the harsher tones of the deep Belt.

"Spent a lot of time playing it when I was here last," Naomi said. "You never forget what you did when you were young, right?"

"Even if you want to." Malikah laughed, and Naomi laughed with her.

Malikah lived in a set of rooms three levels down and thirty degrees spinward from the club. The last time Naomi had been in it, the walls had been draped with silk patterned in brown and gold and the air had been rich with the artificial sandalwood incense that wouldn't clog the air recyclers. Naomi had slept in a bag on the deck for two nights, falling asleep to recorded harp music and the murmuring voices of Malikah and Sam. Only Sam was dead now, and Naomi was back together with Jim, and humanity was heir to a thousand suns within a two-year burn. Being there, laughing with Malikah and the repair crews, Naomi couldn't tell if she was more astounded by how much things had changed or how little.

Malikah touched Naomi's shoulder, her brow furrowed. "Bist ajá?"

"Was thinking," Naomi said, falling into the rhythm of Belter slang only roughly. Golgo wasn't the only thing she was rusty with.

Malikah's mouth turned down at the corners even as the Golgo table erupted in shouts of glee and dismay. For a moment, Sam was there too. Not the actual woman with her red hair and cheerful obscenity and habit of using childish terms—boo-boo, owie—to describe things like meteoroid-breached hulls. Only the space where she had been, and the two women sharing the knowledge that someone was missing.

Paar-or-Pere passed the ball on to the next player—Sakai, the new chief engineer—while the opposing team clapped him mockingly on the back. Naomi moved forward to assess the damage. Being around Belters—just Belters—was weirdly comforting. She loved her crew, but they were two Earthers and a Martian. There were some conversations that she could never have with them.

She could tell when Jim arrived without turning around. The players across the table from her all looked past her as one. Their eyes went wide, and an air of excitement washed over them. No one said it, but they might as well have—*Hey! Look! It's James Holden!*

It was easy to forget that Jim was who he was. He'd started two wars, and played some role in ending them both. He'd captained the first human ship through the Ring, or the first one that survived anyway. He'd been on the alien base in the center of the slow zone and come back. He'd survived Eros Station and the death of the *Agatha King*. He'd been to New Terra, the first human colony on a nonhuman planet, and forged a weird, awkward peace there. It was almost embarrassing, seeing everyone react to that Holden: the one on the screens and in the newsfeeds. She knew Jim was nothing like that James Holden, but there was no point saying it. Some things stayed secrets even when you told them.

"Hello my love," Jim said, putting his arm around her. In his other hand, he had a grapefruit martini.

"For me?" she said, taking the cocktail.

"Hope so. I wouldn't drink it on a dare."

"Hoy, coyo!" Paar-or-Pere said, holding up the steel ball. "Want a throw?"

The laughter around the table was buoyant. Some of it was delight—*James Holden playing Golgo with us!*—and some was cruel—*Watch the big shot suck.* None of it had anything to do with the actual man. She wondered if he knew how much he changed the nature of a room just by walking into it. At a guess, he probably didn't.

"No," Jim said with a grin. "I'm terrible at this. Wouldn't know where to start."

Naomi leaned in toward Malikah. "I should go. Thank you so much for having me." It meant *I am grateful to you for letting me be here with other Belters like I belong.*

"You are todamas welcome, coya-mis," Malikah said. It meant, *Sam's death wasn't your fault, and if it was I forgive you.*

Naomi took Jim's elbow and let him steer her out to the main bar. The music rose as they passed through the doorway, light and sound joining in a sensory assault. On the dance floor, people moved together in pairs or in groups. There had been a time, long before she'd met Jim, when the idea of getting very, very drunk and throwing herself into the press of bodies would have been an attractive one. She could remember the girl she used to be with fondness, but it wasn't a youth she cared to recapture. She stood at the bar and finished her martini. It was too loud to talk, so she amused herself watching people notice Jim, the game of is-it-or-isn't-it in their expressions. Jim, for his part, was amiably bored. The idea that he was the center of attention was foreign to him. It was part of what she loved about him.

When her glass was empty, she put her hand on his, and they pressed out to the public corridor outside the club. Men and women waiting to get in—Belters, almost to a person—watched them leave. It was night on Tycho Station, which didn't mean much. The station was built on three rotating eight-hour shifts: leisure, work, sleep. Who you knew depended on what shift you worked, like three different cities that all occupied the same space. A world that would always be two-thirds strangers. She put her arm around Jim's waist and pulled him in against her until she could feel his thigh moving against hers.

"We need to talk," she said.

He tensed a little, but kept his voice light and airy. "Like man-and-woman talk?"

"Worse," she said. "XO and captain."

"What's up?"

They stepped into a lift, and she pushed the button for their deck. The lift chimed, the doors moving gently closed, as she gathered her thoughts. It wasn't really that she didn't know what needed to be said. He wasn't going to like this any more than she did.

"We need to look at hiring on more crew."

She knew enough about Jim's silences to recognize this one. She looked up into his blank expression, his eyes blinking a fraction more quickly than usual.

"Really?" he said. "Seems to me that we're doing just fine."

"We are. We have been. The *Roci*'s a military design. Smart. A lot of automation, a lot of redundancy. That's why we've been able to run her at a third of her standard crew for this long."

"That and we're the best damned crew in the sky."

"That doesn't hurt. Looking at skills and service, we've got a strong group. But we're brittle."

The lift shifted, the complex forces of station spin and car acceleration making the space feel unsteady. She was sure it was just the movement.

"I'm not sure what you mean by brittle," Jim said.

"We've been on the *Rocinante* since we salvaged her off the *Donnager*. We've had no change in staff. No turnover. Name me one other ship you can think of where that's true. There were runs where the *Canterbury* had a quarter of the staff on their first mission together. And..."

The doors slid open. They stepped out, moving aside to let another couple go in. Naomi heard the others murmuring to each other as the lift doors closed. Jim was quiet as they walked back toward their suite. When he finally spoke, his voice was low and thoughtful.

"You're thinking one of them may not come back? Amos? Alex?"

"I'm thinking that a lot of things happen. Take a high burn, and sometimes people stroke out. The juice helps, but it's not a guarantee. People have been known to shoot at us. Or we've been disabled in a decaying orbit. You remember all that happening, right?"

"Sure, but—"

"If we lose someone, we go from running at a third of a standard crew to a quarter. Add to that the loss of nonredundant skills."

Holden stopped, his hand on the door to their rooms.

"Wait, wait, wait. If we lose someone?"

"Yes."

His eyes were wide and shocked. Little wrinkles of distress gathered at the corners. She reached up to smooth them away, but they didn't go.

"So you're trying to get me prepared for one of my crew dying?"

"Historically speaking, humans are pretty much at a hundred percent on that."

Jim started to say something, faltered, opened the suite door, and walked in. She followed, closing the door behind them. She wanted to let it drop, but if she did, she didn't know when they'd pick it back up.

"If we were running a traditional crew, we'd have two people in every position. If anyone got killed or disabled, someone else would be right there to step in."

"I'm not adding four more people to our ship, much less eight," Jim said, walking into the bedroom. Running from the conversation. He wouldn't actually leave. She waited for the silence and the distress and the worry that he'd made her angry to pull him back. It took about fifteen seconds. "We don't run this like a regular crew because we're not a regular crew. We got the *Roci* when everyone in the system was shooting at us. We had stealth ships blowing a battleship out from under us. We lost the *Cant* and then we lost *Shed*. You can't go through that and just be normal."

"Meaning what exactly?"

"This ship isn't a crew. We don't *run* it like a crew. We run it like a family."

"Right," she said. "And that's a problem."

They looked at each other across the room. Jim's jaw worked, objections and arguments getting stalled at his tongue. He knew she was right, and he wanted her to be wrong. She saw him realize there was no way out.

"Fine," he said. "When the others get back, let's talk about doing some interviews. Taking a couple people on for a mission or two. If they shake down right, we can look at keeping them on permanently."

"That sounds good," Naomi said.

"It's going to change the balance on the ship," Holden said.

"Everything changes," she said, putting her arms around him.

They ordered food from a fusion Indian restaurant, curry and genetically modified rice and textured fungal protein mostly indistinguishable from beef. For the rest of the evening, Holden tried to be cheerful, tried to hide his unease from her. It didn't even start to work, but she appreciated the effort.

After dinner, they watched the entertainment feeds until the time came in the comfortable rhythm of their day that she turned off the screen and drew him back to the bed. Sex with Holden had started off as a thrilling thing, years ago when they were first seeing exactly how stupid a captain and an XO sleeping together would be. Now, it was richer and calmer and more playful. And more comforting.

After, lying on the big gel-form mattress with the sheets in ropes at the foot, Naomi's mind wandered. She thought of the *Roci* and of Sam, of a book of poetry she'd read when she was a girl and a musical group one of the senior engineers had roped her into on the *Canterbury*. Her recollections had started taking on the surreal confusion of dreams when Jim's voice brought her back almost to wakefulness.

"I don't like having them gone."

"Hmm?"

"Alex and Amos. I don't like having them gone. If they get in trouble, we'll be here. I can't even just fire up the *Roci* and go get them."

"They'll be fine," she said.

"I know. I sort of know." He propped himself up on one elbow. "Are you really not worried?"

"A little maybe."

"I mean, I know they're grown-ups, but if something happened. If they didn't come back..."

"It would be hard," Naomi said. "We four have been what we rely on for a lot of years now."

"Yeah," Jim said. And then a moment later, "Do you know who this lady was Amos went back to check on?"

"No. I don't."

"You think she was his lover?"

"I don't know," Naomi said. "I got the feeling it was more of a surrogate mom thing."

"Hmm. Maybe. I don't know why I was thinking lover." His voice had started taking on the fuzzy edges of sleep. "Hey, can I ask an inappropriate question?"

"If memory serves."

"Why didn't you and Amos ever get together? I mean back on the *Cant*."

Naomi laughed, rolled over, put her arm across his chest. Even after shipping with him all this time, she liked the way his skin smelled. "Are you serious? Have you paid any attention at all to his sexuality?"

"I don't think Amos and I are supposed to do that."

"It's not a place you want to be," Naomi said.

"Hmm. Okay. I was just thinking, you know. How much he followed you around back on the *Cant*. And he's never talked about leaving the *Roci*."

"He's not staying on the *Roci* for me," Naomi said. "He's staying for you."

"Me?"

"He's using you as his external, aftermarket conscience."

"No, he's not."

"It's what he does. Finds someone who has a sense of ethics and follows their lead," Naomi said. "It's how he tries not to be a monster."

"Why would he try not to be a monster?" The sleep-slurred words were like a blanket.

"Because he is one," Naomi said, her consciousness flickering across the line. *It's why we get along.*

⚡

The message came two days later, and without warning. Naomi was in an EVA suit, inspecting the work with Chief Engineer Sakai. He was in the process of explaining why they were looking at a different ceramic alloy for the connections between inner and outer hull when a priority message popped into her HUD. She felt a rush of fear, the aftermath of her talk with Holden. Something had happened to Alex. Or Amos.

"Hold on," she said, and Sakai answered with a raised fist.

She started the message. A flat transmission screen popped on with the split circle of the OPA, and when it flickered away, Marco was there. The years had thickened his face a degree, softened the curve of his jaw. His skin had the same richness and depth she remembered, and his hands, folded on the table wherever he'd recorded this, were as delicate. He smiled with the mixture of sorrow and amusement that was like falling backward through time.

The message halted, cut off by the suit's medical systems. Warnings for increased heart rate, elevated blood pressure. She chinned the override, and his voice stuttered softly into her ears, smoothing as the feed cohered.

"I'm sorry. I know you don't want to hear from me. If it helps, I'd just point out that I haven't done it before this. And I'm not doing it lightly now."

Shut it off, she thought. *Stop the feed. Erase it. It would all be lies anyway. Lies or only what parts of the truth served him. Forget it ever came.* Marco looked away from the camera as if he'd read her mind, or known what she would be thinking.

"Naomi, I don't agree with your decision to leave, but I've always respected it. Even when you showed up in the news so everyone knew where you were, I didn't reach out. And I'm not coming to you now for myself."

The words were all crisp and warm and careful: the flawless grammar of someone speaking a second language so well it sounded uncanny. He had none of his Belter patois. So there was another way the years had changed him.

"Cyn and Karal send their love and respect, but they're the only ones who know I'm reaching out. And why. They're on Ceres Station right now, but they can't stay long. I need you to meet their team there and— No. I'm sorry. That's wrong. I shouldn't have put it that way. It's just that I'm at loose ends. I don't know what to do, and you're the only one I can turn to. It's Filip. He's in trouble."

Chapter Four: Amos

His throat ached.

Amos swallowed, trying to force the lump away with a mouthful of saliva, but all that got him was a thick new pain like swallowing sand. The *Roci*'s med bay had shot him full of all the booster vaccines and bacterial prophylactics three months ago, right on schedule. He didn't figure he could be sick. But there it was, a spot in the back of his throat that felt like he'd swallowed a golf ball and it got stuck halfway down.

All around him, the citizens and travelers of the Ceres Station Spaceport milled like ants on their hill, their voices making an undifferentiated roar that was just as good as silence. It amused Amos that this metaphor was one that no one on Ceres would actually understand. Himself, he hadn't seen an ant in close on two decades, but the childhood memories of watching them take down a cockroach or clean the carcass of a rat were vivid and sharp. Like the roaches and the rats, ants had learned to live with their human neighbors without much trouble. When the concrete of human cities spread across the globe and half the animals on Earth were on endangered lists, no one had worried about the ants. They were doing fine, thanks, and spilled fast food was just as plentiful and delicious as dead forest animals had once been.

Adapt or die.

If Amos could be said to have a philosophy, it would be that. The concrete replaces the forest. You get in its way, you get paved over. If you can find a way to live in the cracks, you can thrive anywhere. There were always cracks.

The anthill of Ceres bustled around him. There were people at the top of the food chain buying snacks at the kiosks or tickets for the shuttles and long-flight ships leaving the station. The people in the cracks were there too. A girl no older than ten with long dirty hair and a pink jumpsuit two sizes too small eyed the travelers without staring at them. Waiting for someone to set their luggage or their hand terminal down long enough to be snatched away. She saw Amos looking at her and bolted for a maintenance hatch set low in the wall.

Living in the cracks, but living. Adapting, not dying.

He swallowed again, grimacing at the ache. His hand terminal beeped, and he looked up at the flight board that dominated the station's public space. Bright yellow letters against black, a font designed for legibility over beauty. His long-haul flight to Luna was confirmed for a launch window in three hours. He tapped on his terminal's screen to let the automated system know he'd be on board when it left, and walked off looking for something to kill three hours.

There was a bar by the gate. So that was easy.

He didn't want to get drunk and miss his flight, so he stuck to beer, drinking slowly and methodically and waving at the bartender as he approached the bottom of one glass so that the next was waiting when he finished. He was aiming for fuzzy and relaxed, and he knew exactly how to get there in the shortest possible time.

The bar didn't offer much in the way of entertainments or distractions, so he could focus on the glass, the bartender, the next drink. The lump in his throat thickened with each swallow. He ignored it. The other patrons in the bar were quiet, reading hand terminals or whispering in small groups as they drank. Everyone on the way to somewhere else. This place wasn't a destination; it was something you bumped into in your travels, accidental and forgettable.

Lydia was dead.

He'd spent twenty years thinking about her. The tattoo of her face over his heart was some of that, of course. Every look in a mirror without his shirt on was a reminder. But beyond that, every day had choices in it. And every choice he made started with the little voice in his head asking what Lydia would want him to do. When he'd received the message from Erich, he realized he hadn't seen or spoken to her in over two decades. That meant she was twenty years older than when he'd left. How old had she been then? He could remember the gray in her hair, the lines around her eyes and mouth. Older than him. But he'd been fifteen, and "older than him" had been a wide space most people fell into.

And now she was dead.

Maybe someone twenty years older than the woman he remembered was old enough to die of natural causes. Maybe she'd died in a hospital, or her own bed, warm and comfortable and surrounded by friends. Maybe she'd had a cat sleeping on her feet. Amos hoped that was true. Because if it wasn't—if it was anything *other* than natural causes—he was going to kill every single person even remotely involved. He examined the idea in his mind, rotating it this way and that, waiting to see if Lydia stopped him.

He took another long swallow of beer and burned his throat. He really hoped he wasn't getting sick.

You're not sick, Lydia's voice said in his mind, *you're sad. Grieving. The lump in your throat. The hollow space behind your sternum. The empty feeling in your stomach no matter how much beer you put there. That's grief.*

"Huh," Amos said out loud.

"Need something, buddy?" the bartender asked with professional disinterest.

"Another," Amos said, pointing at the half-full beer he still had.

You don't process grief well, another voice said. Holden, this time. That was the truth. That's why Amos trusted the captain. When he said something, it was because he believed it. No need to analyze it or figure out what he really meant by it. Even when the captain fucked up, he was acting in good faith. Amos hadn't met many people like that.

The only really strong emotion Amos had felt in longer than he could remember was anger. That was always there, waiting for him. Processing his grief that way was simple and direct. He understood it. The man sitting a few stools away at the bar had the rough, rawboned look of a rock jock. He'd been nursing the same beer for an hour. Every time Amos ordered another, the man shot him a glance that was half annoyance, half envy. Coveting his apparently bottomless credit account. It would be so easy. Say something to him, cutting and loud, put him in a position where backing down embarrassed him in front of everyone. The poor fucker would feel obligated to take the bait, and then Amos would be free to process his grief all over the guy. Some time in stir might even be a nice way to unwind.

That guy didn't kill Lydia, Holden's voice said. *But maybe someone else did*, Amos thought. *And I need to find out.*

"Need to cash out here, amigo," Amos said to the bartender, waving his hand terminal at him. He pointed at the rock jock. "Put that guy's next two on my tab."

The rock jock frowned, looking for the insult, but when he couldn't find it he said, "Thanks, brother."

"Anytime, hermano. You be safe out there."

"Sa sa," the jock said, finishing off his beer and reaching for one of the two Amos had just bought. "Do the same, sabe dui?"

Amos missed his bunk on the *Roci.*

The long-haul transport was named the *Lazy Songbird*, but its birdlike qualities began and ended at the white letters painted on its side. From the outside, it looked like a giant garbage can with a drive cone on one end and a tiny ops deck on the other. From the inside, it looked like the inside of a giant garbage can except that it was divided into twelve decks, fifty people to a deck.

The only privacy to be had was thin curtains in the shower stalls, and people only ever seemed to use the head when uniformed crew members were around.

Ah, Amos thought, *Prison rules.*

He selected a bunk, just a crash couch with a little storage under it and a tiny entertainment screen on the bulkhead next to it, as far from the head and the commissary as possible. He tried to stay out of high traffic areas. The people sharing his space were a family of three on one side, and an ancient crone on the other.

The crone spent the entire flight high on little white pills, staring at the ceiling all day and tossing and sweating through fever dreams all night. Amos introduced himself to her. She offered him some pills. He declined. This ended their association.

The family on the other side was much nicer. Two men in their early thirties and their daughter of about seven. One of the men was a structural engineer named Rico. The other a stay-at-home dad called Jianguo. The girl's name was Wendy. They eyed Amos with some suspicion when he first claimed the bunk, but he smiled and shook their hands and bought Wendy an ice cream bar from a commissary vending machine and then didn't follow up by being creepy. He knew what men who had too much interest in little kids were like, and so he knew how not to ever be mistaken for one of them.

Rico was traveling to Luna to take one of the new job openings at the Bush orbital shipyards. "Lots of coyos heading downwell. Beaucoup jobs now, everybody trying to grab a ring for themselves. New colonies. New worlds."

"That'll dry up when the rush dies down," Amos said. He was lying back on his couch, half listening to Rico rattle on, half watching a video feed on his wall screen with the sound off.

Rico gave a Belter shrug of the hands and tilted his head toward his daughter, sleeping in her bunk. "For her, sabe? Later is for later. For now I put some yuan aside. School, ring trip, whatever she needs."

"I hear that. Later is later."

"Oh, hey, they're cleaning the head. Gonna grab a shower."

"What's with that, man?" Amos asked. "What's the rumpus?"

Rico cocked his head, like Amos had asked why space was a vacuum. In fairness, Amos knew the answer, but it was interesting to see whether Rico did too. "Long-haul gangs, coyo. Price of flying on the cheap. Sucks to be poor."

"The crew watches for that shit, right? Anyone gets in a tussle, they gas us all, tie up the perps. No fuss, no muss."

"Don't watch the showers. No cameras. If you don't pay when the shakedown comes, that's where they get you. Better to go when crew is around."

"No shit," Amos said, pretending surprise. "Haven't seen the shakedown yet."

"You will, hombre. Watch Jian and Wendy while I'm out, yeah?"

"Both eyes, brother."

Rico was right. After the first rush of the flight, when the initial bustle of people finding bunks, deciding they hated their neighbor, then finding a new one was over, people were mostly settled in. The Belters bunking on Belter decks. The inners on decks split between Earth and Mars. Amos was on a Belter deck, but he seemed to be the only one mixing.

Prison rules for sure.

On the sixth day, a small group of toughs from a deck up came down the lift together and fanned out through the compartment. With fifty people on the deck, it took them a while to hit everyone. Amos pretended to sleep in his crash couch and watched them out of the corner of his eye. It was a basic scam. A tough walked up to a passenger, explained about in-flight insurance policies, then took a credit transfer with a cheap disposable terminal. All the threats were implied. Everyone paid. It was a stupid racket, but simple enough that it worked anyway.

One of the extortionists who looked like he wasn't a day over fourteen headed their direction. Rico started to pull out his hand terminal, but Amos sat up in bed and waved him off. To the junior extortionist he said, "We're all good over here. No one in this corner pays."

The thug stared at him without speaking. Amos smiled back. He didn't particularly want to be gassed and tied up, but if that's how it had to happen, he'd live with it.

"Dead man," the thug said. He put as much macho as he could into it, and Amos respected the commitment. But much scarier people than a skinny pubescent Belter had tried intimidating him. Amos nodded as if considering the threat.

"So there was this one time I got caught in a reactor crawlspace when a coolant pipe blew," he said.

"What?" the kid asked, baffled. Even Rico and Jianguo were looking at Amos like he'd lost his mind. Amos shifted, and the couch's gimbals squeaked as they reoriented.

"See, the coolant is radioactive as fuck. Hits the open air and it vaporizes. Getting it on your skin ain't good for you, but you can survive that. Washes off, mostly. You don't want to breathe it in though. Get a bunch of radioactive particles down in the lungs where you can't get 'em out? Yeah, you pretty much melt from the inside."

The kid glanced over his shoulder, looking for support dealing with the crazy ranting guy. The rest of team extortion was still busy.

"So," Amos continued, leaning forward, "I had to get into a maintenance airlock, open an emergency locker, and get a rebreather strapped to my face without breathing any of that shit in."

"So what? You still—"

"The point of this little tale of woe is that I learned some facts about myself."

"Yeah?" The situation had gotten weird enough that the kid actually seemed interested in finding out.

"I learned that I can hold my breath for almost two minutes while engaging in stressful physical activity."

"So—"

"So you need to ask yourself, how much damage can I do to you in two minutes before the knockout gas gets me. Because I'm betting it's a lot."

The kid didn't respond. Rico and Jianguo seemed to be holding their breath. Wendy was staring at Amos with a wide-eyed grin.

"There a problem?" One of the junior thug's buddies had finally come over to check on him.

"Yeah, he—"

"No problem," Amos said. "Just explaining to your associate here that this corner of the room doesn't pay for insurance."

"Says you?"

"Yeah. Says me."

The senior thug looked Amos over, sizing him up. They were about the same height, but Amos outweighed him by a solid twenty-five kilos. Amos stood up and spread himself out a little, making the point.

"What crew you run with?" senior thug asked, mistaking him for a rival banger.

"*Rocinante*," Amos replied.

"Never heard of 'em."

"Yeah, you have, but context is everything, ain't it?"

"Might be you fucked up, coyo," the thug said.

Amos gave an expansive Belter shrug of the hands. "I guess we'll find out sooner or later."

"Sooner or later," the thug agreed, then grabbed his junior partner and headed off to the rest of his crew. When they took the lift to the next deck, they left junior behind. He openly stared at Amos from across the room, not trying to hide anything.

Amos sighed and grabbed his towel out of his duffel. "Gonna go take a shower."

"You crazy," Jianguo said. "No crew in there. They'll jump you."

"Yep."

"Then why?"

"Because," Amos said, standing up and throwing the towel over his shoulder, "I hate waiting."

As soon as Amos walked toward the head with his prominently displayed towel, junior started talking on his hand terminal. Calling the troops.

The head was five flimsy sheet plastic shower stalls against one bulkhead, and ten vacuum flush toilets against the other. Sinks lined the bulkhead directly across from the door. The open space in the middle had benches for sitting while you waited your turn in the shower or dressed afterward. Not the best space for hand-to-hand. Lots of hard projections to get mashed into, and the benches were a tripping hazard.

Amos tossed his towel onto a sink and leaned against it, arms crossed. He didn't have to wait long. A few minutes after junior had made the call he and five of the thugs from team extortion filed into the room.

"Only six? I'm a little insulted."

"You not a little anything," the oldest one said. The leader then, speaking first. "But big dies too."

"True that. So how does this go? I'm on your turf, so I'll respect the house rules."

The leader laughed. "You funny, man. Dead soon, but funny." He turned to junior thug and said, "Your beef, coyo."

Junior pulled a shiv out of his pocket. No weapons made it into the passenger compartment through security, but this was a jagged piece of metal torn off of something in the ship then sharpened down. Prison rules, again.

"I'm not going to disrespect you," Amos said to him. "I killed my first guy at about your age. Well, a few guys really, but that's not the issue. I know to take you and that knife seriously."

"Good."

"No," Amos said sadly, "it really isn't."

Before anyone could move, Amos crossed the space between them and grabbed junior's knife arm. The ship was only at about a third of a g thrust, so Amos yanked the kid off the floor and spun, hitting the edge of a shower stall with the kid's arm. His body kept traveling and Amos didn't let go, so the arm folded around the impact point. The sound of tendons in his elbow snapping was like hitting wet plywood with a hammer. The knife drifted to the floor from nerveless fingers, and Amos let go of the arm.

There was a long second where the five thugs stared at the knife on the floor at Amos' feet, and he stared back at them. The emptiness in his belly was gone. The hollow space behind his sternum, gone. His throat had stopped hurting.

"Who's next?" he said, flexing his hands, his face in a grin he didn't know he had.

They came in a rush. Amos spread his arms and welcomed them like long-lost lovers.

"You okay?" Rico asked. He was dabbing at a small cut on Amos' head with an alcohol swab.

"Mostly."

"They okay?"

"Less so," Amos said, "but still mostly. Everyone will walk out of there when they wake up."

"You didn't have to do that for me. I would have paid."

"Didn't," Amos said. At Rico's puzzled look he added, "Didn't do it for you. And Rico? That money goes into the Wendy fund, or I come looking for you too."

Chapter Five: Holden

One of Holden's grandfathers had spent his youth riding in rodeos. All of the pictures they had of him were of a tall, muscular, robust-looking man with a big belt buckle and a cowboy hat. But the man Holden had known when he was a child was thin, pale, and hunched over. As if the years had stripped away everything extraneous and rendered the younger man down into the skeletal older man he became.

It struck him that Fred Johnson had been rendered.

He was still a tall man, but the heavy muscles he'd once had were mostly gone, leaving loose skin at the backs of his arms and on his neck. His hair had gone from mostly black to mostly gray to mostly not there at all. That he could still project an air of absolute authority meant that very little of it had come from his physicality in the first place.

Fred had two glasses and a bottle of something dark on the desk when Holden sat. He offered a drink with a small tilt of his head, and Holden accepted with a nod. While Fred poured, Holden leaned back in his chair with a long sigh, then said, “Thank you.”

Fred shrugged. “I was looking for an excuse.”

“Not the drink, but thanks for that too. Thank you for helping with the *Roci*. The money from Avasarala came, but we have damage we didn’t know about when I wrote the bill. Without our favored client discount, we’d been in trouble.”

“Who says you’re getting a discount?” Fred said as he handed Holden the drink, but he smiled as he said it. He sank into his own chair with a grunt. Holden hadn’t realized coming in how much he was dreading the conversation. Even if he knew it was just good business negotiation, it felt like asking for a handout. That the answer had been yes was good. That Fred hadn’t made him squirm about it was even better. Made him feel more like he was sitting with a friend.

“You look old, Fred.”

“I feel old. But it’s better than the alternative.”

Holden raised his glass. “Those who aren’t with us.”

“Those who aren’t with us,” Fred repeated, and they both drank. “That list is getting longer every time I see you.”

“I’m sorry about Bull, but I think he may have saved the solar system. From what I knew of him, he’d think that was pretty kick-ass.”

“Bull,” Fred said, raising his glass again.

“And Sam,” Holden added, raising his own.

“I’m leaving soon, so I wanted to check in with you.”

“Wait. Leaving? Like leaving leaving, or like Bull and Sam leaving?”

“You’re not rid of me yet. I need to get back out to Medina Station,” Fred said. He poured himself a little more bourbon, frowning down at the glass like it was a delicate operation. “That’s where all the action is.”

“Really? I thought I heard something about the UN secretary-general and the Martian prime minister having a sit-down. I thought you’d be heading to that.”

"They can talk all they want. The real power's in the geography. Medina's in the hub where all the rings connect. That's where the power is going to be for a good long time."

"How long do you think the UN and Mars keep letting you run that show? You have a head start, but they have a bunch of really dangerous ships to throw at you if they decide they want your stuff."

"Avasarala and I are back channeling a lot of this. We'll keep it from getting out of hand." Fred paused to take a long drink. "But we have two big problems."

Holden put down the glass. He was starting to get the sense that him asking for—and getting—the discount on repairs might not actually have been the end of the negotiation after all.

"Mars," Holden said.

"Yes, Mars is dying," Fred agreed with a nod. "No stopping that. But we also have a bunch of OPA extremists making noise. The Callisto attack last year was their work. The water riot on Pallas Station. And there have been other things. Piracy's up, and more of those ships have a split circle painted on them than I'd like."

"I'd think any problems they had would be solved by everyone getting their own free planet."

Fred took another pull of his drink before he answered. "Their position is that the Belter culture is one adapted to space. The prospect of new colonies with air and gravity reduces the economic base that Belters depend on. Forcing everyone to go down a gravity well is the moral equivalent of genocide."

Holden blinked. "Free planets are genocide?"

"They argue that being adapted to low g isn't a disability, it's who they are. They don't want to go live on a planet, so we're killing them off."

"Okay, I can see not wanting to spend six months pumped full of steroids and bone growth stimulators. But how are we killing them?"

"For one thing, not all of them can tolerate that. But that's not really the point. It's that this," Fred said, waving at the space station around them, "is pretty much over once everyone has a planet. For generations, at the minimum. Maybe forever. No reason to dump resources into the outer planets or mining the Belt when we can find the same stuff down a well and get free air and water to boot."

"So once they don't have anything anyone wants, they'll just starve to death out here?"

"That's how they see it," Fred said. He and Holden shared a quiet moment while they drank.

"Yeah," Holden finally said. "Well, they've got a point. But I don't know what they can do about it."

"There are people trying to figure that out. But it's ramping up."

"Callisto and Pallas."

"And more recently they ran an attack on Earth with an old mothballed heavy freighter."

Holden laughed. "I haven't read that Earth got bombed, so that must not have worked."

"Well, it was a suicide attack, and the suicide half worked. The UN fleet in high orbit patrol reduced the freighter to gas a tenth of an AU from the planet. No damage, not much press. But it's possible those were all preliminary. That they're planning some big showy statement about how the Belt can't be ignored. The thing that scares the shit out of me is that no one can figure out what it will be."

⚡

The gently sloping main corridor of the Tycho Station habitation ring was filled with workers. Holden didn't pay much attention to the station schedules, but he assumed the crowds passing him meant it was shift change. Either that, or an orderly evacuation with no alarms sounding.

"Yo! Holden," someone said as they passed.

"Hey," Holden said, not sure who he was saying it to.

Celebrity was not something he'd figured out how to handle,

yet. People would point, stare, whisper to each other when he walked by. He knew it generally wasn't intended as insult. Just the surprise people felt when someone they'd only seen on video screens before suddenly appeared in the real world. Most of the murmured conversations, when he could overhear them, consisted of *Is that James Holden? I think that's James Holden.*

"Holden," a woman walking toward him down the corridor said, "what's up?"

There were fifteen thousand people on Tycho, working in three different shifts. It was like a small city in space. He couldn't remember if the woman speaking to him was someone he should know or not, so he just smiled and said, "Hey, how's it going?"

"Same same," she said as they passed.

When he reached the door to his apartment it was a relief that the only person inside was Naomi. She sat at the dining table, a steaming mug of tea in front of her, a distant look in her eyes. Holden couldn't tell if she was melancholy or solving a complex engineering problem in her head. Those looks were confusingly similar.

He pulled himself a cup of water out of the kitchen tap, then sat across from her waiting for her to speak first. She looked up through her hair at him and gave him a sad smile. Melancholy, then, not engineering.

"Hey," she said.

"Hey."

"So I have a thing."

"Is it a thing I can fix?" Holden asked. "Point me at the thing."

Naomi sipped at her tea, buying time. Not a good sign, because it meant this was something she wasn't sure how to talk about. Holden felt his stomach muscles tightening.

"That's kind of the problem, actually," she said. "I need to go do something, and I can't have you involved in it. At all. Because if you are, you'll try to fix it and you can't do that."

"I don't understand," Holden said.

"When I come back, I promise full and complete disclosure."

"Wait. Come back? Where are you going?"

"Ceres, to start," Naomi said. "But it may be more than that. I'm not sure how long I'll be gone."

"Naomi," Holden said, reaching across the table to take her hand. "You're scaring the shit out of me right now. There's no way you can jet off to Ceres without me. Especially if it's something bad, and I'm getting the feeling it's something really bad."

Naomi put down her tea, and gripped his hand in both of hers. The fingers that had been holding the mug were warm, the others cool. "Except that is what's happening. There's no negotiation on this. So, either I go because you understand and will give me the space to handle this on my own, or I go because we've broken up and you no longer get any vote in what I do."

"Wait, what?"

"Have we broken up?" Naomi asked. She squeezed his hand.

"No, of course not."

"Then thank you for trusting me enough to let me handle this on my own."

"Is that what I just said?" Holden asked.

"Yeah, pretty much." Naomi stood up. She had a packed duffel on the floor next to her chair that Holden hadn't seen. "I'll be in touch when I can, but if I can't, don't read anything into it. Okay?"

"Okay," Holden replied. The whole scene had taken on a vaguely dreamlike feel. Naomi, standing at the end of the table holding her olive-green duffel bag, seemed very far away. The room felt bigger than it was, or else Holden had shrunk. He stood up too, and vertigo made him dizzy.

Naomi dropped the duffel on the table and wrapped both arms around him. Her chin was against his forehead when she whispered, "I'll be back. I promise."

"Okay," he said again. His brain had lost the ability to form any other words.

After one last tight squeeze, she picked up her bag and walked to the door.

"Wait!" he said.

She looked back.

"I love you."

"I love you too," she said, and then was gone.

Holden sat back down, because it was that or sink to the floor. He finally pulled himself out of the chair a minute or an hour later; it was hard to tell. He had almost called Amos to join him for a drink when he remembered Amos and Alex were gone too.

Everyone was.

It was strange how nothing could change while everything did. He still got up every morning, brushed his teeth, put on a fresh set of clothes, and ate breakfast. He arrived at the repair docks by nine a.m. local time, put on a vacuum suit, and joined the crew working on the *Rocinante*. For eight hours he'd climb through the skeletal ribs of the ship, attaching conduit, installing replacement maneuvering thrusters, patching holes. He didn't know how to do everything that needed to be done, but he wanted to, so he shadowed the technicians doing the really complicated work.

It all felt very normal, very routine, almost like still having his old life.

But then he'd return to his apartment eight hours later and no one would be there. He was truly alone for the first time in years. Amos wouldn't come by asking him to hit a bar. Alex wouldn't watch the video streams sitting on his couch and making sarcastic comments to the screen. Naomi wouldn't be there to ask about his day and compare notes on how the repairs were coming. The rooms even smelled empty.

It wasn't something about himself he'd ever had to face before, but Holden was coming to realize how much he needed family. He'd grown up with eight parents, and a seemingly endless supply of grandparents, aunts, uncles, and cousins. When he'd left Earth for the Navy, he'd spent four years at the academy with roommates and classmates and girlfriends. Even after his dishonorable discharge, he'd gone straight to work for Pur'N'Kleen on the *Canterbury* and a whole new loose-knit family of coworkers and friends. Or if not family, at least *people*.

The only two people he'd been close with on Tycho were Fred, so busy with his political machinations he barely had time to breathe, and Sam, who'd died in the slow zone years ago. The new Sam—Sakai—was a competent engineer and seemed to take fixing his ship seriously, but had expressed no interest in any association outside of that.

So Holden spent a lot of time in bars.

The Blauwe Blome was too noisy and too filled with people who knew Naomi but not him. The places close to the docks were full of boisterous workers coming off shift and picking a fight with a famous guy seemed like a great way to blow off steam. Anyplace else with more than four people in it at a time turned into *line up to have your picture taken with James Holden then ask him personal questions for an hour.* So, he found a small restaurant nestled in a side corridor between a residential section and a strip of commercial shopping outlets. It specialized in what the Belters were calling Italian food and had a small bar in a back room that everyone seemed to ignore.

Holden could sit at a tiny table skimming the latest news on his hand terminal, reading messages, and finally check out all the books he'd downloaded over the last six years. The bar served the same food as the restaurant out front, and while it was not something anyone from Earth would have mistaken for Italian, it was edible. The cocktails were mediocre and cheap.

It might almost have been tolerable if Naomi hadn't seemingly fallen out of the universe. Alex sent regular updates about where he was and what he was up to. Amos had his terminal automatically send a message letting Holden know his flight had landed on Luna, and then New York. From Naomi, nothing. She still existed, or at least her hand terminal did. The messages he sent arrived somewhere. He never got a failed connection from the network. But the successfully received message was his only reply.

After a couple weeks of his new bad Italian food and cheap cocktails routine, his terminal finally rang with an incoming voice request. He knew it couldn't be from Naomi. The light lag made a live connection unworkable for any two people not living on the same station. But he still pulled the terminal out of his pocket so fast that he fumbled it across the room.

The bartender—Chip—said, "Had a few too many of my margaritas?"

"The first one was too many," Holden replied, then climbed under the booth looking for the terminal. "And calling that a margarita should be illegal."

"It's as margarita as it gets with rice wine and lime flavor concentrate," Chip said, sounding vaguely hurt.

"Hello?" Holden yelled at the terminal, mashing the touch screen to open the connection. "Hello?"

"Hi, Jim?" a female voice said. It didn't sound anything like Naomi.

"Who is this?" he asked, then cracked his head on the edge of the table climbing back out and added, "Dammit!"

"Monica," the voice on the other end said. "Monica Stuart? Did I catch you at a bad time?"

"Sort of busy right now, Monica," Holden said. Chip rolled his eyes. Holden flipped him off, and the bartender started mixing him another drink. Probably as punishment for the insult.

"I understand," Monica said. "But I have something I'd love to run past you. Is there any chance we can get together? Dinner, a drink, anything?"

"I'm afraid I'm on Tycho Station for the foreseeable future, Monica. The *Roci* is getting a full refit right now. So—"

"Oh, I know. I'm on Tycho too. That's why I called."

"Right," Holden said. "Of course you are."

"Is tonight good?"

Chip put the drink on a tray, and a waiter from the restaurant out front popped in to carry it away. Chip saw him looking at it and mouthed *Want another?* at him. The prospect of another night of what the restaurant laughably called lasagna and enough of Chip's "margaritas" to kill the aftertaste felt like slow death.

The truth was, he was bored and lonely. Monica Stuart was a journalist and had serious problems about only showing up when she wanted something. She always had an ulterior motive. But finding out what she wanted and then saying no would kill an evening in a way that wasn't exactly like every other evening since Naomi left. "Yeah, okay Monica, dinner sounds great. Not Italian."

They ate salmon sushi from fish grown in tanks on the station. It was outrageously expensive, but being paid for by Monica's expense account. Holden indulged himself until his clothes stopped fitting.

Monica ate sparingly, with small precise movements of her chopsticks, almost picking up the rice one kernel at a time. She ignored the wasabi altogether. She'd aged some too, since Holden had last seen her in person. Unlike Fred, the extra years looked good on her, adding a sense of experience and gravitas to her video-star looks.

They'd started the evening talking about little things: how the ship repairs were going, what had happened to the team she'd taken on the *Rocinante* back when the Ring was a new thing, where Alex and Amos and Naomi had gone. He'd found himself talking more than he meant to. He didn't dislike Monica, but she wasn't someone he particularly trusted either. But she knew him, and they'd traveled together, and even more than good food, he was hungry to talk to someone he actually sort of knew.

"So there's this weird thing," she said, then dabbed at the corners of her mouth with a napkin.

"Weirder than eating raw fish on a space station with one of the solar system's most famous reporters?"

"You're flattering me."

"It's habit. I don't mean anything by it."

Monica rooted around in the satchel she'd brought and pulled out a flimsy roll-out video screen. She pushed plates out of the way and flattened the screen out on the table. When it came on, it showed the image of a heavy freighter, blocky and thick, heading toward one of the rings inside the slow zone. "Watch this."

The picture sprang into motion, the freighter burning toward a ring gate at low thrust. He assumed it was the one that led from the solar system to the slow zone and Medina Station, but it could have been any of the others. They all looked pretty much the same. When the ship passed through the gate, the image flickered and danced as the recording equipment was bombarded with high-energy particles and magnetic flux. The image stabilized, and the ship was no longer visible. That didn't mean much. Light passing through the gates had always behaved oddly, bending the images like refraction in water. The video ended.

"I've seen that one before," Holden said. "Good special effects but the plot's thin."

"Actually you kind of haven't. Guess what happened to that ship?" Monica said, face flushed with excitement.

"What?"

"No, really, guess. Speculate. Give me a hypothesis. Because it never came out the other side."

Chapter Six: Alex

Hey, Bobbie," Alex said to his hand terminal's camera. "I'm gonna be downstairs in Mariner for a week or two, stayin' with a cousin. I was wondering if you wanted to get lunch while I'm in town."

He ended the message and sent it, put his hand terminal back in his pocket, fidgeted, took it out again. He started paging back through his contacts, looking for another distraction. With every minute, he came closer to the thin exosphere of home. They were already inside the orbit of Phobos and the now invisibly thin scatter of gravel that people called the Deimos Ring. The drop ship didn't have screens, but from here he'd have been able to see the massive steel of Hecate Base spilling up the side of Olympus Mons. He'd been a boot there after he joined the Navy.

Mariner Valley had been one of the first large-scale settlements on Mars. Five linked neighborhoods that burrowed into the sides of the vast canyons, huddling under the stone and regolith. The network of bridges and tubes that linked them were called Haizhe because the westernmost bridge structures and the trailing tubes made a figure like a cartoon jellyfish. The later high-speed line to Londres Nova was a spear in the jellyfish's crown.

Three waves of Chinese and Indian colonists dug deep into the dry soil there, eking out a thin, perilous existence, pushing the limits of human habitation and ability. His family had been one of them. He'd been an only child to older parents. He had no nieces or nephews, but the variety of Kamal cousins in the Valley were enough that he could go from one guest room to another for months without wearing out his welcome at any one of them.

The drop ship shuddered, the atmosphere outside thick enough now to cause turbulence. The acceleration alarm chimed pleasantly and a recorded voice instructed him and the other passengers to check the straps on their gel couches and put any objects more than two kilos into the lockers set into the wall at their sides. The braking burn would commence in thirty seconds, and reach a maximum burn of three gs. The automated concern made that sound like a lot, but he supposed some folks would be impressed.

He put his hand terminal in the locker, cycled it closed, and waited for the braking rockets to push him back into his couch. In one of the other compartments, a baby was crying. The countdown tones began, a music of converging intervals distinguishable in any language. When the tones resolved into a gentle and reassuring chord, the burn kicked in, pressing him into the gel. He dozed as the ship rattled and shook. The atmosphere of Mars wasn't thick enough to use it for aerobraking on their steep descent path, but it could still generate a lot of heat. Half-awake, he ran through the math of landing, the numbers growing more and more surreal as the light sleep washed over him. If something had gone wrong—a change in the burn, an impact shudder passing through the ship, a shift in the couch's gimbals—he'd have been awake and alert in an instant. But nothing happened, so nothing happened. As homecomings went, it wasn't bad.

The port proper was at the base of the valley. Six and a half kilometers of stone rose up from the pads, the strip of sky above them hardly more than thirty degrees from rim to rim. The processing station was one of the oldest buildings in Mariner, its massive clear dome built with the dual purposes of blocking radiation and providing a view that would impress with its scale. The canyons ran to the east, rugged and craggy and beautiful. Lights glittered from the canyon's sides where the neighborhoods impinged out from the rock, the homes of the insanely wealthy trading the safety of deep stone for the status of an actual exterior window. A transport flier passed, hugging low to the ground where the relatively thick air gave its gossamer wings a little more purchase.

Once upon a time, the data said, Mars had been the home of its own biosphere. Rain had fallen here. Rivers had flowed. Not, perhaps, in the geologic eyeblink of human history, but once. And would, the terraformers promised, again. Not in their lifetimes or their children's, but one day. Alex waited in the customs queue, looking up. The pull of the planet, only about one-third g, felt strange. No matter what the math said, thrust gravity felt different than being down a well. Between the magnificence of the canyons and the eeriness of his weight, Alex felt the anxiety growing in his chest.

He was here. He was home.

The man processing the arriving travelers wore a thick mustache, white with a tinge of red. His eyes were bloodshot and his expression glum.

"Business or pleasure?"

"Neither one," Alex drawled, "I'm here to see the ex-wife."

The man gave a quick smile. "That going to be a business meeting, or pleasure?"

"Let's call it not-business," Alex said.

The processor stroked the screen of his terminal, nodded

toward the camera. As the system confirmed that he was who he claimed to be, Alex wondered why he'd said that. He hadn't said that Tali was a shrew, he hadn't insulted her, but he'd leaned on the assumption for a quick joke. He felt like she deserved better from him. Probably she did.

"'Joy your stay," the processing man said, and Alex was free to enter the world he'd left.

His cousin Min stood in the waiting area. She was ten years younger than him, the last vestiges of youth falling from her and the first comfortable heft of middle age creeping in. Her smile belonged to a little girl he'd known once.

"Hey there, podner," she said, the Mariner drawl probably half a degree thicker than it normally was. "What brings you round these parts?"

"More sentiment than sense," Alex said, opening his arms. They embraced for a moment.

"You got any luggage?" Min asked.

"Traveling light."

"Fair enough. I've got a cart down at the front."

Alex hoisted an eyebrow. "You didn't need to do that."

"They're cheaper than they used to be. The kids aren't back from lower U for another four hours. You got anything you want to do before we've got them underfoot?"

"The only two things I've been looking forward to were seeing people and a bowl of Hassan's noodles."

The look of embarrassment passed over Min's face and vanished again in an eyeblink. "There's a great noodle shop over on the south face. Garlic sauce that'll knock you sideways. But Hassan packed it in about four years ago."

"Ah. No, it's all right. The thing about Hassan's wasn't that they were good."

"Well, now that's truth."

"It's just that they were his."

The cart was a common electric, wider and tougher than the ones they used on stations. The tires were clear polymer that wouldn't streak the floors of the corridors. Alex slid into the passenger's seat, Min taking the controls. They talked about small, domestic things—who in the family was getting married, who was getting divorced, who was moving and where. A surprising number of Min's siblings were on ships headed for the Ring, and though she didn't say it outright, he had the sense that she was more interested in hearing about what he'd seen on the other side of it than in him.

They passed down a long access tunnel and then across one of the linking bridges to Bunker Hill. It was the neighborhood where Alex had grown up. His father's ashes were in the crypt at the synagogue, his mother's had been scattered over the Ophir Chasmata. The first girl he'd ever kissed had lived in rooms two corridors down from the place Min's family was in now. His best friend growing up had been an ethnic Chinese boy named Johnny Zhou who'd lived with an older brother and sister on the other side of the canyon.

Driving along the corridors now, the memories flooded him. The curve of the corridor where the Lone Star Sharabaghar had held weekend dance and drinking contests. The time when he was nine that he'd been caught stealing gum from the bodega at the corner of Dallas corridor and Nu Ren Jie. Getting violently sick in the bathrooms at the Alamo Mall Toll Plaza. A thousand things like them probably happened every day. The only thing that made Alex's experiences different at all was that they were his.

He didn't recognize for a while what was making him uncomfortable. Like the difference between thrust and planetary gravity, the emptiness of the corridors was almost too subtle to notice at first. Even as Min drove deeper into the neighborhood, it was the lights he noticed, and then the locks. All along the corridors, scattered like a handful of thrown sand, rooms and businesses were closed, the windows dark. That in itself didn't mean much, but Alex noticed first one, then a few, then—like flowers in a meadow—a sudden spread of the clunky external locks that landlords and security put on doors when the units weren't in use.

He kept up his end of the banter with his cousin, but he started counting as they drove. In the next hundred doors—homes, businesses, maintenance closets, schools—twenty-one weren't in use.

As Min pulled the cart to a halt at her own doorway, he mentioned it.

"Yup," she said with a lightness that seemed forced. "Ghost world."

Somewhere in the years he'd been gone, Talissa had moved. The old rooms they'd had together were in Ballard, tucked in between the naval station and the old water processing plant. According to the local directories, she was in Galveston Shallow now. It wasn't the neighborhood he'd imagined for her, but things changed. Maybe she'd come into money. He hoped so. Anything that had made her life better, he was in favor of.

The corridors of Galveston Shallow were wide. Half the light came down shafts from the surface, the actual light of the sun strung through a series of transparent shielding to keep the radiation to a minimum. The wide, sloping ceilings gave the place a sense of being natural, almost organic, and the smell of the mechanical air recyclers was nearly hidden by the rich, loamy scents of growing plants. Wide swaths of greenery filled the common areas with devil's ivy and snake plant. The sorts of things that cranked out a lot of oxygen. The moisture in the air was strange and soothing. This, Alex realized, was the dream of Mars made real, if small. The terraforming project would make the whole planet like this someday, if it worked. Flora and fauna and air and water. Someday, centuries after he was gone, people might walk on the surface of Mars, surrounded by plants like these. Might feel the real sun against their skins.

He was distracting himself. He checked his position on his hand terminal against Tali's new address. His heart was going faster than usual and he wasn't sure what to do with his hands.

He wondered what she'd say, how she'd look at him. Anger or joy would both be justified. Still, he hoped for joy.

His plan—find the place, gather himself, and ring the bell—failed because as soon as he turned the last curve to her rooms, he saw her. She was kneeling in among the plants in the common space, a trowel in one hand. She wore thick canvas work pants smeared with soil and a pale brown shirt with a wealth of pockets and loops for gardener's tools, most of them empty. Her hair was a rich brown, so free of gray it had to be dyed. Her face was wider, thicker at the cheeks. Time had been kind to her. She wasn't beautiful. Maybe she'd never been beautiful, but she was handsome and she was Talissa.

Alex felt a smile twitch at his lips, born more from anxiety than pleasure. He pushed his hands into his pockets and ambled over, trying to seem casual. Tali looked up from her work, then down. Her shoulders tensed and she looked up again, staring in his direction. He lifted a hand, palm out.

"Alex?" she said as he reached the edge of the garden space.

"Hey, Tali," he said.

When she spoke, the only thing in her voice was a flat disbelief. "What are you doing here?"

"I had some downtime while my ship's getting fixed up. Thought I'd come back to the old stompin' ground. Touch base with folks. You know."

Talissa nodded, her mouth taking the uneven curl that meant she was thinking hard. Maybe he should have reached out with a message before he came. Only it had seemed to him this was a meeting that should be face-to-face.

"Well," she said. "All right."

"I don't want to interrupt. But, maybe when you're done, I could buy you a cup of tea?"

Tali rolled back onto her heels and tilted her head. "Alex, stop it. What are you doing here?"

"Nothing," he said.

"No. Something. You're here for something."

"Really, I'm not. I just—"

"Don't," she said, conversationally. "Don't bullshit me. No one just shows up at their ex-wife's house out of the blue because they thought a cup of tea sounded nice."

"Well, all right," Alex said. "But I thought..."

Tali shook her head and turned back to digging through the black soil. "Thought what? That we'd get a drink together, talk about old times, get a little maudlin? Maybe fall into bed for nostalgia's sake?"

"What? No. I'm not—"

"Please don't make me be the bad guy here. I have a rich, full, complex life that you *chose* not to be a part of. I have a lot on my plate just now that I don't actually want to share with you, and comforting the guy who walked out on me umpteen years ago because he's...I don't know, having his midlife crisis? It's not my priority, and it's not something that's fair to expect of me."

"Oh," Alex said. His belly felt like he'd swallowed a tungsten slug. His face felt flushed. She sighed, looking up at him. Her expression wasn't cruel. Wasn't even unkind. Tired, maybe.

"I'm sorry," she said. "We're a couple people who used to know each other. At this point, we're maybe even a little less than that."

"I understand. I'm sorry."

"I didn't put you in this position. You put me in it. I was just working with my plants."

"I know. I didn't mean to discomfort you. Not now, and not before."

"Not before? Before, when you walked out on me?"

"It wasn't what I meant to have happen, and it wasn't about you or—"

She shook her head sharply, grimacing as she did.

"No. Not going to do this. Alex? We're talking about the past. That's the conversation I *just said* I don't want to have. All right?"

"All right."

"Okay."

"Sorry if things are...rough."

"I'll be fine," she said.

He lifted his hand again, the same gesture he'd made walking up to her, but with a different meaning now. He turned. He walked away. The humiliation was like a weight on his chest. The urge to turn back, to have one last look in case maybe she was looking at him was almost too much to resist.

He resisted it.

She was right. It was why he'd appeared on her doorstep without warning. Because he'd known that if she said no, he had to respect that, and somewhere in the back of his mind, he'd thought that if they were there, breathing the same air, it would be harder for her to turn him away. And maybe it had been. Maybe what he'd done was actually make it worse for her.

The first bar he came to was named Los Compadres, and the air inside it smelled of hops and overheated cheese. The man behind the bar looked barely old enough to drink, his sallow skin set off by ruddy hair and a mustache that could generously be called aspirational. Alex took a high stool and ordered a whiskey.

"Little early in the day for celebration," the barkeep said as he poured. "What's the occasion?"

"It turns out," Alex said, exaggerating his Mariner Valley drawl just a little for the effect, "that sometimes I'm an asshole."

"Hard truth."

"It is."

"You expect drinking alone to improve that?"

"Nope. Just observing the traditions of alienated masculine pain."

"Fair enough," the barkeep said. "Want some food with it?"

"I'd look at a menu."

Half an hour later, he was only halfway through the drink. The bar was starting to fill up, which meant maybe twenty people in a space that would have taken seventy. Ranchero music played from hidden speakers. The thought of going back to his cousin's and pretending to be cheerful was only a half a degree worse than continuing to sit in the bar, waiting for his self-pity to fade. He kept trying to think about what he could have said or done differently that would have made any difference. So far the best he'd come up with was *Don't walk out on your wife*, which was about the same as saying *Be someone else*.

His hand terminal buzzed. He pulled it up. A written message tagged from Bobbie Draper.

HEY, ALEX. SORRY IT TOOK SO LONG TO GET BACK TO YOU. THINGS ARE WEIRDLY BUSY. YES, IF YOU'RE IN TOWN, I'D LIKE TO MEET WITH YOU. MAY HAVE A FAVOR TO ASK, IF YOU'RE UP FOR IT. SWING BY ANYTIME.

Her address was in Londres Nova. Alex tapped it, and the screen shifted to a map. He wasn't far from the express tube. He could be out there by supper. He touched the bar top with his hand terminal, paid for the drink, and stretched. In the corridor, a cart had broken down, and half a dozen maintenance workers were clumped around it. A woman with skin the color of milk walking past did a subtle double take when Alex nodded. Wondering, he guessed, whether he was the pilot for James Holden. He walked on before she could ask the question.

Yeah. It would be good to see Bobbie.

Chapter Seven: Amos

The spaceport had been built a kilometer outside Lovell City a century before. Now, it was the geographical heart of Luna's largest metropolis, though you wouldn't have been able to tell that from space. Luna boasted very few actual domes. The constant rain of micro-meteors turned a dome into a randomly firing atmosphere ejection port. So as the shuttle descended, the only visible signs of the city were the occasional surface access points and the spaceport itself. The docks weren't the originals, but they were still damned old. The decking had all been white once. Gray pathways marked where years of boots and carts had worn down tracks. The union office looked down over the long hall through pockmarked windows, and the air had the gunpowder stink of lunar dust.

The extortion boys showed up at the disembarking area in force to stare Amos down as he left the ship. He smiled and waved and kept Rico, Jianguo, and Wendy close to him until they were out of the long flight terminal.

"Hermano," Rico said, shaking hands with Amos. "Where you headed to now?"

"Down the well," Amos said. "You fellas take care of that little girl, right? And good luck with the new jobs."

Jianguo hugged Wendy close. "We will. Xie xie usted ha hecho."

Rico and Jianguo stared at him like they expected something else, but Amos had nothing left to say so he turned and walked away toward the terminal for planetary drops. The waiting area was housed in a large false dome designed to impress the tourists. The whole thing was underground, but the massive chamber was covered floor to ceiling with ultra-high-definition video screens showing the outside view. The hills and craters of the lunar surface stretched off in all directions, but it was the blue-and-green half-circle hanging in the sky that drew the most attention. It was beautiful at this distance. The cities nothing but firefly twinkles on the dark side. Where the sun struck the Earth, almost nothing man had made was visible from the lunar orbit. The planet looked clean, unspoiled.

It was a pretty lie.

Seemed like a fact of the universe that the closer you got to anything, the worse it looked. Take the most beautiful person in the solar system, zoom in on them at the right magnification and they were an apocalyptic cratered landscape crawling with horrors. That's what the Earth was. A shining jewel from space, up close a blasted landscape covered with mites living by devouring the dying.

"One ticket to New York," he said to the automated kiosk.

The drop to Earth was short enough that no one tried to run an extortion racket on him, so that was nice. The flight itself was bumpy and nauseating, so that was less nice. One thing about space: it might be a big radiation-filled vacuum that'd kill you in a heartbeat if you weren't paying attention, but at least it never had turbulence. There weren't any windows on the shuttle, but the front of the cabin had a big viewscreen showing the descent through the forward external cameras. New York grew from a gray smudge to a visible cityscape. The spaceport on the artificial land mass south of Staten Island went from a silver postage stamp to a vast network of landing pads and launching rails surrounded by the Atlantic Ocean just past the entrance to Lower New York Bay. Tiny toy ships of suitable size for bobbing in a child's bath grew into the vast solar-powered cargo ships that crawled back and forth across the oceans. Everything visible on the descent was clean and technologically sleek.

That was a lie too.

By the time the shuttle landed he was ready to get into the grunge of the city if only to see something that was honest about itself. When he stood up in the full gravity of Earth to walk off the shuttle, he wanted it to feel wrong, oppressive after all his years away. But the truth was that something deep in him, maybe down at the genetic level, rejoiced. His ancestors had spent a few billion years building all their internal structures around the constant of one g downward pull, and his organism breathed a sigh of relief at the amazing *rightness* of it.

"Thank you for flying with us," a pleasantly nondescript face said from the video screen next to the exit. The voice was carefully crafted to have no specific regional dialect or obvious gender markers. "We hope to see you again soon."

"Go fuck yourself," Amos said to the screen with a smile.

"Thank you, sir," the face replied, actually seeming to look him in the eye. "TransWorld Interplanetary takes your comments and suggestions seriously."

A short tube ride from the landing pad to the spaceport visitors center later and he was in the customs line to enter New York City and officially walk on Earth soil for the first time in twenty-some years. The visitor center stank of too many bodies pressed too tightly together. But under it there was a faint, not-unpleasant odor of rotting seaweed and salt. The ocean, just outside, seeped into everything. An olfactory reminder to everyone passing through the Ellis Island of the space age that Earth was absolutely unique to the human race. The birthplace of everything. The salt water flowing in everyone's veins first pulled from the same oceans right outside the building. The seas had been around longer than humans, had helped create them, and then when they were all dead, it'd take their water back without a thought.

That, at least, wasn't a lie.

"Citizenship, guild, or union docs," the bored-looking man at the customs kiosk said. It appeared to be the only job left in the building not done by a robot. Computers, it seemed, could be programmed to do almost anything but sense when someone was up to no good. Amos had no doubt a full body scanner was looking him over, measuring his heart rate, his skin moisture levels, his respiration. But all of those things could be faked with drugs or training. The human behind the counter would be looking to see if he just *seemed* wrong.

Amos smiled at him. "Sure," he said, then pulled up his UN citizenship records on his hand terminal and the customs officer's computer grabbed them and compared them to the database. The officer read his screen, his face betraying nothing. Amos hadn't been home in almost three decades. He waited to be directed off to the additional security line for a more thorough search. It wouldn't be the first unfamiliar finger up his ass.

"Okay," the customs officer said. "Have a good one."

"You do the same," Amos replied, not able to fully keep the surprise off his face. The customs guy waved an impatient hand at him, telling him to move along. The person waiting behind him in line cleared their throat loudly.

Amos shrugged and moved across the yellow line that legally separated Earth from the rest of the universe.

"Amos Burton?" someone said. An older woman in an inexpensive gray suit. It was the sort of thing mid-level bureaucrats and cops wore, so he wasn't surprised when the next thing she said was, "You need to come with us now."

Amos smiled at her and considered his options. Half a dozen other cops were converging on him in the tactical body armor high-risk entry teams wore. Three of them had tasers out, the other three semiautomatic handguns. Well, at least they were taking him seriously. That was sort of flattering.

Amos raised his hands over his head. "You got me, Sheriff. What are the charges?"

The plainclothes officer didn't respond, and two members of the tactical team pulled his hands behind his back and cuffed him.

"I'm wondering," Amos said, "because I just got here. Any crimes I'm going to commit are theoretical at this point."

"Shush now," the woman said. "You're not under arrest. We're going to take a ride."

"And if I don't want to?"

"Then you'll be under arrest."

The port authority police station was pretty much exactly like every other police station Amos had ever spent time in. Sometimes the walls were industrial taupe; sometimes they were government green. But the concrete walls and glass-fronted offices looking out over a crowded bull pen of desks would have been just as comfortable on Ceres as it was on Earth. Even the burnt-coffee smell was the same.

The plainclothes cop took him past the desk sergeant with a nod and deposited him in a small room that didn't look like the interrogation rooms he was used to. Other than a table and four chairs, the only other furnishing was a massive video screen covering most of one wall. Plainclothes sat him in a chair across from it, then left the room, closing the door behind her.

"Huh," Amos said, wondering if this was some new interrogation technique in the cop playbook. He leaned back in the chair to get comfortable, maybe try to catch some shut-eye after the nauseating shuttle ride.

"What is this? Nap time? Someone wake him the fuck up," a familiar voice said.

Chrisjen Avasarala was on the screen, looking down on him, her face four times its real size on the giant monitor.

"Either I'm not in any trouble, or I'm in all of it," Amos said with a grin. "How you doin', Chrissie?"

"Good to see you too. Call me that again and I'll have an officer beat you gently with a cattle prod," Avasarala replied, though Amos thought he caught a hint of a smile on her face.

"Sure thing, Madam Uber Secretary. This a social call, or...?"

"Why," Avasarala said, all traces of humor gone, "are you on Earth?"

"Came to pay respects to a friend who died. Did I forget to file a form or something?"

"Who? Who died?"

"None of your fucking business," Amos said with a false amiability.

"Holden didn't send you?"

"Nope," Amos replied, feeling the anger start to warm his belly like a slug of good scotch. He tested the restraints, calculating his odds of getting out of them. Of fighting his way past a room full of cops. It made him smile without realizing it.

"If you're here for Murtry, he isn't on Earth right now," Avasarala said. "He claims you beat him half to death in the *Rocinante*'s airlock during the flight back. Do you mean to finish the job?"

"Murtry swung first, so technically, that was self-defense. And if I'd wanted him dead, don't you think he'd be dead? It's not like I quit hitting him because I was tired."

"So what, then? If you have a message for me from Holden just spit it out. If Holden is sending messages to someone else, tell me who and what they are right now."

"Holden didn't send me to do shit," Amos said. "Am I repeating myself? I feel like I'm repeating myself."

"He—" Avasarala started, but Amos cut her off.

"He's the captain of the ship I sail on, he ain't the boss of my fucking life. I've got personal shit to do, and I came here to do it. Now either book me for something or let me go."

Amos hadn't realized Avasarala was leaning forward in her chair until she relaxed back into it. She let out a long breath that turned into a sigh. "You're fucking serious, aren't you?"

"Not known for my comic stylings."

"All right. But you understand my concern."

"That Holden is up to something? Have you met that guy? He's never done anything secretly in his life."

Avasarala laughed at that. "True. But if he's sending his hired killer to Earth, we—"

"Wait, what?"

"If Holden was—"

"Forget Holden. You called me his hired killer. Is that how you guys think of me? The killer on Holden's payroll?"

Avasarala frowned. "You're not?"

"Well, mostly I'm a mechanic. But the idea that the UN has a file on me somewhere that lists me as the *Rocinante*'s killer? That's kind of awesome."

"You say that kind of thing, it doesn't make me think we're wrong, you know."

"So," Amos said, shrugging with his shoulders like an Earther, his hands still behind his back, "we done here?"

"Mostly," Avasarala said. "How was everyone when you left? Good?"

"*Roci* got beat to shit during the Ilus thing. But crew's good. Alex is trying to reconnect with an ex. Captain and Naomi are still rubbing uglies pretty regular. Same same, mostly."

"Alex is on Mars?"

"Well, his ex is. I assume he'd head over there, but he was still on Tycho last I saw him."

"That's interesting," Avasarala said. "Not the part where he's reconnecting with his ex-wife, though. No one ever tries that without seeming like an asshole."

"Right?"

"Well," Avasarala said, then looked up at someone offscreen. She smiled and accepted a steaming cup from a disembodied hand, then took a long sip and sighed with pleasure. "Thank you for meeting with me, Mr. Burton."

"Oh, it was my pleasure."

"Please keep in mind that my name is pretty closely connected with the *Rocinante*, Captain Holden, and his crew at this point."

"So?" Amos said with another shrug.

"So," Avasarala said, then put her steaming cup down and leaned forward again. "If you're about to do something I'll need to cover up later, I'd appreciate a call first."

"You got it, Chrissie."

"Honestly. Fucking stop that," she said with a smile.

The screen went black, and the woman who'd stopped him at the port came in. Amos pointed to the screen with his chin.

"I think she likes me."

The street level view of New York wasn't all that different from the Baltimore streets he'd grown up on. Lots of tall buildings, lots of automated street traffic, lots of people stratified into two distinct groups: those who had someplace to be, and those who didn't. The employed scuttled from public transit to office buildings and back again at shift change. They bought things from street vendors, the simple fact of having currency a mark of status. Those on basic drifted and bartered, living on the excess created by the productive, and adding to it where they could with under-the-table industry too small for the government to notice.

Drifting among them like ghosts, invisible to anyone not from their world, was a third group. The ones who lived in the cracks. Thieves looking for an easy score. Pushers and con artists and prostitutes of every age group, every point on the spectrum of gender and sexual orientation. The kind of people Amos had once been. A corner pusher saw him looking and frowned back, seeing Amos for what he was without recognizing him. It didn't matter. He wouldn't be in town long enough for it to get to anyone who'd come demanding to know where he fit in their ecosystem.

After walking for a couple hours, getting used to the feel of the gravity and concrete beneath his feet, Amos stopped at a hotel he picked at random and checked in. One thing about him had changed, and that was money. Shipping with the *Rocinante*, for all its dangers and drama, had turned out to be a profitable gig. With the shares he'd cashed out, Amos didn't have to worry about how much the hotel would cost; he just asked for a room and told his terminal to pay for anything the hotel charged him.

In his room, he took a long shower. Lydia's face stared back at him from the bathroom mirror as he brushed his teeth and shaved off the short stubble growing on his head. Getting clean had the feeling of ritual. Like preparations made by a holy man before performing some sacred rite.

When he was done, he sat down nude in the middle of the room's large bed and looked up Lydia's obituary.

LYDIA MAALOUF ALLEN, PASSED AWAY WEDNESDAY, APRIL 14TH AT...

Allen. Amos didn't know that name. As an alias it wasn't a very good one, since Lydia Maalouf was the name he'd always known her by. Not an alias then. A married name? That was interesting.

SHE IS SURVIVED BY HER HUSBAND OF ELEVEN YEARS, CHARLES JACOB ALLEN...

Over a decade after he'd left, Lydia had married a man named Charles. Amos probed at that idea, like poking a finger into a wound to see if it was infected. To see if it hurt. The only reaction he found was curiosity.

SHE PASSED QUIETLY IN HER PHILADELPHIA HOME, WITH CHARLES AT HER SIDE...

Charles was the last one to see her alive, so he was the first one Amos needed to find. After reading the rest of the obituary several times, he logged on to the public mass transit site and booked a ticket for that night on the high-speed rail to Philadelphia. Then he lay back on the bed and closed his eyes. He was oddly excited by the idea of meeting Lydia's husband. As if her family was his, and Charles was a person he should always have known, but was only now getting to meet. Sleep eluded him, but the soft bed relaxed the muscles tightening in his back, and the last of the nausea from the shuttle ride faded. The path ahead was clear.

If Lydia had, indeed, died quietly in her own bed with a loving husband at her side, then he would meet this man. See the home she'd lived in. Put flowers on her grave and say his last goodbye. If not, he'd kill some people. Neither possibility excited him more than the other. Either one was fine.

He slept.

Chapter Eight: Holden

Holden ran the video back and watched it again. The ship, an ugly box of metal with additional storage containers strapped to its flanks, made him think of the supply-laden covered wagons in old westerns. It wasn't far from the truth. The *Rabia Balkhi*, registered to Captain Eric Khan out of Pallas, was still just goods and people heading into the frontier to stake a claim. Fewer horses, maybe, but more fusion reactors.

Again, the ship passed through the gate, the image wiggled and jumped, the *Balkhi* was gone.

"So?" Monica asked, her voice rich with anticipation. "What do you think?"

He scratched his arm, deciding what the answer was.

"There are a million reasons an old rust bucket like that might disappear out there," he said. "Loss of core containment, loss of atmospheric pressure, run into debris. Hell, the radio might have just gone out and they're living comfortably on a new planet and hoping someone will drop by to check on them."

"Maybe," Monica said with a nod. "If there was only one. But four hundred thirty-seven ships have passed through the rings into new solar systems over the last year. And of them, thirteen have just vanished. Poof." She spread her fingers out like a tiny explosion. Holden did the math in his head. That was something like a three percent rate of loss. Back when he'd been in the Navy, the budgets had assumed about half of a percent loss to mechanical failure, asteroid impacts, sabotage, and enemy action. This was six times that.

"Huh," he said. "That seems pretty high for ships that were able to fly the year and a half to get to the Ring."

"Agreed. Way too high. If ships blew up without explanation that regularly, no one would ever fly."

"So," Holden said, then paused to order another drink from the table menu. He had a feeling he'd need it. "Why isn't anyone talking about it? Who's keeping track of them?"

"No one!" Monica said triumphantly. "That's the whole thing. No one is tracking them. We have thousands of ships leaving the inner system and streaming toward the gates. They belong to citizens of three different governments, and some who don't think of themselves as citizens of *any* government. Most of these people never even filed a flight plan, they just threw their suitcases in a rock hopper and blasted off for the new worlds."

"Real estate grabs are like that, I guess."

"So here they are, heading off alone or in handfuls, and all of them with the incentive to get wherever it is first. Only something's stopping them. Disappearing them. Or, some of them anyway."

"Clearly," Holden said, "you have a theory."

"I think it's the protomolecule."

Holden sighed and rubbed his face with both hands. His drink arrived, and he sipped at it for a minute. The cold of the ice and the bite of the gin filled his mouth. Monica stared at him, practically bouncing with impatience. He said, "No, it's not. The protomolecule is gone. It's dead. I fired the last processing node into a star."

"How do you know that? Even if it was the last of the ring-building weapon, we know whoever made all this did it with protomolecule tools. And what else can it be? I've read the reports. All those robots and things that woke up on Ilus? The protomolecule attacks us for taking its stuff."

"No, it doesn't," Holden said. "That's not what happened. Without knowing it, I'd brought a node of the original infection with me that was still trying to connect with whatever sent it out in the first place. It woke a lot of stuff up in the process. We shut it down, and, you know, shot it into a star to avoid that happening again."

"How can you be sure?"

At the sushi bar, one of the chefs barked out an announcement, and half a dozen people around him applauded. Holden took a deep breath, letting it out slowly through his teeth.

"I guess I can't be. How do you prove a negative?"

"I know a way that maybe you can," Monica said. The look on her face made Holden think whatever she was about to say next was the entire reason for their conversation. It felt a little like watching a hunting cat track a steak. "Fred Johnson still has what may be the only remaining sample of the protomolecule. The one you took off the secret Mao-Kwikowski ship."

"The one I... Hey, how do you know that?" Holden said. "And how many other people know that?"

"I don't disclose sources, but I think we should get it and see if we can wake it up. Get your ghost Miller to come back and find out if the protomolecule is using the gates to destroy our ships."

Half a dozen responses crashed together in Holden's mind, ranging from *That is the worst idea I've ever heard* to *Are you even listening to what you're saying?* It took a few seconds for one to win out.

"You want me to do a *séance*?"

"I wouldn't call it a—"

"No," Holden said. "Just no."

"I can't just let this drop. If you won't help—"

"I didn't say I wouldn't help. I said I'm not going to go commune with a bit of killer alien goo in hopes that it starts telling me its old cop stories. We don't want to poke that stuff. We should leave it alone."

Monica's expression was open and interested. He wouldn't have been able to see her annoyance and disappointment if he hadn't known to look.

"What then?" she asked.

"You know the old joke about hearing hoofbeats, right?"

"I guess I don't."

"Long story, but the point is that if you hear hoofbeats in the distance, your first guess is that they're horses, not zebras. And you're hearing hoofbeats and jumping straight to unicorns."

"So what are you saying?"

"I'm saying let's go see if we can find some horses or zebras before we start a unicorn hunt."

An intriguing new mystery didn't mean Holden no longer had a day job, but it did give him something to think about other than missing Naomi. And Amos. And Alex. But mostly Naomi. As he crawled along the exposed ribs of the *Rocinante*'s flank with a plasma torch in his hand and looked for cracks, he pondered where ships could go when they disappeared. Monica was right; the number was too high to be just random system failures. There were a lot of other possibilities, even discounting her protomolecule unicorn theory. But Holden had stopped believing in coincidence about when he'd first started spending time with Detective Miller. And the other big thing going on was that radical OPA factions were launching attacks on inner planet holdings like Callisto. And even Earth.

A violent faction of the OPA was dead set against colonization. And, now, colony ships loaded with supplies were vanishing without a trace. Also, Medina Station—nee *Behemoth* nee *Nauvoo* and the hub of all the ring gates—was solidly in the control of the OPA. It made a compelling narrative, even if he didn't have any actual evidence that it was true.

In that scenario, the ships would be boarded by OPA pirate crews, the supplies taken, and the colonists... spaced? A gruesome idea if it were true, and still not the most horrific thing humans had ever done to each other. But that left the ships. They'd keep the ships, and then they'd have to make them disappear. That meant changing the transponder codes. The fact that the *Rocinante* was no longer the *Tachi* was proof that the OPA had that ability.

"Sakai," Holden said, chinning the radio frequency to the private channel he and the chief engineer shared. "Yo, you around?"

"Problem?" he replied in a tone of voice that sounded like he was daring Holden to have a problem. Holden had learned not to be offended by it. Impatience was Sakai's default state.

"More of a riddle."

"I hate riddles," Sakai said.

"Let's say you're trying to figure out if someone has stolen a bunch of ships and changed the transponder codes. How would you find those ships, if you had to?"

The engineer huffed thoughtfully for a moment.

"Don't look for the missing ships," Sakai replied. "Look for the new ones that show up out of nowhere."

"Yes, good. That," Holden said, "is exactly right. Thanks."

He stopped at a cracked weld between the inner hull and one of the ship's ribs and started touching it up with the torch. His faceplate darkened, turning the world into a black place with one bright blue light in it. While he worked, he thought through how you'd track the magically appearing new ships down. The public ship registry was a good place to start, but you'd drown in data trying to do it manually. If Naomi were here, he had no doubt she'd have been able to build a program to find what he wanted in ten minutes on her hand terminal. He, sadly, didn't have her programming skills, but Fred had software engineers on the payroll, and if he—

"Why?" Sakai said. It had been so long since the engineer had spoken that it took Holden a moment to remember the context for the question.

"Why what? Why do I want to know how to find lost ships?"

"Yeah."

"So I have this reporter friend who's looking into some missing ships. I said I'd give her a hand. Just trying to think of ways to actually do that."

"Stuart," Sakai said. It was half statement, half question. "I heard she was on the station."

"Yeah, my old buddy Monica. Truth is, I think she's snipe hunting, but I said I'd help. And I need something to do that isn't feeling lonely and sorry for myself."

"Yeah," Sakai said, then after a long moment added, "So shit hasn't gone weird enough for you to believe in snipes?"

There was a video message light blinking on his home console. Holden tried his hardest not to hope it was from Naomi and still felt a crushing disappointment when Alex's round face appeared on the screen. "Hi boss," the pilot said. "So the thing where I meet up with my ex-wife and we have a tearful reconciliation? Yeah, that was a failure. Probably shoulda thought that one through a little better. But I'm plannin' on stopping by to see Bobbie before I leave, so there's a bright spot. How's my girl? You guys gettin' her all polished up and pretty for my return? I'll check in again when I can. Kamal out."

Holden almost started his reply off by asking for a report on the ex-wife situation, but the little Naomi voice that now lived in his head said *Don't be nosey*, so instead he replied, "Thanks for checking in. Give Bobbie my best. The *Roci*'s still months from ready, so take your time."

He sat for a minute trying to think of something else to say, then just cut the dead air off the end of the message and sent it. It was strange how a person could be so vitally important in your life, and yet you had nothing to say to them when they weren't sharing the same air. Normally, he and Alex would talk about the ship, about the other two crew members, about jobs. With them all split up and the *Roci* in dry dock, there wasn't much left to say that wasn't a personal invasion. Thinking about that looked like the beginning of a long dark road to bitter loneliness, so he decided to go investigating instead.

He kind of wished he had a hat.

"Back so soon?" Fred said when Holden was ushered into his office by one of the OPA leader's minions. "I know my coffee is good, but..."

Holden grabbed a chair and stretched out while Fred puttered with the coffee maker. "So Monica Stuart is on Tycho."

"Yeah. You think someone like that lands on this station without me knowing about it?"

"No," Holden admitted. "But do you know why she's here?"

The coffee maker started hissing to itself, and the office was filled with a rich, bitter smell. While the coffee brewed, Fred leaned over his desk tapping on the terminal. "Something with missing ships, right? That's what our intel team says."

"Have your people looked into it at all?"

"Honestly? No. I'd heard rumblings about it, but we're buried here. Every ship with a functioning Epstein is heading through for the gates. We've got our hands full keeping them from running into each other going through the rings. Most of them are going into unexplored systems with no other ships or stations. We don't hear back from a few, sort of seems like the obvious thing happening."

Holden accepted a steaming mug from Fred with a grateful nod and took a sip. The old man's coffee didn't disappoint. "I get that,"

Holden said after another drink. "And I think her theory on it is pretty far-fetched, but it's the kind of thing that will get public traction if we don't find a better answer first."

"She has a theory already?"

"She thinks it's the protomolecule. The robots and tech waking up on Ilus is her one datapoint."

"You told me that was a onetime thing," Fred said, frowning over his coffee mug. When he spoke again his words blew steam in front of them, like a whisp of dragon breath. "Is Miller back?"

"No, he's not back. As far as I know, there isn't an active protomolecule culture in existence in the universe. But—"

"But I've got the inactive stuff you gave me."

"Right, and Monica knows about it somehow," Holden said.

Fred's frown only deepened at that. "I've got a leak somewhere."

"Yeah, you totally do, but that isn't the part that worries me."

Fred's eyebrows went up in a nonverbal question.

"Monica," Holden continued, "has decided that we should take out the goo and use it like some sort of Ouija board to summon the ghost of Miller."

"But that's stupid," Fred said.

"Right? So I think we should exhaust all other possibilities before we leap right to tinkering with alien viruses."

"First time for everything, I guess," Fred said, only lightly coating the words in sarcasm. "You have alternate theories?"

"I do," Holden said, "but you won't like it."

"I also still have bourbon if we need anesthetic for this operation."

"It may get there," Holden replied, then drank off the rest of his coffee to give himself time. No matter how much Fred had aged over the last half decade, Holden found himself still intimidated by the man. It was hard to broach topics Fred might take offense to.

"More?" Fred asked, pointing at his empty cup. Holden declined with a shake of his head.

"So there's that radical extremist faction of the OPA that you were telling me about," Holden said.

"I don't think—"

"They've had at least two public attacks. One on Martian interests, and one on Earth itself."

"Both of which failed."

"Maybe," Holden said. "But we're assuming we know what their goals were, and that seems like a bad assumption to make. Maybe blowing up a big chunk of a Martian shipyard and forcing the UN home fleet to fire a bunch of missiles at an ancient freighter are wins to them."

"Okay," Fred said with a grudging nod. "Fair enough."

"But there's a third leg to this. Sure, the radicals think Earth and Mars will abandon them once the new worlds are colonized, but that means the colonists themselves are part of the problem."

"Agreed."

"So, what if this radical OPA wing decides that in addition to blowing up some of the inner planets' shit, they can send a message by taking out some colony ships?"

"Well," Fred said, speaking slowly as though he were working out the answer as he said it, "the big problem with that is the location of the attacks."

"Because they happen on the other side of the gates."

"Exactly," Fred continued. "If ships were getting nuked as they passed through the Belt, that would be one thing. But on the other side of the gates? Who has access there? Unless you're thinking the ships were sabotaged in some way. A bomb with a really long fuse?"

"There's another alternative," Holden said.

"No, there isn't," Fred replied, anticipating his next argument.

"Fred, look, I know you don't want to think you've got people working against your interests on Medina. Doctoring records, maybe. Shutting off sensors when there're things they don't want people to see. And I get why that's hard to swallow."

"Medina is central to our long-term plans," Fred said, his words hard as iron. "I've placed all of my very best and most loyal people on that station. If the radicals have a fifth column there, then it means that I can't trust anyone in my organization. I might as well pack it up and retire."

"There are thousands of people on Medina, I doubt you can vouch for every one of them personally."

"No, but the people running the station are *my* people. The most loyal I have. There's no way something like this could be going on without their knowledge and cooperation."

"That's a scary thought."

"It means I don't own Medina Station," Fred said. "It means that the most violent, hard-line, extremist faction of our group controls the choke point of the entire galaxy."

"So," Holden said, "how would one go about finding that out?"

Fred leaned back in his chair with a sigh and gave Holden a sad smile. "You know what I think? I think you're bored, and lonely, and looking for a distraction. Don't dismantle the organization I spent a lifetime building to give yourself something to do."

"But ships are missing. Even if it isn't Medina taking them, something is. I don't know that we can just ignore that and hope it goes away."

"Fix your own ship, Jim. Fix your ship and get your crew back together. This thing with the missing ships isn't your job."

"Thanks for the coffee," Holden said, standing up to leave.

"You're not going to drop it, are you?"

"What do you think?"

"I think," Fred said, "that if you break any of my stuff, you get to pay for it."

"Noted," Holden said with a grin. "I'll keep you in the loop."

As he walked out the door, he could picture Miller smiling and saying, *You can tell you've found a really interesting question when nobody wants you to answer it.*

Chapter Nine: Naomi

Once upon a time there had been a Belter girl named Naomi Nagata, and now there was a woman. Even though the difference between the two had been created a day, an hour, a minute at a time, the Venn diagram of the two almost didn't overlap. What could be cut away, she'd cut years ago. What remained did so in spite of her efforts. For the most part, she could work around them.

"Enjoy your stay on Ceres," the customs agent said, his eyes already flicking to the man standing behind her. She nodded, smiling politely through the spill of her hair, and walked out into the wide corridors of the spaceport. Another face among the millions.

Ceres Station was the biggest city in the Belt. Six million people, more or less, in a hollowed asteroid hundreds of kilometers in diameter. She'd heard that the port traffic alone could add as many as a million transient bodies on a given day. For most of her life, it had been the symbol of inner planetary colonialism. The tower of the enemy on native Belter ground.

Outside the spaceport proper, the corridors were warm bordering on hot, the entropic load of the city trapped by the thermos-bottle vacuum of space. Moisture thickened the air, and the smell of bodies and dried piss was like seeing an old friend's smile. Three-meter-high screens shouted advertisements for machine rigs one second and high fashion the next, their clamor only a thread in the constant, roaring symphony of voices and carts and machinery. A public newsfeed was showing images of fighting somewhere on Earth. Another little insurgent cult or traditional ethnic conflict calling for its due in blood again, important only because it was on Earth. Even for Belters who'd called the float their home for generations, Earth carried a symbolic load. The mother of humanity with her boot firmly on Belter necks. On the screen, a pale-skinned man with blood sheeting down from a scalp wound held up a book. Probably a holy book. He was shouting, his mouth squared by rage. Kill as many people in the Belt, and it wouldn't have been news. Even now.

She turned spinward, looking for a food kiosk serving something appealing. There were the usual corporate products, the same at any station. Now that the OPA ran Ceres, there were also other options. Dhejet and egg curry, cow-style noodle bowl, red kibble. The foods of her childhood. Belter foods. The kitchen on the *Rocinante* had been designed by someone in the Martian Navy, and the food stocks it accepted were always nourishing, usually good, and sometimes excellent. But they weren't *her* food.

She opted for red kibble from a scarred kiosk with adhesive from generations of nightclub flyers caking its sides. It came in a brown pressed-shred container that fit in her left palm with a plastic spatula like a flattened spoon to eat with. The first bite filled her mouth with cumin and her mind with dust-covered memory.

For a moment, she was in her bunk on Tio Kriztec's ship, huddled over the white ceramic bowl she had loved then and forgotten for years, eating quietly while the others sang in the galley. She couldn't have been more than six at the time, but the memory was fresh and bright. She took another bite, savoring it. As she did, she saw the man following her.

He was thin, even for a native. His hair, a dirty gray that flowed back from his head like the folded wings of a bird. He stood maybe fifteen meters away, watching the newsfeed with an air of mild boredom. She couldn't have said what drew her attention to him and left her certain that he was there because of her. Something about the casual way he didn't look toward her, maybe, or the angle of his stance.

Naomi turned spinward again, moving quickly without running, forcing him to keep up. As she walked, she scanned the crowd around her. If she was right, there might be others working in a team. She slid easily through the gaps in the press of bodies, finding the places that opened for a moment as people crossed her path and each other's. She had spent six months on Ceres when she was thirteen and between ships, but the station was still a long way from home territory for her. She did her best, making for a side corridor that she was almost certain ran between the wider pathways.

And maybe she was wrong. Maybe the man, whoever he was, had just happened to be there when she was feeling particularly anxious. She didn't look back until her side corridor rejoined the larger flow of foot traffic from the next gate over. She took the ground in at a glance, and found the place she needed. A currency-changing booth four meters away with opaque privacy walls made a little space in the flow of people like a stone in a river. Without pausing, she walked to the dead space at its far side and leaned against it, her shoulder blades taking in the cool of the metal. The air was thick enough that she was sweating a little, a dampness at her collarbone and the fringes of her hair. She made herself small and unobtrusive, and counted slowly backward from a hundred.

At thirty-two, Wings hurried past her, his chin high, scanning the crowd before him. The bright metallic taste of fear filled her mouth, and she turned back into the booth, and then past it the other way, down the corridor she'd just left. As she retraced her steps, her mind raced through possibilities. Marco had finally decided to end their standoff, and the threat to Filip had been bait for the trap. Or the security forces had been waiting all this time, and she was about to get caught at last. Or someone who'd watched the newsfeeds from Ilus too much had decided to stalk her. Or Marco was just sending his men to check up on her. The last wasn't least likely.

Back in the main corridor, she flagged down a cart and paid for a trip up three levels to an open park. The woman driving the cart didn't look at her twice, which was a relief. Naomi sat back against the hard formed plastic and finished her kibble. The tires hissed against the decking as they took the ramp up, closer to the center of spin and farther from the port.

"Go du-es someplace precise?" the driver asked.

"Don't know where I'm going," Naomi said. "Know when I'm there."

She'd met Marco when she was sixteen and finishing her distributed classwork equivalency on Hygeia Station. On Luna, her work would have gotten her engineering placements at any of the big shipyards. Since it was just an equivalency, she'd known she had another three, maybe four terms before she could get the jobs, even if she already knew how to do the work.

Marco had been part of a salvage and mining crew that based its repairs at Hygeia Station, then looped out into the Belt proper, scraping out rare metals and taking care, sometimes, of the wrecks of old ships that crossed their paths. And maybe, the rumor was, some wrecks that were very, very new. His captain had been an old man named Rokku who'd hated the Inner Planets as much as anyone in the Belt. The crew was the deepest flavor of OPA there was, not a military cell because no one had asked them yet. Naomi had been living with Tia Margolis, another of her adopted aunts, and trading out unlicensed work at the refining station for air, water, food, network access, and a place to sleep. At the time, Marco and his cohort had seemed like a bastion of stability. A crew that had been working the same ship together for seven missions was as good as family to her.

And Marco himself had been amazing. Dark eyes, dark soft hair, a Cupid's bow mouth, and a beard that felt against her palm the way she imagined it would to stroke a wild animal. He'd haunted the corridors outside the station bar, too young still to buy, but more than charming enough to get older people to buy for him on the few occasions he couldn't convince the merchants to bend the rules directly. The others on Rokku's crew—Big Dave, Cyn, Mikkam, Karal—had all outranked Marco on the ship and followed his lead on shore. There hadn't been a particular moment when she'd become part of their crew. She'd just fallen into orbit with the others, been at the same places, laughed at the same jokes, and then at some point she was expected. When they cracked the seal on a storage gate and made it into a temporary invitation-only club, she was invited. And then before long she was helping to crack the seal.

Hygeia Station hadn't been at its best in those days. The Earth-Mars alliance had looked solid as stone back then. The taxes and tariffs on basic supplies hovered just below too expensive to sustain life. And sometimes above it. The ships that ran there ran on air so lean they courted anoxia, and the black market in usable hydroponics was a live and active one. Hygeia Station, while nominally the property of an Earth-based business conglomerate, was in practice a ragged autonomous zone held together by habit, desperation, and the bone-deep Belter respect for infrastructure.

When Marco was there, even the old, cracked ceramic decking seemed a little less crappy. He was the kind of person who changed what everything around him meant. There had been a Belter girl named Naomi who would have sworn she'd follow him anywhere. She was a woman now, and she'd have said that wasn't true.

But here she was.

Bistro Rzhavchina was high up toward the center of spin. Doors of rusted steel painted in sealant blocked the way in, and a bouncer half a head taller than her and twice as wide across the shoulders glowered as she passed through them. He didn't stop her. Up this far, more of the station's spin felt like lateral pull. Water poured on the slant. It wasn't only the cheapness of the real estate that made these corridors thicker with Belters. The Coriolis here started to have an effect just north of subliminal, and that wasn't a thing that Earthers and Martians ever became really comfortable with. Living in spin was a source of Belter pride, a mark of who they were and how they were different.

Dark music filled the place, the rhythm like a constant, low-level assault. The floor was sticky where it wasn't covered with peanut shells, and the smell of salt and cheap beer filled the air. Naomi went to the back, taking a seat sheltered from as many lines of sight as she could manage. Somewhere between fifteen and twenty people sat or stood around the place. She could still feel their gazes on her. Her jaw slid forward a degree, her mouth taking on a scowl that was protective coloration as much as actual displeasure. The wall she rested against vibrated with the bass.

She ordered a drink from the table's system and paid with a preloaded chit. Before the thin-faced boy behind the bar could deliver it, the metal doors to the corridor opened again and Wings came in. His movements were tight and anxious, his expression closed and angry. He hadn't followed her here. This was where he headed back to after he failed. Naomi faded back another centimeter.

Wings sat at the bar, stood up, sat again. A door hidden by shadows at the back of the club opened. The man who came out was huge. The muscles of his neck and torso were so large and defined, she could have used him as an anatomy lesson. His steel-gray hair was cut close to the scalp, white lines of scar crossing behind his left ear like the map of a river delta. A massive tattoo of the OPA's split circle logo decorated the side of his neck. He went to the bar where Wings was waiting. Wings' hands were already out in apology. Naomi couldn't hear what he said, but the gist was clear enough. He'd seen her. He'd lost her. He was sorry. Please don't rip his kneecaps off. She let herself smile a little.

The big man tilted his head, nodded, said something that seemed to relieve Wings enough that he managed a smile. The big man turned slowly, squinting into the gloom of the club. When his gaze reached her, it stopped. The boy at the bar started forward, her drink on a tray. The big man put a hand on the boy's chest, pushing him back. Naomi sat up a little straighter, looking up into the big man's eyes as he reached the table. They were as pale as she remembered.

"Knuckles," he said.

"Cyn," Naomi replied, and then his massive arms were around her lifting her up. She returned the embrace. The smell and heat of his skin was like hugging a bear. "God, you haven't changed at all, have you?"

"Only got better, uhkti. Bigger and brighter."

He put her down with a thump. His smile drew lines all across his face like ripples in a pool. She patted his shoulder and his grin grew wider. At the bar, Wings' eyes were big as saucers. Naomi waved at him. The man sent to follow her hesitated, then waved back.

"So what did I miss?" Naomi asked as Cyn led her to the door at the back of the club.

"Only all of it, sa sa?" Cyn rumbled. "How much did Marco say?"

"Very damned little."

"Always the way. Always the way."

Past the thin door, a corridor snaked back into the raw stone of the asteroid. The sealant was old, gray, and flaking, and cold radiated out from the stone. Three men leaned against the wall, guns in their hands. The oldest was Karal. The younger two she didn't know. She kissed Karal's cheek as she passed. The others looked at her with a mix of distrust and awe. The hidden hallway ended at a steel door.

"Why so secret?" she asked. "You know the OPA runs Ceres now."

"There's OPA and there's OPA," Cyn said.

"And you're that other one," she said, but with warmth in her voice that covered her unease.

"Always," Cyn agreed.

The door slid open, and Cyn ducked to pass through. It was impossible to see around his bulk. Naomi followed.

"Got here and no further," Cyn said over his shoulder. "And best we don't float too long. Plan had us back with Marco a month ago."

"Marco's not here?"

"Nobody here but us chickens." There was a smile in the words.

The chamber they stepped into was wide and cold. A portable scrubber moved stale air and left the smell of rubber. Formed plastic shelves held rations and water. A thin laminate table had five stools around it, and an old network repeater hung from a hook by its wires. A set of bunks leaned against the wall four high. There were bodies curled under the blankets, but if they were sleeping, Cyn didn't take notice of them. His voice carried at the same volume.

"Thing is, better we don't be where anyone can reach us when it all comes down, sa sa?"

"When what comes down?" Naomi said.

Cyn sat at the table, reached out a long arm, and pulled an unlabeled bottle from the shelves. He pulled the cork from its neck with his teeth.

"Ay, Knuckles," he said with a laugh, "you said he didn't tell you much, you weren't singing low, were you?"

Naomi sat on one of the stools as Cyn poured amber liquid into two glasses. The fumes smelled of alcohol and butter and burned sugar. Naomi felt her mouth responding to the scent. The taste was like coming home.

"Nothing like Tia Margolis' brandy," Cyn said with a sigh.

"Nothing, ever," Naomi said. "So, now that I'm here, why don't you fill me in?"

"Well," Cyn said. "It's these pinché ring gates. You know better than anyone. Another thousand inner planets, and a whole new set of reasons they may as well fuck the Belt, que si? And half the Belt sucking the Butcher's cock and making themselves out noble and official and political. So we, and by we I mean Marco, yeah? We decide about two, three years ago—"

"We don't talk about it," a young man's voice said sharply. Cyn looked at the door. Thick with dread, Naomi turned too. The boy looked terribly old and terribly young at the same time. His skin was darker than Marco's, and his hair had more curl. The eyes were the same, though. And the mouth. Something huge—larger than oceans—moved in her chest. Emotions she'd buried rose up, and the rip threatened to pull her away. She tried to hide it, but she had to put a hand flat on the table to steady herself.

He stepped into the room. The sand-colored shirt was large on him, but she could see that his body was in the place between the coltish growth of adolescence and the thickening muscle of a man. One of the figures on the bunk stirred and turned, but didn't otherwise react.

"We don't talk about it until we're safely back. Not even in here. Not at all. Sabez?"

"Savvy mé," Cyn said. "Just thought since—"

"I know what you thought. It passes, but we don't talk about it."

For the first time, the young man's eyes turned to hers. Her own struggle was mirrored in his eyes. She wondered what she looked like to him. What was in his mind and heart where hers was joy and guilt and a venomous regret. This was the moment she hadn't allowed herself to want. She'd known it was coming since the message from Marco arrived on Tycho. She wasn't ready for it. He made a small, quick smile and nodded to her.

"Filip," she said carefully, as if the word were fragile. When he answered, his voice could have been her echo.

"Mother."

Chapter Ten: Amos

The high-speed rail station in Philadelphia was near the center of a middle-income commercial area. Wage earners wandered the streets between strip malls, buying the semi-fashionable clothes and petty luxuries only available to those with currency. Only not too much currency. High-end shopping would be somewhere else, protected by security designed to keep people like these out.

Even on Earth, there were people with money, and then there were people with *money*.

It was weird for Amos to think that he might have enough in his account to pass for the latter. It amused him to imagine wandering over to some highbrow shopping center in his unstylish Belt-made clothes just to give the sales staff a fit when he dropped a couple grand on something useless. Maybe a nice solid platinum drink shaker. For that once or twice a year when he felt like drinking a martini.

Maybe later. After.

He headed out of the mall and toward the residential district that his hand terminal's map said Lydia's old house was in. At the short, tunnel-like exit he was accosted by a boy of eleven or twelve wearing a cheap paper jumpsuit, the kind that basic kiosks dispensed for free with a thumbprint. The boy offered him a variety of sexual services at rock-bottom prices. Amos grabbed the boy by the chin and tilted his face up. There were the fading yellow marks of a not-too-recent beating on his cheek, and the telltale pink around the eyelids of a pixie dust habit.

"Who's your walker?" Amos said.

The boy yanked back away from his hand. "Don't touch for free, man."

"No troubles. I'm not a grabber. Just who's walking you? He around?"

"Don't know what you mean." The boy started looking around for an escape route.

"Yeah, okay. Get lost." Amos watched the boy run off and felt something pressing at his stomach like the onset of a cramp. He couldn't help out every street kid he came across. There were too many of them, and he had other work to do. Frustrating, that. Maybe the kid would find his pimp and tell him about the big scary guy who grabbed his face. Then the pimp would come looking for him, to teach him a lesson about not fucking with the merchandise.

The thought put a smile back on Amos' face and made the knot in his stomach go away.

Lydia's house was thirty-seven blocks from the train station in a low-income neighborhood, but not in a government housing block. Someone was paying actual money for the place, which was interesting. Amos didn't think Lydia could have cleaned up her records enough to qualify for job training. Maybe the husband was a citizen with the skills and clean background to get a straight job. That was interesting too. What kind of guy living an honest citizen's life marries an aging gangster like Lydia?

Amos walked at a leisurely pace, still sort of hoping the pimp would track him down and make an appearance. An hour and a half later his hand terminal told him he'd reached his destination. The house didn't look like much. Just a small one-level that from the street was an almost exact copy of every other small single-story house in the neighborhood. A tiny garden filled the narrow space between the house and the sidewalk. It looked lovingly tended, though Amos couldn't remember Lydia ever owning a plant.

He walked up the narrow path through the garden to the front door and rang the bell. A small, elderly man with a fringe of white hair opened a moment later. "Can I help you, son?"

Amos smiled, and something in his expression made the man take a nervous half step back. "Hi, I'm an old friend of Lydia Maalouf. I just found out she'd passed, and I was hoping to pay my respects." He worked his face for a minute, trying to find a version of his smile that didn't scare little old men.

The old man—Charles, the obituary had said—shrugged after a minute and gestured for Amos to come into the house. On the inside it was recognizably Lydia's space. The plush furnishings and brightly colored wall hangings and curtains reminded Amos of the apartment she'd had back in Baltimore. Pictures lined the shelves and tabletops. Snapshots of the life she'd had after Amos left. Two dogs in a field of grass, grinning and lolling their tongues at the camera. Charles, more hair on his head, but still silvery white, digging in the garden. Lydia and Charles together in a restaurant, candles on the table, smiling over their wineglasses.

It looked like a good life, and Amos felt something in his belly relax when he saw them. He wasn't sure what that meant, but it was probably a good thing.

"You got a name?" Charles said. "Want some tea? Was making some when you rang."

"Sure, I'd take some tea," Amos said, ignoring the first question. He stayed in the cozy living room while Charles banged around in the kitchen.

"It's been a couple months since the funeral," Charles said. "Were you up the well?"

"Yeah, working in the Belt most recently. Sorry it took a while to make it back down."

Charles came back out of the kitchen and handed him a steaming mug. From the flavor, it was green tea, unsweetened.

"Timothy, right?" Charles said, as if he were asking about the weather. Amos felt his jaw clench. Adrenaline dumped into his bloodstream.

"Not for a long time now," he replied.

"She talked about your mom, some," Charles said. He seemed relaxed. Like he knew whatever was going to happen was inevitable.

"My mom?"

"Lydia took care of you after your mom died, right?"

"Yeah," Amos said. "She did."

"So," Charles said, then took another sip of his tea. "How does this go?"

"Either I ask if I can take some of those roses out front to lay on her grave..."

"Or?"

"Or I just take them because no one lives here anymore."

"I don't want any trouble."

"I need to know how it happened."

Charles looked down, took a deep breath, and nodded. "She had what they called an ascending aortic aneurysm. Went to sleep one night, never woke up. I called the EMTs the next day but they said she'd been dead for hours by then."

Amos nodded. "Were you good to her, Charles?"

"I loved her, boy," he replied, a hint of steel in his voice. "You can do what you want here, I can't stop you. But I won't have you questioning that. I loved her from the moment we met to our last kiss goodnight. I still do."

The old man's voice didn't quaver a bit, but his eyes were watery and his hands trembled.

"Can I sit?" Amos asked.

"Suit yourself. Let me know if you want more tea. Pot's full."

"Thank you, sir. I'm sorry about rousting you like that. But when I heard, I worried—"

"I know who Lydia was before we met," Charles said, sitting down on a small couch facing him. "We were always honest with each other. But no one ever bothered us here. She just had a leaky artery and it gave out one night while she was sleeping. Nothing else."

Amos rubbed his scalp for a moment, waiting to see if he believed the old guy. Seemed like he did.

"Thanks. And, again, I'm sorry if I came on strong," Amos said. "So, can I take a few of those roses?"

"Sure," Charles said with a sigh. "Ain't my garden much longer anyway. Take what you want."

"You moving?"

"Well, the guy who was doling Lydia stopped when she died. We had a little set aside, but not much. I'll be going on basic pretty soon, so that means the government block."

"Who was floating her?" Amos asked, already knowing the answer.

"Kid named Erich. Runs a crew in Lydia's old hometown. Somebody you used to know, I guess."

"Used to," Amos agreed. "Does he know about you? That Lydia was married?"

"Sure. He kept in touch. Checked up on us."

"And he cut you off after she died."

It wasn't a question, and Charles didn't answer, just sipped at his tea.

"So," Amos said, standing up, "got a thing I need to go do. Don't start moving out yet. One way or another, I'll make sure you've got the money to keep this place."

"You don't have to do that."

"Sort of do."

"For her," Charles said.

"For her."

The high-speed to Baltimore took less time than the walk to the station had. The city itself hadn't changed at all in the two decades Amos had been away. The same cluster of commercial high-rises, the same sprawl of basic and minimal-income housing stretching out until it hit the orderly blocks of middle-class houses on the outskirts. The same rotting seaweed smell of the drowned eastern shore, with the decaying shells of old buildings sticking out of the murky water like the ribs of some long-dead sea monster.

As much as the realization bothered him, Amos had to admit it looked like home.

He took an automated electric cab from the train station to his old neighborhood. Even at the street level, the city looked the same, more or less. The streetlights had been swapped out for a different, boxy design. Some of the streets had changed from pedestrian-exclusive to mixed use. The thugs and dealers and sex workers were different faces now, but they were all on pretty much the same corners and stoops their predecessors had worked. New weeds growing in all the city's cracks, but they were the same cracks.

He had the cab let him out at a corner coffee stand that was licensed to accept basic ration cards. It was in the exact same location as the last place he'd ever eaten in Baltimore before he left. The cart and the franchise brand were different, but the assortment of rolls and muffins looked identical.

"Tall cup and a corn muffin," he said to the girl working the cart. She looked so surprised when his terminal transferred actual money instead of basic ration credits that she almost dropped his food. By the time his Ceres New Yuan routed through the network and into UN dollars, with every exchange and transfer tacking on fees, he wound up paying triple for his snack.

The muffin tasted like it had been recycled from old, previously eaten corn muffins. And the coffee could have passed for a petroleum product, but he leaned against a wall beside the stand and took his time finishing both. He tossed what was left into recycling and thanked the girl. She didn't reply. His space money and foreign clothes left her staring at him like some sort of alien creature. Which, he supposed, he sort of was.

He had no idea where to start looking for Erich. But he didn't have to walk far before a teenage girl with machine-quality braids and expensive cotton pants drifted out of a shadowy doorway.

"Hey," he said. "You got a minute?"

"For you, Mongo?"

"Name's not Mongo," Amos said with a smile. He could see fear in her eyes, but it was well hidden. She was used to dangerous strangers, but part of that was she knew they were dangerous.

"Should be, brute like you."

"You're local. Help a guy out."

"You need herbage? Dust? I got neuros, that's your thing. Make you fly outta this shithole."

"Don't need your stuff to fly, little bird. Just a question."

She laughed and gave him her middle finger. He wasn't a customer, so he wasn't anything. She was already turning back to her dim doorway. Amos grabbed her upper arm, firmly but gently. There was a spark of real fear in her eyes.

"Gonna ask, little bird. You answer. Then I let you fly."

"Fuck you, Mongo." She spat at him and tried to pull her arm out of his grip.

"Stop that. Just gonna hurt yourself. All I want to know is, who runs your crew? Looking to talk to a guy called Erich. Messed-up arm? If your crew ain't with him, just point me at someone who is, sabe?"

"*Sabe*?" She stopped struggling. "Speak English, asshole."

"Erich. Looking for Erich. Just point me and I'm gone."

"Or maybe I bleed you out," a new voice said. Someone big came out of the same doorway his little bird used. A mountain of a man with scars around his eyes and his right hand inside the pocket of his baggy sweatshirt. "Let her go."

"Sure," Amos said, and turned little bird loose. She bolted for the steps up to her doorway. The walking mountain gave him a nasty grin. Taking Amos' compliance for fear.

"Now get gone."

"Naw," Amos said, smiling back. "Need to find Erich. Big boss now from what I hear. He running your crew? Or can you point me at a crew working for him?"

"I fucking told you to—" Whatever else the mountain was about to say turned into a gurgle after Amos punched him in the throat. While the mountain was trying to remember how to breathe, Amos yanked up the bruiser's sweatshirt and plucked out the pistol he had tucked in his belt. He stomped on the back of the mountain's leg to drop him to his knees. He didn't point the pistol at him, just held it casually in his right hand.

"So, this is how it goes," Amos said in a voice low enough the mountain would hear him but no one else would. Embarrassment was the number one reason people fought. Reduce how embarrassed the mountain was, reduce the likelihood he'd continue fighting. "I need to find Erich, and either you're my friend on that, or you're not. Do you want to be my friend?"

The mountain nodded, but he wasn't talking yet.

"See, I like making new friends," Amos said and patted the thug on his beefy shoulder. "Can you help your new pal find his other friend, Erich?"

The mountain nodded again and managed to rasp out, "Come with me."

"Thanks!" Amos said, and let him up.

The mountain shot a look at the dim doorway, probably signaling little bird to call ahead to someone—hopefully Erich's crew—

with a warning. That was all right. He wanted Erich to feel safe when they met. If he had a lot of guys with guns with him, he'd be more likely to relax and listen to reason.

The mountain led him through his old neighborhood and down toward the docks and the crumbling stone monolith of the failed arcology project there. He was limping a little, like his knee was bothering him. A couple of guys with baggy coats that only sort of hid the heavy weapons underneath nodded at them as they went in, and then fell in step behind them.

"An escort and everything," Amos said to one of them.

"Don't do nothing stupid," came the reply.

"Fairly sure I'm a few decades late on that one, but I take your point."

"Gun," the other guard said, holding out his hand. Amos dropped the pistol he'd liberated from the mountain into it without a word.

From the outside, the old arcology structure was falling apart. But once inside, the look changed dramatically. Someone had replaced the water-damaged flooring with new tile. The walls were painted and clean. The rotting wood doors off the main corridor had been replaced with composites and glass that could take the damp air. It looked like nothing so much as a high-end corporate office building.

Whatever Erich was up to, he was doing well for himself.

They stopped at an elevator, and the mountain said, "He's up on the top floor. I'm gonna bail, okay?" His voice still rasped, but it sounded a lot better.

"Thanks a lot for the help," Amos said without sarcasm. "Take care of that throat. Ice it up when you get back and try not to talk too much. If it's still bugging you in three days, steroid spray'll do it."

"Thanks," the mountain croaked and left.

The elevator dinged and opened, and one of his two remaining guards pointed inside. "After you."

"Gracias," Amos said and leaned against the back wall of the car. The guards followed, one of them sliding a metal card into the elevator controls and hitting the top button.

On the way up, Amos entertained himself by figuring out how he'd get the gun away from the guard closest to him and kill the other. He had a pretty workable strategy in mind when the elevator dinged again and the doors slid open.

"This way," one guard said, and pointed down a hallway.

"The club level," Amos replied. "Fancy."

The top floor had been redesigned with plush furnishings and a maroon velvet carpet. At the end of the hall the guards opened a door that looked like wood but seemed heavy enough that it was probably steel core. Still fancy, but not at the cost of security.

After the luxury of the hallway, the office on the other side of the door was almost utilitarian. A metal desk dominated by screens for a variety of network decks and terminals, a wall screen with an ocean view pretending to be a window, and a big rubber ball instead of an office chair.

Erich always had been twitchy sitting still too long.

"Timmy," Erich said, standing behind the desk like it was a barricade. The two guards moved off to flank the door.

"People call me Amos now."

Erich laughed. "Guess I knew that, right?"

"Guess you did," Amos said. Erich looked good. Healthy in a way he'd never looked as a kid. He even had a middle-aged man's spare tire around the gut. He still had the small, shriveled left arm. And from the way he was standing, he looked like he'd still walk with a limp. But now, surrounded by his success and his well-fed chubbiness, they looked like trophies of a past life instead of disabilities in the current one.

"So," Erich said, "kind of wondering what you're doing in town."

"He beat up Troy," one of the guards said. "And Laci says he manhandled her some too."

"Did he kill anyone?" Erich asked. When neither guard answered, he said, "Then he's still being polite."

"That's right," Amos agreed with an amiable nod. "Not here to mess up your shit, just here to chat."

"So," Erich said, sitting back down on his rubber ball chair, "let's chat."

Chapter Eleven: Alex

Three days after he'd seen Talissa—for what he had to think now was the last time—and gone afterward to eat with Bobbie Draper, Alex knew it was time to go home. He'd had dinners with family and a couple old friends; he'd seen the ways his old hometown had changed and the ways it hadn't. And he'd determined once again that sometimes a broken thing couldn't be fixed. That was the closest he was going to get to having it be okay.

But before he left, there was one more person he was going to disappoint.

The express tube to Londres Nova hummed to itself, the advertisements above the seats promising to make the lives of the riders better in a hundred different ways: technical certifications, improved undergarments, tooth whitening. The facial-recognition software didn't seem to know what to make of him. None of the ads spoke to him. The closest was a thin lawyer in an olive-green suit offering to help people find passages to the new systems beyond the Ring. *Start a new life in the off-world colonies! We can help!*

Across from him, a boy of about seventeen was staring quietly into space, his eyes half-open at the edge of boredom and sleep. When Alex had been about the boy's age, he'd been deciding whether to go into the Navy or apply for upper university. He'd been dating Kerry Trautwine even though Mr. Trautwine was a religious zealot who hated him for not belonging to the right sect. He'd spent his nights playing battle simulations with Amal Shah and Korol Nadkarni.

This boy across from him was traveling the same corridors that Alex had, eating at some of the same restaurants, thinking about sex in likely more or less the same terms, but he also lived in a different universe. Alex tried to imagine what it would have been like to include travel to an alien planet in among his options at seventeen. Would he have still enlisted? Would he have met Talissa?

A gentle, mechanical voice announced their arrival at the Aterpol terminal. The boy's eyes opened, roused back to full consciousness, and he shot a distrustful look at Alex. The deceleration pushed Alex's back, feeling almost like a long attitude burn. Almost but not quite.

Aterpol was the downtown of Londres Nova, the only station with connections to all of the neighborhoods that made up the city. The vaulted ceilings curved over the common areas, the access doors along the walls double-sealed to keep air from leaking into the evacuated tubes. The terminal itself opened into a wide public park with real trees rising from the soil into the artificial twilight. Benches made to look like wood and iron stood scattered along the winding paths, and a pond filled the air with the smells of algae and moisture. The reassuring breeze-murmur of the air recyclers passed under everything like a constant and eternal prayer. Windows rose up along the walls, light streaming out of them or not. The rooms that looked out over Alex as he walked were businesses and apartments, restaurants and maintenance halls.

Alex crossed the park to the farther gates, where the local tubes ran to the other neighborhoods. Innis Shallow, where Bobbie lived, didn't have the best reputation. The worst that Mars had to offer wasn't as bad as an iffy sector on Ceres Station, though, and regardless anyone who took on Bobbie was either suicidal or had an army behind them.

At the Innis Shallow station, Alex shrugged into his jacket and went on foot. There were carts for rent and a girl of no more than fourteen with a scavenged rickshaw calling on the corner. It was a short walk, though, and Alex was dreading the conversation at the end of it.

He'd walked the same path three days before, still smarting from his abortive meeting with Tali, following his hand terminal's directions to Bobbie's rooms. He hadn't seen the former marine since Luna the night that the Ring had lifted itself off the ruins of Venus and flown out toward the far edge of the system, and he'd been looking forward to anything that would distract him from the day he'd been having until then.

Bobbie was living in a very pleasant side corridor with its own greenway in the center and lights that had been fashioned to look like wrought-iron lamps from someone's imagined 1800s London. He'd only had to stand at her door for a few seconds before it opened.

Bobbie Draper was a big woman, and while years of civilian life had lost her a little of her muscle definition, she radiated competence and strength the way a fire did heat. Every time he saw her, he remembered a story from ancient history about the native Samoans armed with rocks and spears driving the gun-toting Spanish conquistadors into the sea. Bobbie was a woman who made that shit seem plausible.

"Alex! Come in. I'm sorry the place is a mess."

"Ain't worse than my cabin at the end of a long run."

The main room was wider than the ops deck back on the *Roci*, and done in shades of terra-cotta and gray that shouldn't have worked together, but did. The dining table didn't seat more than four, and there were only two chairs beside it. Through an archway across from the front door, a wall monitor was set to a slowly shifting spray of colors, like Monet's water lilies animated. Where most places would have had a couch, a resistance-training machine dominated the space, a rack of chrome free weights beside it. A spiral staircase led up and down in the den's corner, bamboo laminate steps glowing warmly in the light.

"Fancy digs," Alex had said.

Bobbie's glance at her own rooms seemed almost apologetic. "It's more than I need. A lot more than I need. But I thought I'd like the space. Room to stretch out."

"You thought you would?"

She shrugged. "It's more than I need."

She put on a brown leather jacket that looked professional and minimized the breadth of her shoulders, then led him to a fish shack with shredded trout in black sauce that had been some of the best he'd ever had. The beer was a local brew, served cold. Over the course of two hours, the sting of Talissa's voice and his feeling of self-loathing lost their edges, if they didn't quite vanish. Bobbie told stories about working veterans' outreach. A woman who'd come in to get psychiatric help for her son who wouldn't stop playing console games since he'd finished his deployment. Bobbie had made contact with the boy's first drill sergeant, and now the kid had a job at the shipyards. Or the time a man came in claiming that the sex toy lodged in his colon was service related. When Bobbie laughed, Alex laughed with her.

Slowly, he'd started taking his turn too. What it had been like on the far side of the Ring. Watching Ilus or New Terra or whatever the hell they wound up calling it as it went through its paroxysms. What it had been like shipping back with a prisoner, which led into the first time they'd shipped a prisoner—Clarissa Mao, daughter of Jules-Pierre and sister to the protomolecule's patient zero, that one had been—and how Holden and Amos and Naomi were all doing these days.

That had been when the ache hit. The homesickness for his crew and their ship. He enjoyed Bobbie's wit and the easy physicality of her company, but what he'd really wanted—then and in the days since—was to be back on the *Rocinante*. Which was why the end of their conversation had been so awkward for him.

"So, Alex," Bobbie said, her attempt to make the words as casual and friendly as everything that had gone before flagging them at once, "are you still in touch with anyone over at the naval yard?"

"I know a few guys still serving at Hecate, sure."

"So I was wondering if I could get you to do a little favor for me."

"Sure, of course," Alex said. And then a fraction of a second later, "What is it?"

"I've got a kind of hobby thing going on," she said, looking pained. "It's…unofficial."

"Is it for Avasarala?"

"Sort of. The last time she was through, we had dinner, and some of the things she said got me thinking. With the new worlds opening up, there's a lot of change going on. Strategies shifting. Like that. And one of the big resources Mars has—one of the things that there's going to be a market for—is the Navy."

"I don't understand," Alex said, leaning back in his chair. "You mean like mercenary work?"

"I mean like things going missing. Black market. We've been through a couple pretty major wars in the last few years. A lot of ships got scrapped. Some of them it seems like we just lost track of. And the Navy's stretched pretty thin. I don't know how much energy they're putting into tracking things right now. You know there was an attack on the Callisto shipyards?"

"Saw something about that, yeah."

"So that's an example, right? Here's a big incident, and the first response is all about identifying who was behind it and rebuilding the defenses."

"Sure," Alex said. "You'd want to do that, right?"

"So figuring out exactly what was lost in the attack is on someone's to-do list, but it's not the top. And with all the shit going on, it may never get to the top. And everyone kind of knows that, even if they aren't saying it."

Alex drank, put down the bottle, and wiped his mouth with the back of his hand. "So if there's a profiteer on the base, they could take the opportunity to lift some equipment that survived, sell it on the black market, and call it lost."

"Exactly. I mean to some degree, that's always happening, but right now, with things a little chaotic and getting weirder all the time?"

"And with Mars losing a lot of its people to colony ships."

"Yeah, that too," Bobbie said. Her expression was hard. Alex sat forward, his elbows on the table. The smell of trout and black sauce still hung in the air, though the plates were gone by then. On the screen at the front of the restaurant, a young woman in a parody of business wear danced to a computer-generated pop tune. Alex hadn't been able to make out the language; at a certain speed every language sounded equally meaningless.

"You're telling me that you're investigating the sources of black market military equipment flowing off Mars."

"Weapons," Bobbie said. "Medical supplies. Ammunition. Power suits. Even ships."

"And you're doing it on your own, for fun, because of something Chrisjen Avasarala said to you."

"I'm kind of working for her."

Alex laughed. "I'm almost afraid to point this out, but you started off saying you needed a favor. You haven't told me what the favor is."

"A lot of the guys on Hecate won't talk to me. I'm a marine, they're Navy. There's that whole thing. But you know them, and even if you don't, you're one of them in a way I'm not going to manage this lifetime. I was wondering, as a favor, if you could help me dig a little."

Alex had nodded at the time, but what he'd said was "Let me think about it."

And now, because it was Bobbie and because he needed something in his life to actually have a moment of real closure, he was going to see her one last time to tell her the answer was no. He had a ship to get back to. If there was something he could do for her from there, he'd be pleased to lend a hand. His first priority now was getting off Mars and not coming back.

He reached the end of her corridor. The iron lanterns were glowing, creating the illusion of a street back on Earth centuries before. The echo of a place that neither he nor Bobbie had ever been, and still it was pleasant and comforting. He walked slowly, listening to the almost-silent chucking of the recyclers as if, just behind them, he could catch the murmur of the flowing Thames.

Somewhere nearby a man shouted once and briefly. It was Innis Shallow after all. Alex walked a little faster. At Bobbie's door, he paused.

It was closed, but not solidly. A black smudge, perfectly round and dented into the flesh of the panel, marked it just where the latch met the frame. A thin line of light at the door's edge showed where the frame had bent, the ceramic shattering. The man's voice came again, a low mutter rising to a final, powerful snap. It was coming from inside Bobbie's rooms.

Alex's heart beat triple time as he pulled out his hand terminal and tapped quickly, quietly to the local system's emergency services link. He thumbed in an alert request and a confirmation, but didn't fill in the details screen. There wasn't time for it. He stood before the door, his hands in fists, wishing as hard as he'd ever wished anything that Amos was there too.

He pushed the door open and rushed in.

Bobbie was at the table, sitting in one of the two chairs. Her arms were behind her. Her legs were splayed out before her, too long for the chair to accommodate. There was blood on her mouth and down the side of her neck. A man in gray coveralls was pointing a gun at the back of her head.

Two other men, dressed in the same gray, turned toward Alex. Both of them had automatic pistols in their fists. A fourth man, this one in a casual suit the color of ash and a bright blue shirt, turned to Alex, his expression equal parts surprise and annoyance. When he saw Alex, his eyes went wide.

"Fuck!" the man in the suit said, the syllable almost lost in the noise of cracking wood. Bobbie moved faster than Alex could follow, shrugging the chair she was bound to into splinters and grabbing the gunman behind her by the wrist. He screamed and something wet happened to his arm.

One of the pistol men fired wildly, the stuttering report assaulting Alex's ears. He rushed forward shouting and barreled into the man in the suit. Together, they staggered back. The other man's knee rammed into Alex's groin, and the world dissolved into blinding pain. Alex slid to his knees, trying to hold the man by his suit jacket. The guns continued their barrage and the stink of spent powder filled the air.

The man in the suit dug for a shoulder holster, and Alex grabbed his arm. The man's wrist was like holding concrete. There was a gun in his fist. Someone shouted, and the roar of gunfire became the roar of something else, deeper and more animal. Alex pulled himself forward, the pain in his testicles fading to merely excruciating. He bit the solid wrist, sinking teeth into the raw silk sleeve and digging until his incisors met. The man in the suit didn't even cry out, just brought his other hand down hard on Alex's temple.

Everything got a little quieter, a little more distant. Alex felt his grip slip off the man's arm, felt himself falling back, landing hard on his tailbone. The pain was there, but foggy. The man in the suit lifted his pistol to point at Alex. The barrel looked wide as a cave.

Oh, Alex thought, *I die like this.*

The man's head twitched forward in a curt nod and he crumpled. Then it was Bobbie standing before him, a six-kilo free weight curled in one hand. The chrome had blood on it and what looked like hair. No one was shooting guns anymore.

"Hey," Alex said.

"You all right?" Bobbie asked, sitting next to him. One of the gunmen staggered past her, cradling his forearm, and bolted out the door. She didn't go after him.

"Little achy," Alex said, then rolled to his side and retched.

"It's okay," Bobbie said. "You did really well."

"Been a long time since hand-to-hand. I probably could have done better if I'd had some practice."

"Yeah, well. There were four of them with guns and two of us without. All things considered, we did okay."

She blew out a long breath, her head sinking low. Alex tried to sit up.

"You all right?"

"Got shot a couple times," she said. "Smarts."

"Shit. You're hurt?"

"Yeah. I'm going to get over to the console there in a minute. Call emergency services before blood loss makes me woozy."

"I already did that," Alex said. "Before I came in."

"Good planning."

"Not sure planning had much to do with it," Alex said. And then, "Bobbie? Stay with me here."

"I'm here," she said, her voice sleepy. "I'm all right."

In the distance, Alex heard the rising tritone of sirens. Breath by breath, they grew closer. For a long moment, he thought the deck was being shaken, then realized it was just his body, trembling. At the side of the room, one of the gunmen lay slumped against the wall. His neck was at a strange angle, and blood was drying on his chest. He wasn't bleeding though. Dead, then. The man in the suit coughed and gagged, choking. The sirens got louder. There were voices now too. A woman identifying herself as police and warning them that people were coming in.

"I was coming to tell you," Alex said. "I'll stay. I'll help."

"Thanks."

"This was about the black market stuff, wasn't it?" Alex said. "I guess you've been asking the right questions."

Bobbie managed a smile. Looking at her now, there was a lot of blood on her shirt.

"Don't know," she said. "All they asked me about was you."

Chapter Twelve: Amos

Want some coke?" Erich asked. "Not synth. Real stuff that came from a plant."

"Nope. But I'd take a drink if one is handy," Amos replied. The pleasantries were just ritual, but ritual was important. In Amos' experience the more dangerous any two people were, the more carefully polite their social interactions tended to be. The loud, blustering ones were trying to get the other guy to back down. They wanted to stay out of a fight. The quiet ones were figuring out how to win it.

"Tatu, bring the El Charros," Erich said, and one of the two guards slipped out the door. To Amos he added, "Been on a tequila kick lately."

"I haven't," Amos said. "Earth is still the only place you can get good tequila. The Belter stuff is undrinkable."

"Not a lot of blue agave up there, I guess."

Amos shrugged and waited. Tatu returned with a tall skinny bottle and two narrow shot glasses. Erich filled both then lifted one in salute.

"To old friends."

"Old friends," Amos repeated and tossed back his shot.

"Another?" Erich asked, pointing at the bottle.

"Sure."

"Seen much of the neighborhood?"

"Just what was between here and the train station."

"Hasn't changed much," Erich said, then paused while they both drank off their shots. He refilled their glasses. "Faces change, but the corners stay the same."

"Funny, I was just thinking that same thing on my way in. Things have changed for you though."

"Not the important ones," Erich said with a grin and wiggled his small, withered left arm.

Amos gestured at the room, the guards, the renovated building around them. "When I left, you were running for your life. So, at least one thing's different."

"You guys can go," Erich said to Tatu and his partner. They slipped out quietly and shut the door behind them. That seemed like a good sign. Either it meant that Erich was sure Amos wasn't there to kill him, or Erich had a way of protecting himself that didn't require other people. It wouldn't be a gun under the desk. That was too direct for Erich. Amos started casually scanning for wires or suspicious lumps on his chair or the floor beneath it.

Erich poured two more shots of tequila then said, "I learned something important from you, when you left."

"Do tell."

"I'll never be the toughest guy in any room, unless I'm by myself," Erich said, waving his small arm again. "But I'm usually the smartest. Executing a plan can be subcontracted out. Making the plan in the first place, not as much."

"True enough," Amos agreed. "It's why I'll never be the captain of a ship."

Erich reacted to that. He didn't change his expression or flinch, but Amos could see the words getting taken in and filed as important.

"But always useful, you," Erich said. "You were always useful. You on a crew now?"

"You haven't seen me in the news?"

"I have. You look different. Shaved your head, got your nose broke a few more times. But I'll never forget a name."

"Well, not this one anyway," Amos said, and then tossed his shot back in a toast to Erich. "Gracias for that, by the way."

"So, you still with that crew?" Erich said.

"I am. Why?"

"Because you're sitting in my office right now drinking my tequila. Still playing that out in my head. Useful guy like you can always get work. If that's what you want, I've got it. But if you're not here looking for work, what are you looking for?"

Amos grabbed the bottle and poured himself another drink. Erich tried very hard not to look nervous. He'd had a lot of practice, because he almost pulled it off. Time can change a lot. Erich had gone from twitchy little hacker with a price on his head to the boss of a respectable chunk of Baltimore's harbor-front property. But some things don't change. Some tells never go away. While Erich sat very still and looked him in the eye without blinking, the tiny hand on his deformed left arm opened and closed like a baby grabbing at a toy just out of reach.

"Went to Lydia's house," Amos said, sipping slowly at the tequila.

"Not Lydia's house anymore. She's dead," Erich said. "That what this is about? I treated her like you would have after you left."

"Yeah?" Amos asked, eyebrows going up.

"Well," Erich admitted with an embarrassed look to the side. "Not exactly like you would have."

"Thank you for that too," Amos said.

"You didn't kill me once when you had every reason to, and

after that, you couldn't have stayed," Erich said, leaning forward. His left hand had stopped clenching. "Walking away from her was part of the favor you did for me. I never forgot that. And she helped me, at first. Helped me build what I have now. Taught me to use brains to beat brawn. She never lacked for a thing it was in my power to give."

"And I appreciate that," Amos repeated. Erich's eyes narrowed and his right hand came up from under the desk with a short-barreled automatic in it. Amos found himself surprised and a little proud of his friend. Erich rested his hand on the desk, the gun pointed away from Amos, more a warning than a threat.

"If you've got some beef you came here to settle," Erich said, "you won't be the first guy to leave this office in a bag."

Amos raised his hands a little in mock surrender. "Not even armed, chief. I came here to talk."

"So talk."

"What you did for Lydia was real nice," Amos said, putting his hands back down slowly but keeping his eye on the gun. "But you're wrong. She's not all dead. Some of her's left."

Erich cocked his head to the side, frowning. "Gonna need to walk me through that one."

"There's an old man loved her and lived with her and kissed her goodnight before she died. A house with a little rose garden they worked together. Maybe some dogs. I saw a picture, but not sure if they're still around."

"I still don't get it," Erich said.

Amos rubbed his thumb against his knuckle, trying to find the words. It wasn't a thought he'd said out loud before, and if he screwed it up and Erich misunderstood, there was a chance they'd wind up trying to kill each other. So it was worth thinking about some.

"It's like this. The old man keeps the house until he dies. He's the only thing she left behind. He's the last bit of her. He keeps the house."

Erich put the little gun flat on the desk and poured himself another drink. He leaned back, holding the glass with his right hand. He couldn't pick the weapon back up without dropping the drink and he couldn't do that faster than Amos could reach him. It was a signal, and Amos felt the tension leave the muscles in his neck and shoulders.

"That's more sentimental than I would have guessed," Erich said.

"I'm not sentimental about much," Amos agreed. "But when I am, I'm pretty passionate."

"So I've heard the request. What's the payoff for me? I had something of a debt to Lydia, but I don't owe the old man shit. What does this win me, I keep him on the dole?"

Amos sighed, and gave his oldest friend a sad smile. "Really?"

"Really."

"I don't kill you, kill those two guys outside. I don't dismantle this organization from the top down and rebuild it with someone who'll owe me a favor."

"Ah," Erich said. "There he is."

Amos had to admit, Erich had grown some stones. He didn't even look down at the gun on the desk as he was being threatened. Just gave Amos his own version of the tragic smile.

"There who is?" Amos asked.

"Timmy."

"Yeah, I guess. It wouldn't be my first choice, though. So how's this go?"

"Costs me almost nothing to keep the old man's house," Erich said, then shook his head as if disagreeing with himself. "But even if it did, I'd still do it. Just to keep Timmy off my streets."

"Again, thanks."

Erich shooed the gratitude away with a wave of his good hand, then stood up and walked to the office's large screen pretending to be a window. The gun still lay on the desk, ignored now. Amos considered it briefly, then leaned farther back in his chair and put his hands behind his head, elbows spread out wide.

"Funny, right?" Erich said, pointing out the window at something Amos couldn't see. "All those new faces and old corners. Shit changes and doesn't. I did, you didn't."

"I live on a spaceship and fight alien monsters sometimes," Amos said with a shrug of his elbows. "So that's different."

"Anything out there scarier than a hype with no money when you're holding his fix? Scarier than a street boss thinks you skimmed?" Erich laughed and turned around, putting his back to the window. "Fuck that. Anything out there scarier than a life on basic?"

"No," Amos admitted.

"So you got what you wanted," Erich said, his voice going flat and dead. "Get the fuck out of my city or it's open season."

Amos stood. He was closer to the gun than Erich now. Could feel it pull at him like gravity. He could pick it up, kill Erich, kill the two guards waiting outside. By the end of the day he'd own a chunk of Erich's old territory and have the muscle and credibility to take the rest. In a flash, the whole scenario played out in his mind.

Instead, he hooked his thumbs in his pants pockets and backed toward the door. "Thanks for the drink," he said. "I forgot how good tequila was."

"I'll have Tatu give you a couple bottles on the way out. To take with you," Erich said.

"Shit, I won't turn that down."

"It was good to see you," Erich said, then paused a moment. "The gun was empty."

"Yeah?"

"Fléchette turret hidden in the light," Erich said, with a flick of his eyes at the inset LED housing above them. "Poisoned darts. I say a word, it kills everyone in the room isn't me."

"Nice. Thanks for not saying it."

"Thanks for still being my friend."

It felt like goodbye, so Amos gave Erich one last smile, and left the room. Tatu was waiting in the corridor with a box full of tequila bottles. The guards must have been monitoring the whole thing.

"Need help on your way out?" the guard asked.

"Naw," Amos replied and hoisted the box over one shoulder. "I'm good at leaving."

Amos let his hand terminal take him to the nearest flophouse and got a room. He dumped his booze and bag on the bed and then hit the streets. A short walk took him to a food cart where he bought what the sign optimistically called a Belgian sausage. Unless the Belgians were famous for their flavored bean curd products, the optimism seemed misplaced. Not that it mattered. Amos realized that while he knew the orbital period of every Jovian moon by heart, he had no idea where Belgium was. He didn't think it was a North American territory, but that was about the best he could do. He was hardly in a position to criticize assertions about their cuisine.

He walked toward the old rotting docks he played on as a child, not for any reason more profound than needing a destination and knowing which direction the water was. He finished the last of his sausage and then, not seeing a convenient recycling bin, he chewed up and swallowed the wrapper too. It was made of spun corn starch and tasted like stale breakfast cereal.

A small knot of teens passed him, then paused and turned to follow. They were in that awkward age between being a victim on legs and capable of real adult crimes. The right age for petty theft and running for the dealers mixed with the occasional mugging when opportunity presented itself without too much risk. Amos ignored them and climbed down onto the rusting steel of an old bayfront jetty.

The teens hung back, arguing in quiet but tense voices. Probably deciding if the reward of a solitary mark with an outsider's credit balance—it being an article of faith that anyone from outside the docks of Baltimore had more money than anyone in them—was worth the risk of taking on a man of his size. He knew the calculus of that equation well. He'd been in on that very argument himself, once upon a time. He continued to ignore them and listened instead to the gentle lap of the water against the pilings of his jetty.

In the distance, the sky lit up with a line of fire like a lightning bolt drawn with a ruler. A sonic boom rolled across the bay a few moments later, and Amos had a sudden and intense memory of sitting on those very docks with Erich, watching the rail-gun supply lifts fired into orbit, and discussing the possibility of leaving the planet.

To everyone outside the gravity well, Amos was from Earth. But that wasn't true. Not in any way that mattered. Amos was from *Baltimore.* What he knew about the planet outside of a few dozen blocks of the poor district would fit on a napkin. The first steps he'd ever taken outside the city were when he'd climbed off a high-speed rail line in Bogotá and onto the shuttle that had flown him to Luna.

He heard quiet footsteps on the jetty behind him. The discussion was over. The yeas outweighing the nays. Amos turned around and faced the approaching teens. A few of them held improvised clubs. One had a knife. "Not worth it," he said. He didn't flex or raise his fists. He just shook his head. "Wait for the next one." There was a tense moment as they stared at him and he stared back. Then, moving as though they'd reached some sort of telepathic consensus, they drifted away in a group.

Erich was wrong about him being the same. The man he'd once been wasn't a collection of personality traits. He was the things he knew, the desires of his heart, the skills he had. The person he'd been before he left knew where the good basement booze was brewed. Which dealers had a consistent supply of quality black market marijuana and tobacco. The brothels that serviced the locals, and the ones that were there only to rob thrill-seeking poverty tourists. That person knew where to rent a gun for cheap, and that the price tripled if you used it. Knew it was cheaper to rent time in a machine shop and make your own. Like the shotgun he'd used the first time he killed a man.

But the person he was now knew how to keep a fusion reactor running. How to tune the magnetic coils to impart maximum energy to ionized exhaust particles, and how to fix a hull breach. That guy didn't care about these streets or the pleasures and risks they offered. Baltimore could look exactly the same, and be as foreign to him as the mythical land of Belgium.

And in that moment, he knew it was his last time on Earth. He was never coming back.

He woke up in his rented flop the next morning with half a bottle of tequila on his nightstand and the first hangover he'd had in years. For a moment he thought he'd been so drunk he wet the bed, but realized that in the stifling heat of the room he'd sweated out about a liter. His throat felt dry and his tongue swollen.

He rinsed off the night's sweat and drank steaming-hot water out of the shower, tilting his head back to let it fill his mouth. After decades of filtered and sterilized ship and space station water, he marveled at all the *flavors* in it. He hoped not too many of them were microbes or heavy metals.

He pulled the remaining tequila bottles out of their box and stuffed them into his duffel bag, wrapping his clothes around them to protect them. Then he picked up his hand terminal and started looking for a hop back to Luna, then a connecting long flight to Tycho. He'd said goodbye to Lydia, or the pieces of her that she'd left behind anyway. He'd said a goodbye of sorts to Erich. There was no one left on the entire planet he gave half a shit about.

Well, no. That wasn't true. Maybe *half*.

He called the number Avasarala had used, and a sculpted young man with a perfect haircut, pale skin, and gigantic teeth appeared.

He looked like an expensive store mannequin. "Secretary Avasarala's office."

"Gimme Chrissie, kid, and make it snappy."

The mannequin was stunned into silence for two long breaths. "I'm sorry, but the secretary can't—"

"Kid," Amos said with a smirk, "I just called on her private line, right? My name is Amos Burton." A lie, but one he'd told often enough it had become a sort of truth. "I work for James Holden. I bet if you don't tell her I'm on the line right now that you're applying for basic by the end of the day."

"One moment please," the mannequin said and then the screen displayed the blue-and-white logo of the UN.

"Burton," Chrisjen Avasarala said, appearing on the screen less than thirty seconds later. "Why the fuck are you still on my planet?"

"Getting ready to leave, chief, but figured I got one more person to check in on before I go."

"Was it me? Because I don't like you enough to consider that charming. I have a flight to Luna waiting on the pad for me so I can go do fucking party arrangements before the Martian prime minister arrives."

"They make you do that?"

"I do everything, and every second I talk to you costs ten thousand dollars."

"Really?"

"No, I just made that number up. But I fucking hate flying to Luna so I've been putting it off to finish other work anyway. Do you need a ride? If it gets you off my planet, I can give you a ride. What? Did I say something funny?"

"Naw, just reminded me of somebody," Amos said. "Anyway, I get the feeling this is the only trip down the well I'm ever going to take."

"I'm crushed," she said.

"Since I'm here, I figured anything I might want to do, better do it now. Anyone I wanted to see, you know," Amos continued. "Where did you guys wind up locking Peaches away?"

"Peaches?"

"The Mao girl. Clarissa. She flew with us for a few months back after she stopped trying to kill the captain. And I have to admit, she grew on me a little."

"You fucked your prisoner?" Avasarala said, her expression evenly divided between amusement and disgust.

"Nah," Amos said. "I don't tend to do that with people I like."

Chapter Thirteen: Holden

The systems that the gate network had opened up were scattered across what everyone was pretty sure was the Milky Way galaxy. Cartography was still working out their relative locations, but even the initial findings put some of the new systems tens of thousands of light-years from Earth and with some distinct weirdness about time and location. Confronted by such unimaginably vast distances, it was easy to forget how much space was in just one solar system. Until you tried to find something in it.

Legally, any spaceship on the move had to register a flight plan and run an active transponder. That made ships traveling from place to place relatively easy to track. And with a transponder pinging away so you knew where to point your telescope, an active drive was visible from across the solar system. But ships would power down for repairs in dock, so transponders disappeared off the grid all the time. Ships were decommissioned, so a transponder might go black and never return for entirely legitimate reasons. Newly commissioned ships showed up with brand-new names and ships that were sold registered name changes. Some were cobbled together from scrap, some were built in shipyards, some were salvaged. And all of it was happening scattered across roughly one hundred quintillion square kilometers of space, give or take a few quadrillion. And that was only if you ignored that space had a third dimension.

So, seventeen ships had vanished going through ring gates, and if Holden was right, they were probably back in the home system with new names. In theory, there was a path to the information he wanted, but unless he was interested in spending several hundred lifetimes sifting through the raw data, he'd need help.

Specifically, he needed a computer plowing through a number of different massive databases on new ships, decommissioned ships, sold ships, repaired ships, and lost ships, looking for anything that didn't add up. Even with a good computer and very smart data sorting software, it was what a programmer would call a nontrivial task.

And, unfortunately, the best software engineer that Holden knew had flown off to parts unknown and wasn't answering his messages. He didn't have the skills to do it himself, the time to learn them, or a crew to do it for him. What he had, was money.

After his shift working with Sakai's people on the *Roci* refit, Holden called up Fred yet again. "Fred, hey, I have a software problem. Can I hire some of your programming wonks for a short-term gig?"

"Your ship need an update?" Fred asked. "Or is this something that will piss me off?"

"Something that'll piss you off. So, who's available for custom script writing?"

Paula Gutierrez had the elongated body and slightly oversized head of a low-g childhood. Her smile was sharp and professional.

She was a freelance software engineer who'd taken a six-month consulting job on Tycho five years before and then just stayed on the station picking up the odd bit of piecework. On Holden's hand terminal, her wide face filled the screen with dark bushy eyebrows and blindingly white teeth.

"So, that's what I'm looking for, and I need it as fast as possible," Holden said after laying out his requirements. "Doable?"

"Very," Paula said. "Tycho keeps all the traffic databases mirrored local, so don't even have to sweat the lag. Gonna cost you for speed, though."

"Cost me what?"

"Fifteen hundred an hour, ten hours minimum. Know up front I don't argue about billing and I don't give discounts."

"That," Holden said, "sounds like a lot."

"That's because I've got you over a barrel and I'm gouging the shit out of you."

"Okay, how soon will I start seeing output?"

Paula shrugged with her eyebrows, then looked down at something off camera. "Call it twenty hours from now before you start getting data sent to you. Want me to collate or stream it as it comes in?"

"Send it straight to me, please. Going to ask me why I want it?"

Paula laughed. "I never do."

⚡

Monica was renting a small suite of rooms on the visitors' level of Tycho. They were expensive, and to Holden's surprise, not any nicer than the company quarters Fred had set aside for his crew. Not many companies treated their own as well as they treated guests. But courtesy dictated that he act like the rooms were something special to make Monica feel good about the investment, so he made impressed noises at the open spaces and quality of the furnishings.

"So what did Fred say?" Monica asked once he took a seat at her dining table and sipped at the tea she'd made.

"He doesn't think there's much to go on, honestly."

"I mean about using the protomolecule sample to try and get in touch with Detective Miller."

"Yeah," Holden replied, putting the tea back on the table and pushing it away. The first sip had left his tongue feeling scalded and rough. "I mentioned that but only so he'd know he had a leak somewhere. That was always a nonstarter as an investigation tool. No one's letting that shit out of its bottle anytime soon."

"Then I'm wasting my time here, is what you're saying."

"No," Holden said. "Not at all. I think the missing ship thing is legitimate. I just don't think it's an alien conspiracy. It's much more likely to be associated with this hard-line OPA wing. I'm looking into it, if that's a story you want to pursue."

Monica spun her hand terminal around on the tabletop, already impatient with him for changing the subject. "I made my name with the story on the *Behemoth*. Aliens and wormhole gates and a protomolecule ghost that only talked to the most famous person in the solar system. I don't think my follow-up to that can be *Humans Still Shitty to Each Other*. Lacks panache."

"So, is this about finding those missing ships? Or is it about finding another batch of alien weirdness to make you more famous?"

"That sounded awfully judgmental for a guy who's managed to shoehorn himself into every major news piece for the last six years."

"Ouch," Holden said, then let the uncomfortable silence stretch a while. Monica kept spinning her hand terminal but not looking him in the eye.

"Sorry," she finally said.

"It's okay. Look, I'm going through this weird empty-nest thing, and it's left me kind of restless. And because I'm looking to latch onto something, I'm going to go find those missing ships. Probably won't be an alien conspiracy, but I'm going to do it anyway. Want to help?"

"Not sure what that looks like, to be honest. I was hoping to just ask the omniscient aliens. Do you know how big space is?"

"I've given it some thought," Holden said. "I have this plan. I talked to Fred about the OPA angle, but he doesn't like that idea so he's rejecting it out of hand. Still, that got me thinking. The OPA isn't going to throw a bunch of ships away. Belters just don't think that way. They recycle everything."

"So?"

"So how do you find pirated ships? Chief Engineer Sakai suggested looking for the new ships that turn up rather than hunting the missing ones."

"*Sakai* suggested..."

"He's a guy I work with on the *Roci* refits. But anyway, I thought that sounded like a great idea so I hired a local data wonk to write a database mining script to track all the new ship names that show up on the registries and try to find an origin point."

"A data wonk."

"Freelance coder. Whatever the name is for that kind of work, yeah, and anytime now I'll start getting a stream of data that includes all the mysteriously appearing ships. Our missing seventeen should be a subset of that. At least it'll be a smaller number of ships than, you know, *all* of them."

Monica stood up and walked away several steps, not speaking. Holden blew on his tea and waited. When she finally turned back around, the look on her face was carefully controlled incredulity. "You've involved Fred Johnson, some engineer here on Tycho, and a fucking *hacker* in this? Are you that stupid?"

Holden sighed and stood up. "I first heard about this from you, so I'll do you the courtesy of letting you know where the investigation goes—"

"And now you're *leaving*?" The incredulous look on Monica's face only deepened.

"Well, funny thing. I don't have to put up with being called stupid by someone I'm trying to help."

Monica lifted her palms in a placating gesture that he suspected she didn't really mean.

"Sorry," she said, "but you just involved three new people, one of whom is the highest-profile member of the OPA, in my...*our* investigation. What on earth made you think that was a good idea?"

"You know me, right?" Holden said, not sitting again but not heading straight for the door either. "I'm not a guy who hides things. I don't think Fred is the bad guy, but if he is then his reaction to our searching will tell us something. Secrecy is the potting soil in which all this conspiracy shit grows. Trust me. The roaches don't like it when you start shining a light on them."

"And what if they decide to get rid of the guy with the light?"

"Well," Holden said with a grin, "that'll be interesting too. They won't be the first ones to try, and I'm still here."

The following day the data from Paula's program began trickling in. He authorized his terminal to transfer the remaining payment for her services and began going through the list.

Lots of new ships were showing up around Mars and Earth, but that was to be expected. The shipyards were cranking out new and refurbished vessels as fast as the mechanics and engineers could make them. Everyone with two yuan to rub together was making a play for the ring gates and the worlds beyond them, and the biggest group of people who like living on planets and were already physiologically adapted to it came from the two inner worlds. Only a tiny fraction of those ships had gaps in their records that Paula's program would flag, but even a brief search led Holden to believe that the flagged ships were mostly paperwork errors, not piracy.

There were also a scattering of suspicious new ships in the Belt. Those were more interesting. If the OPA was stealing ships, then the logical place to hide them was in a region of space thick with ships and other metallic bodies. Holden began going through the Belt list one ship at a time.

The *Gozerian* appeared out of nowhere in the docks at the Pallas refinery in the right date range. The records listed it as a probate transfer, but were vague on who'd died and what relation the new owner had to the old. Holden guessed the answer to those two questions was *person who used to own the ship* and *person who killed them and took it.* The transfer of ownership was sketchy enough that it almost certainly was the result of piracy, but the *Gozerian* was listed as a non-Epstein light-hulled mining ship. A rock hopper. The records from Pallas backed that up, and a search of the list of seventeen missing ships didn't turn up anything matching its description. No one was going to make a run for the edge of the solar system and then all the way in to a new world in something that didn't have an Epstein drive. There were much more comfortable places to die of old age.

Holden checked the *Gozerian* off his list and moved to the next. By the time he'd gone through the entire initial list from Paula it was three a.m., Tycho time, and his shift on the *Roci* started at eight, so he caught a couple hours of rack time and spent a miserable morning trying to trace maneuvering thruster cables through a fog of sleep deprivation.

By the time his shift was over all he could think about was a little dinner and a lot of sleep, but the data stream from Paula was waiting for him with nearly fifty new ships. So he picked up a carton of noodles on his way home and spent the rest of the evening going through the list.

The *Mouse Pie* was a gas freighter and didn't match his missing list. The *Vento* first appeared before the date range he was interested in, and a query to the last dock it had visited confirmed the dates were correct. The *Blasphemous Jester* was listed as Epstein equipped, but a search of the service records showed that the drive had been out of commission for years. Someone had been using it as a short-hop shuttle in teakettle mode ever since.

On and on and on through the names it went. At one point his terminal beeped with an incoming message. Amos checking in with a cryptic "Visited my friend's grave. Went okay, but still got some shit to do. Back later." Holden slurped up another mouthful of noodles that had long since gone cold and now had the consistency of earthworms. How had Miller done shit like this for a living, he wondered. It was shocking to realize how much of investigation was just brute-force solutions. Going through endless lists looking for one thing that doesn't fit. Talking to every single potential witness over and over. Pounding the pavement, as the gumshoes in Alex's neo-noir movies might say.

It was thinking about Alex that twigged his memory, and he went back through the list until he found a ship designated the *Pau Kant*. The last location was marked as 434 Hungaria. A high albedo rock in the Hungaria group, an asteroid group relatively close to the orbit of Mars but with a high inclination. Mars control had caught a ping from the *Pau Kant* and then lost it shortly after. They'd marked the ship as missing.

But prior to that single and short-lived appearance, the *Pau Kant* didn't seem to exist in any other records. He couldn't find any description of her hull type or drive. Nor were there any owner records he could track down. He'd moved it to his list of ships to look into later, but something about Mars and inner Belt asteroids was making his brain itch.

The Hungaria group wasn't a terrible place to hide things. 434 Hungaria was about twenty kilometers across. Plenty of mass to mask ships from radar, and the high albedo of the group would clutter up the results of anyone looking for ships with a telescope. The location was intriguing too. If the OPA radicals were collecting ships to pirate colony transports, the inner Belt was not a bad staging area. They'd also launched an attack on Earth in the recent past. That it had failed didn't mean they weren't planning more. A bunch of stolen ships hiding in the inner ring was exactly the sort of first step another attempt might take.

The Hungaria asteroids were a long way from Tycho's current

location, and Holden didn't have a ship. But they were pretty close to Mars, and Alex was there. If he had access to a ship, it wouldn't be too long a trip to go take a peek. See if the *Pau Kant* was still out there, tethered to the rock and staying dark. And if it matched any of Monica's missing ships? Well, that would be interesting to take back to Fred.

Holden put his terminal on the table, angled up to record his face, and said, "Alex. Hey, hope things are going well out there, and that Bobbie is good. So, I've been looking into this thing with missing ships? And there's a suspicious hit out at 434 Hungaria. Any chance you have access to a ship? If you need to rent one, feel free to pull the funds from my account. I'd like you to go see if a ship named the *Pau Kant* is sitting out there parked and dark. Specs on the transponder code attached to this message."

He put all the information he had on the *Pau* and its most recent location from the Mars control records into a file. It wasn't much to go on, and it felt like a long shot, but Alex would enjoy the flight and Holden was willing to foot the bill so he didn't feel too bad about asking.

He was pretty sure the burst of energy that came from having made progress would be short-lived, but he wanted to share his success and felt wide-awake, so he called Monica. He got her voice mail. He left her a message to call him back, slurped down the last of his cold and nasty noodles, and immediately fell asleep on his couch.

The next morning he wasn't on the duty roster to work on the *Roci*, and Monica hadn't called him back, so he called again. No answer. On his way to breakfast he dropped by her apartment, but she wasn't there either. She'd been a little miffed at him, but he didn't think she'd bail on the whole missing ship story without saying anything. He made another call.

"Tycho security," a young male voice said.

"Hey, this is Jim Holden. I'm checking on a visiting journalist, Monica Stuart. Has she left the station?"

"One sec. No. Records list her as still on board. Her apartment is—"

"Yeah, actually? I'm at her apartment right now and she's not answering here or on her hand terminal."

"My records show that her terminal hasn't connected to Tychonet since early yesterday."

"Huh," Holden said, frowning at her door. The quiet on the other side had taken on an ominous feel. *What if they decide to get rid of the guy with the light?* He wasn't the only one who fit that description. "So she hasn't so much as paid for a sandwich in over a day. That strikes me as not good."

"Want me to send a team?"

"Please do that."

By the time the security team arrived and opened the door to Monica's apartment, Holden was expecting the worst. He wasn't disappointed. The rooms had been methodically searched. Monica's clothes and personal effects were scattered across the floor. The hand terminal she used for interviews had been crushed under someone's heel, but the screen still flickered when Holden touched it. The team found no traces of blood, which was about the only positive sign.

Holden called Fred while the team finished their forensic sweep. "It's me," he said as soon as the OPA chief answered. "You've got a bigger problem than radicals on Medina."

"Really?" Fred said, his voice weary. "And what is that?"

"You've got them on Tycho."

Chapter Fourteen: Naomi

Terryon Lock was supposed to be a new kind of place in the emptiness of the Jovian system. A Belter home world, they figured. Modular, so it could grow or contract at need. Outside the control of Earth or Mars or anybody. A free city in space, with its own governance, its own environmental controls. Naomi had seen the plans when they first spilled out over the networks. Rokku had them printed on thin plastics and stuck to the walls of the ship. Terryon Lock was the new Jerusalem until the security forces at Ganymede shut it down. No colonies without permission. No homes. No safe havens, not even if they built it themselves.

She hadn't even been pregnant when it happened. She didn't know that it would define her.

Filip was eight months old when the *Augustín Gamarra* died. The *Gamarra* had left Ceres Station, burning for a Coalition Navy research station on Oshima with a payload of organics and hydroponic equipment. Ten hours out, burning at a leisurely one-quarter g, the ship's magnetic bottle lost containment, spilling the fusion core into the ship. For a fraction of a second, the *Gamarra* had been as bright as the sun and two hundred thirty-four people died. No wreckage survived, and the official investigation into the event had never been closed because no conclusion could be reached. Accident or sabotage. Mischance or murder.

They had gone from the hidden cell at the back of the club to a private apartment up even nearer the center of spin. The air had the too-clean ozone smell of a recently replaced recycling filter. Filip sat at the small table, his hands folded. She sat on the edge of the tiny foam-and-gel sofa. She looked at the boy's dark eyes and tried to connect them in her mind with the ones she remembered. His lips with the toothless, delighted smile. She couldn't tell if the resemblance was really there, or if it was only her imagination. How much did someone change between not-quite-a-toddler and not-quite-an-adult? Could it really be the same boy? It wasn't anyone else.

The hole wasn't abandoned. There were clothes in the locker, food and beer in the little refrigerator. The pale walls showed chips at the corners where the damage of minor accidents had built up over the course of years. He didn't tell her who the apartment belonged to, and she didn't ask.

"Why didn't you bring the *Rocinante*?" Filip asked. There was a tentative quality to his voice. Like the question was only a stand-in for other ones he wanted to ask. That she wanted to be able to answer. *Why did you go? Didn't you love us?*

"It's in dock for repairs. Will be for months."

Filip nodded once, sharply. She could see Marco in the movement. "That's going to complicate things."

"Marco didn't tell me you wanted the ship," Naomi said, hating the implicit apology in the words. "All he said was that you were in trouble. That you were avoiding the law, and that I could...that I could help."

"We'll have to come up with something," he said.

⁂

The hospitals at Ceres Station were some of the best in the Belt when Naomi had been coming near to term. Neither of them had the money to travel to Europa or Ganymede for the duration of a pregnancy. Ceres had been closer to Rokku's claims than Tycho Station. Childbirth was a greater danger for Belters than for someone who'd lived under constant gravity, and Naomi's pregnancy had already had two scares. She and Marco had lived in a cheap rental near the hospital, one of dozens that catered to Belters who came for the medical care. The terms of the agreement were open-ended, letting them stay until they didn't need the doctors, nurses, expert systems, and pharmaceuticals that the medical complex boasted.

Naomi could still remember the shape of the bed there, the cheap plastic curtains with a printed starscape that Marco hung across the doorway. The smell of it made her sick, but he'd been so pleased with himself she'd tolerated it. And even that late in the process, almost everything made her sick. She'd spent her days sleeping and feeling the baby shifting inside her. Filip had been restless as a fetus. She hadn't felt like a child having a child. She'd felt like a woman in control of her fate.

⁂

"How many do you need to get out?" Naomi asked.

"Fifteen, all told."

"Including you?"

"Sixteen."

She nodded. "Any cargo?"

"No," he said, and then seemed about to go on. After a moment, he looked away.

⚡

Ceres had still been under Earth control back then. Most of the people living on the base were Belters who'd taken contract with one of the Martian or Earther corporations. Earth security by Belters. Earth traffic control by Belters. Martian bioresearch by Belters. Marco had laughed at it all, but the laughter had an edge. He'd called Ceres humanity's largest shrine to Stockholm syndrome.

Everyone flying with Rokku had paid part of their share into the OPA, Naomi included. And the OPA looked after them in the last days of her pregnancy, local women bringing food to the hole, local men taking Marco out to the bars so that he had someone besides her to talk to. Naomi didn't think anything of it apart from being grateful. Those nights when Marco was out drinking with the local men and she was alone in her bed with Filip, her mind moving in the silence had carried an almost transcendent contentment. Or at least that was how she remembered it now. At the time, without knowing what was still to come, the experience might have been different.

⚡

"Where do you need to be?"

"We don't talk about that," Filip said.

Naomi brushed her hair back from her eyes. "You brought me here because it's secure, sa sa? So is it that you don't want to be overheard by someone else, or that you think telling me compromises you? Because if you don't trust me enough to ask for what you want, you don't trust me enough for me to be here."

The words seemed to carry more nuance than they could bear, as if the simple logistical facts also meant something about why she'd left. About who they were to each other. It was like she could feel the words creaking, but she didn't know what Filip heard in them, or what she should have said differently. For a moment, there was a flicker in his expression. Sorrow or hatred or pain, it was gone too quickly to identify. A new stratum of guilt settled onto her, bearing her down. Compared to what she already had, it was trivial.

"He said I should tell you once we were off the station," Filip said.

"Apparently he didn't know I'd be arranging passage on a different ship. Plans change. It's what they do."

Filip's gaze fixed on her, his eyes hard as marbles. She realized she'd been quoting Marco without meaning to. Maybe Filip thought it was a slap, that she was making a claim on his father by using his words. She didn't know. She didn't know him. She had to keep reminding herself of that.

"There's a rendezvous point."

"Is there a time?"

"Yes."

"How long?"

She saw *We don't talk about it* floating in his eyes. When he spoke, his voice was smaller, younger. More vulnerable. "Soon."

"How soon?"

He looked away.

"Very."

She'd known, back then, that there were hard-core OPA factions on Ceres, but it hadn't bothered her. Radical OPA was still OPA, and that made them family. The crazy uncle who got drunk and started fights, maybe, but with Earth cranking up tariffs and Mars lowering the prices it would pay for ore, the sense of being under siege put Belters on the side of Belters first. And after shipping with Rokku for a while, talk of killing Earthers and Martians became a kind of white noise.

The birth had been hard. Thirty hours of labor. The muscles of her abdominal wall, made weaker by a lifetime of inconstant g, had shredded themselves. If they had been in Rokku's ship or even back on Hygeia Station, she might have died, and the baby with her. But the medical complex on Ceres had seen it all before, and worse. A gray-haired woman with a cathedral of tattoos on her hands and arms had been in her room the whole time, singing little tunes in Swahili and Arabic. Naomi could still see her and hear her voice, though she'd forgotten the woman's name. If she'd ever known it.

Filip had drawn his first, exhausted, angry breath at five in the morning, the day after she'd gone into the complex. The pediatric autodoc scanned him, considered for the longest five seconds of Naomi's life, and declared the baby safely within standard error. The gray-haired woman had placed him on Naomi's breast and sung a blessing.

It hadn't occurred to her then to wonder where Marco was. She had assumed he was in a waiting area somewhere, ready to pass out some equivalent of cigars as soon as news of her came. Of her and their son. Maybe that had even been true.

"Do we need to be there, or is off station enough?" Naomi asked.

"Off station at minimum. Better to be there, but not here solid."

"And where are we going?"

"Hungaria cluster." They were a group of minor asteroids. High albedo. No station, but an open-access storage facility. As close to the inner planets as Belt rocks got.

"Are we meeting someone there?"

"Not there. There's a ship a few days in. Sunward. But locked to Hungaria. *Pella*, it's called."

"And after that?"

Filip made the hand shrug of a Belter. Apparently she could know that much, but no more. She wondered what would happen if she pushed, and knew it was an experiment she wouldn't make. *I'm sorry*, she thought. *I loved you more than I have ever loved anything. I would have stayed if I could. I would have taken you with me.*

Filip looked at her and then away.

⚡

She'd spent most of the weeks following the birth in recovery. The baby kept her from sleeping very long at a stretch, but apart from one week of frankly hellish colic, he was neither harder nor easier than she'd been led to expect. The worst thing she suffered was boredom, and Marco helped with that. The local group he'd been drinking with were mechanics and technicians at the port, and Marco brought her engineering problems that they were trying to solve. They were the sort of work consultants would do for half a month's credit. She did them from goodwill and the need to do something intellectually challenging. While Filip napped in the little plastic crib, she customized diagnostic programs for water recyclers. She built virtual timing sequencers for shear force detection units. She designed software overrides for testing the containment limits of magnetic bottles.

The kind of limits that, before long, would fail on the *Gamarra*.

⚡

"All right," Naomi said. "I'll see what I can do."

"Do you have access to another ship?" Filip asked.

"I may be able to charter something."

"You can't just hire a charter. This has to be untraceable."

Meaning, she knew, that whatever was going to happen, it would mean people with guns coming after Filip and Cyn and all the others. Maybe security forces, maybe a rival faction, maybe something else that she hadn't anticipated yet. But there would be consequences. And there would be violence.

"I may be able to charter something discreetly," Naomi said. "If it doesn't work, I'll be sure it doesn't come back to you."

Filip swallowed. For a moment, she saw a glimmer of fear in him. He was sixteen years old now. A year younger than when she'd met his father. Three years younger than when she'd held him to her breasts to feed.

"I would have looked for you if he'd let me," Naomi said. The words came out of her from a need she couldn't control. He was a boy. He was carrying whatever burden Marco had put on him already. Making him responsible for how she felt too wasn't a kindness. She rose to her feet. "You don't need to do anything about that. Just I would have. If he'd let me."

If he'd let me. The words were heavy and toxic as lead. *I would have done what I wanted, except he still controlled me. Still does. After all these years, and all these changes, and everything I have done and become, I wouldn't have left you to him except that Marco still controls me. Constrains me. Punishes me for not letting him rule me outright.*

"All right," Filip said. His expression was empty.

Naomi nodded. Her hands were in fists so tight the knuckles ached. She made herself relax. "Give me a day. I'll know more."

"Come to the club," Filip said. "If we're not there, just wait and we'll make contact. We need to stay moving."

I thought I could stay with you, she thought, and then hated herself for the disappointment she felt. This wasn't a reunion. Her unfinished business with Filip might be what brought her here, but he was doing something else. Something that had brought his long-lost mother back into his world. If she wanted to sit with him and eat sweets and share stories the way they never had, that was her problem.

"Fair enough," Naomi said. She hesitated, then turned to the door. As she reached it, he spoke again, his voice tight. Like the words were hard to say.

"Thank you for coming."

She felt it in her sternum, someone taking a hammer to the bones over her heart. Filip watched her from the table. He looked so much like his father. She tried to imagine that she had ever been that young herself. Tried to imagine that at that age she would have known how to pick words that were that perfectly empty and heartwarming and cruel. She felt the smile press her lips out a millimeter. It was an expression of sorrow more than joy.

"He told you to say that," she said. "Didn't he?"

There were a hundred ways to unpack the boy's silence.

After the *Gamarra*, Marco had come home drunk and happy from his celebration. She'd told him to be quiet, not to wake the baby. Marco had swooped her up in his arms, twirling her in the little room until her ankle hit the bed and she yelped with pain. He'd put her down then, rubbing the little injury. Kissing it. He'd looked up at her with a smile that asked as much as it promised, and she'd thought about whether they could make love quietly enough that Filip would keep sleeping. That was what she'd been thinking of when he destroyed her.

"Managed it, us. You, que si?"

"Managed what?" she asked, leaning back against the gel of the bed.

"Got even for Terryon Lock," Marco said. "Stood up for the Belt. For us. For him."

Marco nodded toward the baby. Filip's thumb had been in his sleep-slack mouth, his eyes so closed they seemed like they'd never open again. She'd known before she understood what she knew. An electric cold washed her heart, her belly, all her body. Marco sensed it. The memory of his quizzical smile looking up past her knee was still burned in her mind.

"What did I manage?" she said.

"Perfect crime," he said. "First of many."

She understood. The *Gamarra* had been killed with her code. The people who died there were dead because of her, and all of Rokku's rough talk and ranting had stopped being empty banter. Marco was a killer now. She was too. They'd gone on to make love anyway, him too warm and dangerous to refuse, her too much in shock even to understand how much she wanted to object. She hated the fact, but they had. It was the beginning of the dark times, but looking back, all the rest of it—the depression, the fear, the loss of Filip, her failed suicide—had all been implicit in that night.

The script over the doors of hell, writ small.

Renting a hole by the port was easy. She had enough money to buy anonymous credit, route it through an off-station exchange, and bring it back to a mayfly shadow account. It only felt strange doing it because she hadn't had to go through those motions in so long. Not since she'd signed on to the *Canterbury*, and that felt like it had been seven lifetimes ago.

She sat on the thin gel bed and waited for the weeping and nausea to stop. They would, even though at the worst of it, they felt like they might not. Then she took a long shower, changed into a fresh set of clothes purchased from a kiosk. Watching the hard puck of compressed cloth expand into a jumpsuit reminded her of an insect pulling itself out of its shell. It seemed like it should be a metaphor for something.

Her hand terminal showed a half-dozen new messages from Jim. She didn't play them. If she had, the temptation to reply—to confess to him and take comfort in him, to talk to someone she trusted completely—would have been too much. And then he would have felt obligated to do something. To come and fix things. To insert himself into the messes that she'd made and the things she'd done. The distance between here and there, between Marco and the *Rocinante*, was too precious to sacrifice. The time for comfort would come later, when she'd done the things she needed to do. When she'd saved Filip. When she'd escaped Marco. So she didn't play the messages. But she didn't delete them either.

Even back on with Rokku, Marco had been cultivating himself as a leader. He'd been good at it. No matter how bad things got, he'd always managed to make it seem like each new hurdle was something he'd factored in, every solution—even ones he'd logically had nothing to do with—was somehow his brilliance. He'd explained once how he managed it.

The trick, he said, is to have a simple plan that more or less can't go wrong so that you always have something, and then stack your risks on that. Have another alternative that won't work but maybe one time in a hundred, and if it happens, you look like a god. And then one that won't work but one time in twenty, that if it lands you look like you're the smartest one in the room. And then one that's only one time in five, but you look like you knew you could do it. And if everything else fails, you've still got the one that would always win.

If there was a single phrase for Marco, that was it: always win.

She wondered more than once over the years where she'd been on that scale. Had she been his one-in-a-hundred or his sure thing? She'd never known, and there was no way that she ever would. It didn't even matter to her anymore, except the way a missing finger itched sometimes.

And now here she was again, doing what he wanted. He'd made her complicit in his plans, whatever they were. This time, though, she knew who she was dealing with. She wasn't the girl who he'd tricked into sabotaging the *Gamarra*. She wasn't a love-struck teenager in over her head. And Filip wasn't a baby that could be spirited away and held as hostage against her good conduct. Her silence.

And so maybe—*maybe*—this was the moment she'd wanted. Maybe calling her in was Marco's mistake. She pushed the idea away. It was too dangerous, too complicated. Too likely to be what Marco had known she would think.

Digging through the station directory, she took the better part of an hour to find the address, even knowing what she was looking for. She didn't know what Outer Fringe Exports did, except that they were shady enough that she hadn't wanted to work with them, and that they were competent enough that they'd known about the Martian claims disputing the salvage of the *Rocinante* before her crew had. Naomi found their physical address—a different berth than the one she'd been at the last time—and caught a cart.

The warehouses near the port were in a constant state of flux. The pressure of commerce and efficiency kept every space in use with as little downtime between rental agreements, loading, and unloading as could be arranged. The sign on the tempered glass door read OUTER FRINGE EXPORTS, but in a week, a day, an hour, it could have been anything.

A young man at the counter smiled up at her. He had close-cropped hair and skin several shades darker than her own. The steel-rimmed glasses could have been an affectation or an interface device. She'd never seen him before.

"Hi," she said.

"Miss Nagata," the man said as if they were old acquaintances. "It's been some time. I'm sorry to say we don't have any work that would be suited to your ship at this time."

"Not what I'm here for," she said. "I need to charter a ship. And I need to do it very quietly."

The man's expression didn't change. "That can be an expensive problem."

"It needs to carry a crew no larger than twenty."

"How long would you need it?"

"I don't know."

"Would it be hauling cargo?"

"No."

The man's eyes lost their focus for a moment. The glasses were an interface, then. Naomi crossed her arms.

One in a hundred, she thought, *I show up with my own warship ready to carry people off Ceres. One in twenty, I know how to find someone who will.* She wondered what the one-in-five plan was. What was the sure thing.

The man's focus came back to her.

"I think we may be able to help," he said.

Chapter Fifteen: Alex

The ride to the hospital was a thing out of a nightmare. As the transport sped through the corridors, the painkillers started to take effect. The combination of ache and sharpness in his body shifted into a deep and troubling sense of simply being wrong. Once, when they were near the emergency admitting entrance, time stuttered as his consciousness slipped away and back again. None of the medics paid him much attention.

They were all focused on Bobbie.

The big woman's eyes were closed, and a pale plastic tube came out of her mouth, keeping her jaw open. From where he rode, Alex could make out only parts of her gurney's readout, and he wasn't sure how to interpret what he was seeing. The medics' voices were clipped and tense. Words and phrases like *attempting to reinflate* and *stabilizing* and *maintaining pressure* pushed Alex toward the edge of panic. Bobbie's body, what he could see of it, was limp. He told himself she wasn't dead. If she were dead, they wouldn't be trying to save her. He hoped that was true.

At the emergency ward, he found himself wheeled into an automated surgical bed not that different from the ones on the *Rocinante*. The scan probably took a minute and a half, but it seemed to go on forever. He kept turning to the side, looking for Bobbie, then remembering she was in a different room now. Even then he didn't understand how much his injuries and painkillers had compromised his mind until the police came and he tried to explain what had happened.

"So how did the woman with the power armor fit into it?" Bobbie asked.

She was sitting up in her hospital bed. Her gown was thick, disposable paper with Bhamini Pal Memorial Hospital printed on it like a pattern, dark blue over light. Her hair was pulled back into a loose bun, and deep bruises darkened her left cheek and her knuckles. When she shifted, the movement was careful. It was the way Alex moved after he'd worked out too hard and felt a little sore. He hadn't been shot twice—once through her left lung, once in her right leg—and he'd seriously considered taking a wheelchair to go between his room and hers.

"I meant you," Alex said. "I was having trouble coming up with your name."

Bobbie chuckled. "Yeah, they're going to want to talk to you again. I think the version they got was a little muddled."

"Do you think...Should we not be talking?"

"We're not under arrest," Bobbie said. "The only one of the other guys that's still breathing lawyered up before he got here. I'm pretty sure they're not going to be looking at us if they want to throw someone in jail."

"What did you tell them?" Alex asked.

"The truth. That a bunch of thugs broke into my rooms, tied

me up, and started taking turns between kicking the shit out of me and asking why I was meeting with Alex Kamal."

Alex pressed his thumb against his upper lip until it ached a little. Bobbie's smile carried a load of sympathy.

"I don't know why that is," he said. "I don't have any enemies on Mars. That I know of."

Bobbie shook her head and Alex noticed again that she was a remarkably attractive woman. He coughed and mentally filed the thought under *horrifically inappropriate given the circumstances.*

"My guess," Bobbie said, "is that it was less about who you are than who you're connected to."

"Holden?"

"And Fred Johnson. And maybe they can even put the two of us together with Avasarala. She shipped on the *Rocinante* for a while."

"For about a minute and a half, years ago."

"I remember. I was there," Bobbie said. "Still, one way or another, the most plausible scenario I've got is that they thought I was reporting something to you or you were reporting something to me. And, even better, the idea scared them."

"Don't mean to look a gift horse in the mouth, but that definition of *even better* has got some mighty long teeth," Alex said. "Did you tell them about your investigation?"

"No, I'm not ready to do that."

"But you think this was related."

"Oh, hell yes. Don't you?"

"It's what I'm hoping for, actually," Alex said with a sigh. Across the hallway, someone shouted words Alex couldn't make out. A nurse stalked by, scowling. "So what are we goin' to do about it?"

"Only thing we can do," Bobbie said. "Keep digging."

"Fair enough. So. What exactly are we looking at?"

Bobbie's expression sharpened. The problem, she said, was ships. The Martian Navy was the newest, best set of ships in the solar system. Earth had more ships, but her Navy was aging, with tech in them that was either generations old or retrofitted, shoehorning more recent designs into older frames. Both fleets had taken heavy losses in the last few years. Whether you called Avasarala's influence prompting or putting her on a mission, Bobbie had started looking, and what she'd found was interesting.

The seven big *Donnager*-class ships were easy to keep track of, but the fleet of corvettes that they carried, ships like the *Rocinante*—they were slippery. Bobbie had started by going back to review the battle data from Io, from outside the Ring, from the incident in the slow zone. Really, when it came to damage reports, there was an embarrassment of riches.

At first, the numbers had seemed to match up. Half a dozen ships lost here, a handful there, the transponder codes decommissioned. But as she looked more deeply, she started running into discrepancies.

The *Tsuchi*, a corvette assigned to the *Bellaire*, had been decommissioned and scrapped after Io. A year later, it appeared in a small-group action report near Europa. The supply ship *Apalala* had been retired from service, and then seven months later, picked up a shipment headed to Ganymede. A load of medical supplies lost to accident appeared briefly on a loading schedule bound for Ceres and then disappeared again. Weapons lost in the fighting around what was now Medina Station appeared in an audit at Hecate Base once and not again.

Someone, Bobbie reasoned, had gone back through the records and doctored the old reports, forging the deaths of ships and then erasing them from the later records, or trying to. She'd found half a dozen hiccups in the data, but any ships that had been successfully erased, she wouldn't see. That meant someone had to be involved high enough up the naval chain of command that they had access to the files.

There was protocol, of course, that laid out who was supposed to have access to the records, but she'd been in the process of looking into how that actually played out in practice when Alex had dropped her a line and suggested dinner.

"If you're up for it," Bobbie said, "that's what I'd want you to look at. Just who could have changed the information. Then I can start looking at them."

"Keep going down the road you were already on," Alex said.

"Only with maybe some friends in the Navy."

"That's one way we can go. It ain't the only one, though."

Bobbie sat forward, caught her breath, and leaned back. "What else are you thinking?"

"Someone hired the gentlemen who messed us up. Seems like findin' out what we can about them might also be worth our time."

Bobbie grinned. "That was the part I was planning to do."

"Well, all right, then," Alex said, and a man stepped into the doorway. He was huge. His shoulders brushed the doorframe on both sides, and his face was thick and heavy with a distress that could have been fear or anger. The bouquet of daffodils in his hand seemed tiny, and would until they were in a vase.

"Hey," he said. "I was just..."

"Come in," Bobbie said. "Alex, this is my brother Ben. Benji, this is Alex Kamal."

"Good to meet you," the massive man said, enfolding Alex's hand in his grip and shaking gently. "Thank you for everything you've done."

"Betcha?" Alex said.

The bed creaked as Bobbie's brother sat at its foot. He looked sheepishly at his sister. Now that she'd said the words, Alex could see the resemblance in them. Bobbie wore the look better.

"The doctor says you're doing well," Ben said. "David wanted me to tell you he's thinking of you."

"That's sweet, but David doesn't think about anything but terraforming and boobs," Bobbie said.

"I've cleaned out the guest room," Ben said. "When they release you from the hospital, you're coming to stay with us."

Bobbie's smile grew sharper. "I don't actually see that happening."

"No," her brother said. "No, this isn't a discussion. I told you from the beginning that Innis Shallow was a dangerous place, especially for someone living by herself. If Alex hadn't saved you—"

"Not sure I was actually saving anyone," Alex said, but Ben scowled and kept right on going over the words.

"—you could have been killed. Or worse."

"Worse than killed?" Bobbie said.

"You know what I mean."

Bobbie leaned forward, resting her elbows on her knees. "Yes, I do, and I think that's bullshit too. I am in no more danger in Innis Shallow than I would be up in Breach Candy."

"How can you even say that?" her brother demanded, his jaw slipping forward. "After what you've just been through, it should be obvious that..."

Alex sidestepped toward the door. Bobbie caught his eye, and the brief smile, gone as soon as it was there, was eloquent. *I'm sorry* and *Thank you* and *We'll talk about the important stuff when he's gone.* Alex nodded and retreated to the hallway, the buzz-saw tones of siblings lecturing each other following after him.

When he got back to his recovery bed, the police were waiting, and this time he gave a statement that was, at least, coherent. Even if he left some of the background issues vague.

For the most part, family was a metaphor on long-haul ships. Now and then, there'd be a group that was actually related by blood, but that was almost always Belters. On military and corporate assignments, there might be a handful of married couples, and now and then someone would have a baby. People would wind up on the same ship who were cousins. They were the exception, and the rule was that family was a way of talking about need. The need for friendship, the need for intimacy, the need for human contact that ran so deeply into the genome that anyone without it seemed not entirely human anymore. It was camaraderie writ large, a synonym for loyalty that was stronger than the concept it echoed.

Alex's experience of real family—of blood relations—was more like having a lot of people who had all wound up on the same mailing list without knowing quite why they signed up for it. He'd loved his parents when they were alive, and he still loved his memory of them. His cousins were always happy to see him, and he was glad of their welcome and their company. Seeing Bobbie and her brother together and feeling even in that brief moment the deep and unbridgeable mismatch of character between them drove something home to Alex.

A mother could love her daughter more than life itself the way the stories told, or she could hate the girl's guts. Or both. A sister and brother could get along or fight each other or pass by in a kind of uncomfortable indifference.

And if real relationship-by-blood shared descent could mean any of those things, maybe family was always a metaphor.

He was still thinking about it when he got to Min's hole. Her boys and the girl that she and her husband had adopted were all there, sharing a meal of fish and noodles when he arrived, and they all greeted him like they knew him, like his injuries were important to them, like they cared. He sat at the table for a little bit, making jokes and minimizing the assault and its aftermath, but what he wanted to do—what he did as soon as his sense of etiquette allowed—was excuse himself and head back to the guest room they'd set aside for him.

A message was waiting for him from the *Roci*. From Holden. Seeing the familiar blue eyes and tousled brown hair was weirdly displacing. Alex felt like part of him was already on the way back to the *Rocinante*, and he was a little surprised not to be there already.

"Alex. Hey, hope things are going well out there, and that Bobbie is good."

"Yeah," Alex said to the playback. "Funny you'd ask."

"So, I've been looking into this thing with missing ships? And there's a suspicious hit out at 434 Hungaria. Any chance you have access to a ship? If you need to rent one, feel free to pull the funds from my account. I'd like you to go see if a ship named the *Pau Kant* is sitting out there parked and dark. Specs on the transponder code attached to this message."

Alex paused the playback, the skin at the back of his neck tickling. Missing ships was turning into a motif to his day, and it made him uneasy. He played the rest of Holden's message, rubbing his chin as he did it. There was a lot less to it than he wanted to know. The records on the *Pau Kant* didn't show it as a Martian vessel, or anything else in particular. Alex set his hand terminal to record, saw what he looked like in the display, combed his fingers through his hair, and started the message.

"Hey, Captain. Got your thing about the *Pau Kant*. I was wondering if I could get a little more information about that. I'm sort of in the middle of somethin' a mite odd myself."

He described what had happened to him and Bobbie in lighter tones than he actually felt. He didn't want to scare Holden when there was nothing the man could do to protect him or Bobbie. Apart from saying that the attackers seemed to have been spooked that Alex had appeared on the scene, he left out the details of Bobbie's investigation and Avasarala's. It might have been paranoia, but transmitting that information without another couple levels of encryption seemed like asking for trouble. He did ask what other ships were supposed to have gone missing, and how it might relate to Mars before he signed off.

Maybe whatever Holden was looking into was just coincidence. Maybe the *Pau Kant* and the missing Martian warships were totally unrelated. Wasn't where Alex would put his money, though.

He checked to see if there was anything from Amos or Naomi, and felt a little let down when there wasn't. He recorded brief messages for the both of them and sent them out.

In the main room of the apartment the kids' voices were loud, three conversations going on at the same time, each fighting to be heard over the others. Alex ignored them, accessing the local directory and looking up old names. People he could think of from his time in the service. There were dozens. Marian Costlow. Hannu Metzinger. Aaron Hu. He checked the directory against them, old friends and acquaintances and enemies, looking for who was still on Mars, still in the Navy, still someone who might remember him well enough to go out for a few beers and talk.

By the end of the evening, he had three, and he sent messages to each of them, then requested a connection to Bobbie. A few seconds later, she appeared on his screen. Wherever she was, it wasn't the hospital. She had on a shirt with a green collar instead of the blue patient's gown, and her hair had been washed and braided back.

"Alex," she said. "Sorry about my brother. He means well, but he's kind of a dick."

"Everybody's related to someone," he said. "You wind up at his place or your own?"

"Neither one," she said. "I need to hire a cleanup crew to get the blood off my floor, and I'm doing a solid security audit to figure out how they got in."

"Yeah. Wouldn't feel safe until that's done," Alex agreed.

"Right? And if there is a follow-up attack, I'm sure as hell not staying where it's going to catch Ben and his wife in the crossfire. I popped for a hotel room. They've got their own security, and I can pay for extra surveillance."

Min's voice rose in the background, calling for calm. There was laughter in her tones, and he heard it echoed in the protests of her children. A tightness like a hand closed over his heart. He hadn't thought about a follow-up attack. He should have.

"They got a spare room at that hotel?" he asked.

"Probably. You want me to find out?"

"Nah, I'll just pack up and head over, if that's all right. They don't, someone will." *And whoever it is, it won't be Min*, he thought but didn't say. "I got a few people I thought I'd try chatting up in the next few days. See if anything seems likely."

"I really appreciate this, Alex," Bobbie said. "We should talk about how to manage that safely. I don't want you walking into a trap."

"Wouldn't make me happy either. Also, you don't have access to a ship, do you?"

Bobbie blinked at the non sequitur. "What kind of ship?"

"Something small and fast," Alex said. "May need to get out to the Belt, take a gander at something for Holden."

"Well, actually, yeah," Bobbie said. "Avasarala gave me the old racing pinnace we took from Jules-Pierre Mao back in the day. It's pretty much just been sucking dock fees, but I could probably get it polished up."

"You're kiddin'. She gave you the *Razorback*?"

"Not kidding. I think it was her way of paying me without actually paying me. She'd probably be confused that I haven't sold it yet. Why? What's up?"

"I'll let you know when I hear more," Alex said. "Maybe something, maybe nothing."

But either way, he thought, *it'll get you and me both where it's hard as hell to have someone make a follow-up attack.*

Chapter Sixteen: Holden

The security footage from Tycho Station covered almost all of the public spaces. The wide, open common corridors, the thinner access ways. Gantries and maintenance corridors. It seemed like the only places the eyes of station security didn't reach were the businesses and personal quarters. Even the storage lockers and tool shops had cameras logging whoever went in or out. It should have made things easy. It didn't.

"This has got to be it," Holden said, tapping a finger against the screen. Under his nail, Monica's doorway opened. Two people came out. They wore light blue jumpsuits with no signs or insignia, dark, close-fitting caps, and work gloves. The crate they wheeled between them was the same formed plastic and ceramic that food and environmental services used to transport biological materials: raw fungal matter to be textured and flavored, then the foods that were made from them, and—when needed—the processed fecal remains taken back as substrate for the fungus. Magnetic clamps held it to the cart, and the indicator on the side showed it was sealed. It was big enough, maybe, to hold a woman. Or a woman's body.

They'd gone in an hour earlier. Monica had gone in twenty minutes before. Whatever happened, she had to have been in that box.

Fred, scowling and hunched over, marked the crate as an item of interest and put a follow order on it. Holden couldn't tell what the older man was thinking, but his eyes were flat with anger. Anger and something else.

"You recognize them?" Holden asked.

"They're not in the system."

"Then how did they get on the station?"

Fred glanced at him. "Working on that."

"Right. Sorry."

On-screen, the two men—Holden was pretty sure they were both men—took the crate to a maintenance corridor, the trace clicking over from camera to camera automatically. In the narrower space, the crate bumped against the walls and tried to bind up where the corridor turned.

"Doors and corners," Holden said.

"What?"

"Nothing."

The security trace showed men and cart entering a warehouse. Pallets of similar crates filled the space. The men guided the cart to a half-filled one, unlocked the clamps, and hauled the crate up and onto the pallet with its siblings. Fred split the display, holding the trace on the cart, but adding one to each of the two men. One panel showed the storage space; the other followed the two figures out to the common corridors.

In the warehouse, a pair of mech drivers came, logged in from lunch, and resumed the task of piling on crates. In the common corridor, the two men went into a lavatory and didn't come out. The trace on them flickered forward until the green border that marked a live feed framed the images. A short call to the warehouse manager verified that the two men hadn't holed up there; they'd just disappeared. The cart, still going through the older records, was buried in among others just like it. Fred advanced the feed. Mech drivers came and went. Pallets filled and were piled on top of each other.

"Present status," Fred said, and the security feed skipped forward without moving away from the warehouse camera. Whatever had been in the crate was still there.

"Well," Fred said, rising to his feet, "this is about to turn into an unpleasant day. You coming?"

The environmental controls in the warehouse showed no anomalies, but Holden couldn't help imagining he smelled something under the oil and ozone. A smell like death. The mech driver was a fresh-faced young woman with straight brown hair the same color as her skin. Her expression as she moved the crates back out from the pallet spoke of excitement and curiosity and barely constrained dread. With every crate that came off, Holden's gut went tighter. Monica had told him that involving other people in his investigation was dangerous. He couldn't help thinking that whatever they found in the next few minutes was going to be his fault.

And so fixing it would be his responsibility. Assuming it could be fixed.

"That's the one," Fred said to the mech driver. "Put it over here."

She maneuvered the container to the empty decking. Its magnetic clamps engaged with a deep thump. The indicator still showed that it was sealed. Even if Monica had been put into the thing alive, her air would have run out hours ago. The mech backed away, settling onto titanium and ceramic haunches. Fred stepped forward, lifted his hand terminal, and tapped in an override. The indicator on the crate shifted. Fred flipped open the lid.

The smell was rich and organic. Holden had a sudden powerful memory of being fourteen at his family compound on Earth. Mother Sophie had kept an herb garden by the kitchen, and when she'd turned the dirt before planting, it smelled just like this. The crate was filled to the brim with the soft, crumbling beige of raw fungal protein. Fred leaned forward, pressing his hand deep. Looking for a hidden body. When he pulled his arm back, dust clung to it up to the elbow. He shook his head no. It was an Earth gesture.

"Are you sure it's the right crate?" Holden asked.

"I am," Fred said. "But let's check anyway."

For the next hour, the increasingly confused mech driver hauled out crates from the pallet and Fred and Holden opened them. When the motes of protein dust in the air set off the particulate warning alarm twice, Fred called a stop.

"She's not here," he said.

"I saw that. So that's kind of weird, right?"

"It is."

Fred rubbed his eyes with his finger and thumb. He looked old. Tired. When he gathered himself, the sense of power and authority was still there. "Either they switched the crates somewhere between her quarters and here or they doctored the feed."

"Both of those would be bad."

Fred looked over at the mech driver as she piled the opened crates into a stack to ship back for reprocessing. When he spoke, his voice was low enough it would only carry to Holden. "Both of which would mean they had a high-level working knowledge of the security system, but not enough access to wipe the records completely."

"That narrows it down?"

"A little, maybe. Could be a UN black ops team. They could have done something like this. Or Mars."

"But you don't think that's it, do you?"

Fred chewed his lip. He pulled up his hand terminal, typed in a series of codes, every tap sharp and percussive. An alert Klaxon sounded and gold-and-green alert icons appeared on every display from Holden's hand terminal to the door controls to the mech status panel. Fred pushed his fists into his pockets with a satisfied grunt.

"Did you just lock down the *station*?" Holden said.

"I did," Fred said. "And I'm keeping it locked down until I've got some answers. And Monica Stuart back."

"Good," Holden said. "Extreme, but good."

"I may be a little pissed off."

The contents of Monica's quarters were laid out on the gray-green ceramic counters of the security lab. No blood, no images, and the background soup of DNA from thousands of people who'd been in contact with the objects in the last week, usually with too small a sample to identify an individual. This was what was left. A clothing bag, its zipper ripped and hanging open in a mindless smile. A shirt Holden remembered her wearing when he'd seen her a few days before. Her crippled hand terminal with its shattered display. All the things that hadn't belonged to the station when it rented her the space. It seemed small, like there wasn't enough there. He realized it was just that he was thinking of it as the collection of a lifetime. Probably she had other possessions somewhere else, but maybe she didn't. If they didn't find her alive, maybe this was all she'd have to leave behind.

"You cannot be fucking serious," Sakai said for what seemed like the third or fourth time. The chief engineer's face was red, his jaw set. He'd arrived at the security station a few minutes after Fred and Holden, and Holden was a little surprised Fred hadn't had him thrown out yet. "I have eight ships inbound within the next week. What am I supposed to do? Tell them to match orbit and float until we decide whether we'll let them in?"

"Seems like a good start," Fred said.

"We have supplies due to ship on half a dozen contracts."

"I'm aware of that, Mister Sakai." Fred's voice was no louder; there was no anger in it. The cool politeness made the hair on the back of Holden's neck rise. Sakai seemed to feel it too. It didn't stop him, but his voice went from accusatory to almost wheedling.

"I've got shipments on two dozen jobs due to go *out*. There are a lot of people counting on us."

For a moment, Fred's shoulders seemed to sag, but his voice was just as strong. "I'm aware of that. We'll open up for business again as soon as we can."

Sakai wavered, on the edge of saying something more. Instead, he made a short, impatient sigh and walked back out as the head of security came in. She was a thin-faced woman Fred called Drummer, but Holden didn't know if that was her first name, her last, or just something she went by.

"How's it going?" Fred asked.

"Nothing we can't handle," she said. Her voice had a crisp accent that Holden couldn't place. She glanced at him, nodded curtly, and turned back to Fred. "Do we have any information we can give on how long we expect the lockdown to be in effect?"

"Tell them the interruption of service will be as brief as possible."

"Yes, sir. Thank you, sir," Drummer said, then turned away.

"Drummer. Close the door when you go, eh?"

Her eyes flickered, cut back to Holden, then away again. She didn't say anything, but she pulled the door closed behind her when she left. Fred gave Holden a mirthless, tired smile.

"Sakai's right. I just shut down the equivalent of a major port city because of one missing woman. Every hour I keep it like this, Tycho's losing thousands of credits in a dozen different scrips."

"So we'll have to find her quickly."

"If they haven't already fed her into the recyclers and broken her down to water and a few active molecules," Fred said. And then a moment later, "I have the sensor arrays sweeping the local area. If she's been spaced, we'll know it soon."

"Thank you," Holden said, leaning against the counter. "I know I don't say it often, but I do appreciate this."

Fred nodded to the door. "You see her? Drummer?"

"Sure."

"I've been working with her directly for three years. Knew who she was for ten before that."

"All right," Holden said.

"If you'd asked me yesterday, I'd have told you I trusted her with my life."

"Now?"

"Now there is exactly one person on this station who I'm certain isn't going to shoot me in the back of the head if I keep pressing on this, and that's you," Fred said.

"That's got to be uncomfortable."

"It really is. So what I mean to say, James, is that while I am glad that you appreciate all I'm doing for you, I'm also taking you on right now as my personal bodyguard. In return, I'll try to keep anyone from shooting you."

Holden nodded slowly. Something in the back of his brain was shifting, like a thought that wasn't quite formed. A wave of vertigo washed over him like he was looking over a cliff. "Two of us against a deep OPA conspiracy."

"Until I have evidence to the contrary, yes."

"That really is an uncomfortable position to be in, isn't it?"

"Not what I would have picked, no," Fred said. "But someone knows how to circumvent my security systems, and whatever your reporter friend was doing was enough to spook them into action direct enough to tip their hand."

"The missing ships," Holden said. "There were a couple of people I mentioned it to."

"That's not something you do."

"In retrospect, I wish I'd played it a little closer to the vest, but—"

"Not that," Fred said. "When you've infiltrated the enemy security structures, you don't do anything that shows that you've managed it. It's basic information warfare. As long as the enemy doesn't know they're compromised, you can keep gathering intelligence. That's not something you give up unless the stakes are unimaginably high or..."

"Or?"

"Or the enemy you've compromised isn't going to be around very long anyway. I don't know if those missing ships spooked someone into making a stupid mistake, or if my position on Tycho is so precarious that it doesn't matter anymore whether I know."

"You seem to be taking it all in stride."

Fred hoisted an eyebrow. "I'm panicking on the inside," he said in a deadpan.

Holden looked over the pile of Monica's belongings as if they might have something to add to the conversation. The hand terminal blinked forlornly. The blouse hung loose and sad.

"Did you pull anything from her terminal?" he asked.

"We can't connect to it," Fred said. "All the diagnostics are disabled or sunk in third-party encryption. Journalists."

Holden picked up the hand terminal. The shattered display was a mess of light scatter. The only sections that still had anything close to recognizable were a blinking red button in one corner and a few letters in a particularly large shard: NG SIG. Holden tapped the red button and the hand terminal flashed once. The button was gone, the letters replaced by something pale brown with a line across it, a single jigsaw puzzle piece floating in a sea of noise-light.

"What did you do?" Fred asked.

"There was a button," Holden said. "I pushed it."

"Jesus Christ. That really is how you go through life, isn't it?"

"But look. It…I think I may have accepted an incoming signal."

"From what?"

Holden shook his head. Then turned back to the pile of Monica's belongings, the tiny half-thought that had been bothering him slipping into his consciousness with something like relief.

"Her video capture," he said. "She has a little wearable interview rig. It's intentionally unobtrusive so that the person she's talking to sort of forgets they're on camera."

"And?"

Holden spread his hands. "It's not here."

Fred moved forward, his lips thin, his eyes shifting over the mess of light from the broken screen. Holden had a sense of movement, as if the image was shifting slightly. Voices came from the far side of Fred's office door. A man's voice raised in anger; Drummer's calm, clipped reply.

"Are you sure we can't get into this hand terminal?" Holden said.

"Positive," Fred said, "but there may be another way. Come on. If we're going to solve this, we're going to need an imaging astronomer."

⚡

Once Fred explained the problem, it took three hours to set up a rig that would capture the glow coming from the scattered screen and an hour more to get the computer to understand its new task. The properties of light coming off extrasolar dust clouds were apparently very different from a busted terminal display. Once the expert systems were convinced that the problem fit inside their job description, the lab went to work matching polarizations and angles, mapping the fissures in the surface of the display, and building a computational lens that couldn't exist in the physical world.

Fred had emptied the lab and sealed it. Holden sat on a chair, listening to the tick-tick-tick of the scanners recording photons and watching the image on the display slowly cohere. Fred hummed to himself, a low, slow tune that seemed melancholy and threatening at the same time. The empty stations and desks highlighted how alone the two of them were in a station filled with people.

A computational run ended. The image updated. It was still rough. Rainbow-colored deformations crossed it and sections were simply missing; it looked like the beginning of a migraine.

But it was enough. Several empty meters, ending in a square metal door complicated by an industrial bolt mechanism. Walls, ceiling, and floor marked with scuffed yellow paint and stippled by guide holes where pallets and crates would stack.

"That's a storage container," Fred said. "She's in a shipping container."

"The way the image moves. Is that her? Is she moving?"

Fred shrugged.

"Because if she's moving, then she's probably alive, right?"

"Could be. If she's alive, it's because they want her alive. And off Tycho. Look at that."

Holden followed Fred's finger. "It's the edge of the doorway?"

"The door's sealed. You don't do that until it's ready to ship. There are probably a quarter million containers like that on the station, but I'd bet we don't have more than a few thousand sealed and ready to go out. Whoever wants her, they want her someplace we can't get her back from."

Holden felt something in his gut relax. She was out there, and she was okay. Not safe, not yet. But not dead. He hadn't realized how much the guilt and fear had settled down on his shoulders until the moment of hope lifted it.

"What?" Fred said.

"I didn't say anything."

"But you made that noise."

"Oh," Holden said. "Yeah, I was just noticing how having everyone I care about gone makes it really important that I not screw up the things I can control."

"Good insight. Well done."

"Are you making fun of me?"

"Little bit. But I'm also running a targeted security scan of the shipping containers on the float. And guess what?" Fred gestured to the display on the desk before him. The great emptiness of the Tycho work sphere was drawn in thin, clean schematic lines. From habit, Holden's gaze went to the *Rocinante*. Fred pointed beyond it to a floating cluster of metal containers. "One of them's warm."

Chapter Seventeen: Alex

Alex had spent a fair amount of his training time at Hecate Base, and going back now was strange in a couple ways. There were the sorts of changes that he'd become accustomed to on Mars—old bars gone, new restaurants in place, the crappy handball courts converted to an administrative center, things like that. But driving his cart through the wide corridors, the thing that struck him most was how young everyone was. Cadets strutted in front of the bar that had once been the Steel Cactus Mexican Grill and sold to-go cups of Thai food now, their chins up and their chests out looking like they were playing dress-up. The ads on the screens were all for weapons and churches, singles services designed for people on tours of duty, and life insurance tailored for the families they left behind. They were the sorts of things that promised control or comfort in an uncertain universe. Alex remembered ads like that from decades before. The styles had changed, but the needs and subterranean fears that fueled them were the same.

Alex had worn the uniform, told the jokes. Or at least the same kind. He'd wondered whether there would be violence when he got out with a mixture of hope and dread. He'd pretended to be tougher than he was in hope of becoming tougher. He remembered how serious it had all been. The time Preston had gotten drunk and started a fight with Gregory. Alex had been pulled into it, and they'd all ended up before the MPs, certain their careers were over. The time Andrea Howard got busted cheating and had been dishonorably discharged. It had felt like someone died.

Now, looking at these kids, of course there was brawling and stupid decisions. They were children. And so he'd been a child when he was there too, and his choices had been made by a guy who didn't know any better. He'd married Talissa when he was about that old. They'd made their blueprints for how he'd serve his tours and then come home. All their plans had been made by kids this young. Looked at that way, it made sense how nothing had worked out.

The other thing that surprised him was that *everyone* seemed to know who he was.

He parked his cart outside a teahouse called Poush that had survived the years since he'd served. The blue-and-gold awning put a gentle shadow over the glassed doorway. Faux-aged paint on the window curved in art nouveau framing with phrases in French. Alex figured the intention was to evoke the idea of some Parisian café of centuries before for people who'd never so much as stepped on the same planet as France. It was strange that the quaint feeling translated so well.

Inside, a dozen small tables with real linen cloth crowded together. The air was thick with the scent of the local qahwa—almonds and cinnamon and sugar. Captain Holden had a thing for coffee, and Alex felt a moment's regret that he was off on Tycho Station where he couldn't smell this. Before he could finish the thought, Fermín boiled up out of his chair and wrapped his arms around him.

"Alex!" Fermín shouted. "Good God, man. You got fat."

"No," Alex said, returning the hug and then breaking it. "That was you."

"Ah," his old friend said, nodding. "Yes, that *was* me. I forgot. Sit down."

The waiter, a young man of maybe eighteen, looked out from behind the kitchen door and his eyes widened. The smile pretended to be the customary politeness, but when he ducked back Alex could hear him talking to someone. He sounded excited. Alex tried not to feel awkward about that.

"Thanks for this," Alex said. "I don't like to be the guy who doesn't keep in touch until he needs a favor."

"And yet," Fermín said. The years had turned his stubble gray and thickened his jowls. Alex felt like if he squinted, he could still see the sharp-faced man he'd served with hidden somewhere in him. It was easier to see him in his gestures when he waved Alex's concern away. "It's nothing. Happy to do a favor for a friend."

The waiter came out of the kitchen, nodding. The wide-mouthed cup in his hand steamed. He put it in front of Alex almost shyly.

"Specialty of the house," the boy said. "For you, Mr. Kamal."

"Ah," Alex said. "Thank you."

The boy nodded again and retreated. Alex chuckled uncomfortably at the cup, and Fermín grinned. "Come on now. You've got to be used to this kind of thing, right? You're Alex Kamal. First pilot through the Ring."

"Naw, just the first one that lived."

"Same thing."

"And I surely didn't want to be," Alex said. "They were shooting at me."

"And that makes it less romantic?"

Alex blew across the surface of the cup and sipped at it. Chai with honey and cardamom and something else he couldn't quite place. "That trip was a lot of things," he drawled. "Romantic wasn't one of 'em. And usually since then I've had the captain around to soak up the attention."

"Probably different elsewhere. But you're a local boy. One of us who got out and made good."

"Is that what happened?"

Fermín spread his hands, the gesture taking in the teahouse, the corridor outside, Hecate Base, and Mars. "I've been here the whole damned time. Made it as far as chief petty officer. Two divorces and a kid in upper university calls me twice a year to borrow money."

"Bet you had fewer people shooting at you, though. It's not as much fun as you make it sound."

"Suppose not," Fermín said. "Grass is always greener."

For an hour, more or less, they sat drinking chai and eating almond cookies—though fewer of those than they had when they'd been younger. Fermín brought him up to speed on half a dozen of the others that they'd known in common back in the day. The chai was good and Fermín jovial. It was hard to say what it was exactly that left Alex melancholy. When the time came to leave, the boy wouldn't take their money. He just said "On the house" when they tried.

The checkpoint into the base proper was manned by a security team that had Fermín glance into a facial recognition setup. Once he cleared, they checked Alex for weapons and contraband and issued him a visitor pass. The process was less than five minutes, and leisurely at that. Alex followed Fermín to a moving walkway and leaned against the rail with him as it drew them forward, deeper into Olympus Mons.

"So this guy," Alex said.

"Commander Duarte? You'll like him. Everyone likes him. Admiral Long's aide. Has been for the last ten years."

"Long hasn't retired?"

"She'll die at her desk," Fermín said. He sounded just on the edge of resentful, but his smile covered whatever it was over.

"I appreciate you setting this up."

"Not a problem. Duarte was excited to meet you."

"Really?"

"Why the surprise? You're pilot of the *Rocinante*. You're famous."

⚡

Winston Duarte's office was plain and comfortable. The desk was simple pressed polycarbonate, a little larger maybe than the receptionist's in the lobby. The screen on the wall was set to a calm semi-abstract piece that flowed in sepia and brown, evoking fallen leaves and mathematical proofs in roughly equal proportions. The only touch of luxury was a shelf of what appeared to be actual printed books on military strategy. The man himself fit in the space like he'd been designed for it. Half a head shorter than Alex with acne-pocked cheeks and warm brown eyes, Duarte radiated politeness and competence. After they shook hands, he took the seat beside Alex rather than cross back behind his desk.

"I have to say I'm a little surprised at the visit," Duarte said. "Most of my dealings with the OPA are formal."

"The *Roci*'s not OPA."

Duarte's eyebrows ticked up a millimeter. "Really?"

"We're more of an independent contractor. We've taken jobs from the OPA, but Earth's paid some of our bills. Private companies too, if the job's a good fit."

"I stand corrected. All the same, I'm honored. What can I do for you, Mr. Kamal?"

"Call me Alex for one thing. I'm not here officially. I mean, I'm on leave from the ship. Came back to the old stompin' grounds for a visit, came across an old friend who needed a hand with something, and one thing led to another."

"Which led you to me," Duarte said. His smile was sudden and warm. "I'll count myself lucky for that. What's on your friend's mind?"

"Missing ships."

Duarte went still, his smile still perfectly in place. For a moment, it was like the man had become a statue. When he moved again, he sat back, leaning into the chair with a barely exaggerated casualness that plucked at Alex's ears. "I'm not aware of any ships that have gone missing. Is there something I should know about?"

Alex folded his hands on his knee. "My friend. She's a marine. Well, ex now. She's been doing a little digging into the black market."

"A journalist, then?"

"A patriotic Martian," Alex said. "She's not looking to stir up anything, and neither am I. But she's found some things that got her back up."

"Things like what?"

Alex lifted a finger. "I'll get there in a minute. Thing is, she's not Navy. Doesn't have friends and contacts on our side. So she asked if I'd ask, and when I did—"

"Chief Petty Officer Beltran sent you to me," Duarte said. "I see."

"Did he make a mistake?"

Duarte was quiet for a long moment, his eyes soft and fixed on nothing. Alex shifted in his seat. These sorts of conversations weren't part of his usual duties, and he couldn't tell if it was going well or poorly. Duarte sighed. "No. He didn't."

"You're... you're seeing things too. Aren't you?"

Duarte stood and moved to the door, not touching it, but looking. His head bent a degree. "This isn't the sort of thing we talk about. I don't break the chain of command."

"I respect that," Alex said. "I'm not asking you to be disloyal to anyone. Only I have some information, you maybe have some too. I'll tell you what I'm comfortable sharing, you do the same. Maybe we can do each other some good."

"I have an investigation in progress."

"Anything I give you, I don't mind your passing on," Alex said. "And maybe it'd be best if it was like that for you too."

Duarte considered, his lips pressing together. "All right. What have you got?"

"Blips in the inventories. Things that got lost or destroyed that showed up again later. Weapons. Medical supplies."

"Ships?"

"Yeah," Alex said. "Ships."

"Give me a name."

"*Apalala.*"

Duarte seemed to deflate. He went to his desk and sank into the chair behind it, but when he spoke, his voice had a relaxed tone that made Alex feel like he'd passed a test. Like the false and cordial ease that had begun the meeting had fallen away like a mask.

"That's one I've been looking at too," Duarte said.

"What are you seeing?"

"I don't know. Not exactly. We're stretched thin. You know that?"

"People heading out for the new planets."

"Inventories are running slow. I think more of them are being dry-labbed than anyone wants to admit. I've been trying to convince the admiral that it's a problem, but either she doesn't understand or…"

"Or?"

Duarte didn't finish his thought. "There has been a pattern of attacks too. They may be political or it may just be theft and piracy. You heard about the attack on Callisto?"

"Heard about it."

"Have you come across anything about it particularly?"

"No."

Duarte clenched his jaw in disappointment. "There was something about that one that bothers me, but I can't put my finger on it. The timing was precise. The attack was well coordinated. And for what? To loot a shipyard?"

"What did they take?"

Duarte's gaze clicked onto Alex. His smile was sorrowful.

"I don't know. Nobody knows. I think nobody will ever know, because I can't even figure out what was there. That's how bad it is."

Alex scowled. "You're telling me that the Martian Navy doesn't know where its own ships are?"

"I'm telling you that the tracking of supplies, ships, and material has all but collapsed. We don't know what's missing because *we don't know*. And I'm telling you that the leadership is so focused on trying not to lose face in front of Earth and the OPA that they're downplaying it."

"Covering it up."

"Downplaying it," Duarte said. "Prime Minister Smith is making a big show *right now* of taking a convoy to Luna to meet with the UN secretary-general and swearing that everything's fine, and he's doing that because it isn't true. If I were a criminal and a black marketeer, all this would look like a permanent Christmas."

Alex said something obscene. Duarte opened his desk and took out a pad of paper and a silver pen. He wrote for a moment, then tore off the sheet and handed it across the desk. In precise, legible handwriting he'd written KAARLO HENDERSON-CHARLES and an address in base housing. The act of physically writing something down, not trusting the information to electronic transfer, felt like either sensible precaution or paranoia. Alex wasn't sure which.

"While you're here, I'd recommend talking to Kaarlo. He's a senior programmer that's been working on a project that was supposed to coordinate the databases. He was the one who came to me first to say he was seeing problems. If you have specific questions, he may be able to give you answers. Or he may be able to point you to where they are."

"Will he help me?"

"He may," Duarte said. "I did."

"Could you…give him cover?"

"No," Duarte said, with his sad smile. "I'm not ordering anyone to do anything with you. No offense. You're not Navy anymore.

Whatever we do, you and I, we do as part of my investigation. And I report all of it, down to the letter, to the admiral."

"Covering your ass."

"Hell yes," Duarte said. "You should do the same."

"Yes, sir," Alex said.

Fermín wasn't in the waiting area when he left, so Alex went out and caught one of the moving walkways heading east, toward base housing. His head felt a little light, like he'd been running the oxygen too lean for too long.

The Navy had always been the thing in his life that didn't change. The permanent factor. His relationship to it might shift. He did his tours, he mustered out, but those changes were all about him. His life, his fragility and mortality and impermanence. The idea that the Navy itself could be fragile, that the government of Mars might stumble or collapse, was like saying the sun might go out. If that wasn't solid, then nothing was.

So maybe nothing was.

Kaarlo Henderson-Charles' hole was in a stretch of a hundred just like it, spare and spartan. There was nothing on the gray-green door to identify it beyond numbers. No flowers in the planter, only dry soil. Alex rang the bell. When he knocked, the door opened under his knuckles. He heard someone grumbling angrily under their breath. No. Not a person. The recyclers on high, scrubbing the air. He caught a whiff of cordite and something like rotten meat.

The body was on the kitchen table in its uniform jumper. The blood had pooled under the chair and spattered along the wall and ceiling. A pistol still hung in the limp right hand. Alex coughed out a laugh of mixed disbelief and despair, then he pulled out his hand terminal and called the MPs.

"Then what happened?" Bobbie asked.

"What do you think? The MPs came."

The hotel lobby was decorated in crimson and gold. A wall

fountain burbled and chuckled beside the couches, giving the two of them something like privacy. Alex sipped at his gin and tonic. The alcohol bit a little. Bobbie pressed her knuckles against her lips and scowled. She was looking solid for any other person who'd been tortured and shot, but still a little fragile for Bobbie. The bandages that covered bullet wounds on her left side made an awkward bump under her blouse, but nothing more.

"They questioned you?" she said, barely even making it a question.

"For about eight hours. Duarte was able to give me a solid alibi, though, so I'm not in prison."

"Small favors. And your friend? Fermín?"

"Apparently his terminal's not on the network. I don't know if he killed the guy or if whoever killed the guy killed him or… anything. I don't know anything." He drank again, more deeply this time. "I may not be good at this whole investigation thing."

"I'm not much better," Bobbie said. "Mostly I've just been shaking the trees and seeing what falls out. So far the only thing I'm really sure about is that something's going on."

"And that people are willing to kill each other over it," Alex said.

"And now that the MPs are involved, they're going to lock down the investigation like it was fissionable. I'm not going to be able to do a damned thing."

"Amateur detective hour does seem to be pretty much over," Alex agreed. "I mean, I can still ask around."

"You did more than enough," Bobbie said. "I shouldn't have gotten you into this in the first place. I just don't like disappointing the old lady."

"I can respect that. But I do kind of wish I knew what was going on."

"Me too."

Alex finished his drink, the ice clicking against his teeth. He had a pleasant warmth in his belly. He looked at Bobbie, saw her looking back at him.

"You know," he said slowly, "just because everything's shut down here, it doesn't mean everything's shut down everywhere."

Bobbie blinked. Her shrug was noncommittal, but there was a gleam in her eyes. "You're thinking about that backwater asteroid Holden was asking about?"

"You've got a ship. There's nothing we can do here," Alex said. "Seems like something we could do."

"Anyone shot at us, at least we'd see it coming," Bobbie said, her nonchalance radiating a kind of excitement. Or perhaps it was the alcohol and the prospect of being in a pilot's chair again making Alex see what he wanted to see.

"We could go," he said. "Take a look. Probably it's nothing."

Chapter Eighteen: Holden

The construction sphere of Tycho Station glittered around Holden, brighter than stars. Ships hung in their berths in all states of undress, the *Rocinante* just one among many. Other ships hung in the center, awaiting clearance to leave. The sparks of welding rigs and the white plumes of maneuvering thrusters blinked into and out of existence like fireflies. The only sound he heard was his own breath, the only smell the too-clean scent of bottled air. The dirty green-gray EVA suit had TYCHO SECURITY stenciled on the arm in orange, and the rifle in his hand had come from Fred's weapons locker.

Station security was on high alert, Drummer and her teams all set to watch each other on the assumption—and Holden was too painfully aware that it wasn't anything more—that if there was a dissident faction within them, they'd be outnumbered by the ones loyal to Fred. When they'd started out from the airlock, Holden had turned on the security system. It highlighted slightly over a thousand possible sniper's nests. He'd turned it off again.

Fred floated ahead of him strapped into a bright yellow salvage mech. The rescue-and-recovery kit looked like a massive backpack slung across the mech's shoulders. A burst of white gas came from the mech's left side, and Fred drifted elegantly to the right. For a moment, Holden's brain interpreted the dozens of shipping containers clustered in the empty space outside the massive warehouse bays as being below them, as if he and Fed were divers in a vast airless sea; then they flipped and he was rising up toward them feetfirst. He turned the HUD back on, resetting its display priorities, and one container took on a green overlay. The target. Monica Stuart's prison, or else her tomb.

"How're you doing back there?" Fred asked in his ear.

"I'm solid," Holden said, then curled his lip in annoyance and turned his mic on. "I'm solid except that this isn't my usual suit of armor. The controls on this thing are all just a little bit wrong."

"Keep you from dying if they start shooting at us."

"Sure, unless they're good at it."

"We can hope they're bad," Fred said. "Get ready. I'm heading in."

As soon as they'd identified the container, Holden had thought they'd send out a mech, haul it into a bay, and open it. He hadn't thought about the possibility of booby traps until Fred pointed it out. The container's data showed awaiting pickup, but the frame that should have said what ship it was slated for was garbled. The image from Monica's feed didn't show anything beyond the access door. For all they knew, she could be sitting on tanks of acetylene and oxygen wired to the same circuit as the docking clamps. What they knew for certain was that the main doors were bolted and sealed. But even those could be wired to a trigger. The lowest-risk option, according to Fred, was to cut a hole into the visible doorframe and send someone in to take a look. And the only someone he was sure he could trust was Holden.

Fred positioned himself in front of the container's doors, and the mech's massive arm reached back and plucked the r-and-r pack loose. Fred unpacked it with a speed and efficiency of movement that made it seem like something he did all the time. The thin plastic emergency airlock, a single-use cutting torch, two emergency pressure suits, a distress beacon, and a small, sealed crate of medical supplies all took their places in the vacuum around him like they'd been hooked in place. Holden had spent enough years bucking ice to admire how little drift each piece of equipment had.

"Wish me luck," Fred said.

"Don't blow up," Holden replied. Fred's mic cut out on his chuckle, and the mech's arms swung into motion with a surgical speed and precision. The welding torch bloomed, slicing through the metal while a sealant foam injector followed to keep the air in the box from venting. Holden opened a connection to the lab and the captured image from Monica's feed. A brightness like a star shone there.

"We've got confirmation," Holden said. "This is the right one."

"I saw," Fred replied, finishing the cut. He smoothed the airlock over the scar, pressing the adhesive against the surface, and then opened the outer zipper. "You're up."

Holden moved forward. Fred held out a bulky three-fingered mech claw, and Holden gave it the rifle, scooping up the medical bag and emergency suit.

"If anything looks suspicious, just get back out," Fred said. "We'll take our chances with a real demolitions tech."

"I'll just pop my head in," Holden said.

"Sure you will," Fred said. The angle of the faceplate made Fred's smile impossible to see, but he could hear it. Holden pulled the outer sheet of the lock over him, sealed it, inflated the blister, and opened the interior sheet. The cut was a square, a meter to each side, black scorch marks with a pale beige foam between them. Holden put a foot on the uncut container door, locking the mag boot in place, and kicked in. The foam splintered and broke inward; the cut panel floated into the container. Dull buttery light spilled out.

Monica Stuart lay strapped in a crash couch. Her eyes were open but glazed, her mouth slack. A cut across her cheek had a ridge of black scab. A cheap autodoc was clamped to the wall, a tube reaching out to her neck like a leash. There didn't seem to be anything else there. Nothing with a big CAUTION EXPLOSIVES sign anyway.

When Holden grabbed the edge of the crash couch, it shifted on its gimbals. Her eyes looked into his, and he thought he saw a flicker of emotion there—confusion and maybe relief. He took the needle out of her neck gently. A tiny spurt of clear liquid bubbling and dancing in the air. He cracked the emergency medical kit open and strapped it over her arm. Forty long seconds later, it reported that she appeared sedated but stable and asked if Holden wanted to intervene.

"How's it going in there?" Fred asked, and this time Holden remembered to turn on the mic.

"I've got her."

Three hours later, they were in the medical bay on Tycho Station proper. The room was sealed off, four guards posted outside and all network connections to the suite physically disabled. Three other beds sat empty, the patients, if there were any, rerouted to other places. It was half recovery room, half protective custody, and Holden could only wonder if Monica understood how much of that security was just theater.

"That wasn't fun," Monica said.

"I know," Holden said. "You've been through a lot."

"I have." The words were slushy, like she was drunk, but her eyes had the sharpness and focus Holden was used to seeing in them.

Fred, standing at the foot of the bed, crossed his arms. "I'm sorry, Monica, but I'm going to have to ask you some questions."

Her smile reached her eyes. "Usually goes the other way."

"Yes, but I usually don't answer. I'm hoping you will."

She took a deep breath. "Okay. What do you have?"

"Why don't we start with how you wound up in that container," Fred said.

Her shrug looked sore and painful. "Not much to tell there. I was in my quarters and the door opened. Two guys came in. I sent an emergency alert to security, screamed a lot, and tried to get away from them. But then they sprayed something in my face and I blacked out."

"The door opened," Fred said. "You didn't answer it?"

"No."

Fred's expression didn't change, but Holden had the sense of growing weight in the angle of his shoulders. "Go on."

"I came to when they were loading me into the crash couch. I couldn't move much," Monica went on, "but I managed to turn my camera rig on."

"Did you hear anyone speaking?"

"Did," she said. "They were Belters. That's what you're getting at, isn't it?"

"It's one thing. Can you tell me what they said?"

"They called me some unpleasant names," Monica said. "There was something about a trigger. I couldn't follow all of it."

"Belter creole can be hard to follow."

"And I'd been drugged and assaulted," Monica said, her voice growing hard. Fred lifted his hands, placating.

"No offense meant," he said. "Do you remember anything specific that—"

"This is about the missing colony ships, isn't it?"

"It's early to say what this is 'about,'" Fred said, and then, grudgingly, "but that's certainly one possibility."

"The OPA's doing it, then. Only you didn't know about it."

"I'm not confirming or denying anything, just at the moment."

"Then neither am I," Monica said, crossing her arms.

"Hey, hey, hey," Holden said. "Come on, you two. We're all on the same side here, right?"

"Not without terms," Monica said.

Fred's jaw went tight. "We just saved your life."

"Thanks for that," Monica said. "I'm included in the investigation. All of it. Exclusive interviews with both of you. I'll give you everything I have about the colony ships and my abduction. Even the parts I didn't tell Holden. And fair warning before I go public with any of this."

"Wait a minute," Holden said. "There were parts you didn't tell me?"

"Final approval before anything sees air," Fred said.

"Not a chance," Monica said. "And you need me."

"Final approval exclusively for issues of security and safety," Fred said. "And two weeks lead time."

Monica's eyes were bright and hungry. Holden had traveled with her for weeks going out to the Ring the first time, and he felt like he knew her. The ruthlessness in her expression was surprising. Fred only seemed amused by it.

"One week lead time, and nothing unreasonably withheld," she said and pointed an accusing finger at Fred. "I'm trusting you on that."

Fred looked to Holden, his smile thin and unamused. "Well, now I've got *two* people I know aren't working for the other side."

⚡

The thing Holden hadn't known— No, that wasn't true. The thing Holden had known, but hadn't appreciated, was the number of ships moving through the rings and out to the vast spread of new planets. Monica's full logs tracked the almost five hundred ships that had made the transit. Many were smaller even than the *Rocinante*, traveling together in groups to make a claim on a new and unknown world or else to join newly founded steadings on places with names like Paris and New Mars and Firdaws. Other ships were larger—true colony ships loaded with the same kinds of supplies that, generations before, humanity had taken out to Luna, Mars, and the Jovian moons.

The first one to vanish had been the *Sigyn*. She'd been a converted water hauler a little newer than the *Canterbury*. Then the

Highland Swing, a tiny rock hopper that had been nearly gutted to put in an Epstein drive with three times the power a ship like that could ever have used. The *Rabia Balkhi* that she'd shown him had the best footage of its transit, but it wasn't the first or the last to disappear. As he went through, he made note of the types and profiles of all the missing ships to forward on to Alex. The *Pau Kant* could be any of them.

There was another pattern to the vanishing too. The ships that went missing did so during times of high traffic when Medina Station's attention was stretched between five or six different ships. And afterward—this was interesting—the ring through which the missing ship had passed showed not a spike in radiation but a discontinuity—a moment when the background levels changed suddenly. It wasn't something that other transits seemed to have. Monica had interpreted it as evidence of alien technology doing something inscrutable and eerie. Knowing what they did now, it looked to Holden more like a glitch left over where the data had been doctored. Like switching the crate that Monica had been taken away in or vanishing into a men's room and never coming out, someone would have had to hide the "missing" ships coming back through the ring. If there was a similar glitch in the sensor data of the ring that led back to humanity's home system—

"Holden?"

The security office around him was empty. Fred had cleared it for his "personal use"—meaning as the center for his private investigation of how deeply he had been compromised. The security personnel Holden had walked past coming in seemed nonplussed to be turned out of their own offices, but no one had raised any objection. Or at least none that he'd heard.

Fred stood in the archway of the short hall that led to the interrogation rooms. He was in civilian clothes, well tailored. A scattering of white stubble dusted his chin and cheeks, and his eyes were bloodshot and the yellow of old ivory. His spine was stiff though, and his demeanor sharp enough to cut.

"Did you hear something?" Holden asked.

"I've had a conversation with an associate of mine who I've known for a long time. Light delay always makes these things painfully slow, but...I have a better idea what I'm looking at. A start, anyway."

"Can you trust them?"

Fred's smile was weary. "If Anderson Dawes is against me, I'm screwed whatever I do."

"All right," Holden said. "So where do we start?"

"If I could borrow you for a few minutes," Fred said, nodding back toward the interrogation rooms.

"You want to question me?"

"More use you as a prop in a little play I'm putting on."

"Seriously?"

"If it works, it'll save us time."

Holden stood. "And if it doesn't?"

"Then it won't."

"Good enough."

The interrogation room was bare, cold, and unfriendly. A steel table bolted to the floor separated the single backless stool from three gel-cushioned chairs. Monica was already sitting in one. The cut on her face was looking much better—little more than a long red welt. Without makeup, she looked harder. Older. It suited her. Fred gestured to the seat at the other side for Holden, then sat in the middle.

"Just look serious and let me do the talking," he said.

Holden caught Monica's gaze and lifted his eyebrows. *What is this?* She cracked a thin smile. *Guess we'll find out.*

The door opened, and Drummer walked in. Sakai followed her. The chief engineer's gaze flickered from Holden to Monica and back. Drummer guided him to a stool.

"Thank you," Fred said. Drummer nodded and walked tightly out of the room. She might have been pissed at being kept out of the proceedings. Or maybe it was something else. Holden could see how something like this could lead to crippling paranoia pretty quickly.

Fred sighed. When he spoke, his voice was soft and warm as flannel. "So. I think you know what this is about."

Sakai opened his mouth, shut it. And then it was like watching a mask fall away. His features settled into an image of perfect, burning hatred.

"You know what?" Sakai said. "Fuck you."

Fred sat still, his expression set. It was like he hadn't heard the words at all. Sakai clenched his jaw and scowled at the silence until the pressure built up and it became too much to bear.

"You arrogant fucking Earthers. All of you. Out here in the Belt leading the poor skinnies to salvation? Is that who you think you are? Do you have any idea how fucking patronizing you are? All of you. *All* of you. The Belt doesn't need Earther bitches like you to save us. We save ourselves, and you assholes can pay for it, yeah?"

Holden felt a flush of anger rising in his chest, but Fred's voice was calm and soft.

"I'm hearing you say you resent me for being from Earth. Am I getting that right?"

Sakai leaned back on the stool, caught his balance, then turned and spat on the decking. Fred waited again, but this time Sakai let the silence stretch. After a few moments Fred shrugged, then sighed and stood up. When he leaned forward and hit Sakai it was such a simple, pedestrian movement, Holden wasn't even shocked until Sakai fell over. Blood poured down the engineer's lip.

"I have given up my life and the lives of people I care for a hell of a lot more than you to protect and defend the Belt," Fred growled. "And I am not in the mood to have some jumped-up terrorist piece of shit tell me different."

"I'm not scared of you," Sakai said in a voice that made it very clear to Holden he was desperately scared. Holden was a little unnerved himself. He'd seen Fred Johnson angry before, but the white-hot rage radiating from the man now was another thing entirely. Fred's eyes didn't flicker. This was the man who had led armies and massacred thousands. The killer. Sakai shrank from his pitiless regard like it was a physical blow.

"Drummer!"

The head of security opened the door and stepped in. If she was surprised, it didn't show in her face. Fred didn't look at her.

"Mister Drummer, take this piece of shit to the brig. Put him in an isolation cell, and be sure he gets enough kibble and water that he doesn't die. No one in, no one out. And I want a complete audit of his station presence. Who he's talked to. Who he's traded messages with. How often he's taken a shit. Everything goes through code analysis."

"Yes, sir," Drummer said, paused. And then, "Should I take the station off lockdown?"

"No," Fred said.

"Yes, sir," Drummer repeated, and then helped Sakai to his feet and ushered him out the door. Holden cleared his throat.

"We need to double-check the work on the *Rocinante*," he said, "because there's no way I'm flying something that guy did the safety inspections for."

Monica whistled low.

"Schismatic OPA faction?" she said. "Well. It wouldn't be the first time a revolutionary leader was targeted by the extreme wing of his own side."

"It wouldn't," Fred agreed. "What bothers me is that they're feeling secure enough to tip their hand."

Chapter Nineteen: Naomi

The beer was vat-brewed: rich and yeasty with a little fungal aftertaste where the hops had been cut with engineered mushrooms. Karal was making hot-plate cousa: thin, unleavened cracker bread heavy with gum roux and hot onion. With Cyn and Naomi and a new man named Miral sharing air with Karal and the hot plate both, the recyclers were working near their top rate for the space. The heat and the spiced air, the closeness of bodies and the just-buzzed relaxation of the alcohol felt like falling backward through time. Like if she opened the door, it wouldn't be the dockside grunge of Ceres Station but Rokku's ship burning for the next claim or the next port.

"So Josie," Cyn said, waving one vast palm. He paused and turned a scowl to Naomi. "Kennst Josie?"

"I remember which one he is," Naomi said.

"Yeah, so Josie sets up shop there, sa sa? Start charging the

Earthers to go down the corridor. Calls it..."—Cyn snapped three times, trying to call up the story's punch line—"calls it a municipal tollway. Tollway!"

"And how long did that last?" Naomi asked.

"Long enough we had to get off station before security grabbed us," Cyn said around a grin. Then he grew sober. "That was before, though."

"Before," Naomi agreed, lifting her glass. "Everything changed after Eros."

"Everything changed after the fuckers killed the *Cant*," Miral said, eyes narrowed at Naomi as if to say *That was your ship, wasn't it?* Another invitation for her to tell her stories.

She leaned forward a degree, hiding behind the veil of her hair. "Everything changed after Metis Base. Everything changed after Anderson Station. Everything changed after Terryon Lock. Everything changed after everything."

"Ez maldecido igaz," Cyn said, nodding. "Everything changed after everything."

Karal looked up. His expression was a mix of camaraderie and regret that meant *Everything changed after the* Gamarra.

Naomi smiled back. It had, and she was sorry too. Being here, with these men, brought up a kind of nostalgia that seeped into everything. All of them would have liked her to tell her stories—being on Eros, riding the first ship through the gate, trekking out to the first colony on the new worlds. Cyn and Karal wouldn't ask, and so the new one followed their lead. And she kept her own counsel.

Filip was asleep in the next room, his body curled into a comma, his eyes merely closed. They weren't the profoundly shut eyes of a sleeping baby. The rest of the cell were in other safe houses. Smaller groups drew less attention, and even if they lost one group, the rest could go on. It wasn't something anyone had said. The strategy was familiar and strange at the same time, like a once-favorite song heard again after years of being forgotten. Karal scooped up the cousa, lifting it off the heating element and spinning it on his fingertips in the same motion. Naomi held out her hand, and he set the cracker down on her palm, their fingers brushing against each other. The simple physical intimacy of close companionship. Of family. It had been true once, and that it was less true now was forgiven by the fact that they all knew it wasn't what it had been. Since she'd arrived, they'd all been careful not to let conversation stray into anything that put too fine a point on the gap of years she'd been absent.

And so when she broke the unspoken covenant, they would know she'd meant to. And as much as she didn't want to undo the fragile moment, the only thing worse than talking about it was leaving it all unsaid.

"Filip is looking well," she said, as if the words carried no extra significance. She bit the cracker, roux and onion flooding her tongue and the back of her nose with salt and sweet and bitter. She talked around it. "He's grown."

"Has," Cyn said, his voice cautious.

Naomi felt years of grief and anger, loss and betrayal at the back of her throat. She smiled. Her voice didn't waver. "How's he been?"

Cyn's glance at Karal was nothing, a flicker almost too fast to notice. They were in dangerous territory now. She didn't know if they were looking to protect her from the truth or Filip and Marco from her. Or if they only didn't want a part of the drama that had been and still was her old lover and their son.

"Filipito's been good," Karal said. "Smart boy, and focused. Ser focused. Marco seen after him. Kept him safe."

"Safe as any of us ever are," Miral said, trying to make the words light. The hunger of curiosity was in the man's expression. He hadn't been there when Naomi and Marco had been together. It was like the rest of them were having a conversation, and half the words Miral couldn't hear.

"Que a mí?" Naomi asked.

"We all told him the truth," Karal said, a hardness coming into his voice. "Not going to lie to our own."

Cyn coughed once. He looked at her sideways, like a guilty

dog. "When he got old enough to ask, him, Marco tells him how things got harsh. Too harsh. His mother, she needed to step away from it. Put ellas kappa together."

"Ah," Naomi said. So that was the story of who she was. The one who'd been too sensitive. Too weak. From where Marco sat, it might even look like the truth.

But then what must it have been to see who she'd become? XO of the *Rocinante*, survivor of Eros Station, traveler to new worlds. Looked at that way, "too harsh" was a strange thing. Unless it meant she just didn't love her son enough to stay. Unless what she'd run from was him.

"Filipito, he's solid," Cyn said. "Be proud of him."

"Nothing but," Naomi said.

"So," Miral said, his voice fighting and failing for casual. "You ship sui James Holden, yeah? What's that like?"

"Steady work. No room for promotion," Naomi said, and Cyn laughed. After a moment, Miral joined in ruefully. Only Karal kept quiet, and that might only have been from concentrating on the hot plate.

Naomi's hand terminal chimed. She picked it up. Two more messages from Jim. Her fingertip was a centimeter from the button to accept them. His voice was a few small movements away, and the thought pulled at her like a magnet. Hearing him now, even just his recorded voice, would be like taking a long shower in clean water. She pushed the messages into her hold queue. Soon, and then all of them. But if she started now, she wouldn't stop, and she wasn't done yet. Instead, she put in a connection request to the address the Outer Fringe Exports representative had given her. A few seconds later, the connection hiccupped to life, a red border marking that the channel was secure.

"Ms. Nagata," the young man said. "How can I help you today?"

"Waiting on the ship," she said. "Need to know where we stand."

The man's eyes unfocused for a moment, then his smile sharpened. "We're waiting for the title transfer to update in the base registry, ma'am."

"So the payment's gone through?"

"Yes. If you'd like, you can take possession now, but please be aware you can't be cleared to leave port until the registry updates."

"That's fine," she said, getting to her feet. "Where's she berthed?"

"Dock six, berth nineteen, ma'am. Would you like a representative present for the handover?"

"No," she said. "Just leave the keys in the ignition, and we can take it from here."

"Of course. It's been a pleasure."

"Likewise," Naomi said. "Have a better one."

She dropped the connection. Cyn and Miral were already gathering their few things. Karal scooped up the last cousa from the hot plate with one hand and unplugged it with the other. She didn't need to tell them to alert the others. Cyn was already doing it. Without changing, the air in the room felt suddenly too thick, the heat from the hot plate and their bodies too oppressive. Naomi stepped through the doorway.

"It's time," she said, her voice gentle. She remembered all the drama feeds and films with a mother waking her child up for school. This was the closest thing she would ever have to that, and against her best judgment, she savored it. "Filip. We can go now."

His eyes opened, and for a moment, he wasn't wholly awake. He looked confused. Vulnerable. Young. And then his focus sharpened, and he was himself again. His new self. The one she didn't know.

They cycled the front door and stepped out into the corridor. The cool rotation breeze smelled of damp and ozone. She was still holding Karal's cousa half-eaten in her off hand. She took another bite, but it had gone cold and the roux was clotting. She dropped what was left in the recycler and tried not to see it as a metaphor for anything else.

Cyn loomed up from the door, his face in its resting scowl. He looked older. Harder. She missed who he'd been when they were young. She missed who she'd been.

"Ready to go, Knuckles?" Cyn asked.

"Hell, yes," she said, and he looked at her more closely. Hearing, maybe, something more in the words than only the affirmation.

The ship was a simple transport skiff so small that the docking clamps holding it seemed about to crush its tarnished sides in. It didn't have an Epstein drive, so most of the hold would be taken up by the propellant mass. It would have to fly teakettle, and even then, a fair stretch of the way they'd be on the float. It was one step better than getting EVA suits and a bunch of extra air bottles, but it would do what they needed. Naomi had bought it at salvage rates, routing money from her share in the *Rocinante* through two anonymized accounts, one on Luna, the other on Ganymede. The final owner of record was Edward Slight Risk Abatement Cooperative, a company that had not existed before it appeared on the registration forms and that would vanish again when the ship was disposed of. The transponders would announce it as the *Chetzemoka*. In all, it represented about half of everything Naomi could call her own, and her name wasn't on any of the paperwork.

It didn't seem like enough. It seemed like too much. She didn't know what it seemed like.

Filip waited in the bay outside the boarding gantry, and so she did too. Cyn and Karal and Miral stood far enough away to give them something like privacy. The berth was a rental space with a red-numbered counter on the wall measuring the minutes left under agreement before its ownership changed. The metal and ceramic walls had the foggy look of sealant breaking down from the constant radiation of space. The air stank of lubricant. Someone had left an old poster on the wall, the split circle of the OPA with a hemisphere of Mars and one of Earth as the circle. Not just OPA, but militant OPA.

They'd been her people, once.

The others arrived. Josie and Old Sandy. Wings, whatever his real name was. A thick-faced, sorrow-eyed woman with one missing tooth that Naomi hadn't seen before. A shaven-headed man with livid scars webbing the dark flesh of his scalp and the limp of an unhealed foot wound. More. Each of them nodded to Filip as they passed, their expressions a mix of respect and indulgence. All of them knew him better than she did. All of them would ship with him when he left. The ache behind her breastbone would have concerned her any other time. Just now, she knew what it was.

Soft tears threatened, but she blinked them back. Bit her tongue to stop them.

"All well?" Filip asked.

She laughed, and the tightness around her heart grew harder. "Well enough. As soon as the registry updates, we can file a plan and go."

"Good."

"Do you have a moment?"

His gaze flickered up to hers, something like anxiety in his eyes. A heartbeat later, he nodded once and pointed to the corner with his chin. They walked together, and the others gave them space. Naomi's heart beat like she was in danger. She could feel her pulse in her throat.

At the wall of the berth, she stopped. Filip turned to face her. The memory of him as an infant, toothless and grabbing onto her finger with a grin of unmistakable pride intruded powerfully into her mind and she took a moment to shove it away.

"It's been good seeing you," she said.

For a moment, she thought he wouldn't answer, then, "You too."

"The ship," she said. "When it's done, it's yours, all right?"

Filip looked over her shoulder toward the gantry. "Mine?"

"I want you to have it. Resell it, keep the money for yourself. Or hold it, if you want. Yours, though. No one else."

He tilted his head. "You're not coming with?"

"I didn't come here to join back in," she said, then sighed. "I came because he said you were in trouble. I came because of you. Whatever he's doing, whatever he's having you do, I can't be part of it. Not before. Not now either."

For a long moment, Filip didn't move. Her throat felt too narrow, like she couldn't get air through it.

"I understand," her son said. Her son who was leaving again. Who was going back to Marco and everything he was.

"Your father isn't a good man," Naomi said, the words spilling out. "I know you love him. I loved him too once, but he isn't..."

"You don't have to justify it," Filip said. "You did this for us, and I appreciate it. This is all you're willing to do, and that's disappointing, but he told me it might happen this way."

"You could come with me." She hadn't meant to say it, but as soon as she did, she meant it to her marrow. "The ship I'm on needs crew. We're independent and we're well stocked. Come do a tour with me, yeah? Get to...get to know each other?"

For the first time, a real expression cracked her son's reserve. Three thin lines drew themselves between his brows and he smiled with what could have been confusion or pity. "Kind of in the middle of something," he said.

She wanted to beg. She wanted to pick him up and carry him away. She wanted him back. It hurt worse than sickness that she couldn't have him.

"Maybe after, then," she said. "When you want it, you say it. There's room for you on the *Rocinante*."

If Marco lets you, she thought, but didn't say. *If he doesn't hurt you as a way to punish me.* And then, a moment later, *God this will be weird to explain to Jim.*

"Maybe after," Filip said, nodding. He put his hand out, and they held each other by the wrist for a moment. He turned first, walking away with his hands in his pockets.

The sense of loss was vast and oceanic. And it was worse because the loss wasn't happening now. It had happened every day since she'd left. Every day that she'd lived the life she chose instead of the one Marco had prescribed for her. It only hurt so badly now because she was seeing what all those days summed to and feeling the tragedy of it.

She didn't see Cyn and Karal coming up until they were there.

She wiped her eyes with the heel of her palm, angry and embarrassed and afraid that a kind word would shatter the composure she still had. A kind word or a cruel one.

"Hoy, Knuckles," Cyn said, his landslide-deep voice low and soft. "So. No chance kommt mit? Filipito's something. Know he's tight and thin right now, but he's still on mission. When he's not running herd, he can be funny. Sweet too."

"I left for reasons," Naomi said, the words feeling thick and muddy and true. "They haven't changed."

"Your son, him," Karal said, and the accusation in his voice was calming because she knew how to answer it.

"You know those stories about a trapped wolf chewing itself free?" she said. "That boy's my paw. I'll never be whole without him, but I'm fucked if I'll give up getting free."

Cyn smiled, and she saw the sorrow in his eyes. Something released in her. It was done. She was done. All she wanted now was to go listen to every message Jim had left her and find the fastest transport back to Tycho that there was. She was ready to go home.

Cyn spread his arms, and she walked into them one last time. The big man folded around her, and she rested her head on his shoulder. She said something obscene and Cyn chuckled. He smelled of sweat and incense.

"Ah, Knuckles," Cyn rumbled. "Didn't have to fall this way. Suis désolé, yeah?"

His arms tightened around her, pinning her arms to her sides. He reared back, lifting her feet off the deck. Something bit at the flesh of her thigh and Karal limped back, needle still in his hand. Naomi thrashed, slamming her knee into Cyn's body. The vicious embrace pressed the air out of her. She bit Cyn's shoulder where she could reach it and tasted blood. The big man's voice was soft and lulling in her ears, but she couldn't tell what the words were anymore. A numbness spread along her leg and up into her belly. Cyn seemed to fall with her locked in his arms, but he never landed. Only spun backward into space without his legs ever leaving the deck.

"Don't do this," she gasped, but her voice seemed to come from far away. "Please don't do this."

"Had to, Knuckles," Cyn said. "Was the plan immer and always, sa sa? What it's all about."

A thought came to her and then slid away. She tried to land her knee in his crotch, but she wasn't sure where her legs were anymore. Her breath was loud and close. Over Cyn's shoulder, she saw the others standing beside the gantry to the ship. Her ship. Filip's ship. They were all turned to watch her. Filip was among them, his face empty, his eyes on her. She thought she might have cried out, but it could only have been something she imagined. And then, like a light going out, her mind stopped.

Chapter Twenty: Alex

When piloting a ship—any ship—there was a point where Alex's sense of his body reached out to subtly include the whole vessel. Coming to know how that individual ship felt as she maneuvered—how the thrust gravity cut out as that particular drive shut down, how long the flip took at the midpoint of a run—all of it made a deep kind of intimacy. It wasn't rational, but it changed how Alex felt about himself. His sense of who he was. When he'd gone from the massive, stately heft of the colony-ship-turned-ice-hauler *Canterbury* to the fast-attack frigate that had become the *Rocinante*, it had been like turning twenty years younger.

But even the *Roci* had tons of metal and ceramic. She could spin fast and hard, but there was an authority behind the movement. Muscle. Piloting the racing pinnace *Razorback* was like strapping onto a feather in a thunderstorm. There was nothing to the ship but a blister the size of the *Roci*'s ops deck strapped to a fusion drive. Even the engineering deck was a sealed compartment, accessible to technicians at the dock. It wasn't the sort of ship the crew was going to maintain; they had hired help for that. The two crash couches huddled close together, and the compartments behind them were just a head, a food dispenser, and a bunk too small for Bobbie to fit in. There wasn't even a system to recycle food, only water and air. A maneuvering thruster could spin the ship around twice in ten seconds with power output that would have shifted the *Roci* five degrees in twice the time.

If piloting the *Rocinante* required Alex to think of the ship like a knight's horse, the *Razorback* begged for attention like a puppy. The screens wrapped around the couches and covered the walls, filling his whole visual field with the stars, the distant sun, the vector and relative speed of every ship within a quarter AU. It threw the ship's performance data at him like it was boasting. Even with interior anti-spalling fabric a decade out of fashion and the grime and signs of wear on the edge of the couches, the ship felt young. Idealistic, feckless, and a little bit out of control. He knew if he spent enough time to get used to her, the *Roci* would feel sluggish and dull when he got back. But, he told himself, only for a little while. Until he got used to it again. The thought kept him from feeling disloyal. For sheer power and exuberance, the *Razorback* would have been an easy ship to fall in love with.

But she wasn't built for privacy.

"...as a community, Mars has got its collective asshole puckered up so tight it's bending light," Chrisjen Avasarala continued behind him. "But the prime minister's convoy has finally launched. When he gets to Luna, I'm hoping we can get him to say something that hasn't already been chewed by half a dozen diplomats playing cover-your-ass. At least he knows there's a problem. Realizing you've got shit on your fingers is the first step toward washing your hands."

He hadn't seen the old woman since Luna, but he could picture her. Her grandmotherly face and contempt-filled eyes. She projected a weariness and amusement as part of being ruthless, and he could tell Bobbie liked her. More, that she trusted her.

"In the meantime, you stay out of trouble. You're no good to anybody dead. And if that idiot Holden's plucking another thread in the same knot, God alone knows how he'll fuck it up. So. Report in when you can."

The recording ticked and went silent.

"Well," Alex said. "She sounds the same as ever."

"Give her that," Bobbie agreed. "She's consistent."

Alex turned his couch to look back at her. Bobbie made hers look small, even though it was the same size as his own. The pinnace was doing a fairly gentle three-quarter-g burn. Over twice the pull of Mars, but Bobbie still trained for full g just the way she had when she was an active duty marine. He'd offered less in deference to her wounds, but she'd just laughed. Still, he didn't need to burn hard.

"So when you said you were working with her?" Alex said, trying not to make it sound like an accusation. "How different is that from working for her?"

Bobbie's laugh was a cough. "I don't get paid, I guess."

"Except for the ship."

"And other things," Bobbie said. Her voice was carefully upbeat in a way that meant she'd practiced hiding her discomfort. "She's got a lot of ways to sneak carrots to me when she wants to. My job is with veterans' outreach. This other stuff..."

"Sounds complicated."

"It is," Bobbie said. "But it all needs doing, and I'm in a position to do it. Makes me feel like I matter, so that's something. Still miss being who I was, though. Before."

"A-fucking-men," Alex said. The lift of her eyebrows told him he'd said more than he'd meant to. "It's not that I don't love the *Roci*. She's a great ship, and the others are family. It's just... I don't know. I came to it out of watching a lot of people I knew and kind of liked get blown up. Could have lived without that."

Bobbie's expression went calm, focused, distant. "You still dream about it sometimes?"

"Yeah," Alex drawled. It felt like confession. "You?"

"Less than I used to. But sometimes. I've sort of come to peace with it."

"Really?"

"Well, at least I'm more comfortable with the idea that I won't come to peace with it. That's kind of the same thing."

"You miss being a marine?"

"I do. I was good at it."

"You couldn't go back?"

"Nope."

"Yeah," Alex said. "Me neither."

"The Navy, you mean?"

"Any of it. Things change, and they don't change back."

Bobbie's sigh was like agreement. The vast emptiness between Mars and the Belt, between the two of them and the distant stars, was an illusion made by curved screens and good exterior cameras. The way the space contained their voices was more real. The two of them were a tiny bubble in a sea immeasurably greater than mere oceans. It gave them permission to casually discuss things that Alex normally found hard to talk about. Bobbie herself was in that halfway space between a stranger and a shipmate that let him trust her but not feel a responsibility to protect her from what he thought and felt. The days out from Mars to Hungaria were like sitting at a bar, talking to someone over beer.

He told her his fears about Holden and Naomi's romance and the panic attacks he'd had on the way back to Earth from New Terra. The times he'd killed someone, and the nightmares that eventually replaced the guilt. The stories about when his father died, and his mother. The brief affair he'd had while he was flying for the Navy and the regret he still felt about it.

For her part, Bobbie told him about her family. The brothers who loved her but didn't seem to have any idea who or what she was. The attempts she'd made at dating since she'd become a civilian, and how poorly they'd gone. The time she'd stepped in to keep her nephew from getting involved with the drug trade.

Rather than trying to fold into the bunk, Bobbie slept in her couch. Out of unspoken solidarity, Alex did the same. It meant they wound up on the same sleep cycle. Bad for rotating watches, good for long meandering conversations.

They talked about the rings and the protomolecule, the rumors Bobbie had heard about the new kinds of metamaterials the labs on Ganymede were discovering based on observation of the Ring and the Martian probes reverse engineering what had happened on Venus. In the long hours of comfortable silence, they ate the rations that they'd packed and watched the scopes as the other ships went on their own ways: a pair of prospectors making for an unclaimed asteroid, the little flotilla escorting the Martian prime minister to Luna, a water hauler burning back out toward Saturn to gather ice for Ceres Station, making up for all the oxygen and hydrogen humanity had used spinning the rock into the greatest port city in the Belt. The tracking system generated tiny dots from the transponder data; the actual ships themselves were too small and far away to see without magnification. Even the high albedo of the Hungaria cluster only meant the sensor arrays picked them up a little easier. Alex wouldn't have identified that particular centimeter of star-sown sky as being different from any other if the ship hadn't told him.

The intimacy of the *Razorback* and shortness of the trip was like a weekend love affair without the sex. Alex wished they'd thought to bring a few bottles of wine.

The first sign that they weren't alone came when they were still a couple hundred thousand klicks out from Hungaria. The *Razorback*'s external sensors blinked and flashed, the proximity reading dancing in and out. Alex closed down the false stars and pulled up tactical and sensor data in their place.

"What's the matter?" Bobbie asked.

"Unless I'm reading this wrong, this is the time when a military ship would be telling us that someone out there's painting us."

"Targeting lasers?"

"Yup," Alex said, and a creeping sensation went up his spine. "Which is a mite more provocative than I'd have expected."

"So there is a ship out here that's gone dark."

Alex flipped through the databases and matching routines, but it was just standard procedure. He hadn't expected to find anything and he didn't.

"No transponder signal. I think we've found the *Pau Kant*. I mean, assuming we can find her. Let's just see what we see."

He started a sensor sweep going in a ten-degree arc and popped open the comms for an open broadcast. "Hey out there. We're the private ship *Razorback* out of Mars. Couldn't help noticing you're pointing a finger at us. We're not looking for any trouble. If you could see your way to answering back, it'd ease my mind."

The *Razorback* was a racing ship. A rich kid's toy. In the time it took her system to identify the ship that was targeting them, the *Roci* would have had the dark ship's profile and specs and a target lock of her own just to make the point. The *Razorback* chimed that the profile data had been collected and matches were being sought. For the first time since they'd left Mars, Alex felt a profound desire for the pilot's chair in the *Rocinante*.

"They're not answering," Bobbie said.

"They're not shooting either," Alex said. "As long as they think we're just some yahoo out joyriding, we'll be fine. Probably."

Bobbie's couch hissed on its gimbals as she shifted her weight. She didn't believe it either. The moments stretched. Alex opened the channel again. "Hey out there, unidentified ship. I'm going to cut thrust here until I hear from you. I'm just letting you know so I don't startle anyone. I'd really appreciate a ping back, just so we all know we're good here. No offense meant."

He cut the drive; the grip of acceleration gravity loosened its hold on him. The gel of the couch launched him gently against his restraints. He could feel his heartbeat in his neck. It was going fast.

"They're deciding what to do about us," Bobbie said.

"That's my guess too."

"Taking them a while."

The *Razorback* announced a visual match, but it wasn't with the data Holden had sent them. The ship with its sights on them wasn't any of the colony ships that had gone missing out in the gates. With an eighty-nine percent certainty, it was a Martian naval corvette, floating dark. Behind him, Bobbie saw the same thing and drew the same conclusions.

"Well," she said. "Fuck."

Profile match completed, the *Razorback* returned to its scanning arc. Another passive contact. If the corvette was the *Pau Kant*, it wasn't out here alone. And then two more. And then six. The *Razorback* picked the nearest one and cheerfully started matching its profile. By reflex, Alex went to activate his point defense cannons. Only, of course, he didn't have any.

"Maybe they'll talk," Bobbie said. He could hear it in her voice that she didn't expect them to. He didn't either. Half a second later, the *Razorback* announced two fast-movers coming from the corvette.

He spun the pinnace away from the missiles and punched the drive. The couch slammed into his back like a blow. Behind him, Bobbie grunted. With a mental apology to her, he pushed them to ten g, and the pinnace leaped forward eagerly.

It wasn't going to be enough.

As light as the *Razorback* was, the missiles were an order of magnitude less mass to accelerate. And they didn't carry anything as fragile as a human body. They could pull a much heavier burn and close the gap to target in a matter of hours. He didn't have countermeasures to shoot them down, and there was nothing to hide behind. He didn't even have a load of cargo to drop out the back in hopes the missiles might blunder into it.

His vision started to narrow, darkening at the edges and dancing gold and fractured in the center. He felt the couch's needles slide into his thighs and neck, the juice like pouring ice water into his veins. His heart labored and he was fighting to breathe, but his vision was clear. And his mind. He had to think. His ship was fast, as ships went, but nothing compared to a missile. There was no cover he could reach in time, and if the missiles were half as good as the ship that fired them, they'd be able to guide themselves right up his drive cone, no matter what he tried to huddle behind.

He could run away, draw the attackers into a line behind him, and then drop core. The vented fusion reaction would probably take out at least the first one. Maybe more. But then they'd be on the float, and at the mercy of a second volley.

Well. A bad plan was better than no plan at all. His finger twitched on the controls. The layout was unfamiliar and the fear that he was coding in the wrong information just because he wasn't on his own damned boat was like a stake in his heart.

Bobbie grunted. He wasn't strong enough to look back at her. He hoped it wasn't pain. High g wasn't a good thing for someone who'd had a bunch of holes pushed through her recently. He told himself it was just the needles feeding her the juice.

An alert popped onto his screen from Bobbie's console. PRIME MINISTER. GUARD SHIPS.

Between the drugs and the panic and the compromised blood flow in his brain, it took Alex a few seconds to understand what she meant. The *Razorback* didn't have point defense cannons or interceptor missiles, but the flotilla heading for Luna did. Alex pulled the data into the plotting system. There was no way they could reach the Martian ships before the missiles caught up with them, but it was just possible—barely—to get inside the range of their antimissile defenses. If he turned course now. If the Martians figured out what was going on and launched almost immediately. And the burn was going to be at the outer limit of what he or Bobbie could handle.

Almost without thinking, he engaged the maneuvering thrusters and the crash couches clicked to match the new vector. The missiles seemed to leap closer, correcting for the new course and anticipating where the pinnace would be. He sent an emergency signal, broadcast on all standard frequencies, and hoped whoever saw it on the flotilla was a quick thinker. The two spheres—time-to-collision and Martian antimissile range—didn't overlap, but there were only a few hundred klicks between them. Barely an eyeblink at their relative speeds. He shifted to medical control and switched Bobbie from juice to life support protocol.

Sorry, Bobbie, he thought. *I'd warn you if I had time, but you're gonna need to take a little nap if we don't want you bleeding out.* He watched her vital signs spike and then drop, her blood pressure and core temperature falling like a stone in the ocean. He pushed the ship to fifteen g.

His head hurt. He hoped he wasn't having a stroke, but it'd be fair if he did. Sustained fifteen g was a stupid, suicidal thing to do. He felt the air pressed out of his chest under the weight of his ribs, his skin. The sound of his gasping was like gagging. But the spheres touched now. Minutes stretched. Then fast-movers from the Martian flotilla. It had taken damned long enough, but the defenses were on the way. He tried to type in a message, warning the Martians that there were more ships out there, a dark fleet. He couldn't keep hold of the thought long enough to send it. His consciousness kept blinking, like the universe stuttering.

The medical system flashed up a warning, and he thought it was Bobbie, her old wounds reopening after all. But it was tagged for him. Something in his gut had ripped free. He canceled the alert and went back to watching death get closer.

They weren't going to make it. The lead missile was too close. It was going to take out the *Razorback* before the rescuers could come. Hadn't he had an idea about that? Something…

He wasn't aware of changing course. His fingers just did it. The spheres didn't touch anymore, until he switched to collision to track the second missile. Then, maybe. Maybe.

He waited. The lead missile closed. Five thousand kilometers. Four thousand. He vented the core.

Two hundred kilometers—

The crush of gravity vanished. The *Razorback*, still hurtling through space, stopped accelerating. Behind him, the lead missile died in the nuclear furnace of the rapidly diffusing core. The second missile jittered and turned to avoid the expanding cloud of superhot gas, and four lights burned before him, streaking across his screens so quickly he only knew them by their afterimages.

A fraction of a second later the Martian antimissile defenses destroyed the pursuing torpedo, but he had already lost consciousness.

Chapter Twenty-One: Naomi

Bist bien, Knuckles?" Karal asked.

The thin, slapped-together galley was too big for so small a crew. Bad design, waste of space. It wasn't worn; it was cheap. She looked at him from behind the veil of her hair and smiled. "Fine, things being," she said, making a joke. "Como sa?"

Karal shrugged with his hands. His hair had gotten gray over the years. And the stubble of his beard. It had been as black as the space between the stars once.

He looked at her eyes and she didn't flinch. "Something to say, me."

"No secrets between us now," she replied, and he laughed. She smiled back. The prisoner flirting with the turnkey, hoping a kind thought in his head would help her later. Maybe it would.

The thing that frightened her most was how well she knew how to play it. From the moment she'd come back to consciousness, she talked when people talked to her, laughed when someone told a joke. She acted like her abduction was just one of those things that happens, like using someone's tools without asking first. She pretended to sleep. Ate as much as she could past the tightness in her gut. And they all treated her like she was the girl she'd been, like they could all ignore the years and the differences, fold her back in as though she'd never gone away. As if she'd never been anyone else. Hiding her fear and her outrage slipped back on so easily, it was as if she'd never stopped.

It made her wonder whether perhaps she hadn't.

"So I was one," he said. "Helped with Filipito. Took care."

"Good."

"No," Karal said. "Before that. Sometimes, he was with me."

Naomi smiled. She'd been trying not to remember those desperate days after she'd told Marco she was leaving. The days after he'd taken Filip. To keep the boy safe, he'd said. Until she got her emotions under control, he'd said. A knot filled her throat, but she smiled past it.

"Those days. *You* had him?"

"Immer, no. But sometimes. Hijo moved, yeah? Night here, two nights there."

Her baby passed around among the people she knew. The manipulation of it was brilliant. Marco using his child as a marker of how much trust he placed in them and at the same time painting her as the crazed one. The dangerous one. Making sure the story in their community was about how solid he was and how close to cracked she'd come. She had the sudden powerful memory of Karal looking in from the kitchen while she broke down in his wife's arms. Souja, her name had been. What must her tears and profanity have looked like to him then?

"Kept it quiet," Naomi said, "and I wouldn't have known. So why say it here?"

Karal's hands shrugged again. "New day. New start. Looking to scrape off some old rust."

She tried to read from his face whether that was true, or if this was just another little cruelty in a form she couldn't call out without looking like the crazy one. If it had been back on the *Roci*, she would have known. But here, now, the balance between fear and anger and trying to control herself swamped little things like truth. It was the beauty of the way Marco had set her against herself. Tell her she was broken as a way to break her, and here they were a decade and a half past, and it still worked.

Then, for a moment, Amos was there, stronger in her memory than the surrounding ship. *It don't matter what's inside, boss. They only care what you do.* She didn't know if it was a memory or just her mind reaching for a place of certainty in an environment where nothing could be relied upon.

If Amos has become my personal touchstone for wisdom, I'm fucked, she thought, and laughed. Karal ventured a smile.

"Thank you for telling it straight," Naomi said. "New start. Scrape off the rust."

And if I ever get the chance to leave you behind in a fire, Karal, then good God *you will burn.*

A chime sounded, then the acceleration warning came on. She hadn't noticed when the ship had made its flip. Might have been when she was asleep, or slowly over the course of hours so that the rotation was subliminal. It didn't matter. She was cargo here. It didn't matter what she knew.

"Strap in, yeah?" Karal said.

"On my way," she said, launching herself gently to the ceiling, and then back to the deck at the crash couch between Cyn and Wings. It had turned out Wings' real name was Alex, but that space was taken in her mind, so he was Wings forever to her. He smiled to her and she smiled back as she strapped herself in against the gel.

The warning went from an amber glow to a ten-count in soft amber numbers, and at zero the couch lurched up against her, folding her a few centimeters in. The deceleration burn had started. When it stopped, they'd be where Marco was.

After the passageway linked the airlocks, she'd thought there would be some kind of farewell. Hugs and lies and all the things people did at the parting after a long journey. When it didn't happen, she understood that it had only been a long journey for her. The flight from Ceres to the empty space sunward of Mars and the Hungaria asteroids was like going from the couch to the head for them.

Filip emerged from the ops deck looking sharp and hard. No, that wasn't true. Looking like a boy trying to look sharp and hard.

"Check her for weapons," Filip said, biting at the words.

Cyn looked from Filip to Naomi and back. "Verdad? Knuckles been packing, she's been for a long time. Doesn't seem—"

"No prisoners on the *Pella* without a check," Filip said, pulling a fléchette gun from his pocket and not pointing it at her in particular. "Way it is, yeah?"

Cyn shrugged and turned to her. "Way it is."

Filip looked at her, his lips pressed thin. His fingers too aware of the trigger on his gun. He should have looked threatening, but he mostly looked scared. And angry. Sending a son on a kidnap job was the sort of thing Marco would do. It wasn't that it was cruel, though it was cruel. It wasn't that it would corrode any relationship that they might have had, though it did that too. It was only that it would work. Even putting Filip on Ceres looked like a manipulation now. *Here is your son, where you left him. Come into the mousetrap and take him back.*

And she'd done it. She didn't know if she was more disappointed in Filip or herself. They were two very different kinds of disappointment, and the one pointed at her had more poison in it. She could forgive Filip anything. He was a boy, and living with Marco in his head. Forgiving herself was going to be harder, and she didn't have much practice.

When the outer airlock cycled, she suffered a wave of disorientation. The passage was the usual design of inflated Mylar and titanium ribs. There was nothing about it that looked strange. It wasn't until they'd nearly reached the other side that she recognized the smell of it: tangy and deep and probably carcinogenic. The outgassing of volatile organics from the cloth.

"This is new?" she said.

"We don't talk about it," Filip said.

"We don't talk about much, do we?" she snapped, and he looked back at her, surprised by the bite in her voice. *You think you know what I am*, she thought, *but all you've got is stories.*

The airlock of the other ship was weirdly familiar. The curve was like the airlock on the *Roci*, and the design of the latch. Martian design. And more than that, Martian Navy. Marco had come into a military ship. Inside, soldiers waited. Unlike the ragged group on Ceres, they wore a rough kind of uniform: gray jumpsuits with the split circle on their arms and breasts. Against the clean design of the ship's corridor, they looked like bad costumes in a play with good set design. The guns were real though, and she didn't doubt they'd use them.

The bridge looked like the *Rocinante*'s younger brother. After the cheap, barely-enough aesthetic of the *Chetzemoka*, military-grade crash couches and terminal displays looked solid and reassuring. And there, in the center of it all like he'd posed himself, floated Marco. He wore something like a military uniform, but without any insignia.

He was beautiful as a statue. Even now, she had to give him that. She could still remember when those lips and the softness in those eyes had made her feel safe. Lifetimes ago, that was. Now he smiled, and a strange relief spread through her. She was with him again, and unquestionably in his power. Her nightmare had come true, so at least she didn't have to dread it anymore.

"I've brought her, sir," Filip said, all his consonants sharp enough to cut with. "Mission accomplished."

"I never had a doubt," Marco said. In person, his voice had a richness that recorded messages lost. "Good work, mijo."

Filip gave a little salute, and spun to leave.

"Ah!" Marco said, pulling the boy up short. "Don't be rude, Filip. Kiss your mother before you go."

"You don't have to do that," Naomi said, but—eyes blank and empty—Filip floated over and pecked her cheek with dry lips before returning to the lift. The guards went with him, except for two that took up stations behind her.

"It's been a long time," Marco said. "You look good. The years have been kind to you."

"You too," she said. "Sound different too. When did you stop talking like a Belter?"

Marco spread his hands. "In order to be heard by the oppressing class, one must speak as a member of it. Not only the language, but the diction. The accusation of tyranny, however well-founded in fact, is dismissed unless it is delivered in the manner that power recognizes as powerful. That's why Fred Johnson was useful. He was already iconic of an authority that the authorities understood."

"So you've been practicing, then," she said, folding her arms.

"It's my job." Marco reached up, pushed his fingertips against the upper deck, and floated down toward the control couches. "Thank you for coming."

Naomi didn't answer that. She could feel him already rewriting the past. Treating her like she'd chosen to join him. Like she was responsible for being here. Instead, she nodded toward the ops deck. "Nice ride. Where'd you get it?"

"Friends in high places," Marco said, and then chuckled. "And strange, strange alliances. There are always people who understand that when the world changes, the rules change with it."

Naomi tugged at her hair, pulling it down over her eyes, and then, angry with herself, pushed it back. "So then. To what do I owe this setup bullshit?"

Marco's hurt expression could have passed for genuine. "No setup. Filip was in trouble, you were in a position to get our son out of a bad place that had the potential to get a whole lot worse."

"And paid for it by being pulled on your ship against my will? I can't really thank you for that."

"You should," Marco said. "We brought you because you're one of ours. To keep you safe. If we could have explained it all, we would have, but things are delicate, and you don't stop to explain why you're protecting someone when the danger's close. The stakes are the lives of millions of Belters, and—"

"Oh please," Naomi said.

"You don't think so?" Marco said, a harshness coming into his voice. "You're the one who killed us. You and your new captain. The minute those gates opened, all the rest of us were dead."

"You're still breathing," Naomi said, but her anger sounded like petulance even to herself. He heard it that way too.

"You didn't grow up down a well. You know how little the inners cared about us. The *Chesed*. Anderson Station. The Cielo mine fire. Belter lives don't mean shit to inners. Never have. You know that."

"They're not all like that."

"Some that pretend they aren't, yeah?" The accents of the Belt slipped into his voice. And a rattling anger with them. "But they can still go down the wells. There're a thousand new worlds, and billions of inners who can just step onto them. No training, no rehab, no drugs. You know how many Belters can tolerate a full g? Give them everything, all the medical care, the exoskeleton support mechs, nursing homes? Two-thirds. *Two-thirds* of us could go be cripples on these brave néo worlds, *if* the inners pulled together and threw all their money at it. You think that's going to happen? Never has before. Last year, three pharmaceutical plants stopped even making their low-end bone density cocktails. Didn't open the patents. Didn't apologize to any ships don't have budget for the high-end stuff. Just stopped. Needed the capacity for colony ships and all the new ganga they're making with the data coming back from the rings.

"We're leftovers, Naomi. You and me and Karal and Cyn. Tia Margolis. Filip. They're moving on, and they're forgetting us because they can. They write the histories, you know what we'll be? A paragraph about how much it sucks when a race of people go obsolete, and how it would have been more humane to put us down.

"Come. Tell me I'm wrong."

It was the same ranting he'd done before, but perfected by years. A new variation of the same arguments he'd made on Ceres. She half expected him to say *The* Gamarra *had it coming. This is war, and anyone who helps choke out the enemy is a soldier whether they know it or not.* Her gut felt like it was made from water. It was a feeling she remembered from the dark times. Something in the back of her head shifted. The serpent of learned helplessness long asleep starting to wake. She pretended it wasn't there, in hopes that if she denied it enough, it wouldn't exist.

"What's it got to do with me?" Naomi asked, less forcefully than she intended.

Marco smiled. When he spoke, it was back in the voice of the cultured leader. The rough-cut Belter thug vanished behind his mask. "You're one of us. Estranged, yes, but one of us all the same. You're the mother of my son. I didn't want you in harm's way."

She was supposed to ask what that meant. The path was laid out before her in lights. *What do you mean, harm's way?* she'd say, and he'd tell her. Watch her eyes go wide. See the fear in her.

Fuck that.

"Didn't want me," she said. "Wanted the *Rocinante*, only that didn't work out. Was it the ship? Or was it Holden? You can tell me. Did you want to show off in front of my new boyfriend? Because that would be kind of sad."

She felt her breath coming fast, adrenaline pumping through her. Marco's expression hardened, but before he could speak, the comms chimed and a voice she didn't recognize echoed on the deck.

"Hast contact," the woman said.

"Que?"

"Little one. Pinnace out from Mars. Talking to the *Andreas Hofer*."

"Scout ship?" Marco snapped.

The pause stretched for seconds. Then, "Looks like just some pinché asshole wrong-placing it. Seen one, seen the whole strike force, though, yeah?"

"How long before the trigger impact?"

"Twenty-seven minutes." There had been no hesitation. Whoever was on the other end of the comms had known the question was coming. Marco scowled at the control panel.

"Couldn't have waited a little longer. Would have been prettier without. But fine. Take out the pinnace."

"Toda?"

Marco looked over at Naomi, his dark eyes on her. A smile touched his lips. Theatrical asshole that he was.

"No. No es toda. Launch the assault on the Martian prime minister's ship too. And tell the hunt group to get ready, so that when the duster runs, we can take him down."

"Sabez," the woman said. "Orders out."

Marco waited, hand out like a challenge. "This is the way," he said. "Make it so they can't forget us. Take chains they fashioned to bind us and use them as whips. We won't go down to darkness. They'll respect us now."

"And do what? Shut down the Ring?" Naomi said. "Start making your cheap bone drugs again? What do you think shooting a Martian politician's going to do for 'our people'? How does that help anybody?"

Marco didn't laugh, but he softened. She had the sense that she'd said something stupid, and it had pleased him. Despite it all, she felt a twinge of embarrassment.

"I'm sorry, Naomi. We're going to have to take this up later. But I really am glad you've come back. I know there's a lot of harsh between us, and that we don't see the world the same way. But you'll always be the mother of my son, and I will always love you for that."

He lifted a fist to the guards. "Make sure she's secure, then get ready for hard burn. We're heading to the fight."

"Sir," one guard said as the other took Naomi by the elbow. Her first instinct was to resist, pull back, but what would the point have been? She pushed off for the lift, her jaw tight, her teeth aching.

"One thing," Marco said, and she turned, thinking he was speaking to her. He wasn't. "When you lock her down, make sure it's someplace she can watch a newsfeed. Today everything changes. Wouldn't want her to miss it, yeah?"

Chapter Twenty-Two: Amos

Reports at this hour are that a massive asteroid has impacted northern Africa. The Oxford Center in Rabat, five hundred kilometers west of the event, is estimating eight point seven five on the Richter scale at the epicenter."

Amos tried again to lean back in his chair. It was an uncomfortable little piece of furniture. Just crappy lightweight plastic to start with, then molded in a factory by a machine that didn't have to sit in it. His first guess was that it had been designed specifically to be awkward and ineffective if you tried to hit someone with it. And then they'd bolted it to the floor. So every five minutes or so, he placed his heels on the textured concrete and pushed back without even knowing he was doing it. The chair bent a little under the pressure, but didn't get more comfortable, and when he gave up, it bounced right back into its old shape.

"—unseen since Krakatoa. Air traffic is being severely affected as the debris plume threatens both civilian and commercial craft. For further analysis of the situation on the ground, we are going now to Kivrin Althusser in Dakar. Kivrin?"

The screen jumped to an olive-skinned woman in a sand-colored hijab. She licked her lips, nodded, and started talking.

"The shock wave hit Dakar just under an hour ago, and authorities are still taking stock of the damage. My experience is that the city is devastated. We have reports that many, many of the local structures have not survived the initial shock. The power grid has also collapsed. The hospitals and emergency medical centers are overwhelmed. The Elkhashab Towers are being evacuated as I speak, and there are fears that the north tower may have become unstable. The sky... the sky here—"

Amos tried to lean back in his chair, sighed, and stood up. The waiting room was empty apart from him and an old woman in the far corner who kept coughing into the crook of her elbow. It wasn't what you'd call a big place. The windows looked out on an uninspiring two hundred meters of North Carolina, bare from the entrance facility to the perimeter gate. Two rows of monofilament hurricane fencing blocked the path to a two-story concrete wall. Sniper nests stood at each corner, the automatic defense and control weapons stiller than tree trunks. The building was low—a single story peeking up out of the ground with administrative offices and a massive service entrance. Most of what happened here happened underground. It was exactly the kind of place Amos had never hoped to be.

Good thing was, when he was done, he could leave again.

"In other news, a distress call from the convoy carrying the Martian prime minister appears to be genuine. A group of unidentified ships—"

Behind him, the admin door swung open. The man inside looked like he was one hundred kilos of sculpted muscle and also tremendously bored. "Clarke!"

"Here!" the coughing old woman said, rising to her feet. "I'm Clarke!"

"This way, ma'am."

Amos scratched his neck and went back to looking at the prison yard. The newsfeed kept on being excited about shitty things going on. He'd have paid more attention to it if the back of his head hadn't been planning the ways he'd have pushed to get out of here if they'd sent him, and where he'd have died trying. From the parts he caught, though, it sounded like a good day for reporters.

"Burton!"

He walked over slowly. The big guy checked his hand terminal. "You Burton?"

"Today I am."

"This way, sir."

He led him to a small room with more chairs bolted to the floor and a table too. The table was solidly made, anyway.

"So. Visitation?"

"Yup," Amos said. "Looking for Clarissa Mao."

The big guy looked up under his eyebrows. "We don't have names here."

Amos opened his hand terminal. "I'm looking for 42-82-4131."

"Thank you. You'll need to surrender all personal effects including any food or beverages, your hand terminal, and any clothing with more than seven grams of metal. No zippers, arch supports, anything like that. While you are inside the prison grounds, you are subject to reduced civil rights, as outlined in the Gorman code. A copy of the code will be made available to you at your request. Do you request a copy of the code?"

"That's all right."

"I'm sorry, sir. I need a yes or no."

"No."

"Thank you, sir. While in the prison, you are required to follow the directives of any guard or prison employee without hesitation or question. This is for your own safety. If you fail to comply, the guards and prison employees are authorized to use any means they deem necessary to ensure your safety and the safety of others. Do you understand and consent?"

"Sure," Amos said. "Why not?"

The big guy pushed a hand terminal across the table, and Amos mashed his thumb onto it until the print read. A little indicator on the side of the form went green. The big guy took it back along with Amos' hand terminal and shoes. The slippers were made out of paper and glue.

"Welcome to the Pit," the big guy said, smiling for the first time.

The elevator was steel and titanium with a harsh set of overhead lights that flickered just a little too quickly to be sure it was really flickering. Two guards apparently lived in it, going up and down whenever it did. So that seemed like a shitty job. At the tenth level down, they let him out, and an escort was waiting for him: a gray-haired woman with a wide face, light armor, and a gun in her holster that he didn't recognize. Something beeped twice as he stepped into the hall, but none of the guards tried to shoot anyone, so he figured it was supposed to do that.

"This way, sir," the escort said.

"Yeah. Okay," Amos said. Their footsteps echoed off the hard floor and ceiling. The lights were recessed into metal cages, making a mesh of shadows over everything. Amos found himself flexing his hands and balling them into fists, thinking about how exactly he'd have to bounce the guard's head against the wall in order to get the gun off her. Nothing more than habit, really, but the place brought it out in him.

"First time down?" the escort asked.

"It show?"

"Little."

From down the hall, a man's voice lifted in a roar. A familiar calmness came over him. The escort's eyebrows went up, and he smiled at her. Her lips turned up in answer, but there was a different assessment behind it.

"You'll be fine," she said. "Right through here."

The hallway was brutal concrete; green-gray metal doors in a line with identical windows of thick green-tinted glass that made the rooms beyond look like they were underwater. In the first, four guards in the same armor Amos' escort wore were forcing a man to the ground. The woman from the waiting room huddled in the corner, her eyes closed. She seemed to be praying. The prisoner—a tall, thin man with long hair and a flowing beard the color of iron—roared again. His arm flashed out, quicker than Amos' eye could follow, grabbing one of the guards by the ankle and pulling. The guard toppled, but two of the others had what looked like cattle prods out. One of them landed on the prisoner's back, the other at the base of his skull. With one last obscenity, the iron-bearded man collapsed. The fallen guard rose back to her feet, blood pouring from her nose as the others teased her. The old woman sank to her knees, her lips moving. She took a long, shuddering breath, and when she spoke, she wailed, her voice sounding like it came from kilometers away.

Amos' escort ignored it, so he did too.

"Yours is there. No exchange of goods of any sort. If at any point you feel threatened, raise your hand. We'll be watching."

"Thanks for that," Amos said.

Until he saw her, Amos hadn't realized how much the place reminded him of a medical clinic for people on basic. A cheap plastic hospital bed, a steel toilet on the wall without so much as a screen around it, a battered medical expert system, a wall-mounted screen set to an empty glowing gray, and Clarissa with three long plastic tubes snaking into her veins. She was thinner than she'd been on the ride back from Medina Station before it had been Medina Station. Her elbows were thicker than her arms. Her eyes looked huge in her face.

"Hey there, Peaches," Amos said, sitting in the chair at her bedside. "You look like shit on a stick."

She smiled. "Welcome to Bedlam."

"I thought it was called Bethlehem."

"Bedlam was called Bethlehem too. So what brings you to my little state-sponsored apartment?"

On the other side of the window, two guards hauled the iron man past. Clarissa followed Amos' gaze and smirked.

"That's Konecheck," she said. "He's a volunteer."

"How'd you figure?"

"He can leave if he wants to," she said, lifting her arm to display the tubes. "We're all modified down here. If he let them take out his mods, he could transfer up to Angola or Newport. Not freedom, but there'd be a sky."

"They couldn't just take 'em?"

"Body privacy's written into the constitution. Konecheck's a bad, bad monkey, but he'd still win the lawsuit."

"What about you? Your... y'know. Stuff?"

Clarissa bowed her head. Her laugh shook the tubes. "Apart from the fact that every time I used them, I wound up puking and mewling for a couple minutes afterward, they've got some other drawbacks. If we pull them out, I'd survive, but it would be even less pleasant than this. Turns out there's a reason the stuff I got isn't in general use."

"Shit. That's got to suck for you."

"Among other things, it means I'm here until... well. Until I'm not anywhere. I get my blockers every morning, lunch in the cafeteria, half an hour of exercise, and then I can sit in my cell or in a holding tank with nine other inmates for three hours. Rinse, repeat. It's fair. I did bad things."

"All that shit the preacher pitched about redemption, getting reformed—"

"Sometimes you don't get redeemed," she said, and her voice made it clear she'd thought about the question. Tired and strong at the same time. "Not every stain comes out. Sometimes you do something bad enough that you carry the consequences for the rest of your life and take the regrets to the grave. That's your happy ending."

"Huh," he said. "Actually, I think I know what you mean."

"I really hope you don't," she said.

"Sorry I didn't put a bullet in your head when I had the chance."

"Sorry I didn't know to ask. What brings you down here, anyway?"

"Was in the neighborhood saying goodbye to a bunch of my past, mostly. Don't see how I'm coming back this way, so thought I'd better say hi now if I was going to at all."

Tears welled up in her eyes, and she took his hand. The contact was weird. Her fingers felt too thin, waxy. Seemed rude to push her away though, so he tried to remember what people were like when they had an intimate moment like this. He pretended he was Naomi and squeezed Clarissa's hand.

"Thank you. For remembering me," she said. "Tell me about the others. What's Holden doing?"

"Well, shit," Amos said. "How much they tell you about what happened on Ilus?"

"The censors don't let me see anything that involves him. Or you. Or anything involving Mao-Kwikowski or the protomolecule or the rings. It might be disruptive for me."

Amos settled in. "All right. So a while back, Cap'n gets this call..."

For maybe forty-five minutes, maybe an hour, he laid out all the stuff that had happened since the *Rocinante* turned Clarissa Mao over to the authorities. Telling stories that didn't have a punch line wasn't something he had much practice with, so he was pretty sure that as story time went, it sucked. But she drank it up like he was pouring water on beach sand. The medical system beeped every now and then, responding to whatever was happening in her bloodstream.

Her eyes started to close like she was going to sleep, but her fingers didn't lose their grip on his. Her breath got deeper too. He wasn't sure if that was part of the medical whatever it was they were doing to her or something else. He stopped talking, and she didn't seem to notice. It felt weird to sneak out without saying anything, but he also didn't want to wake her up just to do it. So he sat for a while, looking at her because there wasn't anything else to look at.

The weird thing was, she looked younger. No wrinkles at the sides of her mouth or eyes. No sagging in her cheeks. Like the time she'd spent down in the prison didn't count. As if she'd never get old, never die, just be here wishing for it. It was probably some kind of side effect of the shit they'd pumped into her. There were kinds of environmental poisoning that did that too, not that he knew the details. She'd killed a lot of people, but he had too, one way and another. Seemed a little weird that she'd be staying and he'd be walking out. She felt bad about all the things she'd done. Maybe that was the difference. Regret and punishment the flip sides of the karmic coin. Or maybe the universe was just that fucking random. Konecheck didn't look like he had a lot of regrets, and he was locked up just the same.

Amos was about to start trying to get his hand free when the Klaxons went off. Clarissa's eyes shot open and she sat up, present and alert and not even sort of groggy. So maybe she hadn't been asleep after all.

"What is that?" she said.

"I was about to ask you."

She shook her head. "I haven't heard that one before."

It seemed like the right time to get his hand back. He went to the door, but his escort was already there coming in. She had her weapon drawn, but not pointing at anything.

"I'm sorry, sir," she said, and her voice was higher than it had been before. She was scared. Or maybe excited. "This facility has been put on lockdown. I'm afraid I'm going to have to ask you to remain in here for the time being."

"How long are we talking about?" he asked.

"I don't know the answer to that, sir. Until the lockdown is lifted."

"Is there a problem?" Clarissa asked. "Is he in danger?"

That was a good move. No guard ever gave a fuck whether the

prisoner was in danger, so she was asking about the civilian. Even so, the escort wasn't going to say a goddamn thing unless she wanted to.

Turned out, she wanted to.

"A rock came down outside Morocco about three hours ago," she said, her sentence curling up at the end like it was a question.

"I saw something about that," Amos said.

"How did it get through?" Clarissa asked.

"It was going very, very fast," the escort said. "Accelerated."

"Jesus," Clarissa said, like someone had punched her in the chest.

"Someone dropped a rock on purpose?" Amos said.

"Rocks. Plural," the escort said. "Another one came down about fifteen minutes ago in the middle of the Atlantic. There're tsunami and flood warnings going out everywhere from Greenland to fucking Brazil."

"Baltimore?" Amos said.

"Everyplace. Everywhere." The escort's eyes were getting watery and wild. Panic maybe. Maybe grief. She gestured with her gun, but it just looked impotent. "We're on lockdown until we know."

"Know what?" Amos said.

It was Clarissa that answered. "If that was the last one. Or if the hits are going to keep on coming."

In the silence that came afterward, they weren't guard, prisoner, and civilian. They were just three people in a room.

The moment passed.

"I'll be back with an update as soon as I have one, sir."

Amos' brain ran through all the scenarios that came easy and didn't see many options. "Hey, wait. I know it ain't for pleasure viewing or nothing, but that screen over there catch newsfeeds?"

"Prisoners only get access in the common area."

"Sure," Amos said. "But I'm not a prisoner, right?"

The woman looked down, then shrugged. She took out her hand terminal, tapped in a few lines of text, and the empty gray screen flickered to life. A pale man with broad, soft lips was in the middle of his report.

"—undetected by the radar arrays, we are getting reports that there was a temperature anomaly that may have been related to the attack."

The guard nodded to him and closed the door. He couldn't hear it lock, but he was pretty sure it had. He sat back in his chair and propped his heels on the side of the hospital bed. Clarissa sat forward, her bone-thin hands knotted together. The feed switched over to a white-haired man talking earnestly about the importance of not jumping to conclusions.

"Do you know where the first one hit?" Clarissa asked. "Do you remember anything from the news?"

"I wasn't paying attention. I think they said Krakatoa? Is that a place?"

Clarissa closed her eyes. If anything, she went a little paler. "Not exactly. It's a volcano that blew itself up a long, long time ago. Sent ash eighty kilometers up. Shock waves went around the world seven times."

"But it's not North Africa?"

"No," she said. "I can't believe they really did it. They're dropping rocks. I mean, who would even do that? You can't...you can't replace Earth."

"Maybe you kind of can now," Amos said. "Lot of planets out there now weren't around before."

"I can't believe someone would do this."

"Yeah, but they did."

Clarissa swallowed. There had to be stairs around here. They'd be locked up so that prisoners couldn't get to them, but Amos figured there'd have to be stairs. He went to the window to the hall and pressed his head against it. He couldn't see anything down the hall either way. Kicking the glass out seemed unlikely too. Not that he was looking to try. Just thinking.

On the screen, a mushroom cloud rose over a vast and empty sea. Then, as a woman's voice calmly talked about megatonnage and destructive capacity, a map was displayed with one bright red dot on North Africa, another in the ocean.

Clarissa hissed.

"Yeah?" Amos said.

"If the spacing's even," Clarissa said, "if there's another one, it's going to be close."

"Okay," Amos said. "Can't do anything about that, though."

The hinges were on the other side of the door too, because of course they were. It was a fucking prison. He clicked his tongue against his teeth. Maybe they'd take it off lockdown and send him on his way. Might happen. If it didn't, though... Well, this was going to be a stupid way to die.

"What're you thinking?" she asked.

"Well, Peaches. I'm thinking that I stayed on this mudball a day too long."

Chapter Twenty-Three: Holden

Holden sat back, light-headed, his eyes still on the screen. The immensity of the news made Fred's office seem fresh and unfamiliar: the desk with the fine black lines of wear at the corner; the captain's safe set into the wall like a little privacy window; the industrial carpeting. It was like he was seeing Fred, leaning forward on his elbows, grief in his eyes, for the first time. Less than an hour earlier, reports had come through with red frames around the feed windows to show how serious everything was. The previous headlines—a meteor or possibly a small comet had struck North Africa—were forgotten. The ships carrying the prime minister of the Martian Republic were being approached by an unknown and apparently hostile force, his escort moving to intercept. It was the news of the year.

Then the second rock hit Earth, and what might have been a natural disaster was revealed as an attack.

"They're connected," Holden said. Every word came out slow. Every thought. It was like the shock had dropped his mind in resistance gel. "The attack on the prime minister. This. They're connected, aren't they?"

"I don't know. Maybe," Fred said. "Probably."

"This is what they were planning. Your dissident OPA faction," Holden said. "Tell me you didn't know about this. Tell me you're not part of it."

Fred sighed and turned to him. The weariness in his expression was vast. "Fuck you."

"Yeah. Okay. Just had to ask." And then a moment later, "Holy shit."

On the newsfeed, images of Earth's upper atmosphere showed the strike like a bruise. The cloud of dust was smearing off to the west as the planet turned under it. The dust plume would keep widening until it covered the whole northern hemisphere—and maybe more—but for now it was just a blackness. His mind kept bouncing off the image, rejecting it. His family was on Earth—his mothers and his fathers and the land he'd grown up on. He hadn't been back in too long, and now—

He couldn't finish the thought.

"We have to get in front of this," Fred said, to himself as much as Holden. "We have to—"

A communication request popped onto the side of the screen, and Fred accepted it. Drummer's face filled a small window.

"Sir, we have a problem," she said. "One of the ships we've got parked out there waiting to dock just put target locks on the main engines and the upper habitation ring."

"Defense grid up?"

"That's the problem, sir. We're seeing—"

The door of the office opened. The three people who came in wore Tycho Station security uniforms. One carried a large duffel bag; the other two had instruments in their hands that Holden struggled to make sense of. Strange hand terminals, or some sort of compact tool.

Or, guns.

Like someone speaking through the radio, a voice in the back of Holden's mind said *This is a coordinated, system-wide attack* just as the first woman fired. The sound alone was like being struck, and Fred toppled back in his seat. Holden scrambled for his own sidearm, but the second woman had already turned to him. He tried to drop down, to take cover behind the desk, but the two women fired almost simultaneously. Holden caught his breath. Something kicked him just below the rib, and he didn't know if he'd hit the edge of the desk or he'd been shot. He fired wild, and the man dropped the duffel bag. The first woman's head snapped back and she dropped to her knees. Someone else was shooting, and it took what seemed like minutes and was probably less than a second to realize it was Fred, supine behind the desk and firing between his feet. Holden had no idea where Fred had acquired a gun in the seconds since the attack started.

The second woman turned her gun toward Fred, but Holden took a breath and remembered how to aim, hitting her in the ribs. The man fled out the office door. Holden let him go and slid to the ground. There didn't seem to be any blood on him, but he still wasn't sure whether he'd taken a bullet. The first woman struggled to her knees, one blood-soaked hand pressing her ear. Fred shot her again. She dropped. Like it was happening in a dream, Holden noticed that the duffel bag had fallen open. It had emergency environment suits in it.

When Fred shouted, his voice was strangely high and very far away. The gunfire had left them both almost deaf. "You're a shitty bodyguard, Holden. Do you know that?"

"No formal training," Holden shouted back. The words felt louder in his throat than they sounded in his ears. He became aware of another voice shouting, but not from here. From the desk console. Drummer. He stooped over Fred, ignoring her. Blood covered the man's side, but Holden couldn't see where the wound was.

"Are you okay?" Holden shouted.

"Just ducky," Fred growled, hauling himself up. He winced, clenched his teeth, and took his seat. On the monitor, Drummer blanched.

"You'll have to speak up," Fred said. "Things got a little loud here. Holden! Secure the goddamn door."

"Doors and corners," Holden said, stepping over the bodies. "Always doors and corners."

Outside, the security office was empty. A light was flashing on the wall. Emergency signal of some kind. Now that he knew to listen for it, he could hear the alarm. Evacuation warning. Someone was evacuating the station ring. That couldn't be good. He wondered if the good guys had sounded the alert, or if it was just part of the plan. A distraction while something even worse happened. He was having a hard time catching his breath. He had to keep checking to make sure he hadn't been shot.

He looked at the gun in his fist. *I think I just killed someone*, he thought. And someone dropped a rock on Earth. And then they tried to kill Fred. It was bad. It was all just bad.

He didn't notice Fred coming up behind him until he took Holden's elbow, leaning against him for support and pushing him forward at the same time.

"Look alive, sailor," Fred said. "We've got to go. They've fired a torpedo at us, and some ratfucker sabotaged my defense grid." Fred was cursing more than usual. The stress of combat waking up the long-dormant marine inside of him.

"They're shooting the ring?" Holden said.

"Yes. And in particular, they're shooting at my office. I'm starting to get the feeling they don't like me."

Together, they struggled forward. In the wide corridor, people were scampering to hardened shelters and evacuation stations.

An older man with close-shaved hair and a mouth set in a permanent grimace saw Fred and the blood. Without a word, he took Fred's far arm across his shoulder.

"Are we heading to medical bay or evac?" Grimace asked.

"Neither one," Fred said. "The bad guys are trying to take engineering. My men got jumped. They're pinned down, and there are two enemy torpedoes on their way to disable the engines. We've got to relieve our people, and get the grid back up. See if we can't start firing back."

"Are you joking?" Holden said. "You've been shot. You're bleeding."

"I'm aware of that," Fred said. "There's a security transfer up here to the left. We can take it. Get to the construction sphere. What's your name, chief?"

Grimace looked at Holden, asking by his expression who Fred was talking to. Holden shook his head. Fred knew his name already. "Electrician First Class Garret Ming, sir. Been working for you about ten years, one way and another."

"Sorry I haven't met you before," Fred said. "You know how to use a gun?"

"I'm a quick study, sir."

Fred's face was gray. Holden didn't know if it was blood loss or shock or the first symptoms of a deeper despair. "That's good."

Tycho Station was built like a ball half a kilometer across. The construction sphere was big enough to accommodate almost any ship smaller than a battleship in its interior space. At rest, the two rings at its equator gave spin gravity to a city's worth of the Belt's best engineers and technicians. The great drives at the sphere's base could move the station anywhere in the system. Or out of it, now. Tycho had overseen the spinning up of Ceres and Pallas. It was the beating heart of the Belt and its loudest boast. The *Nauvoo*, the ship that would have taken humans to the stars, had been too large to fit inside the construction sphere, but it had been built in space next to the massive station. There was no better place for the construction of grand dreams than Tycho. Along with the terraforming of Mars and the farms of Ganymede, it was a living testament to humanity's ambition and skill.

Holden would never have imagined it could feel fragile.

The transfer from ring to construction dome was like taking a particularly awkward lift. They began at the full one-third g of the station, lurched, and their weight began to leach away. When doors opened again, they were in free fall. The blood that had started dripping from Fred's arm was a fluid coating now, the liquid held to his body by surface tension as it gradually thickened into a kind of jelly. Garret was covered with it. Holden was too. He kept expecting Fred to pass out, but the old man didn't lose focus or determination.

Visible from the long translucent tube of the access corridor, the construction sphere looked like a network of purified functionality. Other corridors curved between the ship berths, the walls tiled with a subtly repeating pattern of access panels, power transfers, storage and equipment lockers, and mech parking plates. The steel and ceramic bones of the station showed everywhere, and the light was as bright and harsh as sunlight in vacuum. The air in the access corridor was sweet with the scent of carbon lubricant and electrical discharge. Together, the three of them pulled themselves headfirst toward station south, the engineering decks, and the massive fusion reactors. Holden's body couldn't decide if he was falling down a long, bent well or swimming along an underground river of air.

"Drummer!" Fred snapped. "Report."

The audio feed from his hand terminal was confused for a moment, then the woman's voice came, her syllables clipped, calm, and measured in a way that sounded like the professional version of raw panic.

"Understood. Main engineering has been shut down by the hostiles. They are holding auxiliary engineering with a force of approximately twenty well-armed enemy, sir. We're in a mutual holding action."

"Can you disengage?"

"Not safely, sir. They can't move, but neither can we."

"Do we know—"

Something loud happened on the other end of the terminal, and a second later, a bone-deep ringing shuddered through the corridor. Garret swore under his breath.

"The first torpedo has made impact, sir," Drummer said.

"The ring?"

"No, sir. The drive cone. The torpedo targeting the ring hit a few minutes ago, but failed to detonate."

"Small favors," Fred said. "Do we know the armament of the insurgents?"

"Small automatic weapons. Some grenades."

"Can you shut down their air?"

"There's a manual cutoff, but I haven't had the spare manpower yet."

"I've got an electrician first class with me," Fred said. "Tell me where to take him."

"Understood. We're looking at an access on service deck four. Environment controls Delta-Foxtrot-Whiskey-slash-six-one-four-eight."

"They had vacuum suits," Holden said. "The ones in your office. They had emergency suits. Turning off the air may not matter."

Drummer answered from Fred's hand terminal. "We'll keep them in place until their bottles run out if that's what we need to do."

"Good," Fred said. "We're on our way."

"Don't stop for beer, sir," Drummer said, and the background hiss of the connection dropped. Fred made a small, satisfied grunt and pushed himself farther down the hall.

"It's not going to work," Holden said. "They'll figure out what we're doing and cut through a bulkhead or something."

"You know the difference between a code and a cipher, Holden?"

"What?"

"A code and a cipher. Cipher, you encrypt text so that no one can tell what the words in the message are. A code, you say the words right out in the open, but you change what they mean. Anyone with a smart computer and a lot of time can break a cipher. No one can break a code."

Holden launched himself across a wide intersection where three passageways came together. For a moment, the station extended around him on all three axes. Fred and Garret floated close behind him but pushed off faster, so that they reached the far side before him. Fred turned to his left and gestured for them to follow.

"Service deck four's the other way, sir," Garret said.

"But the four people on the ambush team are this way," Fred replied. His words were getting slushy. "Level six, section fourteen, berth eight. Once we're in position, I'll try to pull the bad guys out, and we'll take them in the flank."

Holden thought for a moment. "You had a whole system set up in case this happened. But what if Drummer had been one of them?"

"I had other systems set up with Oliver, Chu, and Stavros," Fred said. "Secure, open communications with whoever I had left."

"Tricky," Holden said.

"I've been doing this sort of thing for a while."

The ambush team was where Fred said it would be: three male Belters and a woman with the thick build of Earth, all in light armor with riot guns and suppression grenades. Fred gave Garret a short-barreled shotgun and a position at the rear where he could be both useful and safe. One tried to tend to Fred's gunshot wound, but he waved the man away.

Near the bottom of the station, the curve of the corridors was tighter, the horizon close. They were less than ten meters from the doors to auxiliary engineering, and the bent wall offered them cover. When the time came, they'd have to get even closer.

Holden's hand terminal vibrated in his pocket. Around a red frame, the newsfeed announced a third rock had struck Earth. Holden thumbed it off. If he let himself think about what was happening around the rest of the solar system now, he couldn't think about what was about to happen in this corridor. Still, his throat felt thick and his hands had a shudder he couldn't entirely control. His family was on Earth. Amos was on Earth. And Alex was in a tiny ship someplace not too far from the Martian prime minister's convoy. And Naomi was...somewhere. That he didn't know where made it worse.

"Be okay," he murmured. "Just be okay."

"What?" Fred said.

"Nothing. I'm ready."

Fred opened a connection. "Drummer. Killing the air is a no-go. We're going to have to pull in heavy artillery. I have a squad of combat marines I scraped out of a bar. They're coming to relieve you now."

"Understood," Drummer said. Holden thought there was a smile in her voice. "Make it fast, though. We've got two down. I'm not sure we can hold much longer."

"Ten minutes," Fred said, raising his bloodied left hand in the Belter idiom for *Take position*. The ambush team steadied their weapons. Holden did too. It took the people holed up in auxiliary engineering almost five minutes to decide they should make a break for it.

The door popped open, and the first half dozen or so of the enemy streamed out of engineering. They were dressed like normal people: security uniforms, technicians' jumpsuits, the sort of casual clothing Holden would have seen in a bar or in the corridors. They were just people, citizens of Tycho. Of the Belt. They took positions that gave them cover from Drummer's suppressing fire, unaware at first of the second team. At Fred's signal, the six of them opened up, though Holden was aware that he wasn't trying very hard to hit anyone. A second wave tried to get out of engineering as the first one tried to retreat back into it. Drummer's force moved forward with a barrage of gel rounds and suppression grenades that burst into foam and hardened to stone almost instantly.

In half a minute, the fight was over. Fifteen minutes later, the defense grid was back up, and the attacking torpedo boat was burning hard for someplace in among the Trojan asteroids. It was almost an hour before the real cost became clear.

With the station in relative safety, Fred had allowed himself to be taken to the medical bay. The gentle gravity of the ring was still enough to show how weak he'd become. The expert system inserted four needles, inflating him with artificial blood, and the color began to come back to his face. Holden, sitting at the bedside, watched the readouts without really seeing them. He wanted to check the newsfeeds about Earth, and he also didn't. The longer he could put it off, the longer he didn't have to think about it. When Drummer came in with the damage report, it was almost a relief. Another distraction.

"The torpedoes cracked the drive cone," she said.

"How badly?" Fred asked.

"Do you want to fly this thing on a patched-up cone? Badly enough that we're going to manufacture a new one."

"Fair enough," Fred said.

"At least they didn't blow the ring," Holden said. "If that one hadn't been a dud—"

Drummer's face went still. "About that. We were mistaken. The enemy fired a weapon with the hull and drive of a torpedo, but they rigged it with a salvage mech on the end. Ran it into your office, sliced through the exterior decking, and pulled half the wall away with them."

Fred blinked.

"*That* was why they needed EVA suits," Holden said. "I was wondering. But it seems like a pretty weird way to get to you. Peeling your office open like a sardine can."

"They weren't after me," Fred said, then paused and said something obscene.

"What?" Holden said. "What is it?"

Drummer answered. Her voice had the same professional calm she'd used in the firefight. "The enemy took the wall that had

Colonel Johnson's safe. It won't be easy getting it open, but with enough time and resources, we have to assume they will."

"But they already compromised your command structure, right? Any sensitive information they get, they probably already had?"

Holden knew even before Fred said it, but he wanted to give the universe a chance to prove him wrong. Make it so that the worst possible thing hadn't happened.

"They got the sample," Fred said, making it a reality. "Whoever did this? They now have the protomolecule."

Chapter Twenty-Four: Amos

"Wouldn't the density figure in?" Clarissa asked. Whatever crap they'd been feeding into her bloodstream, it had run out. She was starting to look a little better. He could still see the veins under her parchment-thin skin, but she was getting some color back in her cheeks.

"Sure, but that's all energy you'd put in getting the rocks up to speed in the first place. You drop a slug of tungsten out of a ship or a fucking feather pillow, you've still got to get the ship going whatever speed you're aiming for. All that price got paid at the front, energetically speaking."

"But a pillow would have burned up before it hit ground."

"Okay, now *that's* a fair point."

On the screen, the newsfeed showed the strikes again and again, looting footage from as many different sources as they could find—terminals, security cameras, high-orbit mapping satellites. The bolt of ionized air glowed like the trail of a rail gun, and North Africa bloomed a massive rose of fire, again and again. Another beam-like trail in the air, and the Atlantic Ocean went from a vast expanse of slate-blue water to an expanding circle of eerie green and then spewed white and black to the sky. It was like the reporters thought if they all just kept looking at it, it would start making sense.

Millions of people were dead, and millions more would be in the next few hours as the tsunamis and flooding hit. Billions would go in the next few weeks and months. The Earth had become a different planet since he'd gone underground. It wasn't the sort of thing you could make sense of by staring at it, but he couldn't look away either. All he could do was talk to Peaches about trivia and wait to see what came next.

The man doing the voice-over had a gentle European accent and a sense of calm that probably meant he'd sucked down a lot of pills. Or it might have been tweaked and enhanced by the sound techs. "The weapons remained undetected by radar until they entered the Terran atmosphere, less than a second before impact."

The image shifted to an apocalyptic satellite image: five frames in a loop showing the Atlantic impact and the raw shock wave rolling out from it across the ocean. The scale was massive.

"You see," Amos said, pointing a thumb at the screen, "that's how you know they were using radar-absorbing coating on the rocks. Burned off and stopped working after they hit atmo, right? Anyway, you figure it went from the ionosphere to sea level in about half a second, so that's about two hundred klicks per. I'm making this up here, but the kind of bang they're talking about, you could do it with a block of tungsten carbide maybe three and a half, four meters to a side. That ain't big."

"You can figure all that in your head?"

Amos shrugged. "My job has been playing with magnetically contained fusion reactions for a lot of years now. It's the same kind of math, more or less. You get a feel for it."

"I can see that," she said. And then, "You think we're going to die?"

"Yup."

"Of this?"

"Maybe."

On the screen, the newsfeed replayed a five-second clip from a sailing boat. The flash of perfectly straight lightning, the weird deforming lens of the pressure wave bending the air and light, and the image shattered. Whoever had been in the ship, they'd died before they knew what they were looking at. Probably the most common last words that day were going to be *Huh, that's weird*. That or *Oh shit*. Amos was aware in a distant way that his gut hurt, like he'd eaten a little too much food. Probably fear or shock or something. Clarissa made a small sound in the back of her throat. Amos looked over at her.

"I wish I'd seen my father again."

"Yeah?"

She was silent for a moment. Then, "If he'd done it? If he'd figured out how to control the protomolecule? Everything would have been different. This wouldn't be happening."

"Something else would be," Amos said. "And if you'd ever seen that thing up close, you wouldn't think it was better."

"Do you think Captain Holden would ever—"

The floor rose up and punched Amos in the legs. By instinct, he tried to roll, but the attack was too wide. There was no way to get around it. The screen shattered; the lights failed. Something loud happened. For a few seconds, he was rattled around the room like dice in a box, not knowing what was hitting him. Everything went black.

An endless moment later, the amber emergency light flickered on. Clarissa's bed was on its side, the girl poured out of it to the floor. A pool of clear liquid widened around the medical expert system, filling the air with a pungent smell like coolant and alcohol. The thick wire-and-bulletproof-glass window had shattered in its frame and was now opaque as snow. A network of cracks laced the wall. From the corner, Clarissa's half-panicked laughter bubbled up, and Amos felt his own feral smile rise up to meet it. An alarm was sounding, the wail rising and stuttering and rising again. He didn't know if it was supposed to sound like that or if the shock wave had broken it.

"You all in one piece there, Peaches?"

"Not sure. My hand really hurts. May have broken something."

He got to his feet. He hurt everywhere. But long familiarity with pain told him nothing was seriously damaged, so he shoved the hurt to one side and ignored it. Either the ground was still shaking a little or he was. "Well, if you did, that'll suck." The door to the hall was closed, but it looked wrong. Like the frame had warped. He wondered if it would ever open again.

"We're ten stories underground," Clarissa said.

"Yeah."

"If it was like this for us, how bad is it up top?"

"Don't know," Amos said. "Let's go see."

She sat up. Her left hand was already swollen to about twice the size of the right one, so something in it was busted. In her prison gown, she looked like a ghost. Something already dead that hadn't stopped moving yet. Which, he figured, might be accurate.

"We're on lockdown," she said. "We're not going anywhere."

"Thing is, for us to be in lockdown, this has to be a prison. For this to be a prison, there has to be, you know, a civilization out there. I think this just turned into a big hole in the ground with a bunch of dangerous people in it. We should leave."

He kicked the door. It was like punching a bulkhead with a bare fist. He moved over and tried the shattered window. It was only a little bit better. He tried three more times before a voice shouting from outside interrupted him. "Stop that immediately! We're in lockdown!"

"Someone doesn't know this isn't a prison anymore," Clarissa said. She sounded a little drunk. Might be a concussion to go with her broken hand.

"In here!" Amos shouted. "Hey! We're stuck in here!"

"We are in lockdown, sir. You have to stay where you are until—"

"The wall's cracked," Amos shouted back. "It's gonna collapse." It might even have been true.

There was a long moment of quiet, and then a click from the doorway. The door scraped open a couple centimeters and jammed. The escort looked in. Dim emergency lighting from down the hall turned her into a grayscale outline. Even so, he could see the fear in her expression. There were other people behind her, but he couldn't make them out.

"I'm sorry, sir," she said, "but this facility is—"

Amos put his shoulder against the door, not pushing out, but not letting her close it again either.

"In lockdown. I got that," he said. "Here's the thing, though. We need to evacuate."

"You can't, sir, this is—"

"Not just us," Amos said. "You too. You need to get out of here too. Unless you're really looking to die at work, which I would find disappointing."

The escort licked her lips. Her gaze cut to the right. He tried to think what would convince her the rest of the way, but the best he came up with was punching her in the jaw and hoping he could push his way out before anyone shot him. He was cocking back his arm when Clarissa put a hand on his shoulder.

"You've got people on the top, don't you?" she said. "Friends? Family?"

The escort's gaze lost focus, seeing something else. Someone else. Probably someone dead but not cool yet. "I can't...I can't think about that right now."

"Penal regulations say that you have the responsibility to maintain the safety and health of prisoners in your custody," Clarissa said. "You won't get in trouble for leading an evacuation. You'll be a hero."

The escort was breathing heavily, like she was doing some kind of hard physical labor. Amos had seen people do that kind of thing when they were upset about something, but he didn't really understand it. Clarissa moved him gently aside and leaned in toward the escort.

"You can't be part of a relief effort up there if you're buried alive down here," the girl said, softly. Like she was apologizing for something. "There might be aftershocks. The walls might collapse. There's no dishonor in evacuating."

The escort swallowed.

Clarissa leaned in, almost whispering. "There's a civilian in here."

The escort said something under her breath that Amos didn't quite catch, then turned to talk over her shoulder. "Help me get this goddamned door open, Sullivan. The structure's compromised, and we've got a fucking civilian in here that we need to get to safety. Morris, if that bastard tries anything, take him down hard. You understand, asshole? One wrong move, and we'll end you."

Someone in the corridor laughed, and it sounded like a threat. Amos and Clarissa backed up. Two new hands took hold of the door and started hauling it back open.

"Keep the civilian safe? That's what got to her?" Amos asked.

Clarissa shrugged. "It was the excuse she needed. Though you *are* a precious flower."

"Well, sure. Just not used to anybody appreciating it."

The door opened with a shriek, swinging into the corridor only halfway before it stuck fast. Probably permanently. In the hallway, the damage was clearer. A crack ran down the center, three or four centimeters lower on one side than the other. The air was thicker than it had been coming in; Amos felt the reflexive urge to check the air recyclers. Maybe that wasn't even wrong. Being thirty-odd meters underground was a lot like being in vacuum. If things were busted enough, atmosphere was going to be a problem.

The other prisoner—Konecheck—knelt on the ground, a second guard—Morris—standing three paces behind him with a weapon pointed at the man's back. If it was a gun, it wasn't a design Amos recognized. The prisoner's face was swollen all down the left side like he'd lost a boxing match with a very slow ref. The escort, two other guards, Peaches, and this fella.

Konecheck looked up from behind strands of long iron-gray hair and gave a one-millimeter nod. Amos felt a wave of something a lot like comfort pass through him—a looseness across his shoulders, a warmth in his gut. This was going to get ugly before it was over, but it was a scale of violence he understood.

"New plan," the escort said. "We're evacuating these prisoners and the civilian to the surface."

The guard who'd helped pull the door open—Suliman? Sullivan? Something like that—was a thick-necked bull of a man with a single black eyebrow running across his forehead. Morris, the one with the gun, was thinner, older, with bad teeth and missing the last knuckle on his left pinky finger.

"Sure you don't want to put the prisoners in a closet before we go?" Morris asked. "I'd feel a lot better getting out of here if we didn't have these fucking psychos at our back."

"Peaches comes with me," Amos said with a loose shrug. "That's just a thing."

"Might need some help clearing debris," Konecheck said. He'd been the one that laughed before. The words, innocuous as they were, held just as much threat but the others didn't seem to hear it. Amos wondered why that was.

"Elevators are disabled, so we'll get to the stairs," the escort said. "That'll get us out of here. Once we're up top, we can secure the prisoners."

"What about fallout?" the thick guard—Amos was almost sure the name was Sullivan—said.

"That's nukes, asshole," Konecheck growled.

"Rona? Shouldn't you query the captain before we do this?" Morris asked. His eyes hadn't shifted off Konecheck's back. *Competent*, Amos thought, and filed the information away for later.

"Captain's not answering," the escort, Rona, said. Her voice was tight, too controlled to let the panic out. From the way the other two went quiet, Amos guessed they hadn't known that. "Let's head for the stairs. Morris, you take lead, then the prisoners, then me and Sully. You'll need to follow behind, sir."

"I'll walk with them," Amos said.

"Don't trust me with your girlfriend?" Konecheck growled.

Amos grinned. "Nope."

"Let's get moving," Rona said. "Before there's a fucking aftershock."

Fear was an interesting thing. Amos could see it in all the guards without quite being able to point to what it was. The way Morris kept looking over his shoulder, maybe. Or the way Rona and Sullivan walked exactly in step behind them, like they were trying to agree with each other just by the length of their stride. Peaches seemed focused and empty, but that was kind of just her. Konecheck, on Amos' left, was jutting out his beard and making a big show of what a badass he was, which would have been funnier if he didn't have a nervous system redesigned for violence. Guys like that were either scared all the time anyway or so broken they didn't count. Amos wondered whether he was scared. He didn't know how he'd tell. He also wondered if there were going to be more rocks falling, but it didn't seem like the kind of thing he had any say over.

All around them, the prison was in shambles. Cracks ran along the walls like the floor had been shoved out a couple centimeters and pushed back in place. There was a sound of water running through pipes from somewhere. The emergency lights were on, but here and there a few had failed, leaving pools of darkness. Even if the elevators were running, he wouldn't have wanted to take them. One of the things living on a ship for years had done was give him a sense for how the whole vessel was running based on a few local indicators. And if the Pit had been above orbit, he'd have been sleeping in an environment suit, just so as not to be unpleasantly surprised by waking up airless.

"Stop fucking whistling," Konecheck said.

"Was I whistling?" Amos asked.

"You were," Clarissa said, still cradling her swollen hand.

"Huh," Amos said, and started whistling again, consciously this time.

"I said stop it," Konecheck growled.

"Yeah," Amos agreed with a friendly nod. "You did say that."

"Prisoners will maintain silence," Rona snapped behind them. "And the civilian will kindly shut the fuck up too."

Amos considered Konecheck out of the corner of his eyes. Still too early to be sure, but maybe sixty-forty that one of them was going to have to kill the other. Not now, but before it was over. He could hope for the forty.

A shudder passed through the floor like a badly tuned thruster firing. Concrete dust sifted down from the lights like amber snow. Morris said something obscene.

"Aftershock," Rona said. "Just an aftershock."

"Might be," Clarissa said. "Might be the shock wave from Africa. I don't remember how fast that kind of force travels through the mantle."

"Not fucking North Africa," Konecheck said. "No way we'd feel that."

"When the Galveston plant went up, the shock wave was still measurable on its third time around the planet," Clarissa said.

"Oh, the bitch is a history professor now?"

"The prisoners will maintain silence!" Rona shouted. She was sounding a lot more agitated. Around a corner, a light glowed green, the icon of a thick-legged stick man walking up steps. He wondered how many other people were on this level, still in lockdown, waiting on rescue. How many were already trudging up the stairs on their way out. The guards were playing it pretty close to the vest, but he'd have bet good money that there were a whole lot of people making their own decisions right now.

Morris stopped at the door to the stairway. The readout set into the wall beside it showed a red image of a closed lock until he swiped his hand terminal across it and keyed something into the display that opened. The lock switched to green, and the door slid open. Of course a prison would put the locks on the emergency power circuit, Amos thought. He wondered what else was locked.

A landslide of mud, water, rocks, concrete, and rebar spilled into the corridor. Morris yelped and jumped back, then fell to the ground, grabbing one shin. His pants were ripped, and Amos caught a glimpse of a dark wetness between the man's fingers. Blood.

"Morris!" Rona said. "Report!"

"I'm gonna need stitches."

"I'm moving ahead to look," Amos said, leaving *So don't shoot me* as a given. Beyond the door, the stairway was gone. Rubble and dirt were so thick, he couldn't even tell if the stairs still existed under them. He couldn't tell where the water was coming from, but it smelled clean. Which meant it was probably the drinking water. Another tremble shook a few stones and a head-sized ball of concrete loose.

Sullivan was muttering a stream of obscenities under his breath that sounded less like anger and more like the first signs of panic. Amos shook his head.

"No one's getting out that way," he said. "Not without a few months and a digging mech. We're gonna have to find another way up."

"There isn't a goddamn other way up," Rona said. "That's the evacuation route. That right there."

"Peaches?"

Clarissa's voice was calm but still a little slurred. "Hard call, Amos. It's a prison for high-risk criminals. They don't put a lot of easy egress routes in it."

"Fair enough," Amos said. "But say you had to think of something clever?"

"The guards have overrides. If we can get access to the elevator shaft and the car's not blocking it, we might be able to climb up."

"Ten stories at one g on a broken hand?" He didn't mention the possible concussion that was probably screwing with her sense of balance.

"Didn't say it'd be fun."

"The access ladders are all locked down," the escort said. "They put doors across them so no one can get up without permission."

Konecheck gave a wide, mirthless laugh, and Sullivan trained another of the strange not-quite-guns on him.

"Peaches?"

"I don't know. Maybe we could find something else."

Amos stretched his neck, the vertebrae popping like firecrackers. "This," he said, "is getting to be a long fucking day."

Chapter Twenty-Five: Naomi

Hour by hour, history rolled out, every new moment making things worse. The newsfeeds from Earth and Mars, and then reports from Tycho Station and Ganymede filled with reporters and journalists blank with shock or else weeping. The hammering of Earth took most of the bandwidth: images from an apocalypse. Cities along the coasts of the Atlantic with grinding waves shattering fourth- and fifth-story windows. An army of small tornados forming behind the shock wave's leading edge. The planet she was so used to seeing glow as the city lights made it a permanent fire, going dark. The field hospital at Dakar where ash and stones rained down upon row after row of the dead. The shaking UN spokesman confirming the death of the secretary-general. The void between the planets was alive with chatter and speculation, reports and theories and then conflicting reports and theories. With the complexity of light delay, it was almost impossible to put events in order. Everything seemed to be happening at once.

Which, she supposed, was how Marco had wanted it.

The events in other places—things that would have been shattering on any other day—seemed footnotes to the grand thesis of destruction playing out on Earth. Yes, there had been an attempted coup on Tycho Station, but the Earth was dying. Yes, an OPA cell had taken control of the ports on Ganymede, but the Earth was dying. Yes, a battle was going on between Martian escort ships and an unknown force near the Hungaria asteroids, but Earth was dying. The sense that something vast had descended on all humanity was inescapable.

Outside, in the common room, elated voices rose with each new report, cheering with delight. In her assigned quarters, she watched with a growing numbness. And beneath it, something else. After half a shift, she turned the screen off. Her own face reflected in the emptiness that followed looked like another stunned reporter searching for words and failing. She pulled herself out of her crash couch and walked out to the common room. It was so much like the *Roci*'s galley that her brain kept trying to recognize it, failing, and trying again. An utterly unfamiliar space would have been easier than this architectural uncanny valley.

"Hoy, Knuckles," Cyn said, rising from among the crowd. "A que gehst, yeah?"

She made an automatic Belter's shrug, but Cyn didn't sit back down. Not the question of a friend wondering where she was going, but of a guard demanding information of a prisoner. She arranged her expression more carefully.

"This was why, wasn't it? This was why he wanted me?"

"Marco son Marco," Cyn said, and his voice was weirdly gentle. "He thought we should get you, so did, yeah? Why does why matter? Still the safest place to be in the system right here."

Naomi took a long breath and blew it out.

"Lot to take in," she said. "Big."

"Is that," Cyn said. Naomi looked at her hands, her fingers

laced together. *Act like one of them*, she thought. What would she do if she were one of them again? The answer came too naturally. As if she *was* one of them. As if she always had been.

"Ship's got an inventory," she said. "I can do the checks. Be useful."

"I'll join," he said, falling into step with her.

She knew where to go, how the lift would take her, where the machine shop was. In the years she'd been on the *Roci*, she hadn't been aware that she was also internalizing the design logic of the Martian Navy, but she had been. When they reached the shop, she knew where the diagnostic arrays would be stored even though she'd never set foot in the place before.

Cyn hesitated before he opened the cabinets, but only a little. Checking inventory, testing batteries and relays and storage bubbles, was something everyone did in their spare time if they grew up in the Belt. It was as natural as drinking water, and when she picked up an array, he did too. The door to the cargo bay was sealed, but it cycled open for Cyn.

The bay was well-stocked. Magnetic pallets locked to the decks and walls in neat rows. She wondered idly where it had all come from, and what promises had been given in exchange. She went to the nearest, plugged the array into the pallet, and popped it open. The crates unfolded. Batteries. She took the first, snapped it into the array. The indicator went green, and she snapped the battery back out, replaced it, and took the next one.

"All going to be good," Cyn said. "Military grade, this."

"Well thank God militaries never get shit wrong." The indicator went green. She swapped the battery in her hand for the next one. Cyn went to the next crate over, popped it, and started doing as she was doing.

She recognized it as a kindness. He hadn't come down to be her friend, but her jailer. He could as easily have put her back in her cabin and locked the door to keep her there, but he hadn't. He could have stood guard over her while she worked through the batteries, but he didn't. He pretended that they were together on the task, equals. Even if it meant missing beer and Armageddon with his friends. Against her will, Naomi felt a spark of gratitude for that.

"Big day," she said.

"A long time coming," Cyn said.

"Long time," she agreed automatically.

"Got to be weird seeing him again."

She pulled another battery, checked it, put it back, grabbed the next one. Cyn cleared his throat.

"Mé falta," he said. "Shouldn't have said it."

"No, it's fine," Naomi said. "Yes, it's weird seeing him again. Did a lot to get away from him last time. Didn't see ever coming back."

"Bad times."

"Those or these?"

Cyn coughed out a laugh and looked over at her, a question in his eyes. "These? Esá the promised land. Belt standing up. You know how it was before. You remember running thin because we couldn't get enough oxygen. Breaking bones because the meds got taxed too much."

"I do," she said, but Cyn was on a roll now, and he wasn't ready to stop. He put down his array and stared at her. The sympathy had burned out of him, and there was a rage in his eyes. Not with her. With something bigger.

"I got three cousins died because Earth corporations wouldn't sell the good cancer meds to Belters. Gave us the crap left over from the farms on Ganymede. Only vat meats aren't like people, yeah? Don't work the same, but who cares? Tio Bennett got his ship taken away because he was behind on his permitting. He wasn't even in a pinché Earther dock, but he didn't pay, so they boarded him, dropped him on Ceres, and sold his rig. And for what? They protect us from pirates? They protect us from third-rate manufacturers passing off old suits as new? They care if we got shot? If we got killed?"

"I know they don't."

"Didn't, Knuckles. They *didn't*. Because past is the past now. Today," Cyn said, poking the air with his thumb. "You been flying on their side for a lot of years, and maybe not tu falta. Things before, keeping Filipito away, maybe we all did that wrong, yeah? But I'm starting to think you been sharing a couch with an Earth coyo so long you forgot what you *are*. Started thinking maybe you're like them."

No, she wanted to say. *No, I never forgot*. But even as she formed the words, she wasn't sure if they were true. Once, there had been a girl with her name who had belonged here. Who'd felt the rage she saw in Cyn and in Filip. There had been a time when she could have cheered the deaths on Earth. But Jim was from Earth. And Amos. Alex from Mars, which from a Belt perspective was more or less the same thing. And what was she? Their pet Belter? The one that didn't belong? She didn't think so. So then, she was something else.

And still, how well had they known her, really? There was so much she hadn't said. She didn't know what would have changed if she had.

Cyn was scowling at her, his eyes hard, his jaw set. She tried to retreat back behind the curtain of her hair, but it wasn't enough. Not here. Not now. She had to say something; she had to react or it would be the same as confessing, and she was done taking responsibility for things she hadn't chosen. She tried to think what Jim would have said, but imagining him was like touching an open wound. Guilt at keeping her past from him and the grief and longing of being away from him and the fear that something bad had happened to him on Tycho. Or was happening to him, right now, while she could do nothing about it. She didn't know what Jim would do, and didn't dare to imagine him.

All right. Amos, then. What would Amos do?

She took a deep breath, let it out. When she looked up, she brushed her hair away. Grinned. "Well, Cyn. That's one way of looking at things," she said, leaning into the words. "Ain't it?"

Cyn blinked. Whatever he'd expected, it hadn't been that. She checked the last battery on her pallet, replaced it, and shut the box back down. Cyn was still looking at her, his head turned a degree to his left. It made him seem wary of her.

Good.

She nodded at the open pallet at his feet. "You going to check those?" she asked. "Or d'you need some help?"

⚡

By dinner, it seemed like the attacks were done. The feeds, on the other hand, were in full swarm. She sat at a table that, like everything on the ship, seemed too familiar. Cyn sat on her right, and a young woman she didn't know on her left. Her plate was heaped with fried mushroom in hot sauce, the way Rokku used to make it. She ate it one-handed, the way the others did, and wondered whether someone looking over the room would have been able to pick her out as the one that didn't fit.

The screen was set to a feed coming out of Tycho Station. She watched it and tried not to feel anything. When Monica Stuart appeared, she felt a shock of fear that she couldn't quite explain. The woman made an introduction that told Naomi nothing new, then turned to Fred Johnson sitting stiffly across from her. He looked old. He looked tired. She didn't watch him, barely listened to them speak, straining instead at the edges of the screen in case Jim was there. The others were heckling and catcalling anyway. She caught fragments.

"Do you believe that you were the primary target of the attack?"

"That appears to be the case."

"Fucking liar!" someone across the galley shouted, and the others roared their approval. Including Cyn.

Fred moved carefully, and the camera stayed close on his face. He was hurt then, and hiding it. She'd heard once that birds back on Earth would do everything they could to hide that they were ill. Any visible weakness was an invitation to attack. The comparison made Fred Johnson seem vulnerable. Maybe everything was vulnerable now. "The attackers are in custody, and we hope very soon to have a clear idea who was behind this." Something about that caught her. It was odd, knowing Marco, that he hadn't made a press release of it. He'd brought her here to show off, hadn't he?

Or had he? She was supposed to bring the *Rocinante* with her, and they'd been disappointed when she didn't. Was the ship what he'd really wanted? Or Jim? She wondered with a sense of dread what would have happened if she hadn't come alone.

And then, as if thinking had summoned him, Monica Stuart ended the interview with Colonel Fred Johnson, voice of the OPA and director of Tycho Station, and turned instead to Captain James Holden.

Her breath stuttered.

"I understand you were working as a bodyguard for Colonel Johnson," Monica said.

"Yes, that's true," Jim said with a little grimace. He hadn't done a very good job of it apparently. "It wasn't really needed. The people who infiltrated the security team turned out to be a very small minority. He wasn't ever in real danger."

He was lying. Naomi pushed her food away.

"Is it true that there was a secondary target? There are some people reporting that the attack may have been cover for some kind of theft."

Annoyance flashed in Jim's eyes. She wondered if anyone else saw it. Monica was probably pushing into territory that they hadn't agreed on. Or had agreed to avoid. "They're not reporting that to me," Jim said. "As far as I know, apart from some damage to the station, the coup was a total failure." Another lie.

"Switch the feed!" someone shouted. A chorus of agreement rose. Someone called Jim something insulting, and Cyn glanced over at her and then away. Naomi went back to her food. The hot sauce burned her lips, but she didn't mind. The screen switched to a major newsfeed from Earth. The reporter was a young man in a black raincoat. The text said he was in someplace called Porto. The buildings behind him were a mix of ancient and new, with thick, muddy water tearing at them all. On the higher ground behind him, there were rows of sacks. No, body bags.

"That was him, wasn't it?"

She didn't know how long Filip had been standing behind her. The girl to her left nodded to Filip and fled. The boy took the empty seat. Wisps of stubble stretched along the line of his jaw, black against the golden brown of his skin. He turned to look at her, and his eyes took a moment to find her, like he was drunk. "That was the man you left us for, si no?"

Cyn grunted like he'd been hit. Naomi didn't know why. The question was so wrong it was actually funny.

"Not how it played," she said. "But yes. I ship with him."

"He's handsome," Filip said. She wondered whose voice he was echoing. It didn't sound like Marco. "Wanted to say, about your being here? Wanted to say."

But then he didn't go on to actually finish the thought. She wondered whether she saw regret in his eyes, or if she was imagining it because she wanted it to be there. She didn't know what to say, how to answer. It felt like there were many versions of her—the captive, the collaborator, the mother reunited, the mother who went away—and all of them spoke differently. She didn't know which was her real self. If any of them.

Probably, it was all.

"Not the way I'd have chosen," she said, stepping through the words like they were sharp. "But that's true of a lot of things, yeah?"

Filip nodded, looked down. For a moment she thought he'd move away, and didn't know whether she wanted him to stay or go.

"It's me up there now, you know," Filip said. "On the feed? That's me."

The reporter was older than Filip, broader across the face and shoulders. For a moment, she tried to see a resemblance between them, and then like walking into a freezer, she understood.

"Your work," she said.

"Gave it to me as a present," Filip said. "The stealth coating on the rocks? I led the team that retrieved it, me. Without me, none of this."

He was boasting. It was in the corner of his eyes and the tightness of his lips how badly he wanted her to be impressed. To approve. Something like rage shifted in her gut. On the screen, the reporter was listing relief organizations and religious groups. People who were trying to organize help for the refugees. As if anyone on the planet didn't need refuge now.

"Did that to me too," she said. Filip's expression asked the question. "Your father. He put blood on my hands too. Made me complicit in killing people. Thought it would make me easier to control, I guess."

It was the wrong thing to say. The boy flinched, drawing into himself like a snail's feeler touched with salt. The feed changed. The dead and missing on Earth had topped two hundred million. A cheer went up all through the galley.

"Is that why you left?" Filip asked. "Couldn't handle doing the work?"

She sat silent for a long moment. Then, "Yes."

"Better that you went, then," Filip said. She told herself he didn't mean it. It was just something he said to hurt her. It worked. But more than that, she felt a vast sorrow for all the things her baby boy might have been that he wasn't. For the child she could have had in him, if there had been a way. But she'd left her child in the hands of a monster, and the infection had spread. A family of monsters, father and mother and child.

It made it easier.

"Weighed on me," she said. "All those dead people because of what I'd done. I tried to leave. Told him I wouldn't turn him in if he just let me take you and go. So instead he took you away. Said I was acting crazy, and he didn't trust me around you. That if anyone was getting turned in, it would be me."

"I know," Filip said. Spat. "He told me."

"And I was going to have to do it again. And again. And

again. Kill more people for him. I tried to do it too. Tried to push through. Let them die. He tell you I tried to kill myself?"

"Yeah," Filip said. She should stop. She didn't need to put this on him. Her little boy. Her little boy who'd just helped kill a world.

God, she still wanted to protect him. How stupid was that? He was a murderer now. He needed to know.

"I was at an airlock on Ceres Station. Rigged it to open. All I needed to do was step out. It was an old-style one. Blue and gray. And it smelled like fake apple. Something about the recycler there. And, anyway, I did it. I triggered it. Only the station had put in a fail-safe I didn't know about. So." She shrugged. "That was when I knew."

"Knew what?"

"That I couldn't save you. You could have a gone mother or a dead one. Those were all the options."

"Some people aren't meant to be soldiers," Filip said. It was meant to cut, but she was past feeling now.

"The only right you have with anyone in life is the right to walk away. I would have taken you with me if I could. But I couldn't. I would have stayed if I could. But I couldn't. I would have saved you if I could."

"I didn't need saving."

"You just killed a quarter of a billion people," she said. "Someone should have kept that from happening."

Filip stood, his motions wooden. For a moment, she saw what he would look like as a man. And what he had been as a boy. There was a deep pain in his eyes. Not like her own. His pain was his, and she could only hope he would feel it. That he would at least learn to regret.

"Before you kill yourself," she said, "come find me."

He pulled back a centimeter, as if she'd shouted. "Con que I do something stupid like that? Soy no coward, me."

"When it comes," she said, "find me. Nothing can ever take it back, but I'll help you if I can."

"You're merde to me, puta," Filip snapped and stalked away. Around the galley, the others stared or pretended not to. Naomi shook her head. Let them look. She was past caring. She didn't even hurt. Her heart was vast and dry and empty as a desert. For the first time since she'd taken Marco's call on Tycho, her mind was clear.

She'd almost forgotten Cyn was there until he spoke. "Harsh words for his big day."

"Life's like that," she said. But she thought, *This isn't the big day.*

In her memory, Marco spoke. *In order to be heard by the oppressing class, one must speak as a member of it. Not only the language, but the diction.* But he hadn't made his pronouncement yet. Not in any diction. She didn't know his plans. Likely no one but Marco knew all of them.

But whatever his grand design was, it wasn't over yet.

Chapter Twenty-Six: Amos

Sullivan died when they were about fifteen meters up the shaft.

The plan, if you wanted to call it that, was open the elevator shaft doors, then boost up a level and pry those open. Each level could be a staging area for getting to the next, and by the time they got to where the car was stuck at the very top level, they'd have enough experience with the layout they'd maybe be able to find a way to get past it or get the guards posted in it to let them through. Anyway, it was a problem they could solve once they got there.

It took about an hour to get the first set of doors opened. They defaulted to locked, for one thing. For another, the mass of the doors was a lot more than the usual lift gates. In the end, it had taken Amos, Sullivan, and Morris on one door and Konecheck with his modifications on the other to pry them open enough to slip through. Twice, the ground had shaken, and the second time harder than the first; the whole damned planetary mantle was ringing like a struck bell. By the end, Amos was starting to get thirsty, but he didn't see the point in mentioning it.

The shaft was in darkness, which Amos had expected. It was also wet, which he hadn't. Black drops like filthy rain pattered down from above, smearing the walls and making them slick. He couldn't tell if it was leaking through from one of the floors above them or if the building at the ground level had been sheared off. The guards had flashlights, but all the beams showed were dirty steel walls and a recessed track that the car ran on. A set of repeating steel access panels ran along beside the track looking like cabinets stacked one on top of the other, going up forever into the gloom.

"That's the maintenance ladder," Rona said, playing a circle of white light over the cabinet doors. "The doors retract, and there's handholds."

"That's great," Amos replied, leaning out into the empty air. The shaft went down another three meters or so. The black soup at the bottom might have gone deeper than that, but he was hoping not to find out. The air smelled like ashes and paint. He didn't want to think too much about what was leaking into the shaft or where it was coming from. If the whole place was ass-deep in toxic crap, it didn't change what they had to do.

The gap between floors was maybe half a meter. Craning his neck, he could see the lines of the elevator doors set flush into the wall. Not so much as a fingerhold. He thought maybe there was something way at the top of the shaft—a spot of brightness that came and went in an eyeblink.

"Can we get to the next doors?" Clarissa asked from behind him. "What's it look like?"

"It looks like we need a plan C," Amos said, coming back into the prison hallway.

Konecheck chuckled, and Sullivan turned on the man, lifting the gun-like thing to the prisoner's head. "You think that's funny, asshole? You think it's all so fucking amusing?"

Amos ignored the homicidal tension in the air and looked at the gun. It wasn't like anything he'd put his hands on before. The grip was hard ceramic with a contact interface running along the seam. The barrel was short and square and as wide across as his thumb. Konecheck loomed up over Sullivan, his swollen face a mask of rage and defiance, which was fine as long as it stopped there. "You going to use that, little man?"

"What's it shoot?" Amos asked. "Tell me it ain't one of those riot gear things. They give you real bullets down here, don't they?"

Sullivan turned to him, the gun still trained on Konecheck. Amos smiled and very slowly, gently put his hand on the guard's arm and drew it down.

"What the hell are you talking about?" Sullivan asked.

"Plan C," Amos said. "That thing. Shoots real bullets, right? Not gel rounds or some wimpy shit like that?"

"They're live rounds," Morris said. "Why?"

"I was just thinking about how a gun makes a shitty metal punch."

"Where are you going with it?" Clarissa asked.

"Thinking we've got three shitty metal punches," Amos said. "Maybe we can punch some metal."

The guns were biometrically linked to the guards in case someone like Peaches or Konecheck got hold of them, so Amos and Rona lowered themselves down into the muck instead of Amos going alone. The black sludge came up to Amos' ankle, cold and slick. The lowest of the cabinet-like doors had its edge under the dark surface. Amos rapped on the metal with his knuckles, listening to the sound. The beam from the flashlight bounced, filling the shaft with twilight.

"Put a round here," Amos said, putting a daub of muck on the steel. "And here. See if you can get us some fingerholds."

"What if it ricochets?"

"That'll suck."

The first round left a hole in the steel covering maybe a centimeter wide. The second round, a little less. Amos tested the edges with his fingertips. They were sharp, but not knife-sharp. The black rain had soaked the shoulders of his shirt, and the back of it was clinging to his spine.

"Hey, Tiny," he called. "You come down here a minute?"

After a short silence, Konecheck's growl came down. "What'd you call me?"

"Tiny. Just come take a look at this. See if we've got something."

Konecheck landed with a splash, spattering muck on Amos and Rona. That was fine. The prisoner made a big show of flexing his back muscles and stretching out his hands, then stuffed his first two fingers into the bullet holes, braced his other arm against the wall, and pulled. A normal person, it wouldn't have done a damned thing, but the Pit wasn't a place for normal people. The metal flexed, bent, peeled back to show a line of rungs. Curved metal with a little sandpaper texturing for grip. Konecheck grinned, the swelling of his injured face and the jutting beard making him look like something out of a sideshow. His fingertips were red and raw-looking, but as far as Amos could tell, there wasn't any blood.

"All right," Amos said. "It's ugly as hell, but we got a plan. Let's get out of here."

The ladder was narrow and rough, and spending hours hanging off it didn't make sense if they didn't have to do it. Sullivan and Konecheck went up ahead, the guard with his gun to make the fingerholds and the monster to pry away the steel. Amos sat on the concrete floor of the hallway, his legs hanging out into the shaft. Morris and Rona stood behind him with Clarissa between them. Amos' stomach growled. Ten meters up the ladder, the sharp attack of the gun came once, then again.

"I'm surprised it wasn't harder to find a way out," Clarissa said.

"Thing about prison," Amos said. "It's not like it's supposed to keep you in all on its own, y'know? As long as it slows you down long enough for someone to shoot you, it pretty much did its job."

"You've spent time inside?" Rona asked.

"Nope," Amos said. "I just know people."

Another two aftershocks came and went without knocking anyone off the ladder or collapsing the shaft. An hour later, the Klaxon stopped, the silence as sudden and unnerving as the sounding of the alarm had been. With it gone, there were noises in the distance. Voices raised in anger. Twice, gunshots that weren't from the elevator shaft. Amos didn't know how many people were in the Pit, prisoners and guards and whoever else. Maybe a hundred. Maybe more. The prisoners were in cells, he figured. Locked down. If there were other guards, they were making their own decisions, and no one suggested they go find any of them.

Two more gunshots from the shaft, a murmur of voices, and then a scream. Amos was on his feet almost before Sullivan's body fell past. He landed in the muck at the bottom of the shaft. Rona cried out wordlessly, dropping down to him while Morris turned his flashlight up the ladder. Konecheck's feet were two pale dots, his face a shadow above them.

"He slipped," Konecheck called.

"The hell he did!" Rona shouted. Her gun was in her hand, and she was going for the ladder. Amos jumped down and got in her way, his hands spread wide. "Hey, hey, hey. Don't get crazy here. We need that guy."

"Coming up on level four," Konecheck said. "Starting to see light up top. Hear the wind. Almost there."

Sullivan lay in the muck, his leg folded unnaturally under him, and limp as a rag. He still had the gun in his fist. A yellow indicator on the side said he was out of ammunition. Sullivan had lived just long enough to stop being useful, then Konecheck had murdered him.

Asshole couldn't have waited until they were all the way up.

"He slipped," Amos said. "Shit like that happens. Don't do anything stupid."

Rona's teeth were chattering with rage and fear. Amos smiled and nodded at her because it seemed like the kind of thing people did to reassure folks. He couldn't tell if it was doing any good.

"Someone going to come help?" Konecheck called. "Or am I doing all this on my own?"

"Take Morris," Clarissa said. "Two guns. One for the metal, one to guard him. It was a mistake. It won't happen twice."

"And leave you unguarded?" Morris said behind her. "Not a chance. No one goes without a guard."

"I'll keep her out of trouble," Amos said, but the guards didn't seem to hear him.

"Everyone up," Rona said. "Everyone. And if anybody does something even a little bit threatening, I swear to God I'll kill all of you."

"I'm a civilian," Amos said.

Rona pointed toward the rungs with her chin. "Get climbing."

So they climbed up into the darkness, hand over hand. Ten meters up, maybe twelve. Morris first, then Clarissa, then Amos, with Rona coming up last, her flashlight stuck in her belt and her gun in her hand. Konecheck wrestled the next length of ladder open, clanging and cursing and roaring in the effort. The black muck kept dripping down from above, making everything slick. Amos wondered if maybe Sullivan really had slipped, and chuckled to himself quietly enough that no one heard him. Konecheck, at the upper end of the ladder, swung to one side, letting Morris pass next to him. Then two more shots and the two men switched places again. Amos wondered if the rungs had been designed to carry the weight of two men at once. But they didn't bend, so that was one good thing. He spent a lot of time looking at Clarissa's ankles, since that was pretty much what there was to look at. They were thin from atrophy, the skin pale and dusty. He noticed when they started to tremble. If her busted hand bothered her, she didn't say so.

"You all right, Peaches?"

"Fine," she said. "Just getting tired is all."

"Hang on, little tomato," he said. "We're almost there."

Above her, the shaft grew shorter. There was no sign of the car or the guards who'd been in it. Just a pale gray square and a growing howl of wind. Once, when they only had four or five meters still to go, Rona below him made a sound like a sob, but only once. He didn't ask her about it.

And then Konecheck was at the edge, hauling himself up with Morris scrambling after. The black rain was still falling, and it had gotten colder. Clarissa was shaking now, her whole body fluttering like she was too light, and the wind might pick her up and carry her away.

"You can do it, Peaches."

"I know," she said. "I know I can."

She boosted herself up, and then it was Amos' turn. The elevator shaft ended in a clean break, like the hand of God had come and swept everything away. The intake building was gone apart from shattered concrete and splintered wood strewn across the bare field. The fence was gone. The trees on the horizon had been shaved down to stubble. For as far as he could see, there was just earth and scrub. The sky was dark and low, huge clouds scalloped from one side of the world to the other like inverted waves. The wind barreling down out of the east stank of something he couldn't quite identify. It was what he imagined the aftermath of a battle looked like. Only worse.

"Come on," Rona said, pushing at his leg. Then, without warning, Konecheck roared and Morris shrieked. A gun went off as Amos made it up onto the ledge and got his feet under him. Konecheck was holding Morris up off the ground. The guard's head hung slack and boneless in a way that clarified the situation. Clarissa had collapsed at the gray-haired prisoner's feet.

For a fraction of a second, Konecheck's gaze locked with his. Amos saw a base, animal pleasure in the man. The joy of a schoolboy burning ants with his magnifying glass. Faster than anything human, Konecheck dropped the dead guard and surged forward, his feet digging into the slick mud as he ran. Amos stepped into the attack, which wasn't what the guy had expected, and got a solid punch in under his rib cage. But then Konecheck's elbow came out of nowhere and hit Amos' ear hard enough that the world started spinning. Amos stumbled, and the other guy's grip was on his belt and arm. Amos felt himself lifted up over Konecheck's head. He looked down the shaft and saw Rona looking up at him wide-eyed and openmouthed. The black was a long way down. Amos wondered if he'd see Lydia again when he got to the bottom. Probably not, but it was pretty as a last thought.

The gunshot made Konecheck stumble and Amos twisted into the slackness of his grip, falling backward and landing hard. Clarissa was lying over Morris' body, her two hands around the dead man's fist, taking aim again. Blood poured down Konecheck's chest, but before he could launch himself at the girl, Rona's hand came up over the edge of the shaft and grabbed his ankle. Konecheck kicked back, his muscles flickering too fast to see, and Rona yelped. But by then Amos was on his feet again, knees bent deep to keep his center of gravity low. The world was still spinning. He couldn't trust his inner ear to tell him which way was up. But he'd spent a lot of years in free fall. Ignoring vertigo just meant it was a day that ended in *y*.

He landed a straight kick in Konecheck's crotch that probably castrated him, and the man stepped back, eyes wide. He had maybe a tenth of a second to look surprised as he fell back down into the Pit. Then that part was done.

Amos sat down, rubbing his injured ear as Rona crawled up into the bleak half-light. She was crying and turning slowly, taking in the devastation all around them with disbelief and horror. The woman's hands flapped at her sides like she was pretending to be a penguin. Her distress would have been funny if it hadn't been so sincere. Losing everything should at least be dignified.

"Where'd it go?" she shouted over the rushing of the wind, like anyone could answer. And then, "Oh my God. *Esme.*"

Clarissa had rolled onto her back, her arms spread to the filthy rain, her head resting on the dead man like he was a pillow. Her eyes were closed, but he could see her rib cage moving. Amos squinted up at Rona. "Esme? That one of your people?"

She nodded without looking at him.

"Yeah," Amos said. "Look, if you need to go look for her, that's all right with me."

"The prisoner... I have to..."

"It's all right. I'll keep Peaches out of trouble. You know. Until you get back."

The absurdity of it seemed lost on the woman. She stumbled forward, heading for a low hill on the horizon. She wasn't coming back. No one was coming back. There wasn't anything to come back to.

Clarissa's eyes were open now. As he watched, her mouth widened into a smile and she reached up, running damp hands through her hair. When she laughed, it sounded like pleasure.

"Wind," she said. "Oh my God, I never thought I'd feel wind again. I never thought I'd be outside. It's so beautiful."

Amos glanced around the ruins and shrugged. "That's got a lot to do with context, I guess."

He was hungry and thirsty. Wet. They didn't have shelter or clothes, and the only gun they had, they'd need to haul around a dead man to shoot. Until his body got cold, anyway.

"Well, fuck," he said. "Where do we go from here, right?"

Clarissa extended a thin arm, pointing her pale finger to the sky. There, struggling behind the clouds and stratospheric debris, a perfect, pale disk. "Luna," she said. "Staying on the planet's going to mean dying when the food runs out. And the water."

"I was thinking that too."

"There are yachts. I know where the family kept them. But it's a spaceport for rich people. Tons of security. We might need help breaking in."

"I know some people," Amos said. "I mean, y'know. If they're still alive."

"That's a plan, then," she said, but didn't move. Her slur was going away, which meant she probably wasn't bleeding into her brain. So that was one problem he didn't have. Amos shifted, lying back on the dead man's rib cage, the crown of his head touching hers. A little rest seemed like a fine thing, but they'd have to get moving soon. It was a long walk back to Baltimore. He wondered if they could find a car. Or, failing that, a couple of bicycles. His ear was starting to lose its angry throb. He'd probably be able to walk soon.

In the black sky, the pale circle dimmed behind a thicker roil of cloud and ash, then vanished for a moment before struggling back.

"It's funny," Clarissa said. "Most of human history, going to the moon was impossible. A dream beyond anyone's imagination. And then, for a while, it was an adventure. And then it was trivial. *Yesterday*, it was trivial. And now, it's almost impossible again."

"Yeah," Amos said, "well…"

He felt her shift, tuning her head as if to see him better. "What?"

He gestured up toward the sky. "Pretty sure that's the sun. I get what you're saying though."

Chapter Twenty-Seven: Alex

His head hurt. His back hurt. He couldn't feel his legs. It was all distressing until his mind came back enough for him to realize it meant he hadn't died. The medical bay chimed, something cool pumped into his arm, and his consciousness faded away again.

When he woke this time, he felt almost human. The medical bay was huge. Easily five times what they had on the *Rocinante*, but smaller than the full, multiunit hospital of the *Behemoth*. The anti-spalling coating on the walls was the soft brown of bread crusts. He tried to sit up, then reconsidered.

"Ah, Mister Kamal. Are you feeling better?"

The doctor was a thin-faced, pale-skinned woman with eyes the color of ice. Her uniform was MCRN. He nodded to her more out of social habit than because he was feeling better.

"Am I going to be okay?" Alex said.

"Depends," she said. "Keep eating like you're twenty, and it'll haunt you."

Alex laughed and a spike of pain cut through his belly. The doctor grimaced and put a hand on his shoulder.

"You did get a little surgery while you were out. That burn you were on made your ulcer way worse."

"I have an ulcer?"

"You used to. Now you have a reconstructed stem graft, but it's still settling into place. Give it a few days, and it'll be much better."

"Yeah," Alex said, resting his head back on the pillow. "I've been under a little stress lately. Is Bobbie okay?"

"She's fine. They've been debriefing her. I imagine they'll want to chat with you too, now that you're back around."

"What about my ship?"

"We pulled her into the hangar. She's being refueled. You can get her back when we're clear."

That brought him back. "Clear?"

"Those gentlemen who were taking potshots at you? Our escort's back making sure they don't get too happy about following us. Once the relief ships actually get here, I expect you'll be on your way."

"You got some coming, then?"

"Oh my, yes," the doctor said, with a sigh. "Half a dozen of our finest. Probably more than we need, but we're not in a place where anyone wants to take risks."

"I'm right there with 'em on that," Alex said, closing his eyes. The silence felt weird. He opened them again. The doctor stood where she had been before, her smile as it had been, her hands clasped lightly in front of her. There were tears in her eyes.

"Some things happened while you were out," she said. "You should probably know about them."

Bobbie stood up and hugged him hard as soon as he walked into the debriefing room. She wore a flight jumpsuit just like the one they'd provided him. They didn't say anything at first. It felt strange, being enveloped in her arms. She was much larger than him and stronger besides. He would have imagined that being held like that by an attractive woman would have had some erotic element, but all he felt was a deep sense of their shared vulnerability.

He'd never been on Earth. He didn't know it there. Until now, he wouldn't have said he had any particular connection to the place. That he was wrong about that was a revelation. A quarter billion dead between the strikes and the tsunamis. And many more soon. Already the newsfeeds were reporting failures of infrastructure, and surface temperatures were dropping toward freezing in the springtime northern hemisphere under the vast clouds of dust and water and debris. The major cities had fusion reactors for power, but everywhere that still relied on distributed solar was running out of battery reserves. Billions more lights going dark. The secretary-general was dead, as were an unknown number of assembly representatives. The military was calling back ships from all parts of the solar system, making a cordon around the planet in fear of further strikes. The failed coup on Tycho and the dark fleet that they'd stumbled into, it all felt like a footnote to what had happened to humanity's home world.

And the worst thing was no one knew who'd done it all. Or why.

Bobbie let him go and stepped back. He saw the same hollowness he felt reflected in her eyes.

"Holy shit," he said.

"Yeah."

Everything about the debriefing room expressed safety, comfort. The lights were indirect and shadowless. The walls had the same warm brown as the medical bay. Crash couches surrounded a small, built-in table instead of a desk. It was the kind of space Alex associated with psychiatrists' offices in films. Bobbie looked around too, seeming to see the place anew now that Alex was there. She nodded to a small alcove opposite the door.

"You want some tea? They have tea."

"Sure," Alex said. "Okay. Are you all right?"

"I'm fine. I mean, I'm a little shook, but they didn't put me in the med bay," she said. "What kind do you want? They've got orange pekoe, oolong, chamomile—"

"I don't know what any of those are."

"Me either. So. Okay, you get oolong."

The machine hissed. She handed him a bulb. It felt warm in his hand and had a subtle smell of smoke and water. Alex sat at the table and tried a sip, but it was too hot. Bobbie sat beside him.

"That was some pretty amazing flying," she said. "I'm almost sorry I wasn't there to see it."

"I would have warned you, but, you know. Heat of the moment."

She shook her head. "No objections. If I'd been tensed up, I'd have probably popped open an old wound or stroked out or something. I watched the flight data. Seriously, I was in this room wearing a fresh suit and looking at recordings, and there were still a few seconds there I didn't think we were going to make it."

The admiration in her voice felt warmer than the tea. He was pretty sure he was blushing, and hoped it didn't show. "Yeah, it was a squeaker. Good damned thing you remembered the convoy here too. I wasn't coming up with anything. Do we know who the hell those ships are?"

"No. Most of the escort's pulled off to cover us, and so far it looks like it's working. But no transponder signals from the bad guys. No demands or threats or anything."

"Creepy." The tea had cooled enough now. "Any chance they'll let me send a message back to the captain?"

Bobbie sighed and spread her hands. "Eventually, yeah. They've been treating us like friendlies, but it may be a while before they hand us access to the comm arrays. We're still in a fight, even if we're not at the middle of it."

"What did you tell them?"

Bobbie's brow furrowed. "The truth, only it doesn't come out real well."

"Meaning?"

"I said we were out there looking for missing ships hiding under new transponder signals because of a tip from James Holden."

"Huh. Yeah, that does sound a little ominous when you say it out loud, doesn't it?"

"They wanted to know how he knew to look there, and what my relationship was to Holden. I mean, they kind of knew about you, so it was more about why I was shipping with you."

"What was the answer for that?"

"Old friends, and the fact that you were Navy. You know ships. I'm just a ground-pounder. But that got me into talking about looking at black market issues back at home, and you asking around on Hecate for me and the dead guy and the guys who attacked me."

"So the other dead guys."

"Well, yeah. And after that, it seemed like they were a little suspicious when I said I didn't know anything."

Alex leaned forward. His body still felt weak and shaky. "At least they don't think we're part of... you know. That."

The door opened softly, almost apologetically. The man who came in was older, his hair a well-crafted white. He wore a suit instead of a uniform or jumpsuit. He looked like a particularly avuncular lawyer. Two marines came in behind him in full armor. They didn't acknowledge Alex or Bobbie, just took positions at either side of the door. The white-haired man beamed at Alex and then Bobbie and then back at Alex again.

"Mr. Kamal!" he said. His voice matched his appearance. "I'm so glad to see that you're up and around. I was hoping to have a word with you about this present unpleasantness, yes?"

Alex shot a glance at Bobbie. Her shrug was almost invisible. This wasn't someone she knew.

"Of course," Alex said. "Anything I can do to help."

"Good, good, good," the man said, then lifted a finger. "But first."

He sat down at the table, and an oddly mild scowl came over his face. Alex felt like they were about to be gently chided by the head of school. "Sergeant Draper, I was wanting to ask you why the government of Earth is demanding to speak with you. Have you been in contact with them?"

Bobbie's face went gray and pale. Her hand went to her mouth. "Oh, I am so sorry," she said. "You look so different on video. I didn't recognize you, sir. Alex, this is Prime Minister Smith."

Alex hopped to his feet. "Oh! I'm sorry, sir. With everything going on out on Ilus and such, I didn't follow the elections last time."

One of the guards coughed in a way that might have hidden laughter. Prime Minister Smith's scowl shifted to something slightly more authentic and nonplussed. He motioned Alex to sit back down. "Yes, well. No harm, of course. But, to the question. Have you been working with the government of Earth?"

"No," Bobbie said. "I've had some conversations and I have a personal familiarity with one person. Chrisjen Avasarala. But that's all."

The prime minister nodded, his brows knitting. "Yes, I see. With the passing of the secretary-general and disarray of the assembly, Chrisjen Avasarala is the de facto legitimate government of Earth. And she has offered to... I believe the phrase was *massage my balls with a paint scraper* if anything happened to you."

"That sounds like her," Alex said.

"Yes, she is quite colorful. And she is also insisting that she be allowed to speak with you. I wonder what exactly it is you would tell her?"

"Nothing I wouldn't say in front of you, sir," Bobbie said. "I'm not a spy. She brought up some questions and concerns that seemed legitimate and interesting, and I followed up for my own sake. If you'd like, I'd be happy to walk you through everything I did and what I found."

"You are close friends with Chrisjen Avasarala. You are flying with the crew of the *Rocinante*. You seem to have many contacts with Earth and the Belt, Sergeant."

"Yessir," Bobbie said, her gaze forward and slightly down. "Good that we're all on the same side, then."

The silence was longer than Alex liked. The prime minister laced his fingers across his knee. "I suppose it is at that," he said. "So, why don't we all go over what exactly you've found and how we can productively include our mutual friend Chrisjen in all of this."

⚡

The debriefing lasted for hours. They had taken him to a separate room, and he'd told them the story of everything that had happened since the return from Ilus. Then another woman had come, and he'd told her. Then they'd brought him back to where Bobbie was, and asked the two of them questions that, by and large, they couldn't answer. All in all, it had been gentle as interrogations went, and even so, it left him drained.

He had quarters of his own that night. A locker, a crash couch, a screen. Even his hand terminal back. The place was a little larger than his bunk on the *Roci*, tiny compared to the quarters on Tycho, and a little bit better than what he'd had back before he'd mustered out of the Navy. They'd even let him record messages for Holden and Amos and Naomi, though they were vetted by the ship's system before being sent out. After that, he promised himself that he'd keep away from the newsfeeds.

It had been years since he'd smelled the air of an MCRN ship. The astringent bite of the air recyclers brought back memories. His first tour, his last one. A sense of growing melancholy stole over him that he didn't recognize at first. Grief. And fear. All his anxieties over the crew of the *Roci* came back a hundred times over. He imagined being back on the ship without Amos. Or without Naomi. Or never seeing his ship again, never hearing Holden's voice. An hour after he'd resolved to go to sleep, he gave up, turned the lights back on, and opened a newsfeed.

Mars was pledging drops of food and emergency supplies. Ganymede, back in control of her own docks, was diverting crops back to Earth. A group calling itself the Acadian Front had claimed responsibility for the attacks, but were discredited almost as soon as they'd made the claim. And on Earth, the riots had begun. Looting. He turned the feed back off and got dressed.

He opened a connection to Bobbie, and she accepted it almost immediately. Wherever she was, it wasn't her bunk. The walls behind her were too far away, and the sound of her voice echoed a little. Her hair was pulled back from her face, her cheeks were flushed, and she was sweating hard.

"Hey," she said, lifting her chin in a sharp nod.

"Hey. Couldn't sleep. Thought I'd see what you were doing."

"Just got done sparring. The lieutenant's going to let me drill some."

"They know you just got shot a little while ago, right?"

"You think a few bullet holes gets you out of training?" she said with a ferocity that left him wondering whether she was joking. "They're even loaning me a suit."

"You been in powered armor since Io?"

"Nope. So that'll be... I don't know. Either really cool or nightmare inducing."

Alex chuckled, and she grinned. Her smile was like pouring water on a burn. "You heading straight for your bunk, or are you stopping by the mess first?"

"I could stand something to eat probably. Meet you there?"

It was an off-time for the mess. The alpha shift's dinner was done, the beta shift's lunch still an hour away. Bobbie was sitting alone at a table by the far wall, her hand terminal open before her. A group of three men and a woman sat not far from her, casting glances at her back and talking among themselves. Alex felt an instant protective surge, like he was back in lower university and one of his friends was being laughed at by another clique.

He grabbed a cheese sandwich and bulb of water, then came and sat across from her. The remains of meatloaf and gravy she'd wolfed down were on her plate and a familiar voice was coming from her terminal.

"—going to be monitoring anything we fucking say. If you wanted to discuss menstruation at great length and detail, this is probably our best chance. He's always been squeamish about women, and no one likes a Peeping Tom, even if he is prime minister."

"How is she?" Alex asked, nodding toward the hand terminal. Bobbie turned the recording off and frowned at the newly blank screen.

"Heartsick, I think. Devastated. But she'll never let it show. This is what she always feared the most. And now it's happened, and she can't even look away, because she's the one who has to... fix it. Only it can't be fixed, can it?"

"Naw, I guess not."

"They're taking us to Luna."

"I figured as much," Alex said. Something in his voice caught Bobbie's attention.

"You don't want to?"

"Honestly? I want to go home. Get back on the *Roci* with my crew, and after that, I care a whole lot less where we go. Be nice if it was somewhere they weren't shooting at us."

"That would be a plus," Bobbie said. "Don't know where that is."

"Lot of planets out there. My experience with colonies is, ah, a little checkered, but I can see the appeal of a new start."

"There aren't any new starts," Bobbie said. "All the new ones pack the old ones along with them. If we ever really started fresh, it'd mean not having a history anymore. I don't know how to do that."

"Still, I can dream."

"Right there with you."

At the other table, two of the men rose, carrying their trays to the recycler. The man and woman who stayed glanced over at Alex and Bobbie, and then pretended they hadn't. Alex took a bite of his sandwich. The greasy cheese and fake butter were like being young again. Or else like remembering how long it had been since he was young.

"Any word on the assholes who shot at us?"

"They're still fighting with the escort ships. Withdrawing, but not retreating. The escort isn't looking to engage as long as they can keep the bastards from getting close to us."

"Yeah, all right."

"Seem weird to you too?"

"Little bit," Alex said. "Seems like a pretty piss-poor ambush if you don't actually ambush anyone."

"It's because of us," Bobbie said. "You and me. We were in the right place at the right time. We forced the bad guys to make their play too soon. If we hadn't, it wouldn't be just the secretary-general that died. Honestly, I think that's why we're getting treated this well. Smith knows it could have gone a lot worse without us."

"You're probably right. It's just..."

"You're waiting for the other shoe to drop."

"Yeah."

"Me too. We're jumpy. Why wouldn't we be? Someone just broke pretty much all of human civilization overnight."

The words hit Alex like a blow. He put down his sandwich. "They did, didn't they? I don't know who we are now. I don't know what this does."

"Me neither. Or anyone else. But we'll figure it out. And whoever did this, we'll find them. We're not going to let them win."

"No matter what game they're playing."

"No matter what," Bobbie agreed.

Billions were dying right now, and no way to save them. Earth was broken, and even if it survived, it would never go back to what it had been. Mars was a ghost town, the terraforming project at its heart falling to pieces. The aliens that sent the protomolecule hadn't needed to destroy humanity. They'd given humans the opportunity to destroy themselves, and as a species, they'd leaped on it. Alex pushed away an angry tear, and Bobbie pretended she hadn't seen it.

"Yeah," he said. "Still. I'm going to feel a lot better when the relief ships get here."

"Amen," Bobbie said. "Still, I wish it was more than just six ships coming. Well, seven. Six and a half."

"Six and a half?"

"Relief ships picked up a commercial hauler somewhere. Non-military. It's called the *Chetzemoka*?"

Chapter Twenty-Eight: Holden

"Cover for some kind of theft,' " Holden said again. "I mean what the hell was that?"

Fred Johnson kept walking. The gently curving corridor with its view of the construction sphere was like Tycho Station's boast that it had not been destroyed. The people they passed nodded to Fred and Holden. Some wore green armbands in solidarity, and more than a few of those had the OPA split circle with an additional split at ninety degrees to the first. Others had a stylized globe and the words ONE PEOPLE OPA & EARTH. The physical damage to the station was for the most part limited to the engineering and drive levels at the bottom of the sphere and Fred's office on the ring, but Holden couldn't help feeling that the deeper injury was to Tycho's story about itself. Not long ago, Tycho—like Ceres—had been one of the jewels of the outer planets. Part of a greater argument about the independence of the Belt.

Now that Belters had attacked it, it had become something else. The sense of unity with Earth wasn't so much a real sympathy for the government that had so recently been the enemy, than a statement of separation from the OPA. Tycho Station for Tycho Station, and fuck anyone who crossed them.

Or he may have been projecting, since he was feeling more than a little like that himself.

"She was being a journalist," Fred said. "That kind of thing? It's what they do."

"We just saved her life. If it wasn't for us, she'd have been carried off the station to God knows where and…I don't know. Tortured or something."

"That's true," Fred said. They reached the lift, passing through doors that opened in anticipation of them. Fred's rank still had its privileges, and first priority on lifts was one. "But we also lied to her. And she knew it."

Holden bit back an objection because it wasn't much more than *We did not* and he knew that actually they did. It wasn't something he'd have done, just a few years before. Then, he'd have told the truth, the whole truth, and let the chips fall wherever they fell. He didn't know if it bothered him more that he'd changed or that he hadn't noticed it until someone else pointed it out.

Fred looked over to him with a weary smile. "'Be angry at the sun for setting if these things anger you.' A poet named Jeffers said that."

"Yeah, but was he talking about journalists and politicians lying to each other?"

"Matter of fact, he was."

The lift shifted and dropped. Fred leaned against the back wall with a groan.

"We didn't have to do that," Holden said.

"Yes we did," Fred said. "After a loss, the most important thing for a leader to do is be seen. And be seen walking under their own damned power. Sets the narrative."

"Still."

"It's something I can still do," Fred said. "I'm sure as hell going to do it."

Fred's old office was still being repaired. Until its walls and floor didn't open on vacuum, Drummer had set up a space for him near the overfull brig. It was a smaller space, less comfortable and less imposing. Holden couldn't be in it without feeling like Fred had given himself a demotion. Or had accepted without complaint the one the universe had handed to him.

Fred settled in behind his desk and rubbed his eyes with the palms of his hands. "The truth is that almost everything we do here won't even be a footnote in the history books."

"You don't know that. You're just feeling discouraged," Holden said, but Fred was already pulling up his work on the desk monitor.

"I had two messages last night. Well, more than that, but two that were interesting. The first was from Earth. Avasarala was on Luna when it happened, and she's putting together a response."

"A response?"

"A diplomatic conference. The Martian prime minister was already en route. She wants me to be there too. To 'represent the slightly less batshit wing of the OPA.' If humanity really rests on that woman's diplomatic skills... well, that'll be interesting."

"What's the worst that could happen? War?"

Fred coughed out a grim laugh. "I've already talked with Drummer. She's ready to take over operation of Tycho in my absence."

"You're going to go, then?"

"I don't know if I'll go there, but I won't stay here. There's something else I wanted you to see."

Fred opened a message, and gestured Holden toward it. A pale-skinned man with close-cut white hair and the wrinkles of early age competing with acne scars of long-past youth. The date stamp at the lower left corner said it had been sent from Pallas Station.

"Anderson Dawes," Fred said. "You've heard of him?"

"Big mover and shaker in the OPA, isn't he?"

"The man who reached out to me, back in the day. Made me into the inward-facing figurehead of the Belt. Instrumental in the transition of Ceres to OPA oversight. The last few years, he's been negotiating for the OPA to have a stake in Ganymede equal to Earth and Mars."

"All right," Holden said.

Fred started the recording, and the man came to life. His voice was gravelly and low, like he'd been punched in the throat too many times. "Fred. I know this has got to be a hard time for you. For what it's worth, it's pretty shocking to all of us. But so it goes. History's made of surprises that seem obvious in retrospect. I want you to know, I didn't sanction any of this. But I know the men who did, and say what you will about their methods, they're true patriots."

"What the fuck is this?" Holden said.

"Wait for it," Fred said.

"I'm reaching out to you now to make peace within the organization. I know as well as you do how much you've sacrificed and how hard you've worked for the OPA over the years. It's not forgotten. But we're in a new age now, and it carries its own logic. I know you're enough of a man to recognize the difference between justice and the things that have to happen. I'll get you back in the fold. I swear to that. But I'm going to need a token. Something I can take to the new powers to show that you're a reasonable man. That you can negotiate. You've taken a prisoner. Not one of the people who participated in the insurrection. Even they know asking *that* so soon is a bridge too far. But a prisoner of yours nonetheless. His name's William Sakai. As a gesture of good faith, I'm asking that you turn him over to me at Pallas Station, in return for which I will guarantee you a seat at the table when—"

Fred stopped the recording, Anderson Dawes caught with his eyes and mouth half-open.

"You have got to be kidding me," Holden said.

"No one's laughing."

Holden sat down on the edge of the desk, staring at the frozen man, his chest a welter of conflicting emotions: anger, surprise, outrage, amusement, despair. "You could tell him we already threw him out an airlock."

"Would that be before or after we threw him out an airlock?"

"Either way works for me."

Fred smiled and shut down the display. "You say that, but you wouldn't do it. Even angry, you're too decent a man. And it turns out I am too."

"Really?"

"I got soft when I got old. Everything seems…delicate to me now. We're still under lockdown, and I have to open that up. Have to get some semblance of normalcy. That's not the point, though. I have invitations to two tables. The inner planets are in retreat. They're regrouping. The radicals within the OPA are becoming the new leadership."

"But they're crazy mass murderers."

"Yes," Fred said. "And we don't know who they are. Dawes does. I don't."

"Wait a minute," Holden said. "Hold on. Are you about to propose that you trade Sakai to this Dawes guy so that you can feed the names of whoever's behind dropping rocks on Earth to Avasarala? How many times are you looking to change sides in one career?"

"I never changed sides," Fred said. "The sides keep changing around me. I was always the one who wanted order. Peace. Justice, even. What happened at Anderson Station opened my eyes to things I hadn't seen. Or had chosen not to see. Now this…"

"It's done the same thing again."

"I don't know what it's done. That's what I'm trying to decide. There have always been radicals within the OPA. The Voltaire Collective. Marco Inaros. Cassandra Lec. But they were on the margins, where we thought we could control them. Keep them in line, or if not always that, use their excesses to make the mainstream places like Ceres and Tycho seem the least of the available evils. Now, they're in charge. I don't know if the best thing is to declare against them or stand beside them and try to control the fall." He shook his head.

"Your friend Dawes seems to be in bed with them already."

"His loyalty's to the Belt. When the best thing was to find a way to be respected as an equal by the inner planets, that was what he aimed for. My loyalty is to...everyone. There was a long time that meant speaking for the people who had the least voice. Then the protomolecule came and changed the game, and now, if riding beside the radicals gives me the most influence...As long as my people hold Medina, no one can ignore me. I can throw in on whichever side I think it will do the most good to be on, in the long-term."

"That sounds like post hoc realpolitik rationalizing bullshit," Holden said. And then a moment later, "Sir."

"It is," Fred said. "But it's what I've got to work with. If I commission the *Rocinante* to take me to Luna and the meeting with Avasarala, will you accept the job?"

"If we finish checking all of Sakai's work and you bring your own crew, sure. Or, better, we go pick up mine from wherever they've gotten to."

"And if I hire you to take me and the prisoner to Pallas?"

"Then you can go fuck yourself."

Fred chuckled and stood up, checking his sidearm. "I do always enjoy our little chats, Captain. Take the day off. I'll get back to you when I've made a decision. Either way."

"Where are you going now?"

"To talk with Sakai," Fred said. "See if there's anything about this I can glean from him. The prospect of not getting thrown out one of my airlocks might make him more willing to talk with me." He looked at Holden, and his expression shifted to a strange place at the friction point between pitying and pleading. "I try to do the right thing, Holden. But there are times when it's not obvious what that is."

"I agree with you," Holden said. "Right up to the part where you tell me this is one of those times."

⚡

Holden was in a Thai restaurant eating peanut curry that was, as far as he could remember from his childhood on Earth, totally unlike anything served on a planet's surface. A piece of not-chicken floated on top of the not-curry, and Holden was pushing it under with a chopstick and watching it pop back to the surface when two messages came through. The first was from Mother Elise. The family was all right so far. They were under an environmental watch, but no evacuation orders had come. Not, she said with one lifted eyebrow, that there was anyplace to evacuate to better prepared and equipped than the ranch. They were sending the spare reactor down to help with the local grid at Three Forks, and waiting to hear from the Jacksons to see if they needed anything. He knew her well enough to see the depth of anxiety in all the things she didn't say. But when she said goodbye, she promised to be in touch. It was thin comfort, but it was something.

The second message was from Alex.

Bobbie Draper and he were on the prime minister's ship and burning for Luna with the escort fleet watching their backs. Everyone was pretty freaked-out, but he thought they were okay for the time being. The relief ships were on their way and due in a day or two. He hadn't had any word from Naomi, wherever she was. Or, more to the point, from Amos. He made a joke about Amos surviving anything, and how this wasn't the first planet that had blown up on him, but the humor carried the same dread and fear that Holden felt. When Alex signed off, he replayed the whole message from the start three more times, just to hear the familiar voice.

He started to record a response, but the restaurant was too open and too public for the things he wanted to say, so he promised himself he'd get to it when he was back in his quarters. He finished as much of the curry as he could stomach and the restaurant light slowly shifted from yellow to gold, the colors of a false sunset on a planet many of the people there had never seen except on screens. He paid the check and the waiter came, offering a variety of after-dinner desserts or drinks. The man's gaze lingered long enough that, while it was all within the bounds of politeness, it was pretty clear that Holden could have asked for some other things too.

Holden's mind shifted on most of the questions. More food, more drink, more sleep, more sex. Any sex. He was aware of a deep and oceanic cavern of want in his belly. Something that was like hunger or thirst, exhaustion or lust, but that wouldn't be satisfied. He didn't have words for it, except that it left him quick to anger and despair. Lingering behind it all, the fear that he wouldn't ever have his crew back on his ship made him feel gut-punched.

And then the word for it came. He was *homesick*, and the *Rocinante*, wonderful as she was, wasn't home unless Alex and Amos and Naomi were in her. He wondered how long the feeling would last if they never came back. How long he'd wait for them, even once he knew they wouldn't return. The waiter smiled gently down at him.

"Nothing," Holden said. "Thanks."

He walked out to the main corridor, mentally rehearsing what he'd say to Alex and how he'd say it. Anything he said was going to be examined by the Martian communications service, so he didn't want to put anything in it that was open to misinterpretation. The problem with that being that he always knew what he meant by things, and didn't see the other readings until someone made them. Maybe he could just make a few jokes and say that he was ready to have everyone back together.

When his hand terminal buzzed a connection request, he accepted it, his mind primed to expect Alex even though light delay made that impossible. Drummer scowled out at him from the screen. "Mister Holden, I was wondering if you could stop by the auxiliary security office."

"I guess," Holden said, suddenly wary. He still half expected Drummer to turn out to be playing some angle of her own. "Is it something I should know about now?"

A stream of cursing came from the background, growing louder. Drummer stepped aside and Fred lurched into the screen. "If we were talking about it on the network, you wouldn't be coming in here."

"Right," Holden said. "On my way."

In the security office, Fred was pacing, his hands clasped behind his back, when Holden arrived. He nodded sharply by way of greeting. Drummer, at her seat, was a model of the crisp professionalism designed to offer no reason for the boss to yell at you. That was fine. Holden didn't mind being the one who got yelled at.

"What's the matter?"

"Medina went dark," Fred said. "She was supposed to report in this morning, but with everything being at loose ends, I didn't worry. She's missed two opportunities since then. And...Drummer? Show him."

The security chief pulled up a schematic of the solar system. At scale, even Jupiter and the sun were hardly more than a bright pixel. Thousands of dots showed the traffic in-system. Ships and bases, satellites and probes and navigation buoys. All of humanity in a nutshell. With a motion and a syllable, most of the clutter vanished. In its place, a couple dozen green dots with the word UNDETERMINED where the identification codes should be made a rough cloud. Someone's statistics run with a small but significant correlation.

"As soon as the station went dark," Drummer said, "we saw these. Twenty-five new plumes. All of them have drive signatures that match Martian military ships, and all of them are under heavy burn for the Ring."

"Heavy burn?"

"Eight to ten g to start, curving down, which means they're running at the limit of their drives."

Holden whistled. Fred stopped in his pacing, his expression placid in a way that spoke volumes about rage. "Those are my people on Medina. If the station has been compromised, or if these new ships are on their way to do something violent there, it will pose a significant obstacle to my participation with the new direction within the OPA."

"Meaning fuck that noise?"

"Yes."

"It's a long way out to Medina," Holden said. "Even at those burns, it'll take them a while. But I don't think we could beat them there."

"We couldn't do anything if we did. If I took all the ships at my disposal, one Martian frigate could still rain hell on them. And even the *Rocinante* would be badly outgunned."

"Have to wonder where they got Martian military ships," Holden said.

"I'll be sure to ask Dawes about that as soon as I've told him what I think of his good faith prisoner exchange. How long before the *Rocinante*'s ready to fly?"

"Put a rush on it, we could be out of here in five days."

"Mister Drummer, please put all available teams on finishing the repairs and security audit for the *Rocinante*."

"Yes, sir," Drummer said, and shifted her screen to show the work schedules for the construction drum. Fred looked down at his feet and then back up.

"I'm going to be busy the next few days putting Tycho in order for Drummer. I'd like you to oversee the crews on the *Roci*."

"Wasn't going to do anything else."

"Fair enough," Fred said. And then, almost wistfully, "It will be good to see Luna again."

Holden tried to wait until he got back to his quarters, but lost patience when he reached the lift. He opened Alex's message and set up the camera to record his reply.

"Hey, Alex. So, funny thing. Looks like I'm going to be catching up with you sooner than we'd thought…"

Chapter Twenty-Nine: Naomi

She'd known to expect it. Like falling back into a bad habit, the dark thoughts came: which conduits had power lines in them with enough voltage to stop a heart, which rooms were small enough to seal and evacuate, the ways the medical bays could be tricked into administering an overdose. And the airlocks. Always the airlocks. The ideas weren't compulsions, not yet. They were just her brain noticing things that interested her. The worst would come later. If she let it.

So instead, she distracted herself. Not with the newsfeeds that played constantly, everywhere. Those only made her feel more helpless. Not with the conversations with her old friends. At best, those left her feeling like she was lying. At worst, like she was becoming an earlier version of herself for whom the dark thoughts were more natural. What she did have was work. It was all simple tasks like checking inventories and swapping air filters, and always under the watchful eyes of a minder. When she did talk, it was polite and superfluous; the kind of banter anyone crewing the same ship would make. It gave the rest of the crew the illusion that she was one of them in a way that sulking in her bunk wouldn't have. If she had any hope at all, it came from finding a way to leverage her weird non-status with the group. And with Marco.

At first, she'd tried distracting herself by thinking of her real crew. Alex and Amos. Jim. Even her best memories of them were riddled with guilt and pain now, so instead she filled her mind with technical concerns. In the mess, while the others cheered at the images of devastation, she speculated about the reactor's output, starting with the size of the galley, and then guessing at the requirements of the air and water recycling systems, and knowing the rough percentage that the *Roci* put into them. During her sleep shift, as she lay restless in her crash couch, the steady one-third-g burn pressing her into the gel like a hand on her chest, she ran over the power grid from the *Roci*, mapping how the logic of her ship would apply to this one. She thought of it as a meditation because it was too dangerous to admit—even to herself—that she was planning.

And still, small things came together. A toolbox in the machine shop had a bent hasp and, given a few minutes, could be forced open. The Allen wrenches inside would open the access panel on the lift wall between the crew quarters and the airlock, which was where the secondary diagnostic handset for the comm array was stored. With a few uninterrupted minutes, someone could probably broadcast a message. A short one. If there was anything to say, or anyone to say it to.

She had half a dozen schemes like it. A path to sneak between the hulls and take control of a PDC. A way to use a stolen hand terminal to make copies of the engineering software. How to force-cycle an airlock by spoofing the emergency codes from the medical bay. Most of them were fantasies, possible in theory but nothing she had ever had reason to try. A few were fairly solid.

And all of them were defeated by a simple, inescapable fact: the first layer of any security was always physical. Even if she'd found a way to take control of the whole ship using a magnet and a length of Velcro, it wouldn't matter, because Cyn or Aaman or Bastien would put a bullet through her neck before she could manage it.

So she called it meditation and kept the darkness at bay. And sometimes—by being quiet and not making waves and keeping her mind and senses sharp—she heard something she wasn't supposed to hear.

Karal, her minder that shift, was talking up a woman called Sárta while Naomi scraped the crew decking nearby. Truth was the ship was new enough it didn't need it, but it was work. Wings, who'd first hunted her back on Ceres, came out from his quarters in a Martian naval uniform. Naomi looked up from under her hair as Wings saw Karal and Sárta standing together. The flicker of jealousy that passed over him had been the same since humans came down from the trees.

"Hey, y'all," Wings said in a fake drawl. "Víse mé! Bin Marteño, sa sa? Howdy, howdy, howdy!"

Karal chuckled and Sárta looked annoyed. Wings stepped through the narrow hall with an affected bowlegged gait. Naomi shifted aside to give him room.

"You got nothing better to do than play dress up?" Sárta asked.

"Don't wait underwater," Karal said. "Heard we're taking prisoners first. Liano, he ran whispers to Ceres. Tightbeam. Hamechie about the prisoners."

"Not how I heard it," Wings said, too quickly and more to Sárta than Karal. "I heard it's only one. Sakai. And even that..." He shrugged.

"Even that?" Sárta said, and mimicked the shrug. Wings blushed in anger.

"Everyone knows how it is," Wings said. "Sometimes they tell dead men they'll live. Karal, you were there. Andrew and Chuchu? All about how help's coming and then so sorry, so sad?"

"Esa died soldiers," Karal said, but the point hit home. It was in his hands and the corners of his mouth. And then, like he realized his mistake, he looked over to Naomi. She kept her expression blank and bored, her attention on the seam in the deck and the thin plastic spatula she was dragging through it. The cascade of implications couldn't reach her face.

Sakai had been the name of the new chief engineer on Tycho, and if this was the same man, he'd been one of Marco's. And he'd been caught, or they wouldn't have called him a prisoner. She blew the hair up out of her eyes, shifted over to a new seam and started again.

"Back to work, yeah?" Karal said.

Wings grunted his derision, but went back to his quarters to do as he'd been told. Karal and Sárta went back to flirting, but the moment was gone, and pretty soon it was only Karal and Naomi again, passing time.

While she worked, pressing the plastic into the seams, scraping out whatever had gathered there, doing it again, she tried to fit the new information into the larger scheme of things. Marco had hoped she would bring the *Rocinante* to Ceres. But Sakai had known that the ship needed repair, and must have passed that information up to leadership.

She'd thought that Marco had wanted her ship because of who and what *she* was. And maybe that was part of it. Or maybe what he'd really wanted was private access to a ship that would be expected and welcome at Tycho Station. For what, she didn't know. The way he nested plans inside his plans, he might have had half a dozen uses for the *Roci* and for her. And more, there was a question about whether Sakai was in danger. Were they afraid Fred would execute him? Maybe. Maybe something else.

Either way, she knew more now than she'd known before, and, like the bent hasp on the toolbox, it gave her options she hadn't had. She wondered what Jim or Amos or Alex would have done in her place, how they would have taken this one piece of information and used it. An academic question, really, because she knew what Naomi Nagata would do, and it wasn't something any of them could have done.

When the deck was clean, she dropped the spatula into the recycler, stood, and stretched. The thrust gravity made her knees and spine ache, and she wished that wherever they were going, they'd be in a little less of a hurry to get there. It didn't matter.

"Grabbing a shower, me," she said. "Tell him I want to talk."

"Him who?" Karal said.

Naomi hoisted an eyebrow. "Tell him the mother of his son wants to talk."

"You've put him in the field?" Naomi said. "Is that where we are? Child soldiers?"

Marco's smile looked almost sorrowful. "You think he's a child?"

The exercise machines were empty apart from him. On the float, everyone in the crew would have been spending hours in the resistance gel or strapped into one of the mechs. On the burn, most of the crew were getting more than enough from their own weight. But Marco was there in a sheer exercise gown, straps wrapped around his hands, pulling down on wide bands that fought against him. The muscles in his back rippled with every stroke, and Naomi was certain he was aware of it. She had known many strong people in her life. She could tell the difference between the muscles that grew from work and the kind that came from vanity.

"I think he's crowing about how he's responsible for the rock fall on Earth," she said. "Like it's something to be proud of."

"It is. It's more than you or I could have done at his age. Filip's smart and he's a leader. Give him another twenty years, he could run the solar system. Maybe more."

Naomi walked over and turned off the exercise sequence. The wide bands in Marco's hands went slack with a barely audible hiss.

"I wasn't done," he said.

"Tell me that isn't why you brought me here," she said. "Tell me that you didn't abduct me in order to show me what a good father you've been and how well our boy turned out. Because you betrayed him."

Marco's laugh was low and warm and rolling. He started unwrapping his hands. It would have been so easy to hurt him while he did it that she was fairly certain he had a hidden way to defend himself. And if not, the impression that he might was defense enough. She wasn't here to kill him. She was here to push him into saying something.

"Is that what you think?" he asked.

"No," she said. "I think you did it to show off. I walked away from you, and you're such a little boy that you still can't stand it. So when your big moment came, you had to have me here to see it happen."

It was true, as far as it went. She did see a pleasure in him that came from having power over her. Even her weird half-status in the crew was a part of that. Locking her in a cage would have been a tacit admission she was a threat. He wanted her to see that she was powerless, to make the prison walls herself. There had been a time it would have worked. She was betting that he didn't realize that time had passed.

And she was betting that it had passed. When he narrowed his eyes at her, shaking his head, she still felt the tug of humiliation in her throat, familiar as an old habit. So perhaps the truth was more complicated.

"I brought you home to the winning side because you are the mother of my son, and always will be. Anything beyond that is happy coincidence. That we have the chance to find some sense of closure between us—"

"Bullshit. Closure? You lost. It's closed. You only say it wasn't finished because you hadn't won yet. I left. I sacrificed everything because having nothing away from you was better than having it all and being your puppet."

He lifted his hands, palms out, in a mocking gesture of peace. It wasn't working. Not yet.

"I hear that you would have done things differently. I don't blame you for that. Not everyone has the strength to be a soldier. I thought you did. I thought I could count on you. And when the burden bore you down, yes, I took our son someplace I knew he'd be safe. You blame me for keeping him away from you. But you'd have done exactly the same to me, if you'd had the power."

"I would have," she said. "I'd have taken him with me, and you'd never have seen either of us again."

"So how different are we?" Sweat dewed his skin. He took a towel from the rack, dabbing at his face and arms. She knew intellectually that he was beautiful, the way the iridescent wings of a carrion fly would be. She felt the weight of her disgust with herself for letting this man be what he was to her, and knew that was part of what he intended. The dark thoughts stirred in her brain stem. They didn't matter. She was here to solve a puzzle.

He put down the towel. "Naomi—"

"It's Holden then, isn't it? You brought me here as…what? Insurance against him?"

"I'm not afraid of your Earther fuck buddy," Marco said, and Naomi heard the roughness in his voice like an animal scenting a distant fire.

"I think you are," she said. "I think you wanted him off the board before you started this, and I was supposed to lead him into the trap. Because you couldn't imagine that I would come alone. That I wouldn't bring a man to be strong for me."

Marco chuckled, but it had more of an edge to it. He walked across the exercise mat, scooping up his dark robe and shrugging into it. "You're trying to talk yourself into something, Knuckles."

"Do you know why I'm with him?"

If Marco were wise, he wouldn't rise to that bait. He'd walk out, leave her alone among the machines. If she'd managed to make him angry, even just a little bit angry, though…

"I assume you have a kink for powerful men," Marco said.

"Because he *is* what you *pretend* to be."

She saw it land. She couldn't even say what it was that changed in him, but the Marco she'd seen since being brought here—the smooth, world-weary, self-assured leader of the greatest coup in human history—was gone, dropped like a mask. In his place was the rage-filled boy who'd almost destroyed her once. His laugh wasn't low or warm or rolling.

"Well, just wait around, and we'll see how much that does for him. Big Man Holden may think he's unkillable, but everyone bleeds."

There. That was a datapoint. It was working. It might only have been the rhetoric of the squabble, an empty threat. Or he might have just told her that his plans still involved the *Rocinante*.

"You can't do anything to him," she said.

"No?" Marco said, his teeth bared like a chimp. "Well, maybe you will."

He turned sharply, stalking out of the room. Leaving her alone the way he should have a few minutes earlier. Or else a decade and a half before.

"You done?" Cyn asked, nodding at the brick of lentil and rice half-eaten on her plate. On the screen in the mess hall, a Martian general was pounding a table, red-faced with passion that looked a lot like fear. He was describing the cowardice of the person or persons who had committed this atrocity against not only Earth, but humanity. Every third sentence or so, someone at the end of her table would repeat the general's words in a high, quacking voice, like something from a children's cartoon.

She broke off another piece of the lentil brick and popped it in her mouth. "Close enough," she said around it. She put her tray and the rest of the brick into the recycler and walked back toward the lift. Cyn loomed behind her. She was so locked in her own thoughts that she barely noticed he was there until he spoke.

"Heard you had it out with el jefe," Cyn said. "Etwas á Filipito?"

Naomi made a noncommittal sound in the back of her throat.

Cyn scratched at the scar behind his left ear. "Es un bon coyo, your son. I know this is none of what you'd pick, but...Filipito, he heard too. Took it hard."

The lift stopped and she got out, Cyn close behind. "Took it hard?"

"No weight," Cyn said. "Only know it. A man, our Filipito, but not so much he don't want your opinion, yeah? You're his mother."

The heartbreaking thing was that she understood. She only nodded.

In her bunk, her fingers laced behind her neck, she stared up at the blackness on the ceiling. The interface screen at her side was dead. She didn't miss it. Slowly, she put together what she knew.

Marco had made attempts on the lives of the heads of Earth, Mars, and the OPA, but only managed to kill the UN secretary-general. He had tried to get the *Rocinante* before any of those attempts were made. He'd unleashed the worst catastrophe on Earth since the dinosaurs went extinct. He had Martian warships and weapons but didn't show any signs of cooperating with the Martian government or Navy. All things she'd known, nothing new. So what was new?

Three new things, and maybe only that. First, Wings thought the attempts to trade Sakai back might be more to reassure the prisoner than to actually retrieve him. Second, Marco had intimated that Holden was still in danger, and third, that *she* might be the one to hurt him.

And also, underlying everything, her certainty that until Marco had given his speech, made himself the focus of all humanity's attention, the attack was still only half-done. And if Sakai thought he was going to remain a prisoner, it would go wrong. That was interesting. What could Sakai know—

Oh.

Fred Johnson was alive, and Tycho Station wasn't in Marco's hands. Holden was in danger. She would be the one that hurt him.

So that meant that the *Roci*, like the *Augustín Gamarra* before her, had been rigged to have her magnetic bottle fail. Probably in dock. Fred Johnson, James Holden, and incidentally Chief Engineer Sakai and everyone on the station—all of them would die in a fireball whenever the software she'd written a lifetime ago decided that they should.

It was all happening again, and she had no way to stop it.

Chapter Thirty: Amos

They moved on foot. The clouds weren't really clouds, and the rain that spat down at them was as much grit and soot as water. The stink of turned earth and rot was all around them, but the cold pushed it back to where it mostly just smelled cold. From the way the trees were all knocked down in the same direction—leaves roughly northeast, roots pointing southwest—he hoped they'd be heading toward less devastated territory. At least until they got near the coast and the flooding.

In Baltimore, he figured the folks in the least trouble would be in the failed arcology in the middle of the city. It had been designed to hold a whole ecosystem inside its massive steel-and-ceramic walls. That it hadn't worked for shit didn't matter as much as the fact that it had been built tall and designed to last. Even if the bottom few floors went underwater, there'd be plenty of people near the top who rode out the worst of it. When Baltimore was a sea, the arcology would still be an island.

Plus, the arcology was a shit neighborhood. Erich and his thugs owned at least some of it. And so long as the rest wasn't controlled by one of the major players—Loca Griega or Golden Bough—they could probably take it in a determined push. And even if Erich hadn't made it, there'd be someone there to negotiate with. He just hoped it wasn't Golden Bough. Those guys, in his experience, were fucking assholes.

In the meantime, though, there were more immediate problems. Getting there was the goal, and if the idea was to put one foot in front of the other from the Pit in Bethlehem to the arcology in Baltimore, there were some holes in the plan. The expanded district put about three million people between him and where he was going if he took the straightest path. High-density urban centers seemed like a bad idea. He was hoping that they could stay a little to the west of that and make their way around. He was pretty sure there was conservancy zone there they could trek along. Not that he'd spent much of his time on Earth camping. But it was what he had to go with. He probably could have done it, if he'd been by himself.

"How're we holding together, Peaches?"

Clarissa nodded. Her prison hospital gown was mud-streaked from shoulder to hem, and her hair hung long and lank. She was just too fucking skinny and pale. It made her look like a ghost. "I'm fine," she said. Which was bullshit, but what was he going to do about it? Stupid to have asked in the first place.

So they walked, tried to conserve energy, looked for places that might have fresh water. There were a couple emergency stations set up by the highway, men and women with medical armbands and generators to run the lights. It never got more than low twilight, even at noon. The clouds kept some of the heat from radiating out into space, but they blocked the sun too. It felt like early winter, and it should have been summer hot. Every now and then, they came across some new ruin: a gutted building, the walls blown off the steel and ceramic girders, a high-speed train on its side like a dead caterpillar. The bodies they found on the roadside looked like they'd gone in the initial blast.

Most of the dead-eyed, shell-shocked refugees on the roads seemed to be heading for the stations, but Amos tried to steer away from them. For one thing, Peaches was pretty clearly not supposed to be walking free among the law-abiding citizens of Earth, and Amos didn't really feel like having any long conversations about what laws still applied, post-apocalypse. And anyway, the stuff they really needed they couldn't get there. So he kept his eyes open and headed northeast.

Still, it was three days before he found what he was looking for.

The tent was back off the road about seven meters. It wasn't a real tent so much as a tarp strung over a line between a power station pole and a pale sapling. There was a fire outside it though, with a man hunched over it feeding twigs and sticks into the smoky flames. An electric motorcycle leaned against the power station pole, its display dark either because it was conserving power or it was dead. Amos walked over, making sure his hands were always where the other guy could see them, and stopped about four meters away. Peaches stumbled along at his side. He figured that to anyone who didn't know her or who she was, she probably didn't look real threatening.

"Hey there," Amos said.

After a long moment, the other guy nodded. "Hey."

"Which way you heading?" Amos asked.

"West," the guy said. "Everything's fucked east from here to the coast. Maybe south too. See if I can get someplace warm."

"Yeah, things are shit all over," Amos said like they were at a coffee kiosk and chatting about the weather. "We're heading northeast. Baltimore area."

"Whatever's left of it," the guy said. "No offense, but I think your plan sucks."

"That's okay. I was thinking the same about yours."

The man smiled and didn't go for a gun. If he had one. Not so many guns among the law-abiding Earth populace as there were in the Belt. And if the guy was willing to just shoot the shit this long without anyone escalating or making a play, probably he wasn't a predator. Just another accountant or medical technician still figuring out how little his degree was worth now.

"I'd offer to share," Amos said, "but we ain't got shit."

"I'd help, but the tent's only big enough for one."

"I'm small," Peaches joked, but only sort of. Skinny as she was, she had to be feeling the cold worse, and when he paid attention to it, Amos had to agree it was getting pretty damn brisk.

"Word of warning? Head north a few klicks before you cut any farther east," the man said.

"Why?" Amos asked.

"Militia motherfucker. NO TRESPASSING signs and everything. Took a potshot at me when I went to ask for some water. Kind of asshole that's probably pissing himself with glee that the world went to shit and made his stashed guns and paranoia pay off."

Amos felt something in his chest go loose and warm and thought it might have been relief. "Good to know. Take care then."

"Peace be with you."

"And also with you," Peaches said. Amos nodded and turned north, trudging back along the road. About half a klick later, he stopped, squatting down by a tree, and watched the path they'd just walked down. Peaches huddled beside him, shivering.

"What are we doing?"

"Seeing if he follows us," Amos said. "You know. In case."

"You think he will?"

Amos shrugged. "Don't know. Thing about civilization, it's what keeps people civil. You get rid of one, you can't count on the other."

She smiled. She really wasn't looking that good. He wondered in passing what he'd do if she died. Figure something else out, probably. "You sound like you've done this before," she said.

"Shit, I grew up like this. All these folks are just playing catch-up. Thing is, we're humans. We're tribal. More settled things are, the bigger your tribe is. All the people in your gang, or all the people in your country. All the ones on your planet. Then the churn comes, and the tribe gets small again."

He waved a hand at the dark gray landscape. This far out, the trees weren't knocked over, but the weeds and bushes were starting to die from the dark and the cold.

"Right now," he said, "I figure our tribe at about two."

Either she shuddered at the idea or else the cold was getting to her worse. He stood up, squinting down the road. The tent guy wasn't coming. That was good.

"All right, Peaches. Let's get going. We're going to have to head off the road for a bit."

She looked north, up the road, confused. "Where are we going?"

"East."

"You mean where we aren't supposed to go because of some crazy asshole shooting at people?"

"Yup."

The town had been a decent size last week. Cheap little houses on narrow streets, solar panels on all the roofs sucking in the sunlight, back when there had been some. There were still people here and there. Maybe one house in five or six where the tenants were waiting for help to come to them or so deep in denial that they thought staying put was an option. Or they'd just decided they'd rather die at home. As rational a decision as any other, things being what they were.

They walked on the sidewalks even though there weren't many cars. A police van skidded by a few blocks ahead once. A sedan with an old woman hunched in the front seat who carefully ignored them as she passed. When the batteries ran dry there was no power grid to charge them back up, so all the trips were either short or one-way. One house had words painted across the front:

EVERYTHING IN THIS HOUSE IS THE PROPERTY OF THE TRAVIS FAMILY. LOOTERS WILL BE HUNTED DOWN AND KILLED. That left him laughing for a couple of blocks. The supermarket at the center of town was dark, and stripped down to the shelves. So somebody in the place had understood the gravity of their situation.

The compound was on the eastern edge of town. He'd been worried they might walk by it without noticing, but it hugged the road and the signage was clear. PRIVATE PROPERTY. NO TRESPASSING. ARMED SECURITY ON SITE. His personal favorite was NO RELIEF SERVICES.

A wide, flat field of a yard led up to a white modular house. The transport parked in front of it looked like something manufactured to imitate military equipment. Amos had lived in an actual military design long enough to recognize the difference.

He put Peaches in place at the edge of the property first, then walked the perimeter once, taking it all in. The fence had barbed wire all the way around, but nothing electrified. He was about fifty-fifty that there was a sniper's nest in the attic, but it might have just been a bird. Easy to forget that even with the massive burden of humanity, there was still wildlife on Earth. The house itself was prefabbed or else printed in place. Hard to say which. He also saw three tubes coming up out of the ground that looked like they could be ventilation. There were bullet holes in the bark of the trees at the property's edge, and one place where it looked like there was blood on the leaves of the dying bushes.

This was where he wanted to be.

He started by standing at the edge of the property, cupping his hands around his mouth and shouting.

"Hey! In the house! You there?"

He waited a long minute, alert for signs of movement. Something behind the curtains of the front window. Nothing in the sniper's nest. So maybe it was just sparrows after all.

"Hey! In the house! My name is Amos Burton, and I'm looking to trade!"

A man's voice came, shrill and angry. "This is private property!"

"That's why I'm out here fucking my throat up instead of ringing the goddamn doorbell. I heard you were prepped for this shit. I got caught with my pants down. Looking to trade for guns."

There was a long silence. Hopefully the bastard wouldn't just shoot him, but maybe. Life was risk.

"What're you offering?"

"Water recycler," Amos shouted. "It's on the back of my rig."

"I've got one."

"May need another. Don't think they'll be making more anytime soon." He waited to the count of ten. "I'm going to come up to the house so we can talk."

"This is private property! Don't cross the line!"

Amos opened the gate, smiling his biggest goofiest smile. "It's okay! If I was armed, I wouldn't be trading for guns, right? Don't shoot me, I'm just here to talk."

He crossed the line, leaving the gate open behind him. He kept his hands in the air, fingers spread. He could see his breath ghosting before him. It really had gotten cold. That wasn't getting better soon. He wondered if he maybe should have said he had a heater.

The front door opened and the man came out. He was tall and thin with a stupid, cruel face and a long-barreled assault rifle aimed at the center of Amos' chest. It had to be illegal as shit under UN gun laws.

"Hey!" he said with a wave. "My name's Amos."

"You said."

"Didn't get yours."

"Didn't say it."

The man walked forward to take cover behind his pretend military transport.

"Nice rifle," Amos said, keeping his hands up.

"Works too," the man said. "Strip."

"Come again?"

"You heard me. You want to trade with me, prove you're not hiding any weapons. Strip!"

Well, that was unforeseen, but what the hell. Wouldn't be the first guy he'd ever met who got off on feeling powerful. Amos shrugged off his shirt and heeled off his shoes one at a time, then dropped his pants and stepped out of them. The cold air bit his skin.

"Okay!" Amos said. "Unless I've got a pistol up my ass, we can agree I'm not carrying, yeah?"

"Agreed," the man said.

"Look, if you're still worried about it, you can get someone to come out, look through the clothes here. You keep the gun on me, make sure I don't try anything."

"Don't tell me what to do."

That was a good sign. Made it seem more likely that the fella was on his own here. He glanced up at the attic. If there were a second person, that would be the place to put them. Tiny gray-brown wings fluttered into the attic like the answer to a question.

"Where's this cycler?"

"About three miles down the road," Amos said, pointing with his thumb. "I can have it here in an hour, easy."

"That's okay," the man said, lifting the rifle to his shoulder and sighting on Amos. The end of the barrel looked as big as a cave. "I can get it myself."

Before he could pull the trigger, something moved through the field of his yard like a gust of wind. Only this wind had teeth. The man staggered back, then yawped in confusion and pain. With her chemical hormone blockers having faded in the days since they left the Pit, Peaches moved too quickly for Amos' eye to follow. It was like she'd become an angry hummingbird. The man fell to his knees, his assault rifle suddenly gone and one of his fingers broken and bleeding. As he curled to grasp his broken hand, the gun stuttered, opening the man's chest along the side.

And then Peaches went still, her prison gown flapping around her in the breeze, blood spattered down the length of her body, the assault rifle held in one hand. Slowly, she sank to the ground. By the time Amos had his pants back on and got over to her, her eyes had rolled back and she was vomiting. He put his shirt over her and waited until the fit passed. It wasn't more than about five minutes, and since no one else had come out of the house to investigate or take revenge, Amos was feeling pretty confident the dead man had been a bachelor.

She shuddered once, went still, and then the blankness left her eyes.

"Hey," she said. "Did we win?"

"First round," Amos said, nodding to her. "It like that every time?"

"Yup," she said. "It's really not a great design."

"Useful when it's useful, though."

"Is that. Are you okay?"

"Little chilly," Amos said. "Won't kill me. You stay here for a bit, okay? I'm gonna go see what we're looking at inside."

"I'll come with you," she said, trying to sit up. He put a hand on her shoulder. He didn't have to push to keep her down.

"I'll go first. I'd be surprised if it wasn't booby-trapped."

"Okay," she breathed. "I'll just wait here, then."

"Good plan."

The next morning, they set off from the little compound at dawn. They both had professional-grade thermal suits, even if his was a little snug and she had to roll up the cuffs. The bunker under the house had supplies enough to last for a year or two: survival gear, weapons, ammunition, high-calorie rations, a stack of surprisingly boring pornography, and a collection of beautiful hand-carved chess sets. The best find hadn't been in the bunker, though. The garage had a half-dozen unused but well-maintained bicycles, complete with saddlebags. Even with long rifles strapped over their shoulders and their packs weighed down with water and food, they covered the distance from the compound, through the town, and out to the highway in half an hour. By noon, they'd gone farther than three days' walking would have taken them. It was probably seven hundred klicks from the Pit to Erich's office. They'd been able to cover just under thirty on foot. With the bikes, they'd more than double that. Baltimore was maybe nine days away, assuming nothing went wrong. Which, given the context, seemed like a lot to ask. But still.

They stopped for lunch at noon. It was dim enough it could have been the hours just before dawn. His breath was pluming in the air now, but between the exercise and the thermal suit, Amos didn't feel the cold. Peaches seemed about a thousand times better too. She was smiling, and there was color in her cheeks. They sat on an old bench beside the road, looking east. The view was mud and a scattering of debris.

And still on the horizon, the glow of something huge—a city or a fire—lit the clouds from below, gold on gray. So maybe even the end of the world had its moments of beauty.

Peaches took a bite of her ration bar and sipped the water from her self-purifying canteen. "Is it bothering you?"

"What?"

"What we did."

"Not sure what that was, Peaches."

She looked at him, her eyes narrowed like she was trying to decide if he was joking. "We invaded a man's home, killed him, and took his stuff. If we hadn't come through, he might have made it. Lived until the sun came back. Survived."

"He was gonna shoot me for no reason except that I had something he wanted."

"He wouldn't have done it if we hadn't gone there. And we lied to him about wanting to trade."

"Seems like you have a point to make, Peaches."

"If he hadn't been ready to pull the trigger, would you have let it go? Or would we still be here, with these guns and this food?"

"Oh, we were taking his shit. I'm just pointing out both sides of the argument had the same plan."

"Then we're not exactly the good guys, are we?"

Amos scowled. It wasn't a question that had even crossed his mind until she said it. It bothered him that it didn't bother him more. He scratched his chest and tried to imagine Holden doing what they'd done. Or Naomi. Or Lydia.

"Yeah," he said. "I should really get back to the ship soon."

Chapter Thirty-One: Alex

You're in a good mood," Bobbie said as Alex sat down across from her. Her breakfast was oatmeal with an egg-like protein crumble, sausages, and hot sauce. Her hair, pulled back in a tight ponytail, was wet with sweat, and her cheeks were flushed from recent exertion. Just looking at her made him feel out of shape. But she was right. He was in a good mood.

"Captain's bringing my girl to Luna."

Bobbie frowned. "Your…girl?"

"The *Roci*."

"Oh. Right," she said. "For a second, I just thought…Yeah. It'll be good to see Holden too. And Avasarala."

"Be good to be on my own damn ship," Alex said, tapping pepper onto his plate of reconstituted eggs. "Now if we can just get Amos and Naomi back. Whoa. Did I say something?"

The shadow that had come over Bobbie's expression vanished

again and she shook her head. "Nothing. Just... I don't know. Envy, I guess. It's been a while since I had people."

She stabbed one of the sausages with a fork and glanced around the mess hall as she ate it. Alex's eggs were chalky and tasted more of yeast than something that came from a chicken, and it brought decades of memory with it. "Being back around active-duty folks making it hard to look forward to civilian life?"

"Sort of."

"Things change," Alex said.

"And they don't change back," she said, quoting him back to himself.

Alex broke off a piece of toast, popped it in his mouth, and talked around the crust. "We still talking about the service?"

Bobbie smiled. "No, I guess we're not. I still can't really get my head around it. Earth's never going to be Earth again. Not like it was."

"No, it won't."

"Mars either," Bobbie said. "I think about my nephew. Smart kid. Book smart, I mean. He hasn't really been in the world except for going through university and then the terraforming project. That's his whole life. He was one of the first people I knew to really get what off-world colonies meant for everything back here."

"Yeah. It makes everything different," Alex said.

"Except how we deal with it," she said, then racked an imaginary shotgun and fired it off with a popping sound.

"Amazing how much we've managed to do, considering how we're doing it all with jumped-up social primates and evolutionary behaviors from the Pleistocene."

Bobbie chuckled, and he was glad to hear the sound. There was something about making the people around him feel better that left him feeling lighter himself. Like if the others on his crew could be upbeat, whatever it was couldn't be that bad. He understood the flaw in that logic: if comforting them comforted him, maybe comforting him comforted them, and they could all drive the ship into a rock while they smiled at each other.

"I heard the relief ships are here," Alex said.

"Yeah, that may not be as good as we'd hoped," Bobbie said around a mouthful of sausage. "They were talking about it at training this morning. The relief ships should be getting in operational range right around now, but the scuttlebutt is the crews are all green as hell. Like first-mission green."

"*All* of them?" Alex said.

"The good crews are all back at Hungaria covering our six."

"Well. Better a bunch of teenagers flying with us than just the two frigates," Alex said. "But you'll excuse me if I'd hoped the cavalry coming over the hill was a little more experienced."

"They probably said the same thing about us when we started up."

"You know they did. First mission I flew solo, I almost dumped core by mistake."

"Seriously?"

"Got flustered."

"That's military-grade flustered, all right," Bobbie said. "Well, hopefully, this'll be a milk run to Luna."

Alex nodded and took a sip of coffee from his bulb. "You think that'll happen? You really think it's over?"

Bobbie's silence was an answer.

They spent the rest of the meal on less fraught subjects: how training for marines and Navy were different and which one was better; Alex's stories from Ilus and the slow zone; speculation about what exactly Avasarala was going to do once they got the prime minister to Luna. It was all shop talk, and Alex found it easy and pleasant. He hadn't crewed with her in years, but she was good to talk to, good to be around. In another life, he could imagine shipping with her. Well, in the military anyway. He couldn't quite place her on a water hauler like the *Canterbury*, and he wondered what it would have done to have her on the *Roci*. Part of what made the *Rocinante* home was that the crew was so small, and had so much shared context. There was an intimacy that living in quarters with the same handful of people for so long gave.

Anyone coming in—even someone as competent and smart and easygoing as Bobbie—would have had to contend with that, and there was nothing that screwed up a crew like having one person who felt excluded.

He was still thinking about that, chewing the next-to-last mouthful of so-called eggs and listening to Bobbie tell a story about free-climbing on the Martian surface, when the Klaxons went off.

"All hands to battle stations," the calm, crisp voice said between whoops of the alarm. "This is not a drill."

Alex was up and heading toward his crash couch before he fully registered what was going on. Bobbie was beside him. They both threw their breakfast trays and drink bulbs into the recycler on the way out, long training identifying anything that wasn't bolted down as a potential projectile if the ship's vector changed too suddenly. The staccato vibration of the PDCs was already ringing in the decks, but Alex couldn't imagine what could have gotten near enough for that kind of close combat without being noticed. The alarms were still going off when they reached the corridor and one of the marines—Sergeant Park, his name was—gathered them up.

"No time to get you to your quarters. There are some spare couches we can put you up in over here."

"What's going on?" Alex said, trotting to keep up.

"The relief ships are firing on us," Park said.

"What?" Bobbie snapped.

Park didn't break stride, opening a hatch into an empty meeting room and ushering them in. Alex dropped into the embrace of a crash couch, strapping himself down with an efficiency of long habit and deep training. His mind was tripping over itself.

"Someone faked military transponder codes?" he said.

"Nope, they're our birds," Park said, checking Alex's straps.

"Then how—"

"We hope to beat that answer out of them when the time comes, sir," Park said. He switched to Bobbie's chair and checked her straps too while he spoke. "Please remain in your couches until we signal that it's safe to get out. Not sure what we're looking at, but I expect this may get—"

The ship lurched hard, snapping the gimbals of the couches forty-five degrees to the deck. Park shifted, bracing just before he hit the wall.

"Park!" Bobbie shouted, reaching for the straps that held her in. "Report!"

"Remain in your couch!" the marine shouted from behind Alex and below him. The press of thrust gravity sank him deep into the gel. A needle slid into his leg, pumping a cocktail of drugs into his bloodstream that would lessen the danger of stroke. *Jesus, this was more serious than he thought.*

"Park!" Bobbie said again, and then a string of obscenities as the marine stumbled out the door and into the corridor, leaving them behind. "This is fucked. This is so fucked."

"Can you get anything?" Alex shouted, even though she was only a meter and a half away. "My control panel's locked out."

He heard the sound of her breath over the distant vibrations of the PDCs, the deeper tones of missiles launching. "No, Alex. I'm getting the stand-by screen."

A loud fluting groan passed through the deck, rattling the couches as they shifted again. Whoever was at the helm, they were putting the ship through its paces. Along with the deep, recognizable reports of the ship's weapons, there were other sounds, less familiar ones. Alex's mind turned all of them into damage from the enemy, and at least some of the time, he was sure he was right. His throat was tight, and his gut hurt. He kept waiting for a gauss round to pass through the ship, and every second it didn't happen made it feel more likely that it would.

"You doing all right?" Bobbie said.

"Just wish I could see what was going on. Or do somethin' about it. Don't mind fighting, but I hate being spam in a can."

His stomach lurched, and for a long moment, he mistook the sudden weightlessness for nausea. His crash couch shifted to his left, Bobbie's to her right, until they could almost see each other.

"Well," Bobbie said. "They got the drive."

"Yup. So that thing where you and Avasarala thought maybe someone was appropriating MCRN ships and supplies?"

"Look pretty smart now, don't we?"

The couches shifted again as maneuvering thrusters on the ship's skin fought against the massive inertia of steel and ceramic. The throbbing of PDCs and report of missile launches made a rough background music, but it was a quiet that caught Alex's attention.

"The bad guys," he said. "They stopped shooting."

"Huh," Bobbie said. Then a moment later, "Boarding action, then?"

"What I was thinking."

"Well. How long do you want to stay in these couches before we go try to scare up some weapons?"

"Five minutes?"

"Works for me," Bobbie said, taking out her hand terminal. "I'll set a timer."

The door of the meeting room cycled open at three minutes, twenty-five seconds. Three marines floated through in light battle armor, bracing against the doorframe and holding assault rifles at their sides. The first one—a thin-faced man with a scar running down the side of his nose—moved forward. It struck Alex that if the bad guys, whoever they were, had Martian warships, they probably also had Martian armor, but the thin-faced man steadied himself against the desk.

"Mister Kamal. Sergeant Draper. My name's Lieutenant de Haan. The ship's going to be maneuvering, so we'll need to be careful, but I need you to come with me now."

"Roger that, sir," Bobbie said, popping the straps on her couch loose and shifting to launch for the door. Alex was only a beat behind her.

The marines moved through the weightless halls with practiced efficiency, cover to cover with one always in firing position at the back, another at the front, and Bobbie and Alex in the center of the formation. Twice, the ship lurched with Alex in the middle of a jump from one handhold to the next. The first time, he caught himself on a different support, but the second, he bounced off a bare length of deck, spinning through the air until one of the marines grabbed him and hauled him to safety. The one-sided sounds of battle grew first louder and then more distant. One bulkhead failed to open, reporting vacuum on the other side, and they had to backtrack. Like a restless dream, the journey seemed to go on forever and also be over almost as soon as it had begun.

On the bridge, the captain was strapped into her couch, the prime minister in the couch beside her. All around, the crewmen at their stations were rattling information to one another, and Alex caught bits of it, his mind forming a picture of their situation almost without knowing what exactly he'd heard to inform it. The main drive was down. The comm array was unable to transmit either broadcast or tightbeam. There were hull breaches near engineering, the armory, and aft storage. Missiles could still be fired, but the guidance systems were down. No one mentioned the two frigates that had been flying with the ship since the main escort had been pulled away. Alex figured that meant they were dead.

"We are under attack and being boarded," the captain said, her voice remarkably calm. "The original escort force is also now under concentrated attack, and will be unable to come to our relief. We have put out a broad distress call, but it seems unlikely in the extreme that anyone could make it here in time to affect the outcome of the conflict. We are preparing to offer a vigorous defense, but if we are unable to assure your safety, it may become necessary for you to evacuate."

"Into the middle of a firefight?" Alex said.

"It isn't optimal," the captain said. "With respect, my first priority has to be the safety of the prime minister."

"Of course, Skipper," Bobbie said at the same time that Alex said, "That's sounding a mite ominous." The captain ignored both of them.

"We have half a dozen rescue pods prepped. Protocol is to give each of you an armed escort in the pod, and release them all at once, in hopes of distributing enemy attention and giving each of you the best possible chance of being overlooked."

"That's a shitty plan," Alex said to the captain, then turned to the prime minister. "You know that's a shitty plan, don't you, sir?"

Smith nodded. His face was flushed, and a thin sheen of sweat danced across his neck and jowls, surface tension adhering it to his skin.

"Yeah," Bobbie said. "Pods don't have an Epstein. You'd be dropping us out there to get shot. And we have a racing yacht right here. The *Razorback*'s built for speed."

The captain raised her hand, demanding silence. "What I was going to say? We can commandeer the *Razorback* for the prime minister, give her a pilot and an escort guard, but that means I'm still dropping two civilians into a meat grinder."

"Why the hell would you do that?" Bobbie interrupted. "We've got a pilot and an escort right here. Don't we? We can put Prime Minister Smith in the bunk and take the couches. Alex has more experience piloting that ship than any of you, and—all respect to Lieutenant de Haan—I can shoot as straight as anyone you've got. It'll be tight, but it's totally possible."

"That's where I was going, yes," the captain said, her voice buzzing with annoyance. "In addition, the prime minister has made it clear that for political reasons, the presence of Sergeant Draper is required on Luna, so—"

"They said yes, Captain Choudhary," the prime minister snapped. "Take *yes* for an answer."

"Lieutenant?" Bobbie said. "If I'm acting escort on this mission, I'd really like to have a weapon."

The thin-faced man smiled, his eyes glinting and cold. "I can arrange that, Gunny. Captain?"

The captain nodded sharply, and Lieutenant de Haan launched for the lift, Bobbie close behind him. Alex's heart was beating double-time, but the fear was tempered by a growing excitement.

Yes, he was in danger of losing his life. Yes, an unknown enemy had them surrounded and were likely about to storm the ship itself. But he was going to get to fly in battle again, and some immature, juvenile part of his soul could hardly wait.

"We will use our PDCs to cover you as long as we can," the captain said, and Alex interrupted her again.

"Not going to be enough. If we're burnin' all the way to Earth...we can probably outrun the enemy ships, but their missiles don't have to worry about keeping anyone inside from getting squished by thrust. And it ain't like there's anything out here to hide behind."

"You'll have to think of something," the captain said.

"All right," Alex said. "Set a bunch of missiles to match the frequency of the *Razorback*'s comm laser. Launch as many as you can with us when we go, and Bobbie can use our laser to target incoming fire. We'll outrun their ships and shoot down their missiles. Unless there's someone between here and Luna or we run out of missiles, we should be fine."

As long as we don't get shot the second we launch, he didn't add.

The captain blinked and shot a glance at the prime minister. There was a question in the politician's eyes. Captain Choudhary shrugged. "He thought of something."

"You mean—"

"No," the captain said, "that might...that might work."

"Captain!" A voice came from behind them. "We have confirmed enemy contact at decks seven and thirteen. Permission to use heavy weapons?"

"Permission granted," the captain said, then turned to Alex. "I think that's your cue to head out, Mister Kamal."

"Thank you, Captain," Alex said. "I'll make this work if I can."

The prime minister unstrapped and floated up out of his couch until one of the two remaining marines grabbed him and pulled him back into orientation. The prime minister and the captain shook hands as another voice interrupted.

"Captain, we're getting a message from the attacking force. From the *Pella*."

"Their command ship," the prime minister said to Alex.

"More demands of surrender?" the captain asked.

"No, sir. It's broadcast, not tightbeam. It's...well, holy shit."

"Give it to me, Mister Chou," the captain said. "From the start."

An audio feed clicked on. Thick static crackled, vanished, then crackled again. Someone grunted, and it sounded like pain. When the voice finally came, it was focused and serious. And it hit Alex like a kick to the belly.

"If you receive this, please retransmit. This is Naomi Nagata of the *Rocinante*..."

Chapter Thirty-Two: Naomi

She knew it was coming before it came. Before she even knew what it would be. The feeling of the ship changed without any of the details shifting, at least not at first. The crew still watched the newsfeeds and cheered. She was still under constant guard and treated like a mascot: James Holden's tame girlfriend brought back to the cage where she belonged. Marco was polite to her, and Filip was caught between approaching and avoiding her. But there was a difference. A tension had come into the ship, and she didn't know yet if they were all anticipating news of another atrocity or something more personal and concrete. All she was sure of at first was that it made it harder for her to sleep or eat. The dread in her gut was too heavy.

No one told her anything, and there was no single moment when she drew her conclusions. Instead, she looked back, and details filtered through from her days in captivity. A few remained, trapped by a nearly occult sense of importance. Wings showing off in his Martian uniform, a broad-shouldered girl hardly older than Filip exercising with the steady focus of someone preparing for something she knew she wasn't prepared for, Karal steering her own inventory busywork toward the armory and its store of powered armor, the seriousness with which Cyn tried the weight of each of the guns in his hands. Like the sediments of dust that built up in a badly maintained duct, the small things came together over time into a shape that was almost the same as knowledge. They were going into battle. And more than that, they were ambushing a Martian force.

When she found Miral and Aaman sitting knee-to-knee in the corridor outside the medical bay, she knew the moment was almost on her, and the hope she'd been hiding even from herself bloomed up in her throat, as wild as anger.

"This is the *Pella*," Miral said, concentrating on each syllable. "Confermé course match."

"Confirming," Aaman said gently.

Miral balled his hands into fists and tapped the deck with them. "Fuck. What did I say?"

"Confermé. You want confirming."

"Again," Miral said, then cleared his throat. "This is the *Pella*. Confirming course match."

Aaman grinned. "Course match confirmed, *Pella*."

Miral looked up, noticed Naomi and Cyn approaching, and grimaced. Naomi shook her head. "You sound great," she said. "Very Martian."

Miral hesitated, caught, she guessed, in the uncertainty of what she knew and was supposed to know. When he smiled, it was almost sheepish. Naomi smiled back and kept walking, pretending that she was one of them. That she belonged. Cyn, beside her, made no comment but watched her from the corners of his eyes.

The mid-shift meal was refried noodles and beer. The newsfeed was set to a system-wide report, and she watched it avidly for the first time, not for what it said, but what it didn't. Food and water reserves were running out in North America and Asia, with Europe only a few days better. Relief efforts from the southern hemisphere were hampered by a growing need for supplies locally. She didn't care. It wasn't Jim. Medina Station had gone dark; the basic carrier signal remained, but all queries were being ignored, and she didn't care. The Martian minority speaker of parliament back in Londres Nova was calling for the prime minister to return immediately to Mars, and she only cared a little. Every story that wasn't about a ship blowing up at Tycho Station was a victory. She ate fast, sucking down the sweet, pale noodles and slamming back the beer, as if by hurrying her meal, she could rush the ship, the attack.

Her opportunity.

She and Cyn spent the next half shift going through engineering and the machine shop, making sure everything was locked down. In a ship full of Belters, she had no doubt it all would be, and it was. The ritual of it was reassuring, though. The sense of order and control over a ship's environment was a synonym for safety. Belters who didn't triple-check everything had been weeded out of the gene pool fast, and seeing the regularity of the shop gave her an almost atavistic sense of comfort. And also, without being obvious, she checked the location of the flawed toolbox with its misshapen hasp and then carefully didn't look at it again. She felt obvious, sure that by so clearly cutting the box out of her awareness, she was actually calling Cyn's attention to it.

The relationship between the dark thoughts and the nearly unbearable swelling of excitement in her heart didn't occur to her until Cyn's hand terminal chimed and he called the work to a halt.

"Wrócić do tu crash couch, yeah," he said, touching her shoulder. His hand was gentle but strong. She didn't pretend ignorance, didn't try to disguise her anxiety. It would just read as being scared of the battle anyway.

When they got to her quarters, she strapped in and Cyn checked her. Then, to her surprise, he sat by her side for a moment, his mass shifting the balance of the couch. His muscles rippled under the skin with even his smallest movements, but he still managed to seem boyish and shy, like his body was a costume. "Zuchtig tu, sa sa?"

Naomi smiled the way she imagined she would have if she'd meant it. "Of course I'll be careful," she said. "Always am."

"La, not always, you," Cyn said. He struggled with something. She didn't know what. "Close quarters, means a lot of maneuvering. Don't have a couch to catch you, then you get a wall, yeah? Maybe a corner."

Fear flooded her mouth with the taste of copper. Did he know? Had he guessed? Cyn flexed his hands, not able to meet her gaze.

"En buenas mood, you. Happy, ever since you and Marco. So I'm thinking maybe you think there's something to be happy for, yeah? Maybe a way out don't have doors."

Suicide, she thought. *He's talking about suicide. He thinks I'm going to unstrap in the middle of the battle and let the ship beat me to death.* While she hadn't consciously considered it before, it was the kind of thing the dark thoughts would have brought her. And worse, the thought brought no surprise with it, but only a sense of warmth. Almost of comfort. She wondered whether that had been in her mind, whether the danger inherent in her plan was its drawback or a covert way for the bad thoughts to find their expression. That she wasn't sure unnerved her.

"I plan to be here when this is over," she said, biting the words as if to convince herself as much as her guard.

Cyn nodded. The ship's system sounded the maneuvers warning, but the big man didn't get off the couch. Not yet. "Esá? Hard for us and you both. We come through, yeah? All of us, and you too." He was staring at his hands now like something might be written there. "Mi familia," he said at last. "Remember that. Alles lá son family, y tu bist also."

"Go strap in, big guy," Naomi said. "We can finish this after."

"After," Cyn said, shot a smile at her, and rose. The second warning came, and Naomi leaned back into the gel, just as if she meant to stay in its cool embrace.

On the bridge, Marco was no doubt being smooth and calm, playing the part of the Martian captain, reassuring everyone he could that everything was under control now that he was there. They'd believe him too. He was in a Martian ship with a solid, known transponder. He was probably using Martian military encryption. That he could be anything other than what he seemed would be as inconceivable to them as it was obvious to her.

She wanted to care, but she didn't. She didn't have time.

The sound of missiles firing and the mutter of PDCs came as the room lurched thirty degrees to the left, her couch hissing on its gimbals. She popped the straps loose and sat up, pulling her leg away from the needle. If she'd been sure it wasn't a sedative, she'd have waited for the injections. Too late. The couch shifted back to neutral position. She hopped down to the floor and walked quickly and steadily for the corridor. She kept her arms wide, fingertips against the walls on either side, and slid her feet across the deck. *Knees bent, center of gravity low*, she told herself.

Be ready for the change when it comes. The ship twitched around her. The walls and deck showed nothing, her eyes promising her that everything was solid, quiet, and stable as her own mass pushed her, falling toward one wall and then the next, and then—worst—forward where there was nothing to catch herself against. It was worse than weightlessness. The struggles of a mind to interpret up and down in the absence of gravity could be disorienting, but this was something else. She rattled down the hallway like dice in a cup, moving forward when she could, bracing herself against the walls when the motion was too violent.

In the lift, she selected the machine shop and gripped the handholds as the mechanism dropped her down the body of the ship. A concussion rattled her. The Martians fighting back. That was fine. Let them. She couldn't give that struggle her attention. Not until hers was done.

The machine shop was empty, all the tools locked in place, but with enough tolerance that when the ship lurched, they all rattled: metal against metal like the ship itself was learning to talk. She went for the compromised toolbox, but the deck fell away under her. She stumbled, her head crashing against the metal shelves. For a few seconds, the rattling seemed to recede. She shook her head, and drops of blood pattered on the wall and the deck.

Not a big deal, she told herself. *Head wounds always bleed a lot. It doesn't mean it's serious. Keep moving.*

The PDCs chattered, the sound moving through the body of the ship. She found the toolbox, popped open the restraint, pulled it out, and sat on the deck, cradling it. For a long, sick second, she thought the lock was different, solid, unapproachable, but that was wrong. A trick of the mind. It was fine. She pulled at the latch, worked her fingertips into the crevice that shouldn't have been there, then pulled it wider, and pushed in again, driving her own skin and bone into it like a wedge. It hurt like hell, but she ignored it. The pressure of her body against the deck suddenly grew terrible. They were accelerating. She didn't know why. Her back ached. It had been years since her spine had been asked to support her body during a heavy burn. Usually, she was lying on her back in gel around now.

With an indignant pop, the latch gave. The toolbox flew open, but nothing spilled. All the wrenches, epoxy welders, voltage meters, and cans of air and lubricant were strapped in place. She flipped through the close-packed layers to a line of Allen wrenches and plucked out the 10 mm. It was one of the advantages she had over Marco and his crew. She'd been living in a Martian ship for years. Knowing what tools opened which access panels was like recognizing the back of her own hand. She gathered up a voltage tester, a wiring crimp, and a light-duty soldering iron and stuffed them in her pockets. With any luck, she'd only need the wrench, but—

The deck drifted away under her, gravity suddenly gone. She couldn't tell if she was spinning through the air or the ship was turning around her. She reached for the deck, the walls, but nothing was within reach besides the floating toolbox. That was good enough. She grabbed it in close to her belly, then pushed it away as reaction mass, and twisted to grab the workbench. Down came back, and the toolbox crashed down behind her as she stumbled. Another low boom rattled the ship. Knees and spine aching, she ran for the lift.

Gravity vanished again as she got into it. The PDCs were still chattering, but less now. She didn't remember the last time she'd heard a missile fire. The battle was winding down. She willed the lift to travel faster. If the all clear sounded and other people got out of their couches before she was done, then Holden and the *Rocinante* and possibly a fair percentage of Tycho Station would die. With every slow meter the lift took her, she imagined it: the drive cycling up and then spilling out, a fire brighter than light that ate everything. The ship moved, slamming her against the wall hard enough to bruise, then released her to float free again. She killed the lift between the crew quarters and the airlock, bracing herself so that the deceleration didn't leave her trapped in the middle of empty air.

The access panel was fifteen centimeters high and forty wide and opened on the major electrical routing through the center of the ship. If she'd cut through all the cables there with a welding torch, all the traffic would have rerouted instantly to other channels. Apart from a few warning indicators, nothing would happen. That was fine. She didn't want to break the ship. She wanted to use it. Braced with both feet and one hand in the wall handholds, she worked the Allen wrench. The screws were integral to the plate and didn't come free, but she felt it when the metal threads lost their grip. Three connections came off. Four. Five.

Six.

She could see the handset through the gap where the plate was beginning to come free. The ship shuddered under her, turning. She squeezed the wrench in her fist, seeing it fall away down the shaft even though it wasn't happening. A thick red-black clot of blood slipped free of her hair, smearing itself across the pale wall. She ignored it. Seven connectors were loose. Eight. She heard voices from the crew quarters. A woman saying something she couldn't make out, and a man answering no. Nine. Ten.

The plate came free. She scooped up the handset, checking its charge. The batteries were nearly full. Connection read good. She didn't know which circuit was the broadcast and the first one she tried threw an error code. Cursing musically under her breath, she set it to diagnostic mode and started querying. It seemed to take forever before it came back. She cycled through the report with her thumb until she found it. Channel eighteen was a comm array using the D4/L4 protocols that the *Rocinante* did for broadcast. She thumbed in the override code that would let her send thirty seconds of diagnostic tones out, then deleted the file that held the tones. When the error came up, she told it to override to manual. She was almost weeping now. Her right foot slipped, and she grabbed for the open access panel. Her knuckles scraped something sharp and toothy. She grunted in pain and put her annoyance aside. No time.

"If you receive this," she said, pressing the handset close to her lips, "please retransmit. This is Naomi Nagata of the *Rocinante*. Message is for James Holden. The software controlling the magnetic bottle has been sabotaged. Do not start the reactor without reloading the hardware drivers from a known good source. If you hear this message, please retransmit."

Halfway through the last word, the handset chirped that the thirty seconds were up and returned to the base menu. She let the handset go, let herself go, floated back from the wall. She spread her arms wide and let the Allen wrench go. She hoped it had worked. It was the middle of a battle. There could be jamming to contend with if Marco wanted to keep what was happening unclear, but it was just as likely he was enjoying being a spectacle. And if she was right, if they were going after the Martian prime minister, the data coming off the battle would be gone over by the best intelligence services that still existed.

Jim wasn't safe, not yet. She knew it, but for a moment, she didn't feel it. The darkness would come back; the bone-crushing anxiety, and the guilt and the fear. She didn't doubt that, but now, right now, she felt only light. She'd made her plan, and it had worked. Her warning would reach him or it wouldn't. Either way, there was nothing more she could do. And on the bridge, right now, Marco was figuring out what exactly she'd done. The laughter that came boiling out of her throat felt like victory.

The voices from the crew quarters grew louder, more confused. Even though the all clear hadn't been called, she heard people moving around. She recognized Cyn's voice, raised in alarm. Her leg brushed against the wall, and she reached out to hook her wrist into the handhold. No point bothering with the lift. Hand over hand, she pulled herself along the shaft and then into the corridors. The faces that peered from the doorways were wide-eyed. One man started back when he caught sight of her. Naomi launched herself along the hallway with a kick and flew straight as an arrow, not even touching the handholds along the way to steady herself. Her shoulder ached. The wound on her scalp was bleeding again. She felt serene.

Cyn hauled himself around a corner, then braced and watched her, his jaw slack, his eyes round. She lifted a fist in greeting as she floated by.

"Anyone needs me," she said, "I'll be in my quarters, yeah?"

Chapter Thirty-Three: Holden

Most of human history had static maps. Even in times of change and chaos, when civilizations had fallen in the course of a single night, the places remained more or less the same. The distance between Africa and South America was going to stay what it had always been, at least over the span of human evolution. And whether you called it France or the Common European Interest Zone, Paris was closer to Orléans than Nice. It was only when they moved out to Mars and then the Belt and the worlds beyond it that the distance between the great centers of human life became a function of time. From Tycho Station, Earth and Luna were almost on the far side of the sun. Mars was closer, but retreating with every hour. Saturn was closer than either and the Jovian moons farther away. That everything came closer and then farther apart was a given in Holden's life; uncommented and unremarkable. It was only times like this that facts of orbital periodicity started to seem like a metaphor for something deeper.

As soon as Fred made the decision to go to Luna, Holden had moved his things back to the *Rocinante*. And then the rest of the crew's possessions too. He'd found Amos' clothes neatly folded and regimented in a rough canvas bag. Alex's had been thrown haphazardly in a case, half in a mesh bag and half not, though which set was clean and which bound for the laundry, Holden couldn't tell. Naomi's things had been in his suite. A spare pair of boots, an unpaired sock, underwear. She'd left a model of a Martian combat mech—bright red and flat black and no bigger than his thumb—on the bathroom counter. He didn't know if it held some special meaning to her or if she would even remember where she'd gotten it from. He was careful to take it with him, though. Careful to wrap it and put it in a cushioned box. It was the closest thing he had to taking care of the woman it belonged to, so that was what he did.

Being back in the *Rocinante* was like coming home, except that it was too empty. The narrow corridors of the crew deck seemed too wide. The occasional ticking and popping of the expansion joints adjusting to shifts in temperature were like the knocking of ghosts. When the repair team were somewhere he could hear them, Holden resented the voices and footsteps that weren't his crew's. When they were gone, the silence oppressed him.

He told himself it was temporary. That before long, he'd have Alex back in the cockpit and Amos down in engineering. Naomi beside him, telling him gently what he was screwing up and how to do it better. He'd go to Luna, and they'd be there. All of them. Somehow.

Except he still hadn't heard from Naomi. He'd gotten a short text-only message from Mother Tamara that his parents were all right for now, but that ash was falling on the ranch like snow in winter. And nothing from Amos.

Sometimes people knew when they were saying their last goodbyes, but not always. Not often. Most people's last parting of ways were so small, the people involved didn't even notice them. Now, in the darkness of the command deck with a half-liter bulb of bourbon floating beside him and the audio system playing twelve-bar blues, Holden was pretty sure he'd said a couple of his own final goodbyes and not known it. He replayed everything in his head, his memories becoming less authentic and more painful every time he did.

"We're all that's left," he said to the ship. "You're all I've got."

The *Rocinante* didn't answer for a long moment, and then, weirdly, it did. A bright yellow incoming request alert appeared on his console. Holden wiped his teary eyes with a sleeve and accepted it. Fred Johnson appeared in a window, his brows furrowed.

"Holden?"

"Fred?"

"Are you all right?"

"Ah. Yes?"

Fred leaned forward, his head growing massive on the screen. "I've been trying to reach your hand terminal for the past fifteen minutes."

Holden looked around the command deck, then nodded. "I may have left it in my pants. In my quarters. I think I did."

"Are you drunk?"

"I think I am." He had to concentrate not to slur.

"And you're not wearing pants?"

"I'm not ready to take our relationship there yet."

"Well, have the med bay give you something to sober you up and get your ass covered. I'm sending the flight crew over."

Holden turned up the lights and killed the music feed. "What's going on?"

"We're getting reports. The Martian prime minister's under attack. The ships your man Alex found were decoys to draw off the escort."

"But," Holden said, "the new escort ships—"

"Are the ones shooting at him."

Holden cursed under his breath. "Alex is on that ship. Did we hear from Alex?"

"We haven't heard from anybody. I was keeping some radio telescopes pointed that direction, and this is what they're getting. I checked with Drummer and the engineering staff. They said the *Roci*'s got a clean bill of health, and I'm less and less interested in sitting around here waiting for whoever's behind all this to take another swing at me."

Holden undid the straps on his couch, floating forward. His head was a little swimmy. He looked around at the command deck. It was like some part of his brain was still expecting to see Alex and Naomi and Amos there with him. He hadn't realized it was a habit, to look for his people before the *Roci* got under way. This, he realized, was the first time ever that they wouldn't be there. It felt like a bad omen.

"Okay," he said. "I'll clean up for company. When are you looking to go?"

"How soon is as soon as possible?"

"The reactor's cold, and we'd want to top up the air and water," Holden said. The alcohol fumes seemed to be burning away already, but he wasn't entirely sure if that was true or if it just felt that way. "Plus I'm reliably informed that I need to get something from the med bay to sober me up and get my ass covered."

"Glad you were paying attention," Fred said. "So two hours?"

"I think we can manage that."

"Let's do."

Holden pulled himself down the lift shaft hand over hand. A new crew coming onto his *Rocinante.* It was the obvious thing, of course. It had always been the plan, but now the prospect filled him with dread. Unfamiliar faces at the controls and in the crew quarters. Voices in the ship that weren't the ones he'd gotten used to in the years since the *Donnager.* Even when they'd been carrying passengers, his crew had been at the heart of the ship. This was something else, and he didn't like it.

He stopped at the med bay on the way to his quarters. Sober, the symbolic implications of a new temporary crew for the trip to Luna didn't seem quite as ominous, but the thought stayed at the back of his mind: without Naomi—without all his crew—the *Rocinante* wasn't going to be what she had been. When he checked his hand terminal, the only messages were from Fred. Alex's silence didn't help.

The transport tube's connection to the airlock was a gentle thump, like Tycho Station clearing its throat. Holden was at the airlock to let them in. Eight people—six Belters, and two who looked like they'd come from Earth, all wearing Tycho Station flight suits and hauling small personal kits—floated into the space among the lockers. Drummer was with them, wearing her security uniform.

"Captain Holden?" Drummer said. "I'd like to introduce Captain Foster Sales and his crew."

The man who floated up, arms braced, looked too young to be a captain. Close-cropped black hair transitioned into a glossy beard that tried and failed to lend the boyish features some gravitas. He was introduced to the others—pilots Arnold Mfume and Chava Lombaugh, engineers Sandra Ip and Zach Kazantzakis, weapons technicians Gor Droga and Sun-yi Steinberg, communications specialist Maura Patel. By the end of the little ceremony, Holden was pretty sure he'd already forgotten all of their names.

Drummer seemed to read his unease, because when the crew broke to their stations, she lingered and drew him aside. "They're good people, Captain. I vetted all of them myself. None of them are the bad guys."

"Yeah," Holden said. "That's good."

Her smile was weirdly gentle. "It's weird for me too."

"Yeah?" he said.

"On my watch, they broke into the station, stole the fucking protomolecule. They tried to kill the boss. I'm spending all day projecting an attitude of calm and control, and come sleep shift, I'm grinding my teeth and staring at the wall. Now the old man's leaving? Honest to God, I'm shitting bricks here."

Holden blew out a long breath. "Thanks for that."

"Anytime, sir. Everyone you meet's fighting a hard battle."

"Should I know anything about..." He nodded toward the door. Drummer briefed him in quick, simple sentences. Ip's roommate had been one of the turncoats, and she still felt betrayed. Steinberg and Mfume both had a hard time losing face, and while it wasn't usually a problem, if they got into a spat, someone would have to step in and deescalate. Droga had family on Earth, and he was worried and angry and grieving. Holden made a note to speak to the man if he had a chance. With every small detail, every fault and vulnerability, every strength and peculiar virtue, Holden felt something in his chest grow calmer.

Okay, these men and women weren't his family, but they were his crew. They wouldn't ever mean what Alex and Amos and Naomi meant, but for the next weeks, he was their captain. And that was enough.

For now, that was enough.

When Fred came through the airlock, Drummer was just finishing her rundown of Maura Patel's insomnia problem. Fred landed feetfirst on the wall, ankles hooked into the handholds like he'd been born in the Belt. He stood at ninety degrees to them, a rough smile on his face and a small personal kit strapped to his back.

"Well, what are you two doing?"

"Drummer is very gently telling me how to put on my big-boy pants," Holden said.

"Really?" Fred asked.

"It's possible I was getting a little maudlin."

Fred nodded. "Happens to the best of us from time to time. Where do we stand?"

Drummer answered. "The crew's initiating the warm-up. We haven't had anyone reporting trouble, so you should be good to go on schedule."

"Excellent," Fred said. "Of course, they've probably taken all the good bunks by now."

"All the bunks are the same," Holden said. "Except mine. You can't have mine."

"Wouldn't think of it, Captain," Fred said. "The Martian convoy's put out a distress call. The original escort's trying to burn back toward them, but the mystery ships are engaging in force now. As ambushes go, this one's looking pretty effective."

"Sorry to hear that," Holden said. "Still nothing from Alex."

"Well. We can hope for the best," Fred said. "Latest intel shows the attackers have stopped firing. So that makes it look like a boarding action."

Holden's blood went cold. "Protocol is they blow the ship if boarders get close to taking engineering or the CIC."

"That's so that the enemy doesn't compromise your codes," Drummer said. "They rode in on Martian naval ships. That damage is already done."

The three were silent for a moment. When Fred spoke, his voice was low and mordant. "Well, that's cheerful. You coming to help this along, Captain?"

Holden looked at Drummer. She held herself professionally at attention, but he thought he saw a glimmer of unease in her eyes. Fred Johnson had run Tycho Station for almost two decades, and now he was leaving. He might not come back. And Holden might not either.

Everyone you meet is fighting a hard battle.

"Let's give this part to Foster," Holden said. "Let him get a feel for the ship. There's something I need to take care of on the station before we go."

⚡

Monica was in new rooms. To look at her, sitting on the couch, it was like she was meeting him for the first time. The months they'd spent—her crew and his—shipping out to the Ring, the desperate work she'd done on the *Behemoth* back before it became Medina Station, her abduction and his rescue of her. All of it was gone. Her expression was polite, and it was closed.

"So," Holden said. "I'm about to take off. I'm not sure when or even if I'll see you again. And I feel like we're not good."

"Why do you feel like that?"

"Off the record?"

The silence cooled the room, then Monica took her new hand terminal out of her pocket and tapped it twice. It chimed and she rested it on her thigh. "Fine. Off the record."

"Because I lied to you, and you know it. And you're angry about it. And because you tried to get me to talk about things I didn't want to talk about by springing questions on me in the middle of an interview, and I'm angry with you about that."

Monica sighed, but her face softened. She looked older now than when they'd first met. Still camera-ready and perfect at all times, but worn by the universe. "What happened to you, Holden? You used to be the man who didn't hide anything. You were the one voice everyone could trust, because even if you didn't know all of it, you'd at least tell the truth you did know. This reading the press release thing? It's not you."

"Fred asked me not to say that he'd been targeted."

"Or that they got away with the protomolecule sample," Monica said, then held up her hand terminal. "We're off the record. Do me the courtesy of not lying to me now too."

"And that they got away with the protomolecule," Holden said.

Monica's face softened. She scratched her arm, fingernails hissing against the cloth. "That's critical. That's the scariest thing that's happened since this all started. Don't you think that people have a right to know the danger they're in?"

"Fred knows. He's told Avasarala and Smith. Earth and Mars know. The OPA knows. Panicking people for no reason—"

"Panicking at this point isn't unreasonable," Monica said. "And deciding for people what they should get to know so they do what you think they should do? That isn't how the good guys act, and you know it. It's paternalistic, it's condescending, and it's beneath you. Maybe not them. The political movers and shakers. But it's beneath *you*."

Holden felt a warmth rising in his chest. Shame or anger or something more complicated, he couldn't say. He remembered Mother Tamara saying *It hurts most if there's something true in it.* He wanted to say something mean. To hit back. He laced his fingers together. "Does what you do matter?"

"What?"

"Reporting? Telling things to people. Does it have any power?"

"Of course it does."

"Then how you use that power matters too. I'm not saying that we were right to put the protomolecule thing under the rug. I'm saying that telling everyone about it—especially right now while whatever the hell this is is still going on—is worse. When we were in the slow zone, you were the voice that pulled us all together. You gave a shape to that moment of chaos. And it made people safer and calmer and more rational. More civilized. We need that again. I need that again."

"How can you say—" Monica began, and her hand terminal buzzed. She looked down at it in annoyance, then did a double take. She lifted a finger to him. Just a second.

"What is it?" Holden said, but she was reading her terminal, her eyes getting wider. "Monica? If this is some kind of object lesson about how shitty it is to withhold information, I admit it's weirdly elegant. But if you could stop it now—"

"The attack ships. The ones going after the Martian prime minister. The command ship put out a message." She looked up at him. "It's for you."

Naomi's voice on the hand terminal was thin and tinny and like waking up from a nightmare into something worse. "If you receive this, please retransmit. This is Naomi Nagata of the *Rocinante*. Message is for James Holden. The software controlling the magnetic bottle has been sabotaged. Do not start the reactor—"

She kept talking, but Holden already had his hand terminal up. His knuckles ached, and he had to force himself to stop squeezing the device. He put out a connection request to Drummer. His heart beat against his ribs and he felt like he was falling, like he'd stepped off a tower and hadn't quite caught the ledge on the way down. Monica was cursing quietly under her breath. It sounded like prayer.

If the reactor came up and the bottle failed, the *Rocinante* would die in a fraction of a second. Tycho Station might survive. Some of it, anyway.

"Drummer here," his hand terminal said. "How can I help you, Captain?"

"Have you started the reactor?" Holden said.

Drummer went silent for maybe half a second. It felt like years. "Yes, sir. We're at sixty percent, and looking great."

"Shut it down," Holden said. "Shut it down right now."

There was a moment of silence. *Don't ask me why,* Holden thought. *Don't argue or ask me to explain. Please don't.*

"Done. The core is down," Drummer said. "So can I ask what this is about?"

Chapter Thirty-Four: Alex

…Do not start the reactor without reloading the hardware drivers from a known good source. If you hear this message, please retr—"

The message cut off.

"We have to get this out," Alex said. "We have to get that to Holden."

"I'll take care of it," the captain said. "You and the prime minister need to evacuate. Right now."

Alex looked at her, confused. Naomi was on the attack ships. The *Roci* had been sabotaged. He felt like the moment of stillness between being hit in the head and the bloom of pain. His first semi-coherent, irrational thought was *If Naomi's with them, maybe they're not so bad.*

"Mister Kamal?"

"No, I'm fine. It's just—"

Prime Minister Smith looked at him, the man's gentle, innocuous eyes seeming utterly out of place. "Does this change anything for us?"

"No," Alex said. "I just…No. No, we should go. Wait. Bobbie…"

"Gunny Draper knows where you're going," Captain Choudhary said. "I'll see she doesn't get lost."

They moved to the lift, the two marines before and behind them. The lift car gave Alex a moment of orientation as it pushed them down into the heart of the ship. It only took a few seconds to match velocity and go back to floating, but it was enough of a cue that his mind made one direction into down, the other into up. The lift car was wide enough for three times the load. The marines took stations at the door, ready to face danger if there was any. The prime minister took a place at the side near the front, where there was a little cover. No one commented on it. It was just a thing that happened. The dynamics of political power as positions in an elevator.

Naomi was here. *Right* here. Maybe less than ten thousand kilometers away. It was like he'd turned a corner and she was there. Except, of course, that she wasn't. Even close-quarters battle meant distances that were vast in any other context. If the ship had been transparent, the enemy vessels would only have been visible by their drive plumes—dots of light in a sky filled with them. The *Pella* could be as far from him right now as Boston was from Sri Lanka, and it would still be almost intimate in the vast scale of the solar system.

"You're thinking of your friend," Smith said.

"Yes, sir," Alex said.

"Do you know why she would be on the *Pella*?"

"I don't know why she wouldn't be on the *Rocinante*. And no offense, but I'm wondering why I ever got off my ship too. Longer I'm away, the worse an idea leaving it turns out to have been."

"I was thinking the same about my house," Smith said.

One of the Marines—taller, and with a slushy accent that Alex couldn't place—nodded. "You should take cover, sir. We're going to have to pass through some territory we might not control."

He meant that the enemy had already cut off the path between them and the hangar. Alex pressed himself against the wall that the prime minister hadn't claimed and braced. The lift slowed, what had been down became up, then even that gentle gravity went away again. The marines stepped back, raised their weapons, and the doors opened. An eternal half second later, they moved out into the corridor, Alex and the prime minister following.

The corridors of the ship were empty, the crew strapped in their couches for the battle or else on the move elsewhere, keeping these halls safe while the four of them moved down them. The marines took turns moving forward from doorway to intersection to doorway. The distance behind them grew greater with every little jump, and Alex was deeply aware of the doors they'd passed that could open without any guards between him and whoever came out. The marines didn't seem worried, so he tried to take comfort in that.

The halls had the same anti-spalling covering that the bridge and the mess had had, but marked with location codes and colored strips that would help navigate the ship. One line was deep red with HANGAR BAY written in yellow Hindi, English, Bengali, Farsi, and Chinese. Where the red line went, they followed.

They went quickly and quietly and Alex was almost thinking they'd make it to the bay without trouble when the enemy found them.

The ambush was professional. The slushy-voiced marine had just launched forward when the firing started. Alex couldn't see where it was coming from at first, but he braced automatically and risked looking forward. At the intersection ahead of them, he caught the flare of muzzle flashes and the small circle of helmets. The attackers were standing on a bulkhead looking up the corridor, like they were shooting into a well. Even if he'd had a gun, there was a very small area to target.

"We're taking fire," the other marine said, and it took Alex a quarter second to understand he wasn't talking to them. "Tollivsen's shot."

"Still in the fight," the slushy accent shouted.

Across the corridor from Alex, Prime Minister Smith was huddled behind the lip of a doorway. Most civilians tried to press against the wall and ended up launching themselves into the middle of the firing lines. Smith hadn't done that. So score one for training.

Another burst of fire sang past, tearing long black strips from the walls and deck and filling the air with the smell of cordite.

"Oyé," one of the attackers called. "Hand up Smith y we let you go, sa sa?"

The first marine fired three rounds in fast succession, and the attackers' laughter followed it. Alex couldn't be sure, but he thought the people firing at him were wearing Martian military uniforms and light armor.

"Hey!" Alex called. "We're not going to be any good to you dead, right?"

There was a lull, like a moment of surprise. "Hoy, bist tu Kamal?"

"Um," Alex said. "My name's Kamal."

"Knuckles' pilot, yeah?"

"Who's Knuckles?"

"Pinché traitor's who," the voice said. "You get to hell, tell her Salo sent you."

"Grenade incoming," the slushy-voiced marine said, his voice weirdly calm. "Employing countermeasures."

Alex turned his face to the wall and pressed his hands to his ears. The shock of the explosion was like being slapped all across his side. He fought to breathe. Flecks of something like snow swirled through the air, and the stink of plastic and spent explosive was thick enough to choke. The stutter of gunfire seemed to come from far away.

"Grenade mitigated," the marine shouted. "But we could use some backup here."

The prime minister had a bright line of red across the backs of his hands, blood soaking into the white of his cuffs and floating in tiny dots through the air of the hallway. Alex felt the wall shudder under his hand as something on the ship detonated too far away to hear. Someone at the head of the corridor was laughing and whooping something in Belter chatter too fast to follow. Alex ducked his head out and back again, trying to get a glimpse of the corridor ahead. A crackle of gunfire drove him back into his shallow cover.

The laughter ahead of them turned to screams, the sharp, flat reports of gunfire into something deeper and more threatening. The marines opened fire, and the corridor rose to pandemonium. A body cartwheeled by, limp and dead, its uniform sopping up blood from a dozen wounds. Alex couldn't tell which side the fighter had belonged to.

The gunfire stopped. Alex waited a long moment, ducked his head out and back again. Then leaned out for a longer look. The intersection where the enemy had been was misty with smoke and blood and the anti-grenade countermeasure. Two bodies floated in the middle space, one dead in light combat armor, the other in full marine recon gear. The power-armored figure lifted its hand in the sign for all clear.

"We cleaned that up for you," Bobbie called, her voice seeming to come from miles away and with all the treble stripped out. "You can come on up. Might want to hold your breath through here, though. There's some particulates."

Alex pulled himself forward, the prime minister following close behind. They passed Bobbie and four new marines that swelled their escort to six. He hadn't seen Bobbie in armor since the fight on Io. With the other marines around her, the massive armor adding to her normal bulk, she seemed at home. And more than that, she seemed wistful, knowing that it was an illusion.

"Looks good on you, Draper," Alex called as he passed. Half-deafened by the firefight, he only felt the words in his throat. Bobbie's smile told him that she'd heard them.

In the hangar, the *Razorback* hung in clamps built to accommodate ships much larger than she was. It was like seeing an industrial lathe with a toothpick in it. The flight crew hung on to handholds around it, gesturing Alex and Bobbie and the prime minister on. By the time Alex got to the ship, the massive hangar doors were already starting their opening cycle. The flight chief was pushing a vacuum suit at him and shouting so he could hear her.

"We're coordinating with fire control. The PDCs'll try to get you a clear run, but be careful. You run into our own rounds, and that'd just be sad."

"Understood," Alex said.

She gestured toward the hangar doors with her chin. "We're not taking the time to evacuate the bay completely, but we'll get you down to maybe half an atmosphere. Little bit of a pop, but you shouldn't spring a leak."

"And if I do?"

She held out the environment suit again. "You'll have some bottled air to suck on while you figure something out."

"Well, not a great plan, but it's a plan."

"Imperfect circumstances," the flight chief agreed.

Alex shrugged the suit on as the prime minister, already wearing his, slipped into the pinnace and toward the back bunk. The *Razorback* was a yacht. A hot rod, made for zipping around outside an atmosphere, the philosophical descendant of ships that didn't lose sight of the shore. And more than that, she was old. The girl who'd first flown her had been dead or something stranger for years, and the ship had been old before she went. Now they were going to fly it through an active battle zone.

He checked the last of the seals on his suit, and started for the *Razorback*. Bobbie was in the entry, looking in. When she spoke, it was through the suit radio.

"We've got a little problem, Alex."

He squeezed in beside her. Even before she'd been in combat armor, Bobbie had made the interior of the ship seem a little undersized. Looking from her to the second couch now, she made it look ridiculous. There was no way she was going to fit.

"I'll have them stop the launch sequence," Alex said. "We can get you in a normal EVA suit."

"There are boarders on the ship. Looking for us. For him," Bobbie said. "There isn't time." She turned to look at him. On the other side of the helmet, her expression was rueful. "I'm only seeing one option here."

"No," Alex said. "You're not staying. I don't give a shit. I'm not leaving you behind."

Bobbie shifted, her eyes wide. "What? No, I meant take out the couch and use the suit motors to brace me. Did you think I was—"

"That. Do that. Now," Alex said.

Bobbie leaned forward, the magnetic boots locking onto the deck of the *Razorback*, and one hand clamped against the frame. With the other, she gripped the base of the crash couch and lifted. The bolts sheared off like she was tearing paper, and she tossed the couch out into the hangar. The gimbals shifted and turned under the spin. Bobbie scuttled in, pressing hands and feet against the walls and deck and pushing until the suit was wedged in as solidly as if it had been part of the superstructure.

"Okay," she said. "I'm good."

Alex turned back to the flight chief. The woman saluted him, and with his heart in his throat he returned it. The marines who'd escorted them—who'd risked their lives to get them this far—had already gone. Alex wished he'd thought to thank them.

"I'll get to my station, and then we'll get you out," the flight chief said. "You be careful out there."

"Thank you," Alex said. He pulled himself into the ship, closed the hatch, and started running through the checklist. The reactor was hot, the Epstein drive showing green across the board. Air and water were at capacity, and the recyclers ready. "You in place back there, sir?"

"Ready as I'm likely to get," the man replied.

"You hang on tight," Alex said to Bobbie. "This might get rough, and you're not in a crash couch."

"Yeah I am," she said, and he could hear the mischievous grin in her voice. "I'm wearing mine."

"Well," Alex said softly. "Okay, then."

The clamp lights went from engaged to warning to open, and the *Razorback* was on the float. Emergency Klaxons sounded, the noise softened by the thinned atmosphere, and the massive hangar door began to open. The change in exterior pressure rang the pinnace like a hammer blow. Alex aimed for the widening gap full of darkness and stars, and hit it. The *Razorback* leaped out into the vacuum, eager and hungry. The display marked a dozen ships too small for his naked eye to see, and the long, curving shapes of PDC fire like tentacles waving through the void.

"Taking control of the comm laser," Bobbie said.

"Roger that," he said. "This is going to get bumpy."

He threw the *Razorback* out the hangar doors at full speed and into the narrow lane between the battleship's PDCs firing on full auto. He spun the pinnace between the lines of high-velocity tungsten, hoping they were enough to stop any missiles the ambushing ships fired at them from point-blank range. And then, from behind them, fast-moving bogies in wave after wave. The *Razorback*'s display turned into a solid mass, the density of the missile swarm too much for the screen to differentiate between them. The entire arsenal of the battleship launched all at once, and keyed to target on the pinnace's comm laser frequency.

"We've got our escort," Alex said. "Let's get out of here. How many gs can you take back there, Draper?"

"If I break a rib, I'll let you know."

Alex grinned, spun the pinnace toward the sun, and accelerated—two g, three, four, four and a half—until the system started complaining that it couldn't inject him with anything through the EVA suit. He hit the suit's crude helmet controls with his chin and injected himself with all the amphetamine it had in its tiny emergency pack. The enemy ships seemed unsure what had just happened, but then they began to turn, thin red triangles on the display. Exhaust plumes competed with the stars behind him as he fell toward the sun, toward Earth and Luna and the rattled remnants of the UN fleet. Alex felt a bloom of joy welling up in his chest, like shrugging off a weight.

"You can't take the *Razorback*," he said to the tiny red triangles. "We are gone and gone and gone." He switched the radio to general. "How's everyone doing back there?"

"Fine," the prime minister gasped. "But will we be accelerating like this for much longer?"

"Bit longer, yes, sir," Alex said. "Once we get some breathing room, I'll cut us back to just a g."

"Breathing room," the prime minister said, the words labored. "That's funny."

"Five by five here, Alex," Bobbie said. "Is it safe to pop my helmet? I'd rather not run through all my bottled air when there's fresh in the ship."

"Yeah, that's fine. Same back there, Mister Prime Minister."

"Please. Call me Nathan."

"You got it, Nate," Alex said. The sun was a sphere of white. He pulled up the nav computer and started plotting in paths to Luna. The fastest would take them inside the orbit of Mercury, but the pinnace wasn't rated for more than half an AU from the coronal surface. So that was going to be a little tricky. And Venus wasn't anyplace that he could gracefully use to slingshot. But if Avasarala was sending out an escort to meet them, she might be able to get a boost off the planet. So heading that direction might make sense.

"Alex?" Bobbie said.

"I'm here."

"That thing about not leaving me behind? You really meant that, didn't you?"

"Of course I did."

"Thank you."

He felt a blush rising even against the pressure of the burn.

"Welcome," he said. "I figure you're crew now, right? We look out for each other."

"No soldier left behind," she said. It might have been the gs, but something about her tone made it sound like she meant something deeper by the words. Like she'd made a promise. She grunted. "Alex, we've got fast-movers coming in. I think the bad guys are throwing missiles at us."

"You ready to disappoint them, Gunny?"

"Oh hell yes," Bobbie said. "How many bullets have we got in this magazine?"

Alex switched the display. The cloud of escort missiles resolved into a numbered list, all in white with identifying serial numbers beside each of them. Even the list filled the screen. He switched to a field summary. "A little shy of ninety."

"That should get us where we're going. Looks like pretty near all their ships are burning hard for us too. How would you feel about taking a few potshots at them by way of discouragement?"

"It'll keep them at a distance, anyway. I figure their PDCs'll probably take them down before they can do any real damage, but apart from that I'm not opposed," Alex said. "Except...hold on." On his list, he switched to the enemy flotilla. It took him a few seconds to find what he was looking for. He marked the *Pella*. "Not that one. We don't shoot that one."

"Understood," Bobbie said.

No soldier left behind, Alex thought. *That goes for you too, Naomi. I don't know what the hell's going on out there, and I don't see how this plays out yet. But I'll be damned if I'm just leaving you behind.*

Chapter Thirty-Five: Naomi

Back before, when she had been a girl and not known any better, it had been hard for her to cast Marco as the bad guy in their pairing. Even after the *Gamarra*, it had been difficult. Even after he'd taken Filip away. She'd grown up around poverty. She knew what bad men looked like. They raped their wives. Or beat them. Or their children. That was how you knew them for what they were. Marco was never that. He never hit her, never forced himself on her, never threatened to shoot her or throw her out an airlock or pour acid in her eyes. He'd pretended kindness so well she would doubt herself, make herself wonder if she was the one being unreasonable, irrational, all the things he implied she was.

He never did anything that would have made it easy for her.

After she'd reached her quarters, the door had locked. She hadn't bothered trying to raise help or leave her little room since. She knew a cell when she was in it, and she'd known with a certainty like her own mortality that sooner or later, Marco would come.

He sat across from her now, still in his Martian military uniform. His eyes were soft, his lips pressed into a smile of amusement and regret. He looked like a poet. A man well bruised by the world, but still capable of passion. She wondered if he practiced the expression in a mirror. Probably, he did.

The wound on her head had stopped bleeding. Her joints all ached, and a vast bruise was blooming on her left hip. Even her fingertips felt like she'd scraped the first layers of skin off them, leaving them weeping and raw, though actually they just looked a little pinker than usual. She drank the same version of chamomile tea that the *Rocinante* made, and it felt like having a secret ally. She recognized that wasn't a perfectly sane thought, but comfort was comfort.

The mess was empty, the screens turned off and the crew sent away. Even Cyn and Karal were absent. The implication was that whatever they said there was private, but it probably wasn't. She could imagine Filip on another deck, watching. It felt like a setup. Everything about Marco felt like a setup. Because everything was.

"I don't know why you do these things to me, Naomi," Marco said. There was no anger in his voice. No, that wasn't true. The anger was there, but hidden behind the mask of disappointment. "You used to be better than this."

"I'm sorry. Did I upset your plans?"

"Well, yes," Marco said. "That's the thing. Used to be, you knew better. Used to be you at least tried to understand what was going on before you jumped in. Professional. This, though? Took a difficult thing and made it worse. Now what could have been gentle is going to be hard. I just want you to understand why I'm going to do what I'm going to do so you see I didn't have a choice."

There was a smart thing to do. She knew it. A wiser woman would have cried, begged forgiveness. That it would be insincere was the point. It was a mistake to give Marco anything real. Better to be thought weak. Better to be underestimated and misunderstood. She knew that, but she couldn't do it. When she tried, something deep within her pushed back. Maybe if she pretended to be weak, it was too possible that it would become true. Maybe she was pretending to be strong.

Naomi spat on the deck. There was a little blood along with her saliva. "Save the air."

He leaned forward, taking her hand in his. His grip was strong, like he was showing that he could hurt her, even if he wasn't doing it right now. She thought, *Well, that's one way to make your subtext physical*, and then chuckled.

"Naomi, I know we aren't good, du y mé. I know you're angry. But I know we were something once. We're one body, you and me. Much as we try to be apart, our son means we will never be totally separate."

She tried to pull her hand back, but he kept hold of it. She could pull harder or let him touch her, control her body even if it was only that much. The glimmer in his eyes was pleasure. His smile was a little more genuine, and it had an edge.

"You've got to understand what I'm doing here, it's not for me. It's for us."

"Us?"

"Belters. All Belters. It's for Filip. So when his turn comes, there's still a place for him. Not just a footnote. Once upon a time there were a people who lived on moons and asteroids and the planets where life didn't evolve. But then we found the gates, and those people died out because we didn't need them. It's why I have to do this. You don't like my methods. I understand that. But they're mine, and the cause is righteous."

Naomi didn't speak. The food processor let out a high whine that meant its water supply was getting low. She wondered if Marco knew that, or if it was just another meaningless noise for him.

"Pretty speech. But it doesn't explain why I'm here. You didn't need me here in order to break the system. Needed me for something else. You want to know what I think?"

"You told me," Marco said, his grip on her hand tightening just a degree. "So the great James Holden wouldn't come blow my house down. Seriously, you think too much of him. He's not that impressive."

"No, it's worse than that. I think you wanted the *Roci.* I think you wanted my ship flying at your side when you did all this. But when I didn't bring her, you fell back. Had Sakai rig her to blow. Because there is nothing original about you at all."

His smile was as warm, but his eyes were cold now. Unamused. "Don't follow," he said.

"You start the conversation with *Why do you make me hurt you when I love you so much?* and now we're at *If I can't have you, no one can.* You can pretend we're talking about the ship if you want. Doesn't matter to me."

Marco let her go and stood. He wasn't as tall as she remembered him. "You got it wrong from the start. I wanted Fred Johnson—Butcher of Anderson Station, who killed people like you and me and Filip just because we were Belters. I wanted him isolated. Keep your ship out of his hands. Tried to get it brought, but no. Had Sakai try to disable her. *Disable*, sa sa? Had it rigged to blow at three percent power. Blown off her aft, maybe didn't even hurt anyone."

"I don't believe you," she said, but he was on a roll now, pacing the length of the mess, his arms spread wide like a man giving a speech to an invisible crowd.

"Killing the ship wasn't my plan. That's what *you* pushed me into. What happens to Holden is your fault, not mine. That's what you need to see. How things get worse when you start acting like you know. You don't know, Naomi. You don't know because I haven't told you."

She took a sip of her tea and shrugged. "So tell me."

Marco grinned. "You notice when we cut thrust for a few minutes? Strange thing to do in the middle of a chase, don't you think?"

The truth was, she hadn't noticed. In her bunk, nursing her wounds, the shifts in ship gravity hadn't been on her mind.

"Docking procedure," he said and pulled his hand terminal from his pocket and chose something. The speakers on the screens clicked, hissed. No image appeared on them, but a voice came.

Her voice.

"This is Naomi Nagata of the *Rocinante*. If you get this message, please retransmit. Tell James Holden I am in distress. Comm is not responding. I have no nav control. Please retransmit."

Marco touched something else on his hand terminal, and the screens sprang to life. Exterior cameras, probably connected to the point defense. The *Chetzemoka* burned not more than a hundred meters away, a docking tube clinging to her airlock like an umbilical cord. A ship that, if they dug hard enough, would trace back to her. The payments that had come from her accounts.

"Put it on intersecting course, more or less," Marco said, his voice weary and sorrowful in a way she was certain hid glee. "Set the bottle to fail when the proximity sensors ping a ship. Didn't have to be this way, but it does now."

A real despair rose up in her throat, and she pushed it back down. It was what Marco wanted, so she would do *anything*, feel *anything* except that. She considered the screen. The ship looking like a box held together with one line of solder and some epoxy.

"You're stealing it from your own son," she said. Marco frowned. Naomi pointed toward the screen with her chin. "The *Chetzemoka*. I told Filip he could have it when we were here. That's his ship. You're stealing it from him."

"Necessity of war," Marco said.

"Shitty parenting."

His jaw slid forward. His hands balled in fists. For a moment, she thought he was going to make it easy. He'd show whatever audience he was playing for who and what he really was. He got his temper back in time, and she wasn't sure if she was relieved or disappointed.

"If you'd stayed in your place, James Holden would have lived. But you stepped out. Put yourself where you didn't belong. Because of you, he's going to die."

Naomi stood up, rubbed her eye with the back of her hand. Her false voice repeated through the mess hall—"Tell James Holden I am in distress..."

"Anything else?"

"You pretend you don't care," Marco said. "But you do."

"You say so." She shrugged. "I got a little bump. It's giving me a headache. Or something is. Going to med bay get it fixed, yeah?"

"You can pretend—"

"Can I pretend in the med bay? Or do you need to go on impressing me?" It was too much. She felt a flood of words hammering up behind all she'd said. *You are an egomaniac and a sadist* and *I can't believe I ever thought I loved you* and *If Jim dies, I will by God find a way to make the bottle on this ship fail and we'll all go to hell behind him.* But engaging was also a trap, so she didn't. She let the silence break the rhythm of Marco's performance and saw his shoulders shift when he gave up and stepped off the stage in his head.

"Miral!" he yelled, and as the sounds of one of the crew moving from the quarters grew louder, "You abused the freedom I gave you. You can't expect to keep it."

"Too dangerous to leave free?" she asked, then licked her fingertip and ticked off a mark on an imaginary board. "One point for me, then."

In the med bay, a woman she didn't know ran tests to make sure Naomi wasn't bleeding in her brain; that none of the bruises she had were crush wounds bad enough to kill the muscle, flood her body with potassium, stop her heart. Miral leaned against the supply cabinet, reciting obscenities—bitch, puta, cunt—with a half-focused rage. After spending all those days running inventory, Naomi knew everything in the cabinet. First drawer: gauze and bandages. Second drawer: one-use blood cards for maybe a hundred different field tests. Third drawer: emergency medical supplies like decompression kits, adrenaline shots, defibrillating tape. Naomi stared at Miral as he recited his litany. He glanced away, and then returned the stare, enunciating each word a little more sharply.

The medic had her sit up, the cushion of the medical table crackling under her shifting weight. The analgesic was a spray that went in Naomi's mouth. It tasted like fake cherry and mold.

"Maybe take it easy for a couple days, yeah?" the medic said.

"Best I can," Naomi agreed, hopping down from the bed. She straight-kicked Miral in the crotch, sending him sprawling into the cabinet and cracking two of her toes. She ignored the stab of pain in her foot and launched herself onto him, pounding at his head and neck. When he rolled, she rolled with him. The cabinet doors were open, spilling test cards and preloaded hypodermics across the floor. Miral's elbow swung up, glancing off her jaw but still hard enough to make her ears ring.

She fell to the side, her belly to the deck, decompression kits the size of her thumb pressing into her face as Miral writhed around to kneel on her back. The medic was screaming. Naomi tried to turn, tried to evade the punches, but she couldn't. The pain bloomed between her shoulder blades. And then, like time skipping, the weight was off her. She rolled to her side. Karal had Miral in a submission hold. He struggled and cursed, but the old Belter's eyes were flat and dead.

"Be angry con sus séra that she got you unexpected," Karal said. "Marco pas beat her down, you sure as fuck don't, sabe pendejo?"

"Sa sa," Miral said, and Karal let him go. The medic, standing in the corner, was a picture of silent rage. Miral rubbed his neck and glared at Naomi where she still lay on the deck. Karal walked over to look down at her.

"Bist bien, Knuckles?"

She nodded, and when Karal put out his hand, she took it and let him help her up. When she started for the door, Miral began to follow. Karal put a hand on the man's chest. "I got this, me."

Naomi hung her head as they walked, her hair falling over her face like a veil. The steady pressure of acceleration left her knees and spine aching even more than her wounds. All through the ship, malefic faces turned to her. She could feel the hatred coming off them like heat from a fire. When she passed through the mess, the *Chetzemoka* was still on the screen, the docking umbilical linking them. They'd need to cut thrust when they unhooked it, or it would fall to the side, trailing along the ship like a limp tentacle. That would be how she knew she was too late. It hadn't happened yet.

At her quarters, Karal came in behind her and closed the door. With two of them in the tiny space, it felt cramped and uncomfortably intimate. She sat on the crash couch, arms crossed, her legs tucked under her, and looked at him, her expression carrying the question. Karal shook his head.

"You got to stop this, Knuckles," he said, and his voice was surprisingly gentle. "We're in king shit here. Esá la we're doing? History, yeah? Changing everything, but for us this time. I know you and him ain't right, but tu muss listen him. Yeah?"

Naomi looked away. She just wanted him to leave, but Karal didn't go. He sank down, his back against the wall, his knees to his broad chest.

"I heard the plan where we gehst con du? Bring you in? Fought it, me. Mal cóncep, I said. Why cut open the scar? Marco said was worth it. Said you were going to be in danger when it all came, and Filip, he deserved to see his mother, yeah? And Marco's Marco, so si."

Karal rubbed his palms over his head. It made a soft hissing sound, almost too faint to hear. Naomi felt an inexplicable urge to touch him, to offer some comfort, but she didn't. When he spoke again, he sounded tired.

"We're little people in big times, yeah? Time for Butchers and Marco—men and history-book things. Other pinché worlds. Who wants that? Just you let this pass, yeah? Maybe your Holden, he doesn't take the bait. Maybe something else trips before he gets here. Maybe you get small and you live through this. That so bad? Doing what needs to live through?"

She shrugged. For a time, the only sound was the clicking of the air recycler. Karal lifted himself up with a grunt. He looked older than she thought of him. It was more than just the years, she thought. For a moment, she was young again, back on Ceres with Filip bawling in his crib while she watched the news of the *Augustín Gamarra*. It occurred to her for the first time that everyone on that ship had watched Earth die in real time the way she'd seen the firefly light of the *Gamarra* rise and fade on the newsfeed, looped a dozen times while the reporter spoke over it. She wanted to say something, but she couldn't, so she just watched as Karal opened the door then closed it behind him. The lock slid closed. She wiped the wet from her eyes, and—once she was sure he wasn't coming back—spat the decompression kit into her hand.

Wet with her saliva and no bigger than her thumb, it was the sort of thing any mech driver kept with her. A tiny ampoule of injectable oxygenated artificial blood, and a panic button that would make an emergency medical request for an airlock to cycle. Military ships like the *Pella* and *Roci* ignored that sort of request as basic security. The *Canterbury* and other commercial ships usually allowed it, filled as they were with civilians who posed a greater threat to themselves than pirates or boarders did. She didn't know how the *Chetzemoka* would respond to it, but there was only one way to find out. The only other things she needed were an EVA suit and a clear idea of when the ships would cut thrust.

Then it was a matter of taking control of the ship, maybe blowing the core, and getting the hell away from Marco. Again. She felt a pang of regret at the thought of Filip—and Cyn and Karal and all the people she'd known once and cared for. Even loved. It was an echo of greater pain, and she could ignore it.

"Didn't break me when I was a girl," she said to the tiny black kit. "Don't know why he thinks he can break me now."

Chapter Thirty-Six: Holden

Holden wanted badly to sleep, but sleep wouldn't come. The most he'd been able to manage was a few hours' unconsciousness that left him groggy and ragged. He'd been given the option of moving back into quarters on the station, but he'd refused. Even though he slept better with gravity holding him to the mattress, he didn't want to leave the ship. He wasn't sure how long it had been since he'd shaved, but the patchwork of stubble on his cheeks and neck itched a little. During the work shifts, it wasn't so bad. The new crew checked the systems they'd all checked before, looking for sabotage they hadn't seen last time, and it gave him something to do. People to talk to. When they left, he ate in the galley, tried to sleep for a while, then wandered through the ship like he was looking for something but couldn't remember what it was.

And then, inevitably and against his better judgment, he checked the newsfeeds.

"With the silence from Medina Station, all contact with the colonial planets has been lost. We can only speculate on the significance of the partial report from the Fólkvangr settlement concerning alien activity in the southern hemisphere of New Triton—"

"A spokesman for the port authority said that Ganymede's neutrality was a reflection of its universal importance and not a political statement—"

"UN forces are en route, but it is not clear whether Prime Minister Smith is actually aboard the racing ship or if this is a distraction to pull the enemy's attention away from a more traditional evacuation. Regardless, acting secretary-general Avasarala has announced a security zone covering the flight path of the pinnace, and all ships in the area have been advised to move beyond weapon range until such time as—"

Light speed, he decided, was a curse. It made even the farthest corners of humanity's reach feel close, and the illusion was a kind of poison. The delay between Tycho Station and Earth was a little less than a quarter of an hour, but to travel that far would take days. If Alex or Naomi died, he could know within minutes that they were gone. He floated in his restraints, the cabin lights turned off, and flipped through the feeds, jumping back and forth in case anything had happened, knowing that if it had, there was nothing he could do. He felt like he was standing on a frozen lake, looking down through the ice while the people he cared about most drowned.

If he couldn't know, if everything that was happening could happen someplace he couldn't watch, then maybe he could look away. Maybe he could close his eyes and dream about them, at least. When a connection request came on his hand terminal, he was glad to get it.

"Paula," Holden said.

"Holden," the hacker replied. "Wasn't sure what schedule you're on. I was afraid I was calling in your sleep shift."

"No," Holden said. He didn't know why he felt defensive about being awake, but he did. "It's fine. I'm fine. What have you got?"

She grinned. "I have a smoking gun. I can transmit a report to you—"

"No. I mean, yes. Do that. But am I going to understand what I'm seeing?"

On the screen, she stretched, grinning. "I was about to head out to dinner. Meet me at La Fromagerie and I'll walk you through the whole thing."

Holden pulled up the station directory. It wasn't far. If Naomi died right now, the news would reach him just about when he got there. Maybe before. He pressed his palm against his sandpaper-dry eyes. "Sounds like a plan," he said.

"Meal's on you."

"You've got me over a barrel, yeah, yeah. Be right over."

The restaurant was small, with what appeared to be real wooden tables but were certainly pressed bamboo from station hydroponics; no one charging even vaguely reasonable prices for the meals would have been able to afford something from an actual tree. Paula was at a table against the wall. The bench she sat on looked normal for her. When he sat across from her, his feet didn't quite touch the deck.

"Boss," Paula said. "I already ordered."

"I'm not hungry. What have you got?"

"Take a look," she said, passing her hand terminal over to him. The screen was filled with a structured scatter of code, structures nested inside structures with repeated sections showing variations so subtle as to approach invisibility. It was like seeing a poem written in an alphabet he didn't know.

"What am I looking at?"

"These two lines," she said. "This sends the stop code to the bottle. These are the conditional statements that call it. For you, if you'd gotten to ninety-five percent, you'd have been a star. If you'd been in dock, which you probably would have, it would have taken a fair bite out of the station too."

"And the new software? The one that the ship's running now?"

"Not in it," Paula said. "This is where you get to be impressed with me finding two lines of uncommented code in a fusion reactor's magnetic bottle driver."

"Very impressive," Holden said, dutifully.

"Thank you, but that's not the cool part. Take a look at the trigger line. You see all those calls set to null? They're all other system parameters that weren't being used."

"Okay," Holden said. From the brightness in her expression, he had the sense he should have seen something more in her words. Maybe if he'd been able to sleep...

"This is an all-purpose trap. You want something to blow when they've been out of port for six days? Set that call there to about half a million seconds. You want it to go when the weapons systems are armed? This call right here set to one. There's maybe a dozen different ways to set this thing off, and you can mix and match them."

"That's interesting—"

"That's a smoking fucking gun," Paula said. "Bottle containment failures don't leave much by way of data. Not supposed to happen ever, but sometimes they do. The story has always been that accidents happen, what can you do? Ships blow up sometimes. This shows that someone built a tool specifically to make it happen. And to make it happen again and again and again, wherever they could sneak their code into the ship they decided had to die. What we have here is key evidence in maybe thousands of murders no one even knew *were* murders until right now."

Excitement tightened her voice, brightened her eyes. The unease in his gut grew thicker.

I need to go do something, Naomi said in his memory. *And I can't have you involved in it. At all.*

Was this it? Was this what she'd been trying to keep separate from him, from the *Rocinante*? And what did it mean if it was?

Paula was still looking at him, expectation in her eye. He didn't know how to respond, but the silence was getting awkward.

"Cool?" he said.

Fred was sitting at Drummer's desk, his elbows resting on the tabletop, his hands cradling his chin. He looked as tired as Holden felt. On the screen, Drummer and Sakai were in one of the interrogation rooms. The table that was usually between them had been moved askew, and Drummer was leaning back in her chair and resting her feet on it. Prisoner and guard were both drinking what looked like coffee. Sakai laughed at something and shook his head. Drummer grinned impishly. She looked younger. Holden realized with a start that she was wearing her hair down.

"What the hell is this?" he asked.

"Professionalism," Fred said. "Building rapport. Establishing trust. She's halfway convinced him that whoever he was working for was willing to crack the station open with him still inside it. Once he's come around, we'll own him. That man will tell us everything we ask and then try to remember something we didn't think to dig for if we give him time. No one's as zealous as a convert."

Holden crossed his arms. "I think you're overlooking the beat-him-with-a-wrench stratagem. I favor it."

"No you don't."

"In this case, I'd make an exception."

"No. You wouldn't. Torture's for amateurs."

"So? I don't do this professionally."

Fred sighed and turned to look up at him. "The reckless tough-guy version of you is almost as tiring as the relentless Boy Scout was. I'm hoping your pendulum swings hit middle sometime soon."

"Reckless?"

Fred shrugged. "Did you find anything?"

"Yeah," Holden said, "but it's not in the fresh driver. We have a clean bill of health."

"Unless there's something else."

"Yup."

"Sakai says there wasn't."

"Not entirely sure I know how to respond to that," Holden said. Then, a moment later, "So, I've been thinking."

"About the message from the *Pella*?"

"Yeah."

Fred stood up. His expression was hard, but not without compassion. "I was expecting this fight, Holden. But there's more at stake here than Naomi. If the protomolecule is being weaponized, or even just set loose again—"

"That doesn't matter," Holden said. "Wait, no. That came out wrong. Of course that matters. It matters a lot. It just doesn't change anything. We can't..." He paused, swallowed. "We can't go after her. I've got one ship, they've got half a dozen. Everything in me wants to fire up the engines and burn like hell after her, but it won't help."

Fred was silent. The distant sound of Sakai's laughter filtered through from the screen. They both ignored it. Holden looked at his hands. He felt like he was confessing something. Maybe he was.

"Whatever's going on here?" Holden said. "Whatever she's involved with, I can't fix it by putting on my shining armor and riding into battle. The only way I can see to do her any good at all is to do what we had planned. Get you to Luna. If you can use Dawes and Sakai and Avasarala to open some kind of communication with these sons of bitches, Naomi can be a bargaining chip. We can trade her for some of the people you've got in the brig. Or Sakai. Or something."

"That's the conclusion you've reached?"

"It is," Holden said, the words tasting like ashes.

"You've grown up some since the first time we met," Fred said. Holden heard the sympathy in it. The consolation. "It's making me regret my 'reckless' comment."

"I'm not convinced that's a good thing. Have you ever done

this? Loved someone like they were part of you and then left them in danger?"

Fred put a hand on Holden's shoulder. For all the frailty that age and trouble had put in the older man's face and body, his grip was still firm. "Son, I've grieved for more people than you've met. You can't trust your heart on this. You have to do what you know, not what you feel."

"Because if I do what I feel..." Holden said, thinking that the end of the sentence was something like *I'd beat Sakai's teeth in* or *I'd get us all killed*. Fred surprised him.

"Then we lose her."

"Course set," Chava Lombaugh said from the cockpit. "On your order, sir."

Holden tried to lean back into his crash couch, but without thrust gravity to give him weight, it ended up as just a straightening of the neck. His heart was racing, adrenaline ticking coolly through his veins.

It wasn't supposed to be like this. The command deck felt too full. Sun-yi, serious and relaxed, was at weapons. Maura had comm controls up, monitoring them because that was what she did more than from any actual need. It should have been Alex's voice. It should have been him and Naomi in the couches.

He shouldn't have been scared.

"All right," he said. "Let's do this."

"Sir," Chava said. The warning light went from amber to red and Holden fell back into his couch. Tycho Station fell away behind them. It wouldn't be an hour before it was too small to make out without assistance. Holden waited for three long, shuddering breaths. Four.

"How are we looking, Mister Ip?"

From the engineering deck, Sandra Ip—who should have been Amos—said, "All systems are within tolerance."

"Meaning not all blowed up," Holden said.

There was a pause on the channel. "Yes, sir. Not all blowed up, sir."

Holden hated it that he wasn't sure of his own ship. The *Rocinante* had been nothing but solid for him since the day he'd gotten aboard her. He'd trusted the ship with his life the way he trusted his heart to beat. It was more than instinct. It was automatic. To do anything else would have been strange.

But that was before. Sakai's sabotage hadn't killed him, but it hadn't left him unscathed either. It would be a long time before Holden was sure that there were no more unpleasant surprises hidden in the ship. Software waiting for the right moment to evacuate the air or throw the ship into a fatal acceleration or any of the other thousand ways a ship could fail and kill its crew. They had looked everything over and found nothing, but they'd done that before and nearly died from their oversights. There was no amount of double-checking that would ever prove that nothing had been missed. From now on—maybe for a long time, maybe forever—he would wonder about things he hadn't before. He was resentful, even angry, that his faith had been shaken.

He wondered if he was still thinking about the *Rocinante*.

"All right," he said, unstrapping. "I'm going to get some coffee. You folks try not to break anything, and if you do, let me know."

The chorus of *yessirs* was oddly disheartening. He wished they'd known he was joking. Or felt comfortable enough to joke back. Their formality was just another way it didn't feel like his ship anymore.

He found Fred in the galley, talking into his hand terminal, recording a message that was clearly meant for Anderson Dawes. Holden got his coffee quietly between phrases like *lines of communication* and *profound lack of trust*. When Fred finished, he folded his hands and looked over.

"I'd take one of those too. Cream, no sugar."

"Coming up," Holden said. "Anything new?"

"Two of the original Martian escort surrendered."

"Seriously?"

"They were too far from the action to affect the outcome, and they were getting hammered. I don't like it, but I won't second-guess their command."

"Is it just my imagination, or are these people handing us our asses on a plate?" Holden said, bringing the coffee mugs to the table. "Are they really this good, or do we all just suck a lot worse than I thought we did?"

Fred sipped the coffee. "Ever heard of the Battle of Gaugamela?"

"No," Holden said.

"Darius the third, emperor of Persia, had two hundred thousand soldiers under his command. Bactrians, Arachosians, Scythians. Some Greek mercenaries. On the other side, thirty-five thousand soldiers, and Alexander of Macedon. Alexander the Great. Five Persians to every Macedonian. It should have been a slaughter. But Alexander pulled so much of the enemy out to the flank that a gap opened in the middle of the Persian lines. Alexander called his men to form a wedge, and leading with his own cavalry, he pushed through and headed straight for the emperor. There were vast forces to either side, surrounding him. But it didn't matter, because he saw how to reach Darius. Alexander saw something no one else had seen.

"These people? This little faction of the OPA? Between Earth and Mars and me, we outnumber them. We outgun them. All this has happened because someone saw an opportunity that no one else did. They had the audacity to strike where no one else would even have considered an attack. That's the power of audacity, and if a general is lucky and strong-minded, they can take that advantage and keep the enemy on their back foot forever."

"You think that's their plan?"

"It would be mine," Fred said. "This isn't someone making a play to control the Belt or the Jovian moons. This is someone trying to grab all of it. Everything. It takes a certain kind of mind to succeed in something like that. Charisma, brilliance, discipline. It takes an Alexander."

"That sounds a little discouraging," Holden said.

Fred held up the coffee cup. The name TACHI hadn't quite worn off the side, red and black letters half-erased by use. But not gone. Not yet. "I understand better now how Darius felt," Fred said. "Having power, position, advantage. Especially when you think you know how wars work. It blinds you to other things. And by the time you see them, there's a Macedonian cavalry with spears set coming right at you. But that wasn't how Darius lost."

"It's not? Because the story you just told me sounded a lot like that's how he lost."

"No. He ran."

Holden drank. From the crew quarters, the murmur of unfamiliar voices was a reminder that things were wrong. That the patterns of the past were broken, and might never be put right. "He was going to get killed if he didn't, though. Alexander would have killed him."

"Maybe. Or maybe Darius would have withstood the charge. Or maybe he would have fallen and his army would have crushed Alexander's in rage and grief. The end of an emperor isn't always the end of an empire. I look at Earth and what happened there. I look at Mars. At what happened on Tycho, and what I'm afraid happened on Medina. I'm seeing Alexander's wedge bursting through the line at me. The same shock as Darius, the same dismay. The fear. But I'm not Darius. And I think Chrisjen Avasarala isn't either."

"So you don't think we're screwed?"

Fred smiled. "I don't know what to think yet. I won't until I know more about the enemy. But looking back through history, there are a lot more men who thought they were Alexander the Great than men who actually were."

Chapter Thirty-Seven: Alex

They burned across the emptiness, and the enemy came hard behind them. Four Martian military ships with target locks on Alex's drive burned toward him as they all dropped toward the sun. The other two had stayed behind to continue the attack on the main force. More than half the attackers had peeled off to come for him. Alex hoped it was enough to let Captain Choudhary get a toehold. Nothing he could do about that from here, though, but watch and hope.

For the first few hours, it had all been hard burn and dodging. Once he'd opened up some distance between the *Razorback* and the attackers, the nature of the chase altered. It wasn't about catching or being caught anymore. Alex had the lead, had seventy-two missiles left flying around him in a cloud, a path to Luna, and reinforcements burning out to join him. If nothing went wrong, he'd be safe in less than two days.

The enemy's job now was to make something go wrong.

"You've got another couple PDC arcs coming in," Bobbie said.

"That's cute," Alex said. "I'm moving to avoid. You want to let the missiles know?"

"Already done."

The tungsten slugs of the enemy point defense cannons were meant to chew through missiles at close range. At the distances they were holding now, they were something between an invitation for the crew of the *Razorback* to blunder into them by mistake and an uplifted middle finger. Alex tracked the incoming fire and braced as the maneuvering thrusters pushed them down and to the left to avoid the gently curving arcs of enemy fire, then up and right to correct to the original course. Around him the cloud of missiles parted to let the slugs pass through their flock of exhaust cones and warheads.

"Any enemy missiles following that up?" he asked.

A moment later Bobbie said, "Nope."

"Keep an eye out. Our friends there are gettin' antsy."

"Happens when you're losing," Bobbie said. Even without turning, Alex could hear the smile in her voice.

From the cabin in the back, Smith's voice came in staccato gasps. Even the relatively modest one-g flight was three times what the man was used to. He'd been burning up the tightbeam for hours. Sometimes, Alex caught Chrisjen Avasarala's recorded voice, other times a man's warm drawl. Someone on Mars, he figured.

The *Razorback* had been a toy once, and while the screens were decades out of date, they still had some bells and whistles. He set the wall screens to match external cameras, and the wide starscape bloomed around them. The sun was bigger and brighter here than it would have been on Earth, but constrained by the limits of the screen to a burning whiteness. The curves of the Milky Way glowed all along the plane of the ecliptic, the billions of stars made soft by distance. Being surrounded by missiles was like floating in a cloud of fireflies, and behind them, bright as seven Venuses in an Earth twilight, the drive plumes of the attackers who wanted them dead.

And also Naomi.

Bobbie sighed. "You know, a thousand of those stars out there are ours now. That's like, what? Three ten-thousandths of a percent of our galaxy? That's what we're fighting over."

"You think?"

"You don't?"

"Nah," Alex said. "I figure we're fighting over who gets the most meat from the hunt and first access to the water hole. Mating rights. Who believes in which gods. Who has the most money. The usual primate issues."

"Kids," Bobbie said.

"Kids?"

"Yeah. Everyone wanting to make sure their kids have a better shot than they did. Or than everyone else's kids. Something like that."

"Yeah, probably," Alex said. He shifted his personal screen back to tactical, pulling up the latest data on the *Pella.* It still had the strange, cheap-looking civilian craft tethered to it. Alex couldn't tell if they were taking something off it or putting something on. So far, it was the only craft in the little force that wasn't clearly military design. There hadn't been any more contacts from Naomi. He didn't know whether that was a good thing or a problem, but he couldn't help checking on the ship every five minutes like he was picking at a scab.

"You ever worry about your kid?" Bobbie asked.

"Don't have one," Alex said.

"You don't? I thought you did."

"Nope," Alex said. "Never really had the situation for one, you know? Or I guess I did, and it didn't fit. What about you?"

"Never had the urge," Bobbie said. "The family I've got has been more than enough."

"Yeah. Family."

Bobbie was silent for a moment. Then, "You're thinking about her."

"Naomi, you mean?"

"Yeah."

Alex turned in his couch. Bobbie's armor reached against both walls, servomotors locked in place to brace her. She looked crucified. The wound in the deck where she'd pulled out the crash couch made it seem like she'd burst through the bottom of the ship. Her expression managed to be both sympathetic and hard.

"Of course, I'm thinking about her," Alex said. "She's right there. And probably she's in trouble. And I can't figure out how the hell she got there in the first place. It's not going to be too long before the cavalry gets here to save us, and when they do, I don't know if I should be helping to attack the *Pella* or protect her."

"That's hard," Bobbie agreed. "But you know we've got our mission. Get Smith to Luna. We've got to stand our watch."

"I know. Can't help thinking about it, though. I keep putting together schemes where we use the missiles we've got left to make them turn her over to us."

"Any of them even remotely plausible?"

"Not a one," Alex said.

"There's nothing worse than keeping to your duty when it means leaving one of your own in danger."

"No shit." Alex looked at the readouts from the *Pella*. "You know, maybe—"

"Stand your watch, sailor. And heads up. We've got more PDCs coming in."

Alex had already seen them and started laying in the course corrections. "Optimistic little shits. Got to give them that."

"Maybe they think you'll get sleepy."

The overloading of the pinnace was awkward and strange. Moving from the pilot's seat to the head meant both Alex and the prime minister of Mars squeezing past Bobbie's power armor. Or, for Bobbie, exiling Smith to the empty space where her couch had been while she used the tiny cabin to break down her armor or climb back into it. No one even suggested that they sleep by hot-bunking in the cabin.

Smith himself seemed like a personable man, polite and thoughtful. *Inoffensive* was a word that came to mind. Alex had stopped following Martian politics sometime around the slow zone, so he didn't come in with any preconceptions about the man or his policies. When they did talk, it was usually about small things—the popular culture of Mars when they were both growing up, Smith's gratitude for the efforts he and Bobbie were putting into keeping him alive, some questions about what Ilus had been like. Alex had the sense that Smith was, if anything, a little starstruck by him. Which was pretty thoroughly odd, when he thought about it.

Still, when Smith popped his head out of the cabin to tell Bobbie that there was a message specifically for her from Avasarala, it had the sense of a secretary who was vaguely uneasy interrupting his boss. Alex felt a weird impulse to reassure the man it was all right, but wasn't sure how to say it without being even more awkward.

Bobbie thanked him, and for a while she was silent. Alex kept his eyes on the enemy and the sun and the data from the incoming UN escort ships that were still hidden by the sun's corona.

"Alex?" Bobbie sounded frustrated.

"Yup."

"I can't make this thing's incoming feed talk to my suit. Can you put this up on a screen for me? I'd do it myself, but—"

He switched over to the comm system, opened a panel on the wall screen, and sent the message to it. Chrisjen Avasarala appeared. She looked older than Alex remembered her. There were dark circles under her eyes and a grayness to her skin that didn't belong there. Her sari only made her look paler. When she spoke, though, her voice was just as sure as ever.

"Bobbie, I need any data you have about the missing Martian ships. I know, you're going to tell me how you've already given me everything, and of course I trust and believe all that you say, blah blah fucking blah. But I need it. Now. I've got confirmation of two dozen Martian military vessels that are burning hard for the Ring. Everything from the *Barkeith* to a couple resupply barges. It's like a little fucking fleet all its own. Smith says he's looking into it, which could mean anything from he knows exactly what's going on and doesn't want to tell me to Mars is in the middle of a coup and he doesn't want to tell me. One way or the other, he's locked up tight as a rat's asshole."

"Sorry about this," Bobbie said over her shoulder.

"It's nothing she hasn't said to my face," Smith replied.

"You want me to stop the playback?" Alex asked, but Avasarala was already talking again.

"If these are more ships that got sold to whoever's chasing you, I need to know. If they're all MCRN vessels with actual Martian Navy crews, that's something very different. And since they're not answering, I'm stuck trying to peep in the windows. If you've held something back—something sensitive, something that made you uncomfortable to share with me—I absolutely understand. Your patriotism and loyalty to Mars has been a thorn in my fucking side since the day I met you, but I respect it. It speaks well of you as a soldier and as a person, and now it's time to get the fuck over it.

"Also, Nathan, if you're listening, and I assume you are, I'm the best and only friend you've got. Give her permission to share what she has, or I swear to God I'll have you turning tricks out of a prefab shed on the side of the highway. I'm trying to save humanity here. It would be just fantastic if someone would *help*."

Her voice broke on the last word, and tears appeared in her eyes. Alex felt a tightness in his chest and a sense of sorrow he'd managed to ignore until it now welled up in him. Avasarala took a deep breath, sneered, and turned her gaze back to the camera. She wiped her eyes with the back of her hand angrily. Like they'd betrayed her.

"So. No more fucking around. I love and adore you, and I can't wait for you—all of you—to be where I can keep you safe. Be careful. And send me the fucking data. Now."

The message ended. Bobbie let out a long, shuddering breath. Alex was pretty sure if he looked back, she'd be weeping too. Smith's voice came from the door to the cabin.

"I've told her all I know about them," Smith said. "The ships were not listed as missing. The crews aboard them all check out as Martian citizens. But so did the false escort ships. Until I have a complete audit of the military's personnel and supply databases, I don't know what I'm looking at."

Alex coughed to clear his throat before he spoke. "Avasarala's not always the most trusting person, Nate. It ain't just you."

"She's thorough," Smith said. "And she's in a hard position. Sergeant Draper?"

There was a long silence. When Alex looked back, Bobbie's expression was closed. Her lips pressed to a single line. "On my own initiative and without direction from Avasarala I...When I found evidence that something had gone missing, I checked to see what commanding officers were in charge of that materiel. I didn't see any pattern in it, but someone else might. If they saw it."

Alex closed the panel Avasarala had been in. The air seemed fragile. Smith took a short breath, made a small, noncommittal sound in the back of his throat. "Please see that I get a copy too, Sergeant Draper."

He closed the door to the cabin behind him. Alex sat up in his couch. "You know," he said, "you have a really weird relationship with treason. On the one hand, I think you may be the most patriotic person I've ever met, and on the other hand—"

"I know. It's been confusing for me too. For a long time now."

"Your loyalty to the corps and your loyalty to that woman ever really come to blows, it'll be a hard day."

"It won't happen," Bobbie said. "She won't let it."

"No?"

"She'd lose," Bobbie said. "She hates losing."

The message from the *Pella* came three hours later. From the first instant, it was clear that it was a press release. The answer to the questions everyone had been asking: Who did all this, and why? The man was seated at a desk, two different banners showing the split circle of the OPA on the wall behind him. His uniform was crisp and unfamiliar, his eyes soulful and gentle to the point of being nearly apologetic, his voice low and rich as a viol.

"My name," he said, "is Marco Inaros, commander of the Free Navy. We are the legitimate military voice of the outer planets, and we are now in a position to explain both to the oppressors on Earth and Mars and also to the liberated people of the Belt the terms on which this new chapter of human liberty, dignity, and freedom are founded. We recognize the right of Earth and Mars to exist, but their sovereignty ends at their respective atmospheres. The vacuum is ours. All travel between the planets of the solar system are the right and privilege of the OPA and will be enforced by the Free Navy. All taxes and tariffs imposed by Earth and Mars are illegal, and will not be respected. Reparations for the damage done by the inner planets to the free citizens of the system will be assayed, and failure to repay them for the benefit of the full human race will be considered a criminal act."

A throbbing had come into the man's voice without it ever seeming to make his words affected or musical. He leaned in toward the camera, and it felt both intimate and powerful.

"With the opening of the alien gates, we are at a crossroads in human history. We have already seen how easy it would be to carry our legacies of exploitation, injustice, prejudice, and oppression to these new worlds. But there is an alternative. The Free Navy and the society and culture of the Belt are representatives of that new pathway. We will begin again and remake humanity without the corruption, greed, and hatred that the inner planets could not transcend. We will take what is ours by right, yes, but more than that, we will lead the Belt to a new, better form. A more *human* form.

"As of now, the gates to the other worlds are closed. The inner planet colony ships will be redirected to existing stations in our system, and the goods they carry contributed to building the strong outer planets that we have always deserved. We no longer recognize or accept the yoke of the inner planets anywhere in the system. The moons of Saturn and Jupiter are ours by right. Pallas Station, Ceres Station, every pocket of air in the Belt with even one human in it, all are the natural and legal property of their inhabitants. We pledge our lives to protect those people, citizens of the greater humanity, against the historical and established crimes of economy and violence they have suffered at the gun barrels of Earth and Mars.

"I am Marco Inaros. I am commander of the Free Navy. And I call upon all free men and women of the Belt to rise up now in joy and glorious resolve. The Free Navy pledges you all the safety of our protection. This day is ours. Tomorrow is ours. The future of humanity is ours. Today, and forevermore, we are free."

On the screen, Marco Inaros lifted his hand in the Belter idiom of greeting, militarizing the motion with his precision and focus. His face was an icon of resolve and strength and masculine beauty.

"We are your arm," he said. "And we will strike your enemies wherever they are. We are the Free Navy. Citizens of the Belt and of the new humanity, we are yours."

A rising chord picked up and broke into a traditional Belter protest song transformed into something martial and rousing. The new anthem of an invented nation. The image faded to a split circle and then to white. The crew of the *Razorback* were quiet.

"Well," Bobbie said. "He's pretty. And he's really charismatic. But, wow, that speech."

"It probably sounded good in his head," Alex said. "And really, when your prelude is you kill a couple billion people, anything you say is going to sound a little megalomaniacal and creepy, right?"

Smith's voice was calm, but the dread in it carried through. "He wasn't talking to us." He stood in the door to the cabin, his arms stretched to brace against the frame. His amiable smile hadn't changed, but its meaning had. "That was meant for the Belters. And what they heard in him—what they saw in him—won't be anything like what we did. For them, he just declared victory."

Chapter Thirty-Eight: Amos

Ash sifted down, coating everything with a few millimeters of gray. Everything stank of it. They got off the road to let relief convoys go by twice, and then once when an old electric service truck whined by, its bed filled with six or seven huddled figures. They slept when it got too dark to see, hauling the bikes into the bushes or alleys. The dead guy's emergency rations tasted like crap, but they didn't seem to be toxic.

After four days, the plants along the roadside started showing signs of dying: green leaves turning brown and curving toward the earth. The birds, on the other hand, were going crazy. They filled the air with chirps and trills and songs. It was probably sparrow for *Holy shit, what's going on, we're all gonna die*, but it sounded pretty. Amos tried to keep clear of the bigger cities, but there wasn't a lot of space left in that part of the world that wasn't paved.

Passing through Harrisonburg they were followed by a dozen dogs for about ten kilometers, the pack building up its nerve to attack. He let Peaches go ahead for that part, but it never got serious enough to make him spend bullets. When they started getting in toward Baltimore, there stopped being a way to keep clear of people.

They were still about a day from the arcology, and the smell of the world had changed to salt water and rot, when they ran into the other crew. They were moving down a commercial street, the bikes making their soft chain-hiss, and he caught sight of the others in the gloom, heading toward them. Amos slowed down, but didn't stop. Peaches matched him. From the smear of light in the east, he guessed it was about ten in the morning, but the darkness still made it hard to be sure how many of them there were. Four he could see for sure. Maybe more trailing a little way behind. Hard to say.

They were smeared with ash, the same as everything. If they had weapons, Amos didn't see them. Handguns, maybe. So he had them for range if he wanted to start shooting. They were walking, so outrunning them was also an option, if it came to that. Thing was, Peaches didn't look like anywhere near the threat she was, and pretty much everyone was going to be going off appearances. It was that kind of misunderstanding that got people killed.

The other group slowed down, but didn't stop. Wary, but not disinterested. Amos stood up on his pedals.

"Peaches? How's about you hang back a little."

"Draw down on them?"

"Nah. Let's be neighbors first."

Her bike slowed and fell behind. Ahead on the street, the others made their own calculations and came to a different conclusion. All four stepped out toward Amos together, chins raised in a diffident greeting. No trouble unless there's trouble. Amos smiled amiably, and it occurred to him this was exactly the kind of situation that had taught him how to smile like that.

"Hey," he said.

"Hey." One of the four stepped closer. He was older. He moved gracefully, center of gravity low. Maybe a veteran. Maybe just someone who'd boxed some. Amos pointed his smile at the guy, then the other three. Tension crept up the back of his neck and into his shoulders. He breathed through it, forcing himself to relax. "Coming from Baltimore?"

"Monkton," the fighter said.

"Yeah? Towers or the flats?"

The fighter's mouth twitched into a little smile. "Z tower," he said.

"Zadislaw," Amos said. "Had a friend lived there once. Long time ago. How is it up there?"

"It's ten thousand people in a box with no food and not much water."

"Not so great, then."

"Power supply's all fucked up. And Baltimore's worse. No offense meant, but I'd say you're heading the wrong way." The fighter licked his lips. "Nice bikes."

"They do what we need 'em to," Amos agreed. "Only gets worse south of here. We're walking away from the strike."

"Keep going south, though, it gets warm again. That's where we're headed. Baja complex."

One of the others cleared her throat. "I've got a cousin down there."

Amos whistled between his teeth. "That's a hell of a walk you got there."

"Walk there or freeze here," the fighter said. "You and your friend there ought to come with us."

"I appreciate the invite, but we've got people we're meeting up with in Baltimore."

"You sure about that?"

"It's more like a working hypothesis, but it's the plan for now."

The fighter's gaze flickered down to the bike again, then up to Amos' face. The man studiously avoided looking at the rifle hanging on Amos' back. He waited to see which way they were going. The other man nodded.

"Well, good luck to you. We're all going to need it."

"That's truth," Amos said. "Tell Baja hi for me when you get there."

"Will."

The fighter started off down the street, the others with him. Amos loosened the strap that held the rifle, but he didn't draw the weapon. The four walkers moved down the ash-gray road. Peaches rode up, passing them. The last in their formation turned to watch her pass, but no one made a move.

"Everything all right?" she asked.

"Sure," Amos said. The shadows of the other crew faded into the gloom.

"Talked them out of any unpleasant actions?"

"Me? Nope. They did most of that themselves. Best defense we've got right now is everyone's in the habit of not killing each other and taking their shit. Pretty soon, people are just going to start assuming anyone they don't know is out to slit their throats. If they're lucky."

She looked at him. Her face was smooth, her eyes intelligent and hard. "You don't sound upset at the prospect."

"I'm comfortable with it."

With every kilometer traveled they came closer to the sea and the stink of rot and salt grew worse. They hit the high-water mark: the place where the charge of the floodwaters had broken. The line of debris was so clear and distinct it looked deliberate. A short wall made of wreckage and mortared with mud. Once they passed it, the ash was thick with mud and the roads were covered in broken wood and construction plastic, ruined clothes and waterlogged furniture, blackened plants killed by darkness and ash and salt water. And the bodies of dead people and animals that no one was going to bother cleaning up. The bikes threw up gobbets of the muddy road and they had to push harder, bearing down with all their weight, to keep the wheels spinning.

When they were still about twenty klicks from the arcology, Amos ran into a pit filled with water and covered over with a scum of ash. It bent the bicycle's front rim. He left it where it lay, and Peaches dropped hers beside it.

He was aware of voices around him. Every step of the way, they were being watched. But between having rifles and not seeming to have anything much else, no one tried to stop them. All around, the ground floors of the buildings were gutted, walls cracked by the pitiless water, and the contents of the stores and apartments and offices puked out into the streets. Some places, the second story was just as bad; some places it was better. Above that, the city seemed almost untouched. Amos kept imagining the place like it was a healthy-looking guy with exposed bone and gangrene from the ankle down.

"Something funny?" Peaches asked.

"Nope," Amos said. "I was just thinking."

The arcology was no different. It loomed up among the ruins, towering over the debris-choked streets now the way it had over the maintained streets before. The reactor that powered the vast building seemed to still be running, because lights glowed in half of the windows. If he just put his hand over the bottom layer, Amos could almost pretend the ash was snow, and all this was nothing more than the worst Christmas in history.

They trudged into the lowest level. Icy mud stuck his pants to his skin up to the knee. Glass pipes and footprints showed where people had been but there was no one standing guard. At least no one they saw.

"What if your friend's not here?" Peaches asked as Amos poked at the elevator's call button.

"Then we think of something else."

"Any idea what?"

"Still nope."

He was more than half-surprised when the elevator doors opened. Flood damage could have ruined the mechanism. Of course it could also get stuck halfway up, and they could die in it.

When he selected the club level, the screen clicked to life. A broad-faced woman with a scar across her upper lip sneered out at him.

"The fuck you want?"

"Amos. Friend of Erich's."

"We got no fucking handouts."

"Not looking for any," Amos said. "Want to talk about a job."

"No jobs either."

Amos smiled. "You new at this, Butch? I have a job. I'm here to see if Erich wants in. This is the part where you go tell him there's some psycho in the elevator wants to talk with him, then he says who is it, and you say the guy calls himself Amos, and Erich tries not to look surprised and tells you to let me up and—"

"For fuck's sake!" Erich's voice was distant, but recognizable. "Let him up, or he'll talk all day."

Butch scowled into the screen and blinked out to the blue arcology menu system. But the car started up.

"Good news is he's here," Amos said.

Erich's office looked the same as the last time Amos had been in it—the same wall screen showing the same ocean view, the rubber ball instead of a chair, the desk encrusted with decks and monitors. Even Erich didn't look different. Maybe better dressed, even. It was the context that changed it all. The screen showed an ocean of gray and white, and Erich's clothes looked like a costume.

Butch and the four other heavily armed thugs with professional trigger discipline who'd escorted them from the elevator walked out, closing the door behind them. Erich waited until they'd gone before he spoke, but the tiny fist of his bad arm was opening and closing the way it did when he was nervous.

"Well. Amos. You're looking more alive than I'd expected."

"Not looking too dead yourself."

"As I recall the way we left it, you weren't ever coming back to my city. Open season, I called it."

"Wait a second," Peaches said. "He said if you came back here, he'd kill you?"

"Nah," Amos said. "He broadly implied that one of his employees would kill me."

Peaches hoisted an eyebrow. "Yeah, because that's different."

"If this is about the old man, I haven't checked to see if he made it or not. Deal was he kept the house, and I did that. More than that, and I've got other problems."

"And I got no trouble to cause," Amos said. "I figured things had changed enough maybe the old rules weren't a great fit for the new situation."

Erich walked over to the wall screen, limping. A few seagulls circled, black against the colorless sky. From the last time he'd been there, Amos knew the buildings that should have provided a foreground. Most of them were still in place close in. Out toward the shoreline, things were shorter now.

"I was right here when it happened," Erich said. "It wasn't a wave like a wave, you know? Like a surfer wave? It was just the whole fucking ocean humping up and crawling onto shore. There's whole neighborhoods I used to run just aren't there now."

"I didn't see anything happen," Amos said. "The newsfeeds and the mess after were bad enough."

"Where were you?"

"Bethlehem," Peaches said.

Erich turned back to them. There was no anger in his face, or fear, or even wariness. That was good. "So you're headed south, then? How bad is it up there?"

"Not that Bethlehem," Amos said. "The one in the Carolina admin district."

"Where the Pit is," Peaches said, raising her hand like a kid in a classroom. Then a second later, "Was."

Erich blinked and leaned against his desk. "Where the third strike hit?"

"Close to there, yeah," Amos said. "Lost that tequila you gave me with the hotel, so that sucked."

"All right. How are you still alive?"

"Practice," Amos said cheerfully. "Here's the thing, though. I've got a job. Well, Peaches has a job, and I'm in. Could use some help."

"What kind of job?" Erich asked. A sharpness and focus came into his voice, talking business. It was like watching someone wake up. Amos turned to Peaches and waved her on. She hugged stick-thin arms around her torso.

"Do you know Lake Winnipesaukee?"

Erich frowned and nodded at the same time. "The fake lake?"

"Reconstituted, yeah," she said. "There's an enclave on Rattlesnake Island. The whole place is walled. Independent security force. Maybe fifty estates."

"I'm listening," Erich said.

"They have a private launchpad built out onto the lake. The whole point of the place is that you can drop there suborbital or down from Luna or the Lagrange stations, and be walking distance from home. Everyone there has a hangar. Probably nothing with an Epstein, but something that could get us to Luna. Going through the road, you couldn't get past the checkpoints, but there's a way in from the water. The boathouse locks are compromised. Put in the right code, and they pop open even if the security chip's not in range."

"Which you know how?" Erich said.

"I used to summer there. It's how we got in and out when we went slumming."

Erich looked at Peaches like he wasn't sure how she'd gotten in the room. His laugh was short and hard, but it wasn't a no. Amos picked up the pitch. "Idea is we get in, grab a ship, and head for Luna."

Erich sat down on the ball, his legs wide, and rolled a few centimeters back and forth, his eyes half-closed. "So what's the score?"

"The score?" Peaches asked.

"What are we taking? Where does the money come in?"

"There isn't any," Peaches said.

"Then what do I get out of it?"

"You get out of here," Amos said. "Place was kind of a shithole before someone dropped the Atlantic on it. It's not getting better."

Erich's wasted, tiny left arm squeezed tight to his body. "Let me get this straight. You've got a score where I go seven, maybe eight hundred kilometers, sneak past some private mercenary death squad, boost a ship, and the payoff is that I get to leave everyone and everything I've got here? What's next? Russian roulette where if I win, I get to keep the bullet?" His voice was high and tight. He bit the words as he spoke them. "This is my city. This is my place. I carved my life out of the fucking skin of Baltimore, and I spent a lot doing it. A lot. Now I'm supposed to put my tail between my legs and run away because some Belter fuckwit decided to prove he's got a tiny little dick and his mama didn't hug him enough when he was a kid? Fuck that! You hear me, Timmy? *Fuck* that!"

Amos looked at his hands and tried to think what to do next. His first impulse was to laugh at Erich's maudlin bullshit, but he was pretty sure that wasn't going to be a good idea. He tried to think what Naomi would have said, but before he came up with anything good, Peaches stepped toward Erich, her arms out to him like she was going to give him a hug.

"I know," she said, her voice choked with some emotion Amos didn't place.

"You *know*? What the fuck do you *know*?"

"What it's like to lose everything. How hard it is, because you keep thinking it can't really be gone. That there's a way to get it back. Or maybe if you just act like you still have it, you won't notice it's gone."

Erich's face froze. His bad hand opened and closed so fast, it looked like he was trying to snap the tiny pink fingers. "I don't know what you're talking—"

"There was this woman I knew when I went in. She killed her children. Five of them, all dead. She knew it, but she talked about them all like they were still alive. Like when she got up tomorrow, they'd be there. I thought she was a lunatic, and I guess I let that show, because she stopped me one day at the cafeteria and said, 'I know they're dead. But I know I'm dead too. You're the only bitch here thinks she's still alive.' And as soon as she said that, I knew exactly what she meant."

To Amos' astonishment, Erich started to weep and then blubber. He fell into Peaches' open arms, wrapping his good arm around her and crying into her shoulder. She stroked his hair and murmured something to him that could have been *I know, I know*. Or maybe something else. So clearly something sweet and touching had just happened, even if he wasn't clear what the fuck it was. Amos shifted from one foot to the other and waited. Erich's wracking sobs grew more violent and then started to calm. It must have been fifteen minutes before the man pulled himself out of Peaches' embrace, limped to his desk, and found some tissue to blow his nose.

"I grew up here," he said, his voice shaking. "Everything I've ever done—every meal I ever ate, every toilet I ever pissed in, every girl I ever rolled around with? It's all been inside the 695." For a second, it looked like he was going to cry again. "I've seen things come and go. I've seen shit times turn into normal and turn back to shit, and keep telling myself this is like that. It's just the churn. But it's not, is it?"

"No," Peaches said. "It isn't. This is something new."

Erich turned back to the screen, touching it with the fingertips of his good hand. "That's my city out there. It's a mean, shitty place, and it'll break anyone who pretends different. But...but it's gone, isn't it?"

"Probably," Peaches said. "But starting over's not always bad. Even the way I did it had some light in it. And what you've got is better than what I had."

Erich bowed his head. His sigh sounded like something bigger than him being released. Peaches took his good hand in both of hers and the two of them were silent for a long moment.

Amos cleared his throat. "So. That means you're in, right?"

Chapter Thirty-Nine: Naomi

She didn't have days. Hours maybe. For all she knew, minutes. And the plan still had holes in it.

She sat in the mess, hunched over a bowl of bread pudding. People passed through from the crew quarters, some wearing Martian uniforms, some their normal clothes, a few in a new Free Navy uniform, but the other tables stayed empty apart from her and Cyn. Before she'd been almost crew. Now she was a prisoner, and as a prisoner, her schedule had changed. She'd eat when other people weren't eating; she'd exercise when other people weren't exercising; she'd sleep in the dark with her door locked from the outside.

She was grateful for it. She needed the quiet of her own mind now, and strangely, she felt comfortable there. Something had happened in the last days. She couldn't put her finger on when or how, but the dark thoughts had either vanished or else grown so vast she couldn't see their horizons. She didn't think she was crazy. She had felt her mind fishtailing out from under her one time and another in her life, and this was very different. She understood she might die, that Jim might die, that Marco might sail from success to success, that Filip might never forgive or even understand her. And she could tell that all of those facts mattered to her, and mattered deeply. But they didn't overwhelm her. Not anymore.

The umbilical linking the ships was fifty meters at full extension. Not even as wide as a soccer field. The link between the ships was between the cargo-level airlocks, where it was easier to access engineering and move supplies, which left the crew-level airlocks unused. There were EVA suits in the lockers there. With a strip of welding tape or a crowbar, she could get one in only a couple of minutes. Get into the suit, out the *Pella*'s airlock, force the airlock on the *Chetzemoka* all in the time between the drives cutting off and the *Chetzemoka* firing her maneuvering thrusters. There were no calculations for it. It would be very, very close, but she thought it was possible. And since it was possible, it was necessary.

There were problems, of course, that needed solving. For one thing she didn't have welding tape or a crowbar, and with her escorts now treating her as untrustworthy, her opportunity to steal either while running an inventory was gone. Second, once Marco saw she'd taken an EVA suit and made the jump, she had no way to keep him from firing a missile at the *Chetzemoka*. Or worse, finding some way to disable the proximity trap and come back for her. If she could get a suit on the sly, though, so that the inventory said they still had a full complement, they might think she'd killed herself. If she was dead, she posed no threat. She knew the inventory system well enough, she thought she could force an update. She knew she could, given enough time and access. But she only had hours. Maybe hours. Maybe less.

A familiar, sharp voice came from the screen where a newsfeed was still playing to the empty room. "Secretary-General Gao was more than the leader of my government. She was also a close personal friend, and I will miss her company deeply."

Avasarala's expression was careful, composed. Even through the screen and a couple hundred thousand kilometers, she radiated certainty and calm. Naomi knew it might all be an act, but if it was, it was a good act. The reporter was a young man with close-cut dark hair who leaned forward and tried to look up to the task of interviewing her. "The other casualties of the war have—"

"No," Avasarala said. "Not war. Not casualties. These aren't casualties. They're murders. This isn't a war. Marco Inaros can claim to be an admiral in command of a great navy if he wants. I can claim to be the f—Buddha. That doesn't make it true. He's a criminal with a lot of stolen ships and more innocent blood on his hands than anyone in history. He's a monstrous little boy."

Naomi took another bite of bread pudding. Whatever they used to make the raisins wasn't convincing, but it didn't taste bad. For a moment, her thoughts weren't on welding tape and inventory cheats.

"So you don't consider this an act of war?"

"War by who? War is a conflict between governments, yes? What sort of government does he represent? When was he elected? Who appointed him? Now, after the fact, he's scrambling to say he represents Belters. So what? Any petty thug in his position would want to call it war because it makes him sound serious."

The reporter looked like he'd swallowed something sour and unexpected. "I'm sorry. Are you saying this attack isn't *serious*?"

"This attack is the greatest tragedy in human history," Avasarala said, her voice deep and throbbing. She dominated the screen. "But it was carried out by shortsighted, narcissistic criminals. They want a war? Too bad. They get an arrest, processing, and a fair trial with whatever lawyer they can afford. They want the Belt to rise up so they can hide behind the good, decent people who live there? Belters aren't thugs, and they aren't murderers. They are men and women who love their children the same as any of us. They are good and evil and wise and foolish and *human*.

And this 'Free Navy' will never be able to kill enough people to make Earth forget that shared humanity. Let the Belt consult its own conscience, and you'll see compassion and decency and kindness flourish in any gravity or none. Earth has been bloodied, but we will *not* be debased. Not on my fucking watch."

The old woman sat back in her seat, her eyes fiery and defiant. The reporter glanced into the camera and then back to his notes. "The relief effort on Earth is, of course, a massive undertaking."

"It is," she said. "We have reactors in every major city on the planet running at top efficiency to provide power for—"

The screen went blank. Cyn put his hand terminal down on the table with an angry click. Naomi looked up at him from behind her hair.

"Esá bitch needs sa yutak cut," Cyn said. His face was dark with rage. "Lesson á totas like her, yeah?"

"For for?" Naomi said, shrugging. "Kill her, and another one will take her place. She's good at what she does, but even if you did slit her throat, there'd just be someone else in the same chair saying the same things."

Cyn shook his head. "Not like that."

"Close by."

"No," he said, his chin jutting a centimeter forward. "Not like that. Alles la about big social movements y ages of history y sa? Stories they make up later so it makes sense. Not like that, not real. It's people do things. Marco. Filipito. You. Me."

"You say so," Naomi said.

"Esá coyo on Mars who traded us for all the ships and told us where to find supplies? He's not 'Martian economic despair' o 'rising debt ratios' o 'income and access inequality.' " With each pretentious invented term, Cyn wagged his finger like a professor lecturing a class, and it was funny enough that Naomi chuckled. He blinked at the sound, and then smiled a little shyly. "La coyo la is just some coyo. He's a man made a deal with a man who talked up some otras, and we did things. Who people are, it matters, yeah? Can't replace them."

His gaze was on her now, not a professor lecturing a class, but Cyn lecturing her. She scooped the last bite of pudding into her mouth. "Get the feeling you're saying something," she said around it. Cyn looked down, gathered himself. She could see the effort more than she could understand it.

"Filipito, he needs you. No sabez la, but he does. You and Marco are you and Marco, but no you take the coward's out."

Her heart jumped a little. He thought she was in despair, that she might give in to the dark thoughts. She wondered what brought him to the conclusion, and whether it was a mistake he was making or something he could see in her that she couldn't. She swallowed. "You telling me not to kill myself?"

"Be a bad thing to say?"

She stood up, her soiled bowl in her hand. He rose with her, following as she headed for the recycler. The weight of her body was reassuring. There was still time. They hadn't cut the drives yet. She could still figure her way over. "What should I do, then?"

It was Cyn's turn to shrug. "Come with. Be Free Navy. We go where they need us, do what needs doing. Help where they need help, yeah? Already eight colony ships on target."

"Target for what?"

"Redistribué, yeah? Alles la food and supplies they got heading out for the Ring? Más a anyone ever gave the Belt. Take that, feed the Belt, build the Belt. See what es vide when we're not scrabbling for air y ejection mass. Gardens in the vacuum. Cities make Tycho Station look some rock hopper's head. New world without a world to it, yeah? None of this alien bok. Blow the Ring. Burn it. Get back to people being people, yeah?"

Two women walked by, heads bent toward each other in passionate conversation. The nearer one glanced up, then away, then back. There was venom in her gaze. Hatred. The contrast was stark. On one hand, Cyn's vision of a future where Belters were free of the economic oppression of the inner planets—of the central axioms that had formed everything in Naomi's childhood. In her life. Civilization built by them and for them, a remaking of human life. And on the other, actual Belters actually hating her because she had dared to act against them. Because she wasn't Belter enough. "Where does it end, Cyn? Where does it all end?"

"Doesn't. Not if we do it right."

⚡

There was nothing in her cabin that could help her, but since she was confined there and alone, it was where she searched. Hours. Not days.

The crash couch was bolted to the deck with thick steel and reinforced ceramic canted so that any direction the force came from was compression on one leg or another. Any individual strut might have been usable as a pry bar, but she didn't have any way to unbolt the couch or break one free. So not that. The drawers were thinner metal, the same gauge, more or less, as the lockers. She pulled them out as far as they would open, examining the construction of the latches, the seams where the metal had been folded, searching for clues or inspiration. There was nothing.

The tiny black thumb of the decompression kit, she kept tucked at her waist, ready to go if she could just find a way. She felt the time slipping away, second by second, as she came up blank. She had to find a way. She would find a way. The *Chetzemoka* was so close to still be too far away.

If she didn't try to go when they pulled the umbilical? If she could sneak across now and hide there until they separated...If she could get to the armory instead, and maybe find a demolition mech that could act as an environment suit...or that she could use to cut through the bulkheads fast enough that no one shot her in the back of the head...

"Think," she said. "Don't spin and whine. Think."

But nothing came.

When she slept, it was for thin slips of minutes. She couldn't afford a deep sleep for fear of waking to find the *Chetzemoka* gone. And she lay on the ground with her hand clutching the base of the crash couch so that it would tug her awake if they went on the float.

What would Alex do? What would Amos do? What would Jim do? What would she do? Nothing came to her. She waited for despair, the darkness, the sense of overwhelming failure, and didn't understand why it didn't come. There was every reason to be devastated, but she wasn't. Instead there was only the certainty that if the dark thoughts did return, they would come in such strength that she wouldn't stand a chance against them. Oddly, even that was comforting.

When she knocked to go to the head, Sárta opened the door. Not that it mattered. She followed Naomi down the hall, then waited outside. The head didn't have anything of use either, but Naomi took her time in case inspiration came. The mirror was polished alloy built into the wall. No help there. If she could take apart the vacuum fans in the toilet...

She heard voices from the other side of the door. Sárta and someone else. The words were too soft to make out. She finished washing her hands, dropped the towelette in the recycler, and stepped into the corridor. Filip looked over at her. It was her son, and she hadn't recognized his voice.

"Filip," she said.

"Cyn said you wanted to talk to me," Filip said, landing the words equally as question and accusation.

"Did he now? That was kind of him."

She hesitated. Her hands itched with the need to find some way to put her hands on an EVA suit, but something in the back of her mind whispered *If they think you're alive, they'll come for you.* Anger and diffidence made the planes and angles of Filip's face. Cyn already thought she was bent on self-slaughter. It was why he'd sent Filip.

Her belly went heavy almost before she understood why. If Filip thought it too, if when she went missing, her son went to Marco and stood witness to her suicidal bent, it would be easier to believe. They might not even check to see if a suit was missing.

"Do you want to talk here in the hallway?" she said, her lips heavy, her mouth slow. "I have a little place nearby. Not spacious, but there's some privacy."

Filip nodded once, and Naomi turned down the hall, Sárta and Filip following her. She rehearsed lines in her mind. *I'm so tired that I just want it to be over* and *What I do to myself isn't your fault* and *I can't take it anymore*. There were a thousand ways to convince him that she was ready to die. But beneath those, the heaviness in her gut thickened and settled. The manipulation was cruel and it was cold. It was her own child, the child she'd lost, and she was going to use him. Lie to him so well that what he told Marco would be indistinguishable from truth. So that when she disappeared to the *Chetzemoka*, they would assume she'd killed herself, and not come after her. Not until it was too late.

She could do it. She couldn't do it. She could.

In the cabin, she sat on the couch, her legs folded up under her. He leaned against the wall, his mouth tight, his chin high. She wondered what he was thinking. What he wanted and feared and loved. She wondered if anyone had ever asked him.

I can't take it anymore, she thought. *Just say I can't take it anymore.*

"Are you all right?" she asked.

"Why wouldn't I be?"

"I don't know," she said. "I worry about you."

"Not so much you wouldn't betray me," he said, and that untied the knot. Yes, if she lied to him, it would be betraying him, and for all her failures, she'd never done that. She could. She could do it. It wasn't that she was powerless before the decision; it was that she chose not to.

"The warning I sent?"

"I have dedicated my life to the Belt, to freeing the Belters. And after we did everything we could to keep you safe, you spat in our faces. Do you love your Earther boyfriend that much more than your own kind? Is that it?"

Naomi nodded. It was like hearing all the things Marco was

too polished to say out loud. There was real feeling behind them in a way she would never hear from Marco. Maybe never had. He'd soaked up all his father's lines, only where Marco's soul was safe and unreachable in its deep self-centered cyst, Filip was still raw. The pain that she had not only left him, but left him for a man from Earth lit his eyes. *Betrayal* wasn't too strong a word.

"My own kind," she said. "Let me tell you about my own kind. There are two sides in this, but they aren't inner planets and outer ones. Belters and everyone else. It's not like that. It's the people who want more violence and the ones who want less. And no matter what other variable you sample out of, you'll find some of both.

"I was harsh to you the day the rocks dropped. But I meant everything I said. Your father and I are now and always were on different sides. We will never, ever be reconciled. But I think despite everything, you can still choose whichever side you'd like. Even now, when it seems like you've done something that can't be redeemed, you can choose what it means to you."

"This is shit," he said. "You're shit. You're an Earth-fucking whore, and always have been. You're a camp follower, looking to sleep your way into anybody's bed who seems important. Your whole life's that. You're nothing!"

She folded her hands. Everything he said was so wrong it didn't even sting. It was like he was calling her a terrier. All she could think of it was, *These are the last words you're going to say to your mother. You will regret them for the rest of your life.*

Filip turned, pulled open the door.

"You deserved better parents," she said as he slammed it behind him. She didn't know if he'd heard.

Chapter Forty: Amos

Between walking and biking, scrounging up food, and picking a route that avoided the dense populations around the Washington administrative zone, the seven-hundred-odd kilometers between Bethlehem and Baltimore had taken them almost two weeks. The four-hundred-odd klicks from the arcology to Lake Winnipesaukee took a couple hours. Erich sent out Butch—whose name was something else that Amos couldn't remember even after they told him—and two others, then sent him and Peaches to wait in another room while he had some conversations.

Twenty minutes later, Amos and Peaches and Erich and ten men and women were standing on the roof of the arcology loading into a pair of transport helicopters with the Al Abbiq Security logo on the side. Erich didn't say if they were stolen or if he'd been paying off the security force, and Amos didn't ask. Pretty much an academic issue at that point.

The landscape they passed over was bleak. The ash fall had slowed, but not stopped. The sun was a ruddy smear on the western horizon. Below them, cities bled into each other without so much as a tree or a swath of grass between them. Most of the windows were empty. The streets and highways were filled with cars, but few of them were moving. They swung out to the east as they passed by New York City. The great seawall had been shattered, and the streets flooded like canals. Several of the great towers had fallen, leaving holes in the skyline.

"Where is everyone?" Peaches shouted over the chop of the rotors.

"They're there," Erich shouted back, gesturing with his bad arm and holding on to the strap with his good. "They're all there. It's just there's not as many as there were last week. And more than there are going to be."

Over Boston, someone fired a missile toward them from the roof of a commercial shopping district, and the copters shot it down. The sky to the east was the low bruise-dark that made Amos think of storm clouds. In the west, the sunset was the color of blood.

"We gonna have trouble with the rotors icing up?" Amos asked the pilot, but he didn't get an answer.

They set down at an airfield a few klicks south of the lake, but Amos got a look before they landed: low hills holding the water like it was being cupped in a massive palm. There were maybe a dozen islands scattered across the lake, some as crowded with buildings as the shore, others with little tame forests if someone rich enough for the luxury lived there. The landing platform was a square of floating ceramic with red and amber lights still blinking for visual landings.

When they actually got to the water's edge, it wasn't as pretty. The water stank of dead fish and a coating of ash lay across the surface like someone had sifted chalk dust over the whole place. Erich's people waded in up to their thighs and dropped three packages that unfolded into hard, black pontoon boats. By the time they started toward the enclave on Rattlesnake Island, the sky was a perfect black. No stars, no moon, no backsplash of light pollution. The night was like sticking his head in a sack.

They spun to the north side of the island where a wide bridge on a coated steel pier ran out toward the launching pad. Hangars and boathouses encrusted the shore, boxes for the toys of the wealthy as big as basic housing blocks for a thousand people. The pontoon boat they were in surged forward over the chop of the water. The boathouse they chose was painted bright blue, but outside the circles of their lights, it could have been anything. It only took a minute to find the keypad on a pole that poked up from the dark water. Peaches leaned over, stretched her thin arm, and tapped out a series of numbers. For a second, it looked like it hadn't worked, then the boathouse doors silently rose and automatic lights came on. The interior was all wood paneling, rich red cedar, and enough room for a tennis court. An angry barking came out from the darkness as they steered inside.

A wolfhound stood on the deck of a little powerboat, its paws on the rail. The pontoon boats snugged up in the space next to the powerboat. Amos hauled himself up and the wolfhound darted toward him, growling and snarling. It was a beautiful animal, genetically engineered, he figured, for the gloss of its fur and the graceful lines of its face.

"Hey there," Amos said, squatting down to its level. "Someone didn't bother taking you along when they left, huh? That shit's gotta suck."

The dog shied back, uncertain and frightened.

"How about this," Amos said. "Don't start anything with us, we won't shoot you."

"It doesn't talk," Erich said as the dog retreated, barking over its shoulder.

"How do you know? Assholes with this much money, maybe they put some kind of translator into its brain."

"They can't do that," Erich said, then turned to Peaches. "They can't, can they?"

"This is the Cook estate," Peaches said. "Darwa and Khooni lived here. I used to sleep over on Wednesday nights in the summer." She shuddered a little and Amos cocked his head. "It's a long time since I've been here. It seems like it should have changed more."

"You know how to get to their hangar?" Erich asked.

"I do."

But when they got there, the space was empty. When they crossed the broad gravel yard to the next hangar over—the Davidovics'—it was empty too. The third one didn't have a ship, but it did have a dozen people. They stood in the center of the space with handguns and the kind of cheap suppression sprays they sold over the counter at grocery stores. The man in front was maybe fifty with graying hair and the beginnings of a new beard.

"You, all of you, stay back!" the man yelled as Amos and Butch and three more came in through the side door. "This is private property!"

"Oh, it belongs to you?" Butch sneered. "This all your place?"

"We work for the Quartermans. We have a right to be here." The man waggled his handgun. "You, all of you, get out!"

Amos shrugged. Another half dozen of Erich's people had come in, most of them with assault rifles held calmly at their sides. The servants were all huddled together in the middle of the room. If they'd had any skill or practice, there would have been two or three snipers up in the rafters, ready to start picking the bad guys off while these folks kept their attention low, but Amos didn't see anyone. "I kinda don't think the Quartermans are coming back. We're going to take some of their stuff. But anything we can't use, you should feel welcome to."

The man's face hardened, and Amos got ready for there to be a lot of dead people. But before Erich's people lifted their guns, Peaches interrupted.

"You're...you're Stokes, right?" The front man—Stokes, apparently—lowered the gun, confused as Peaches stepped forward. "It's me. Clarissa Mao."

"Miss Clarissa?" Stokes blinked. The gun wavered. He heard Butch mutter "Fucking seriously?" under her breath, but no one started firing. "Miss Clarissa! What are you doing here?"

"Trying to leave," Peaches said, with a laugh in her voice. "What are you here for?"

Stokes smiled at her, and then nervously at Amos and Erich and all the others, shining his teeth at them like the beam from a deeply insecure lighthouse. "The evacuation order came when the second rock came down. The Quartermans all left. Took the ship, and gone. They all went. The Cooks, the Falkners, old man Landborn. Everyone, they took their ships and left. Told us the security would keep us safe until relief came. But there's no relief, and the security? They're thugs. They tell us we have to pay them since the Quartermans are gone, but what do we have?"

"All the Quartermans' shit," Amos said. "Which brings me back to my first point."

"Are there any ships?" Peaches said. "We need a ship. Just to get us to Luna. That's why we came here."

"Yes. Yes, of course. The Bergavins left the *Zhang Guo*. It is in their hangar. We can take you there, Miss Clarissa, but—"

A sharp whistle came from the side door. From the street outside it. Butch met Amos' gaze. "Company," she said.

The streets on the island were wide. Roomy. Big enough to haul a ship down to the bridge. The security patrol car had the claw-and-eye logo of Pinkwater. Its headlights cut a wide cone through the darkness. Erich stood with his good hand up to shield his eyes. Two men were swaggering up toward him.

"Well now," the first man said. "What have we got here?"

Erich backed away, limping. "No trouble, sir," he said.

"How about if I determine that," the lead man said. "Get on the fucking ground." He had a cowboy hat on and his hand on the butt of his pistol. Amos smiled. The warmth in his belly and his arms was the same kind he got when he heard a familiar song after a long time. It was just pleasant. "I said get on the ground you crippled sonofabitch! You do it now, or I'll fuck your fucking eyeholes!"

"Peaches?" Amos called as he strode out into the light. The two security men drew their pistols and pointed them at him. "Hey, Peaches, you back there?"

"Yes?" she said. It sounded like she was in the side door. That was fine. He saw the pair of security men clock the rest of Erich's people in the gloom. They were mostly silhouetted, but their bodies went tense. Always a bad moment, seeing you brought a knife to a gunfight.

"See, this is what I was talking about," Amos called. "Things start falling apart, and the tribes get small. These guys, probably good upstanding folks when there's a boss to answer to. Clients. Shareholders." He turned to the man in the hat and grinned amiably. "Hey," he said.

"Um. Hey," Hat said.

Amos nodded and called back toward the hangar. "Thing is you take that away, they're guys with guns. They *act* like guys with guns. Do guys-with-guns stuff. Right?"

"I follow you," Peaches said.

"You should put your guns down," Amos said to Hat. "We've got just a shitload more of them than you do. So really."

"You heard the man," Butch said. "Guns on the ground, please."

The security men glanced at each other.

"We could have just shot you," Amos said. As Hat and his partner slowly lowered their guns to the pavement, Amos raised his voice again. "So Peaches, these guys? They go from being protectors of this big tribe with what's-his-name and them inside the tribe to being protectors of their own little tribe, and those folks on the outside of it. It's all about who's in and who's out."

Hat lifted his hands, palms out, about shoulder high. Amos hit him in the jaw. It was a solid punch, and his knuckles ached from it. Hat staggered back, and Amos stepped forward twisting his body into the kick. It landed on Hat's left kneecap and the man screamed.

"Thing is," Amos called, "most of us don't got room in our lives for more than six"—he straight-kicked Hat in the middle of the back as he tried to stand up—"maybe seven people. You get bigger than that, you got to start telling stories about it."

Hat was crawling back toward the car. Amos put his knee on the man's back, leaned down, and started emptying Hat's pockets and belt. Chemical mace. A Taser. A wallet with ID cards. A two-way radio. He found the unregistered drop gun strapped to the guy's ankle. Each thing he took, he threw out to the edge of the water, listening for the splash. Hat was weeping, and Amos' weight made it hard for him to breathe. The other one was standing perfectly still, like if he didn't move Amos wouldn't notice him. Wasn't like he had a better strategy at this point.

Amos grinned at him. "Hey."

The guy didn't say anything.

"It's okay," Amos said. "You didn't say you were gonna skull-fuck my friends, right?"

"Right," the other one said.

"Okay, then." Amos stood up. "You should probably get him to a doctor. And then whoever else you've got on this shithole of an island, tell them what I did, and how I didn't fuck you up because you hadn't fucked with me. Okay?"

"All right."

"Great. And then don't come back around here."

"I won't."

"We won't," Amos said. "You mean *we* won't. Not you and not your tribe."

"We won't."

"Perfect. No problems, then. And give Butch your stuff, all right? Drop gun too."

"Yes, sir."

Amos walked back toward the hangar. Sure enough, Peaches was standing in the doorway, her arms crossed. He wiped his hand. His knuckles were bleeding.

"See, that's what civilization is," he said. "Bunch of stories. That's all."

"So what if it is?" Peaches said. "We're really good at telling stories. Everything just turned to shit, and we're already finding ways to put it back together. Stokes and the other servants were ready to fight us or get killed, but then I knew his name and he remembered me, and now there's a story where he wants to help us. You go out there and you send a message about how those guys should leave us alone. All of us. More than just six or seven. And, side note here, you know the Pinkwater guys are going to come back and try to kill you for that, right?"

"Just need 'em to take a long time gearing up," Amos said. "Figure we'll be off the ground by then."

Stokes leaned in from behind Peaches, his expression apologetic. "About that? There is a small problem."

⚡

The hangar was as tall as a cathedral, and the *Zhang Guo* stood in the middle of it like a piece of gargantuan art. The surface of the ship was worked to look like gold-and-silver filigree over a body of lapis. The drive cones had golden ideograms written on them in something that looked like gold but apparently didn't melt at high temperature. He could tell from looking it didn't have an Epstein drive. Twice as big as the *Rocinante* and maybe—*maybe*—a quarter as functional, it was as much an orbital shuttle as it was a confession of decadence.

And, more to the point, it didn't run.

"The house power supplies are exhausted," Stokes explained. "Without power, there's no water recyclers. No heat. No network connections."

"So," Amos said. "You figured the smart move was to get a bunch of people who've never seen a working fusion drive to just fire one up so you could top off the batteries? That's the kind of suicidal optimism you just don't see every day."

Stokes shrugged. "The ship was here only because it needed repair. We were never able to make it run."

Amos clapped the man on the shoulder. "You just go get me all the tools you were using. This is something I know how to do."

Stokes trotted away, shouting to the others from his group. Erich's people seemed to be equally divided between setting up a defensive perimeter and looking for the most expensive things that would fit in their pockets. Erich and Peaches came to stand beside him.

"How fucked are we?" Erich said.

"Don't know," Amos said. "First guess, there's something hinky with the power supply. Too much noise. A bad coupler. Something that's triggering the safety shutdown. But I've got to get between her hulls and take a peek."

"I'll help you ring the circuits," Peaches said. Erich looked over at her, confused. "I spent a few months as an electrochemical technician," she said.

"Well of fucking course you did," Erich said.

"You bring a deck?" Amos asked.

"Sure," Erich said. "Why?"

Amos pointed at the drive cone with his chin. "You can get the diagnostics running, and I can tell you what the output means."

Erich frowned and scratched his neck thoughtfully with his tiny arm. "Sure. Figure I can do that."

Peaches coughed once, then chuckled. "Erich? Did you ever, you know, *kill* anyone?"

"I run a drug empire in Baltimore," Erich said. "Of course I've killed someone. Why?"

"Nothing," she said. "It's just here we are, three murderers, and what's going to save our asses if anything does is that we happen to have the skill set to repair a fusion drive."

Erich smiled. "We are kind of well suited to this, aren't we?"

"Well, we'd better set up some lookouts while we do it, though," Amos said. "My plan to get out of here before trouble comes back may not work out."

"I can have Stokes help with that too," Peaches said. "They can't fight, but they can watch. And I can get a few of the savvy ones to help us put the ship together if you want."

"More the merrier," Amos said. "Long as they don't touch anything unless we tell them."

"When we go, are we taking them with us?" Peaches asked.

"Yup," Amos said.

She smirked. "Because they're tribe?"

"Shit no. My tribe is the crew on the *Roci*, maybe you two, and a dead woman. I don't actually give a shit if every damned one of 'em dies."

"So why take them?"

One of Erich's people called out. Another one laughed, and one of the servants tentatively joined in. Amos rubbed the raw spots on his knuckles and shrugged. "Seems like the sort of thing Holden'd do."

Chapter Forty-One: Naomi

Naomi lifted the handles of the resistance machine over her head then let them slowly down. Sárta sat on the box of resistance gel and watched her like someone a little bit bored at a zoo. Naomi didn't care. They didn't talk. For every purpose but the ones that mattered most, Naomi was alone.

The trick, she'd decided, was not to remove just one EVA suit, but all of them. Corrupt the data, and no one would know whether she'd taken something or not. But if she only broke the inventory for the suits, that would be telling too. She lifted the handles. The muscles in her arms and shoulders ached. She let the handles down, savoring the pain. If she could get one of the scanners she'd used before, she might be able to feed false data into the system. Fill it with a few thousand phantoms. A million EVA suits filling every square centimeter of the ship. Then even if she couldn't erase the data, she could render it useless. The problem was—

The warning Klaxon sounded. Naomi's heart sank into her belly. They were preparing to go to free fall. She was out of time. She wasn't ready. Outside the ship right now, the umbilical was still in place. As soon as it was hauled in, the *Pella* and the *Chetzemoka* would peel apart, and all her fragile hopes would die. She let the handles drop. The cable pulled them back into place, ready for the next person.

She wasn't ready. She wasn't going to *be* ready. It didn't mean she wouldn't try.

She walked the few steps to the resistance gel and nodded at the guard. "Going to the head."

"Just been, you."

"Going again," she said, turning away.

"Hell you are. Hey!" Naomi pretended to ignore the woman, listening as she scrambled down to come after her. She'd been a model prisoner up to now, and the defiance took Sárta by surprise. Well, it was meant to. The warning sounded again, and the count. Zero g in three. Two. Naomi put both hands on the doorframe. One. Up and down vanished, and she pulled her body into a tight curl and exploded out toward Sárta. Both her feet hit the guard in the belly, sending her back through the wide empty air of the room. She grabbed Naomi's left shoe, prying it off as she spun away. It would take her seconds to reach the other side of the room and something to push against. That was her head start. Sárta was already shouting.

Naomi flipped herself through the hatch, then down the hall, too fast for safety. She had minutes. She had less than minutes. Had she really thought she could pry open a locker, pull on a suit, and cycle the airlock? The math had worked at the time. She couldn't imagine it now.

Sárta was somewhere behind her, shouting. Raising the alarm. But Naomi was already around the corner. With sight lines broken, Sárta would have to guess where she'd gone. With luck, it would buy her a few more seconds. She only needed seconds. She only had them. The crew airlock was closed. She cycled the inner door open, then started pulling at lockers. If someone—anyone—had slipped up. Left one unlocked. The metal clanked and rattled under her fingertips as she tugged and tugged and tugged. Was the umbilical unhooked yet? Were they pulling it in? It seemed like they must be.

There were voices raised from down the hallway. Men and women shouting. One of them was Sárta. Another one was Cyn. She felt herself sobbing and ignored it. She couldn't fail. She couldn't. Not this time. Not now.

For a sickening second, she didn't feel the decompression kit at her waist. She slapped the place where it had been pressed against her skin, and it was there. If she could just get a *suit*. She tried another locker. Her heart skipped as it opened. A simple EVA suit hung there, suspended in the null g by thin bands of elastic. She reached for it.

She stopped.

They'll know the suit is missing, a small voice said in the back of her mind. *They'll know where you've gone. They'll come after you.*

Her breath was heavy and fast, her heart racing. The thing she'd been trying not to think for the last hours came to the front of her mind like an old friend. *Fewer than fifty meters. It isn't far. You can make it.*

She closed the locker. The inner door of the airlock was open now. She launched herself toward it, forcing herself to pant. To hyperoxygenate. She couldn't tell if the dizziness she felt was from too much oxygen or a kind of existential vertigo. She was really going to do this. Naked in the void. She braced her palms against the outer door of the lock. She expected it to be cold. That it was the same temperature as any decking seemed wrong.

Fifty meters in hard vacuum. Maybe less. Maybe it was possible. She couldn't depressurize first. The long seconds matching the airlock to the outer nothingness would take more time than she had. She'd have to blow it out. Full pressure to nothing in a fraction of a second. If she held her breath, it would pop her lungs. She would have to blow herself empty first, let the void into her. All around her heart. Even if it worked, it would do her damage.

She could handle that.

The voices were loud and getting louder. Someone shouted, "Find the fucking bitch!" Cyn sloped in past the lockers. His eyes widened. Sárta was behind him. *Good*, she thought. *Perfect. Let them see.* The indicator went from green to red under her thumb. Cyn launched across the room with a wordless cry as the inner door started to close. For a moment, she thought he wouldn't make it, but his hands caught the edge of the door and hauled himself through. She tried to push him back, but he forced his way in.

The airlock door closed behind him, the magnetic seals clacking. Naomi held the handhold by the control panel, waiting for him to hit her. To kick. To put her in a chokehold. The lock was small enough he could put flat palms on both doors. She couldn't get away from him if he attacked, but he didn't. On the other side of the door, Sárta was shouting. Naomi thumbed the emergency override. Three options appeared: OPEN SHIP DOOR, OPEN OUTER DOOR, RETURN TO CYCLE.

"Knuckles, no you hagas eso." His hands were spread before him, wide and empty. "Bist bien. Bist bien alles."

"What are you doing?" Naomi said, surprised to hear the pain in her voice. "Why did you do that?"

"Because you my people, yeah? We're Belt. Born on the float. You, me. Alles la." Tears were welling up in his eyes, waves sheeting over pupil and iris with no gravity to fight the surface tension. "We travel so far, vide—uns the promised land. And we go all of us together. Tu y mé y alles."

"You aren't saving me," she said.

The big man crossed his arms. "Then I'm die trying. You're my people. We look out for each other. Take care. Not going to stand by while you die. Won't."

She should have been panting, forcing oxygen into her blood. She should have been flying across the emptiness. Cyn floated, turning slowly clockwise a degree at a time, his lips pressed tight, daring her to deny him. Daring her not to see that she was loved here, that she had family here, that she belonged.

Someone hit the inner door of the lock. The voices were louder. More numerous. Naomi knew she could open the door, but if she did, Cyn wouldn't be the only one going out it. If he'd wanted to, he could have beaten her down by now. That he hadn't meant he'd chosen not to. Naomi's heart felt trapped between stones. She couldn't blow the door. She had to. She couldn't kill Cyn. She couldn't save him. *Whatever you do now*, she thought, *you will regret it forever.* Seconds passed.

Another voice. Filip on the other side of the airlock door. She could hear him shouting, telling her to open the door. He sounded frantic.

How the hell did she keep getting into these situations?

"Be strong," Cyn said. "For Filipito, be *strong*."

"Okay," she said. She pushed her jaw forward in a yawn, opening her throat and her Eustachian tubes. Cyn yelped as she hit OPEN OUTER DOOR. Air tugged at her once, hard, as it evacuated. Adrenaline flooded her blood as she was assaulted invisibly on every square centimeter of flesh. The breath in her lungs rushed out of her, trying to pull her lungs along with it. Cyn grabbed at the airlock frame to keep himself inside, spun, screaming, was gone.

With her lungs empty, there was no reserve. She wasn't holding her breath, surviving off the gas held inside her. Someone could hold their breath for a couple minutes. In the vacuum, she could make it maybe fifteen seconds unaided.

One thousand one. Naomi shifted, hand over hand, to brace against the inner door and look out. The void was there, the great dome of stars. The *Chetzemoka* glowed in sunlight brighter than the Earth had ever seen. The umbilical hung to her left, too bright to look at directly and more than halfway retracted. Her ribs ached; her eyes ached. Her diaphragm tugged at her gut, trying to inflate lungs squeezed to knots. If she'd had an EVA suit, it would have had attitude thrusters. Without them, she had one chance and no time to think about it. *One thousand two.* She launched.

For a moment, she saw Cyn in the corner of her eye, a flicker of pale movement. The sun was below her, vast and bright. Radiant heat pressed against her throat and face. The Milky Way spread out, arching across the endless sky. Carbon dioxide built up in her blood; she could feel it in the burning drive to breathe. The *Chetzemoka* grew slowly larger. *One thousand five.* Shadows streaked its side, every protrusion and rivet cutting the sunlight into strips of darkness. Everything fell slightly out of focus as her eyes deformed. The stars shifted from diamond points of light to halos to clouds, like the whole universe dissolving. She'd thought it would be silent, but she heard her heartbeat like someone hammering in the next deck.

If I die here, she thought, *at least it's beautiful. This would be a lovely way to die. One thousand eight.*

The lines of the *Chetzemoka*'s airlock became clear enough to make out. Without magnetic boots, she'd have to reach it with bare handholds, but she was close. She was almost there. The world began to narrow, lights going out in her peripheral vision even as the bright ship grew larger. Passing out. She was passing out. She plucked the black thumb out of her belt, twisted it to expose the needle, and slammed it into her leg. *One thousand ten.*

A coldness spread through her, but the colors came back as the sip of hyperoxygenated blood poured through her. An extra bit of breath without having the luxury of breathing out first. The airlock indicator on the *Chetzemoka*'s skin blinked, the emergency response received, the cycle starting. The ship loomed up. She was going to hit, and she couldn't afford to bounce. She put her hands out fingers first, and prepared to crumple as she struck. There were handholds on the surface—some were designed, but others were the protrusions of antennae and cameras. She hit with all the same energy she'd kicked off with, the ship slamming into her. She'd known to expect that. She was ready. Her fingers closed on a handhold. The force of the body wrenched her shoulder and elbow, but she didn't lose her grip. *One thousand thirteen.*

Across the gap, the umbilical was in the *Pella.* Maneuvering thrusters lit along the warship's side, an ejection mass of super-heated water glowing as it jetted out. Cyn's body—he would have lost consciousness by now—was out there somewhere, but she couldn't see it. He was already lost, and at least Sárta and Filip and maybe others had seen them both. Cyn and Naomi in the airlock without suits, and then gone. Spaced. Dead.

Not dead yet. She had to get moving. Her mind had skipped a fraction of a second. She couldn't do that. Naomi pulled herself carefully, skimming along centimeters from the skin of the ship. Too fast, and she wouldn't be able to stop. Too slow and she'd pass out before she reached safety. All she could do was hope there was a golden middle ground. *One thousand...* She didn't know anymore. Fifteen? Her whole body was a confusion of pain and animal panic. She couldn't make out the stars at all anymore. The *Pella* was a blur. The saliva in her mouth bubbled. Boiled. A high, thin whine filled her ears, an illusion of sound where no sound was.

A lot of things happen, she thought, vaguely aware she'd said it to someone else, not long ago. *Even this.* She felt a wave of peace wash over her. Euphoria. It was a bad sign.

The airlock was there, five meters away. Then four. Her mind skipped, and it was flashing past her. She shot out her arm, grabbing for it, and the frame hit her wrist. She clutched for it, snatching the way Cyn had. She was spinning, the impact turning all her forward momentum angular. But she was over the airlock. Its pale mouth rose up from under her feet and vanished overhead, and back again, and back again. When she reached out, her hand was actually inside the ship, but she couldn't touch the frame. Couldn't pull herself in. The *Pella* was drifting away, losing its color as her consciousness began to fade. So close. She'd come so very close. Centimeters more, and she might have lived. But space was unforgiving. People died there all the time. The *Pella* loosed another plume from its maneuvering thrusters, as if in solemn agreement.

Without thinking, she drew up her leg, the spin increasing as she bent tight. She pulled off the shoe that Sárta hadn't gotten. Her hands felt weird. Clumsy, awkward, more than half numbed. When she stretched back out, the spin slowed to what it had been. She tried to judge the timing, but too little of her mind was left. In the end, she saw the *Pella* at the end of a distant and darkening hall and threw the shoe at it as hard as her failing strength allowed.

Ejection mass. The spin slowed. Her hands reached farther into the airlock. She was drifting in. Her heel hit the steel frame and the pain was excruciating and very far away. Her mind blinked. She had an impression of the airlock control panel, the lights trying to impart some critical information. She couldn't see the colors or the symbols on the pad. Her consciousness faded and was gone.

Naomi woke herself up coughing. The deck was pressing against her face. She couldn't tell if she was desperately weak or under high burn. The edges of the airlock around her were fuzzy. She coughed again, a deep wet sound. Images of hemorrhaging lungs filled her mind, but the fluid she brought up was clear. Her hands were almost unrecognizable as hands. Her fingers were thick as sausages, filled with plasma and fluid. Her skin was too hurt to touch, like a bad sunburn. Her joints ached from her toes to the vertebrae in her neck. Her belly felt like someone had kicked her in the gut a couple dozen times.

She forced a breath. She could do that. Inhale, exhale. Something gurgled in her lungs. Not blood, though. She told herself it wasn't blood. She rolled onto her side, tucked her legs up, rose to sitting, and then lay back down again as the world swam. That was more than a g. That had to be more than a g. She couldn't be that weak, could she?

The *Chetzemoka* hummed under her. She realized vaguely that she was hearing words. Voices. A voice. She knew that didn't make sense, but she didn't know why. She pressed her hands to her face. A storm of emotions ran through her—elation, grief, triumph, rage. Her brain wasn't working well enough yet to associate them with anything. They just happened, and she watched and waited and gathered her scattered self together. Her hands and feet started hurting, tortured nerve endings screaming at her. She ignored them. Pain was only pain, after all. She'd lived through worse.

Next time, she made it to her feet. The little black thumb of the decompression kit was still lodged in her leg. She pulled it out, lifted it to shoulder high, and dropped it. It fell like maybe one and a half, two gs. That was nice. If she'd felt this bad at just one g, she'd have been worried. She should probably have been worried anyway.

She cycled the inner door open and stumbled out to the cheap locker room. The lockers hung open, EVA suits hanging in them or scattered on the floor. The air bottles were all gone. The voice—it was just one voice, but her ears seemed to have lost all their treble and left only an incomprehensible soup of bass tones—was familiar. She thought she should know it. She moved through the abandoned ship. She wondered how long she'd been unconscious, and if there was any way to know where she was, what heading she was on, and how fast she was already traveling.

She reached a control panel and tried to access the navigation system, but it was locked down. As was the comm, the system status, the repair and diagnostics. She laid her forehead against the panel more from exhaustion than despair. The direct contact of bone on ceramic changed the voice, sound conduction through contact, like pressing helmets together and shouting. She knew the voice. She knew the words. "This is Naomi Nagata of the *Rocinante*. If you get this message, please retransmit. Tell James Holden I am in distress. Comm is not responding. I have no nav control. Please retransmit." She chuckled, coughed up the clear fluid, spat it on the deck, and laughed again. The message was a lie built by Marco to lure Jim to his death.

Every bit of it was true.

Chapter Forty-Two: Holden

Arnold Mfume, who wasn't Alex, came out of the crew quarters still drying his hair. When he saw Holden and Foster—the two captains—by the coffee machine, he grimaced.

"Running a little late there, Mister Mfume," Foster Sales said.

"Yes, sir. Chava just pointed that out to me. I'm on my way."

"Coffee?" Holden said, holding out a freshly brewed bulb. "Little milk, no sugar. Might not be how you take it, but it's ready now."

"I won't say no," Mfume said with a fast, nervous smile. Holden couldn't place his accent. Flat vowel sounds and swallowed consonants. Wherever it came from, it sounded good on him.

As Holden handed over the bulb, Foster cleared his throat. "You know it's a bad habit to be late for your shift."

"I know, sir. I'm sorry, sir. It won't happen again."

And then, Mfume was gone, bolting up the ladder toward the

cockpit faster than the lift would have taken him. Foster sighed and shook his head. "It's good being young," he said, "but some people wear it better than others."

Holden tapped in an order for another coffee. "I wouldn't want people to judge me by what I did in my twenties. What about you? Can I get you one?"

"More of a tea man, myself," the other captain said. "If that's an option."

"Don't know that I've ever tried."

"No?"

"There was always coffee."

The morning meeting had started off as just part of the shakedown. Between the new crew and the uncertainty surrounding the ship, it had seemed like a good idea for Holden and Foster Sales to touch base with each other, compare notes, make sure that everything was the way it was supposed to be. The care Foster took to treat the *Roci* with respect had helped Holden. The new crew wasn't his, and he didn't feel comfortable with them, but they weren't going through the real crew's lockers while no one was looking. And day by day, their presence was growing more familiar. Less strange.

When he called down to engineering and Kazantzakis or Ip replied, it didn't seem as wrong anymore. Finding Sun-yi and Gor wired into gaming goggles shooting the crap out of each other in simulated battles—because as weapons techs with no one to shoot at they were getting antsy—stopped being weird and edged into sort of endearing. Maura Patel was spending her insomniac, sleepless shifts upgrading the tightbeam system. Holden knew it was something Naomi had on her list of projects, but he let Maura do it anyway. And after the long, quiet days in the dock, sleeping in his couch and waking to an empty ship, part of him even appreciated the company. They might be the wrong people, but they were people. Having guests in his house kept him from descending into his fear and anxiety. He was only putting on a brave face, but it actually made him feel a little braver.

"Anything else I should be aware of?" Foster asked.

"Just I want to know if anything happens with the *Razorback* or the *Pella*," Holden said. "Or if we get a message from Earth. Amos Burton or my family, either one." As if they were different.

"I think you've made that clear to the crew," Foster said solemnly, but with a glimmer of amusement in his eye. Probably Holden had made the point a few times. To everyone. The coffee machine chimed and gave Holden a fresh bulb. Foster made his way to the ladder, and then down toward the torpedo bays where Kazantzakis was cleaning things that were already clean. Holden waited a few seconds and then headed up to the ops deck. Chava, coming down, met him, and they did a little awkward no-you-first dance before they got past each other.

Fred was in the crash couch that he'd appropriated as his office. The hatch to the cockpit was closed, but Holden could still hear the wailing of the raï that Mfume liked to listen to during his shift in the pilot's seat. Between that and the coffee, he wouldn't be sleeping, but Fred had put headphones on and so didn't hear Holden coming. The image on his screen was familiar. Marco Inaros, the self-styled head of the Free Navy and public face of the devastation of Earth. And—Holden tried the thought carefully in case it hurt too much to think it—if Naomi was dead, the man who'd probably killed her. His chest contracted painfully and he pushed the idea away. Thinking about Amos and Naomi was too dangerous.

Fred turned sharply, noticing him, and pulled off the headphones. "Holden. How long have you been there?"

"Just came up."

"Good. Hate to think I'm getting too feeble to know when there's someone in the room. Everything all right?"

"Apart from being in the middle of a system-wide coup with half of my crew missing? Peachy. I mean, I'm not sleeping, and when I do it's nightmares from start to finish, but peachy."

"Well, it was kind of a stupid question. Sorry about that."

Holden sat on the couch beside Fred's and leaned in.

"What do we know about this guy?"

"Inaros?" Fred said. "He was on my short list of possibilities when the rocks dropped. Not the head of it, but in the top five. He leads a splinter group of high-poverty Belters. The kind of people who live in leaky ships and post screeds about taxation being theft. I've spoken to him a time or two, usually to deescalate a situation he wanted to set on fire."

"You think he's the one behind it all?"

Fred sat back, his couch gimbals hissing as they shifted. From the headphones, Holden could hear the man's voice even over the murmurs of raï—"We will begin again and remake humanity without the corruption, greed, and hatred that the inner planets could not transcend..."

Fred grunted and shook his head. "I don't see it. Inaros is charismatic. And he's smart. Watching his press release, he certainly thinks he's in charge, but he'd have to. The man's a first-rate narcissist and a sadist besides. He'd never knowingly share power with anyone if he could help it. This level of organization? Of coordination? It seems beyond his reach."

"How so?"

Fred gestured toward the screen. The light from it glowed in his eyes; tiny images of Inaros giving his salute. "It doesn't feel right. He's the kind of man who carries a lot of weight in a small circle. Playing at this scale isn't what he does best. He isn't a bad tactician, and the timing of the attacks was showy in a way that seems like he was likely behind them. And he's charming at the negotiating table. But..."

"But?"

"But he's not a first-class mind, and this is a first-class operation. I don't know how to put it better than that. My gut says that even if he's taking credit for it, he has a handler."

"What would your gut have said before the rocks dropped?"

Fred coughed out a laugh. "That he was an annoyance and a small-time player. So yes, it may just be sour grapes on my part.

I'd rather think I was outplayed by someone who's a genius at something grander than self-mythologizing."

"Do you have any idea why Naomi would be on his ship?"

Fred's gaze shifted from the hazy middle distance of thought to directly on Holden. "Is that someplace we want to go right now?"

"Do you?"

"I don't. But I can speculate. Naomi is a Belter, and what I know of her says she grew up in the same circles as Inaros and his crew. I have to assume they crossed paths before and had some unfinished business. Maybe they were on the same side, maybe they were enemies, maybe both. But not neither."

Holden leaned forward, elbows on his knees. As general as they were, as gently as he'd said them, the words were like little hammer blows. He swallowed.

"Holden. Everyone has a past. Naomi was a grown woman when you met her. You didn't think she'd popped out of the packaging right when you set eyes on her, did you?"

"No, of course not. Everyone on the *Canterbury* was there because they had a reason. Including me. It's just if there was something big, like 'part of a cabal that went on to destroy Earth' big, I don't know why she wouldn't have told me."

"Did you ask?"

"No. I mean, she knew that I was interested. That she could tell me whatever she wanted to tell me. I figured if she didn't want to, that was up to her."

"And now you're upset that she didn't. So what changed? Why are you entitled to know things now that you weren't entitled to know before?"

The raï from the cockpit paused, silence filling the ops deck. On Fred's screen, the playback had reached the split circle as it faded to white. "I may," Holden said, "be a small, petty person. But if I'm going to lose her, I at least need to know why."

"We'll see if we can't put you in a position to ask her yourself," Fred said. The music from the cockpit kicked in again, and

Fred scowled up at the hatch. "If it's any comfort, I think we have a chance. I don't think it'll be long before he's ready to open negotiations."

"No?" Holden said. It was such a thin sliver of hope, but he felt himself jumping to it all the same.

"No. He got the jump on us tactically. I will absolutely give him that. But the next part is where he has to actually consolidate and hold power. That's not tactics. That's strategy, and I don't see anything in him that leads me to think he has a handle on that."

"I do."

Fred waved a hand like Holden's words had been smoke and he was clearing the air. "He's playing a short-run game. Yes, his stock's high right now, and probably will be for a little while. But he's standing in the way of the gates. All of this is to stop people from going out and setting up colonies. But the hunger is already out there. Smith couldn't stop Mars from depopulating itself. Avasarala couldn't put the brakes on the process, and God knows she tried. Marco Inaros thinks he can do it at the end of a gun, but I don't see it working. Not for long. And he doesn't understand fragility."

"You mean Earth?"

"Yes," Fred said. "It's the blind spot of being a Belter. I've seen it over and over in the past few decades. There's a faith in the technology. In the idea of maintaining an artificial ecosystem. We're able to grow food on Ganymede, so they think humanity's freed from the bonds of Earth. They don't think about how much work we had to do for those crops to grow. The mirrors to concentrate the sun, the genetic modifications to the plants. The process of learning to build rich soil out of substrate and fungus and full-spectrum lights. And backstopping all of that, the complexity of life on Earth. And now these new worlds... well I don't have to tell you how much less hospitable they are than it says on the box. Once it becomes clear that he's got it wrong—"

"He doesn't, though," Holden said. "Yeah, okay, the ecological part maybe he hasn't thought all the way through, but when it comes to the Belt, he *isn't* wrong. Look at all the people who just pulled up stakes and headed out for the rings. Ilus or New Terra or whatever the hell you want to call it? It's a terrible, terrible planet, and there are people living on it. All those colony ships that left Mars to go try terraforming a place that's already got air and a magnetosphere? A lot of those people are really, really smart. Even now, just now, you said how the pressure to get out to the new systems is more than this guy expects or is prepared for. That means he's doomed, maybe. But that doesn't make him wrong. We have to make him be wrong."

"You think I don't know that?" Fred said. "What I was doing with Medina Station would have—"

"Would have made a place for all the people living on Medina Station. But asteroid prospectors? Water haulers? The crews that are barely eking by? Those are who Marco's talking to, and he's right because no one else is taking them into account. Not even you. They're looking at the future, and they're seeing that no one needs them anymore. Everything they do will be easier in a gravity well, and they can't go there. We have to make some kind of future that has a place for them in it. Because unless we do, they have literally nothing to lose. It's all already gone."

The system chimed and Maura's voice came over the speakers. "Captain Holden, sir?"

"I'm here," Holden said, still looking at Fred's angry scowl. "And aren't you supposed to be off shift, Mister Patel?"

"I am off shift, sir. But I couldn't sleep, so I was running some diagnostics. But Captain Sales said you wanted an alert if the situation changed with the *Razorback* and its pursuers?"

Holden's mouth flooded with the metallic taste of fear. "What's going on?"

"We're getting reports that the Free Navy ships have broken off, sir. The UN forces are still half a day out, but the thought is the Free Navy vessels are trying to steer well clear of any large-scale confrontation."

"The *Pella*?" Holden said.

"With the Free Navy fleet, sir, but when they made the course change, a civilian ship broke off from the grouping, turning the other way. It's got a lot of inertia to overcome, but unless it changes its acceleration profile, it looks to be on a course that will bring it within a million klicks of us."

"That's not accidental," Fred said.

"It isn't, sir," Maura said. "The vessel's registered at the *Chetzemoka*, and it's broadcasting a message on loop. Message follows."

Holden's knuckles hurt and he forced himself to relax his fists. Naomi's voice filled the ops deck, and it was like being on the verge of passing out from dehydration and being handed a glass of water. As dire as the message was, Holden still felt every syllable untying his knots. When Naomi's message was done, he fell back in his couch, limp as a rag. She was in trouble, but it was trouble they could fix. She was on her way back toward him.

"Thank you, Mister Patel," Holden said. "In thanks, you may now have all my stuff. I don't care about any of it anymore."

"Including the coffee maker, sir?"

"Almost all my stuff."

When Fred spoke, his voice was hard. Sharp. Unrelieved. "Mister Patel, what relief ships are in the vicinity?"

"Transponder data shows nothing, sir. The inner system's been pretty much shut down. UN order."

Holden rolled to his side and called up a connection to Mfume. Music blared out of the console. Mixed with the sounds filtering through the deck, it made the ops deck seem larger than it was. "Mfume!" Holden shouted, and then a few seconds later, "Mister Mfume!"

The music turned down, but not off. "Sir?"

"I need you to take a look at the flight path for the *Chetzemoka*. See what it's going to take to match orbits with her."

"What ship?" Mfume said.

"The *Chetzemoka*," Holden said. "Just check the newsfeeds. It'll be there. Let me know what you figure out as quickly as you possibly can. Like now would be good."

"I'm on it," Mfume said, and the music turned off both on the console and from the hatch. Holden took a deep breath, then another, then laughed. The relief wasn't an emotion. It was too physical and profound for that. It was a state of being. It was a drug that poured invisibly through his veins. He started laughing and it turned into a moan that sounded like pain, or else pain's aftermath.

Fred clicked his tongue against his teeth. "So. If I were to suggest that we not rendezvous with that ship?"

"I would be happy to let you and your friends off anywhere between here and there," Holden said. "Because unless you've decided to turn to piracy and throw me out the airlock, that ship is where we're going."

"I thought as much," Fred said. "Can we at least agree to be careful approaching it?"

Holden felt a little bubble of rage rise up in him. He wanted to shout at Fred, to punish him for taking this moment and soiling it with doubt. With the possibility that it was a trap and not Naomi coming home at last. Holden took the great glowing sense of release and tried to put it aside and his anger with it.

"Yes," he said. "You're right. It could be a trap."

"It may not be," Fred said. "I hope it isn't. But..."

"But we're living in interesting times," Holden said. "It's okay. I get it. I'll be careful. *We'll* be careful. But if it is her, and she really is in trouble, she's my first priority. That's just the way it is."

"I know," Fred said, and the way he said it meant *I know, and everyone who knows anything about you does too. Which is why you should be careful.*

Holden turned to the monitor and pulled up the nav data. As he watched, Mfume laid in the course that would get him to Naomi. Or whatever else was on that ship. Fred's seed of doubt had already taken root. He didn't know whether to be grateful or resent the old man. Between the distances and their respective velocities, it looked like it would be tricky. Naomi had been burning hard toward Earth, and the speed the *Chetzemoka* had built up was almost all in the wrong direction to reach him. If it wasn't a trap and Naomi was in trouble, he could still be too late. The UN force might be able to help, but she was already peeling away from their flight path.

Which still didn't leave him entirely without resources. He flipped to comms and started recording.

"Alex, since you're in the neighborhood and it went so well the last time I asked you to check out a mystery ship, I was wondering if you'd be interested in making a little detour."

Chapter Forty-Three: Alex

The worst thing was not knowing. The newsfeeds were awash with information, but very little of it matched up. Four billion were dead on Earth. Or seven. The ash and vapor that had turned the blue marble to white was starting to thin already—much sooner than the models predicted. Or the surface of the Earth wouldn't see daylight and blue skies for years. It was the dawn of a resurgence of natural flora and fauna driven by the human dieback or it was the final insult that would crash a perennially overstressed ecosystem.

Three more colony ships had been captured on their way to the ring gate and turned back or boarded and the crews spaced, or else seven had, or it was only one. Ceres Station's announcement that Free Navy ships could use the docks was a provocation or a proof that the OPA was unified or the station administration was giving in to fear. All around the system, ships were turning off their transponders, and the systems for visual tracking of the exhaust plumes were getting dusted off and reprogrammed in languages that contemporary systems could parse. Alex told himself it was temporary, that in a few months, maybe a year, everyone would run with transponders again. That the Earth would be the center of human civilization and culture. That he would be back on the *Roci* with Holden and Naomi and Amos.

He told himself that, but he was getting less and less persuasive. Not knowing was the worst thing. The second-worst thing was being chased by a bunch of top-of-the-line warships that really wanted to kill you.

In the display, one of their escort missiles went from green to amber to flashing red.

"Shit," Bobbie said. "Lost one."

"It's all right. We've got plenty more."

In the past hours, the *Pella* and her pack had come up with the bright idea of coordinating their comm lasers to hit a particular missile and then pumping energy into it until the controls overheated. The missiles failed inert, or they would have figured the enemy strategy out when the escorting cloud had cooked off in a massive chain reaction. Instead, they'd lost four missiles in half an hour and put together what was happening. Bobbie and the *Razorback*'s antiquated and underpowered system had designed a rolling pattern formation for the missiles that kept any one of them from being in an uninterrupted sightline for more than a few seconds at a time. Watching it on the cameras reminded Alex of documentaries he'd seen about deep sea fish on Earth, vast schools roiling and yet staying together. Only for him, it was their little group of remaining missiles.

Ever since the announcement by the Free Navy, the prime minister had been back in the cabin, using their own tightbeam for what sounded like a hundred furious conversations that all seemed to have the same timbre. Alex couldn't quite make out all the words and he made conscious effort not to listen in case someone asked later what he knew. But the phrases *not substanti-*

ated and *significant failure* and *still investigating* all came through enough times that Alex started to recognize them, kind of like hearing a song often enough that the lyrics became clearer.

His monitor was divided between a large-scale map of the solar system highlighting the parts of it critical to him—the *Razorback*, the UN military escort burning out to meet them, the *Rocinante*, the *Pella* and its pack, Tycho Station, Mars, Earth, Luna—and a smaller inset that was the *Razorback*'s internal systems diagnostics. The little pinnace hadn't been intended for full interplanetary travel, and with Earth and Mars where they were, they were going to be cutting it pretty close. The reactor had enough fuel pellets to burn for months, but once they ran out of ejection mass, the drive wouldn't do them much good. So far, they were still inside the error bars. Which, for him, meant that even if they ran out, they'd be going slow enough that someone could come throw a tether on them. Rescued by professionals was still firmly in his win column.

The navigation system threw an alert to his monitor. He opened it.

"What've you got?" Bobbie asked.

"The *Pella* and her little friend there cut their drives again," Alex said. "And...Hey! I think...Some of the ships are peeling off. I think they're giving up!"

Bobbie whooped and Smith stopped his conversation in the back long enough to come see what was going on. By the time Alex had explained it all, the *Pella* had its drive on too, and was turning with the others. Not a full flip-and-burn, but a kind of fishtail slide that kept a good fraction of their momentum while still setting them on a course for the Belt and, give or take a few million kilometers, the Jovian system. The *Chetzemoka* peeled off in the opposite direction. Whatever mission the *Pella* was on, it was leaving the *Razorback* behind.

A tension Alex hadn't been consciously aware of started to evaporate along with Bobbie's occasional whoops and laughter. The UN escort force checked in. The solar flares weren't even coming close to intersecting with their path. The *Razorback*'s heat sinks were coping with the radiant heat well enough. Alex let himself relax.

It lasted almost half an hour.

"This is Naomi Nagata of the *Rocinante*. If you get this message, please retransmit. Tell James Holden I am in distress. Comm is not responding. I have no nav control. Please retransmit..."

And then forty minutes after that:

"Alex, since you're in the neighborhood and it went so well the last time I asked you to check out a mystery ship, I was wondering if you'd be interested in making a little detour. I'm having my temporary pilot figure out a fast burn that will get me to Naomi, but you're closer and you're going in nearly the same direction. There's a chance this is the bad guys trying to trick us, so keep your eyes open. If it is Naomi, though, make sure she's still breathing when I get there. Let me know what you think."

Alex's jaw was clenched hard enough his teeth ached. He already knew what Bobbie was going to say, so instead of starting the conversation, he started quietly feeding data into the nav system and seeing what options were open depending on how hard he wanted to burn and how much fuel he had left, and what telemetry said about the little ship and the convoy it broke off from. The wall screens were set to mimic the exterior view, so when he looked up from the navigation data, he could pick out the dot of light that was her drive plume. He also pulled up an audio feed matched to the broadcast from it. "This is Naomi Nagata of the *Rocinante*. If you get this message, please retransmit..."

He could feel the disapproval radiating up from behind him. Bobbie didn't say anything at first, didn't even make a grunt or a noise. It didn't matter. Alex knew. When she finally did speak, it was almost a relief to have it out in the open.

"What are you doing there, sailor?" Bobbie asked.

"Figuring the best way to go after Naomi."

"Any reason you're doing it?"

"Because we're going after Naomi."

"We're almost at the flip part of the flip-and-burn. Any course changes we make are going to eat up a lot of fuel."

Alex didn't look back. Just gestured at the screen. "The way I figure, that's a distress call. We logged it. We're obligated to stop."

"Don't," Bobbie said.

"That's the rules."

"Don't throw the rule book at me. We've got a mission here. I don't like it any more than you do, but we need to stand our post. We've got orders."

Alex's jaw hurt worse. He tried yawning to stretch the ache away. It didn't work. He turned his crash couch to face her. With her helmet off and her hair pulled back in a tight, functional ponytail, her head seemed small. The power armor was still locked in place, hands in fists against each side of the ship. If she decided to disable him and take command of the pinnace, she was just going to win. Also, he needed to keep in mind that she was jerry-rigged in place, and probably couldn't actually take a really high-g burn without coming loose.

"We do," he said. "We've got orders. But you've got orders from Nate and Avasarala, and I absolutely respect how you look out for both of those. But I got orders from my captain, and the watch I need to stand is over that way and getting farther from us."

"You're not thinking with your head," Bobbie said. "Look at the risk profile, Alex, because if we go, we're taking a risk. If we win, we get Naomi Nagata out of trouble. If we lose, the leader of one of the most important political organizations in the human race dies at a time when unity and leadership is critically important. No, stop. I know what you're thinking. I've thought it too, just about some other people. Naomi's yours. She's one of the people in your circle, and fuck if you're going to risk her, much less sacrifice her for some kind of vague greater good, right?"

Alex closed his mouth, paused. "Right."

"I understand that," Bobbie said. "I do. I had to train a lot to understand that isn't what we do. You had that training too. Whether we're on active duty or not doesn't matter. We serve Mars because we swore an oath. If doing the right thing was the same as doing the easy thing, we wouldn't have had to swear. We have the prime minister of Mars in this ship. We have a military escort coming to get him safely to Luna."

"And we have the enemy out there," Alex said, hating the words as he said them. "It's a trap, isn't it?"

"I don't know," Bobbie said. "It could be. Disable someone and shoot the responders is a dirty trick, but I wouldn't put it past these bastards."

"I don't see how going after her would put us in more danger than holding course," Alex said. "If they've got a rail gun pointing at us, they can hole us right here just as well as over there."

"Trojan horse," Bobbie said. "Pack that thing full of soldiers. If we dock with her, all these missiles aren't going to help a damned bit. Or if the *Rocinante* gets to it, they take Fred Johnson."

"The odds of—"

"Don't think about the odds," Bobbie said. "Think about the stakes. Think how much we lose if we take the risk and it goes wrong."

Alex's head felt thick, like the first stages of illness. He looked back at his nav panel. The distance between the *Razorback* and *Chetzemoka* increased with every second. He took a deep breath, blew out. Naomi's voice came softly from the feed. "Tell James Holden I am in distress. Comm is not responding. I have no nav control..."

The voice that came from the cabin space was soft, gentle, conversational. "An interesting analysis, but incomplete."

Nathan Smith stood in the doorway. His hair was greasy and disarrayed. His clothes looked like they'd been slept in. His eyes were bloodshot, the rims red and angry. Alex thought he looked a decade older than when they'd taken off. The prime minister smiled at Alex, then Bobbie, then Alex again.

"Sir," Bobbie said.

"You've neglected a term, Sergeant. Consider what we stand to lose if we don't make the attempt."

"The reason for doing this," Alex said. "The reason for doing any of this. If there's a chance—and I think there's a pretty damned good one—that Naomi managed her own escape, and she's out there and in distress, and she's called for help, you know what the rules are? That we stop and help. Even if she's not someone we know. Even if it was someone else's voice. That's the rule, because out here, we help each other. And if we stopped doing that because we're more important or because the rules don't apply to us anymore, I can make a decent case that we've stopped being the good guys."

Smith beamed. "That was beautiful, Mister Kamal. I had been thinking of explaining to Chrisjen Avasarala that we'd left our only solid witness to the *Pella* behind, but I think I like your version better. Set course and alert the UN escort to our change of plans."

"Yes, sir," Alex said. When the door closed, he turned to Bobbie. "Sorry."

"Don't be," Bobbie said. "It's not like I didn't want to go after her."

"And if it turns out the ship's full of soldiers?"

"I can take this suit out for a drive," Bobbie said. "Won't hurt my feelings."

It only took a few minutes to set the optimal intercept course and fire off a flight plan to the UN escort ships. Afterward, he recorded a tightbeam message for Holden. "Hey there, Cap'n. We're on our way, but we'll be careful. Get in, take a good look, and if anything's getting our hackles up, we won't board. Meantime, you tell that pilot you've got that whoever makes rendezvous first owes the other fella a beer."

Chapter Forty-Four: Naomi

Even a steady one g could be unpleasant for her. The constant press of two was a slow torture. It began as a deep ache in her knees and the base of her spine, then progressed quickly to sharp pain, like a needle stuck into the joints. Naomi surveyed the *Chetzemoka* in stages, moving through a deck, then lying down until the pain lessened, then the next deck. Her hands and feet hurt even as the swelling subsided. Her cough didn't get better, but it didn't get worse.

The first disappointment was that the controls were in lockdown. She tried a few passwords—FreeNavy and Marcoisgreat and Filip—but even if she got it right, there was no reason to expect that they'd left the biometrics profiles turned off.

The lockers by the airlock hung open and empty. The three EVA suits that remained didn't have batteries or air bottles. The emergency rations were gone. She expected the toolboxes to be gone from the machine shop, but they'd taken out the racks that held them too, the drawers from the cabinets, the LEDs from the wall lights. The crash couches were all slit open, gel and padding pooled on the deck beside them. The drug delivery system and reservoirs were gone. The only water was in the drives; ejection mass to be spit out the back of the ship. The only food was the residue in the recyclers that hadn't been processed back into anything edible. The stink of welding rigs and burning still hung in the air, so the air recycler was probably running unfiltered.

Naomi lay on the deck, her head resting on her hands, and her eyes closed. The ship had been constructed for one use and as an insurance write-off. Its working life had begun with it being disposable, and it had been looted from there. Even the physical panels and monitors had been salvaged and carried away. As presents to Filip went, it was actually pretty crappy. The deck shook under her, the vibration of thrust setting up resonances that no system even tried to damp down. Between the high g and the vacuum damage leaking fluid into her lungs, breathing took more effort than it should have.

The ship wasn't a ship. She needed to stop thinking of it that way. It was a bomb. It was what she'd done to the *Augustín Gamarra* years ago and had carried with her ever since like a weight around her throat. Jim had known the kind of person that landed on water haulers like the *Canterbury*. He'd said that everyone there had reasons for being there. There were reasons the ship she'd tried to give to her son was stripped empty and triggered to kill. Not just her but anyone who came close to her. There were reasons. If she could defuse it, undo the threat, then she could follow it back, though. Take it to Ceres, where it had all started. There should be a way through the machine shop. All machine shops were supposed to be connected at the back.

She reached out her hands, only they weren't her hands. She was dreaming. She forced her eyes open and rolled to her back with an exhausted sob.

Okay. If she stopped moving now, she was going to sleep. That was good to know. She sat up, rested her head against the wall. *Sleep later. Sleep when you're dead. Or even better, sleep when you're safe.* She grinned to herself. Safe. That sounded like a good plan. She should try that for a change. She balled her hands into tight fists. The joints all screamed in pain, but when she opened them, her fingers moved better. That was probably a metaphor for something.

She had to set priorities. She didn't have a lot of resources. If she just grabbed at the first idea that came to her, it would be easy to exhaust herself without getting the critical work done. She needed to get food and water and make sure the air supply was reliable. She needed to warn anyone coming to save her not to approach. She needed to disarm the trap. Maybe dump core, maybe replace the drivers with a copy that didn't carry her poisoned code.

And she needed to do it before the ship blew up. At two g. Without tools or access to the controls. Or…was that right? Access to the controls was going to be hard, but she should be able to improvise some tools. The EVA suits weren't powered and didn't have bottles, but they had seals and reinforcement. She could take the cloth apart, and salvage some lengths of wire. Maybe something solid enough to cut with. And could she use the helmet clamps as a kind of vise grip or clamp? She wasn't sure.

Even if she could, what would that gain her?

"More than you've got now," she said aloud. Her voice reverberated in the empty space.

All right. Step one, make tools. Step two, drop core. Or warn anyone coming in. She stood up and forced herself back to the airlock lockers.

⚡

Five hours later, she was on the ship's perfunctory little engineering deck, sealing the hatch manually. Two of the EVA suits had given up what little they had to offer to make a tiny, sketchy tool kit. Doing anything with the controls had failed. So she could be a rat in a box, or she could take out the middleman. After all, the controls all connected to machinery, and the machinery—some of it—was where she could put her hands on it.

The space between the hulls was in vacuum, and she didn't have any great faith that the outer hull was actually sealed. The one remaining suit held about five minutes' worth of air without a bottle and she could set the radio to passive and pick up the faintest echo of her own voice making the false message with the residual charge in the wires. The lock that should have let her get into and out of the maintenance access had been hauled off as salvage, but she could turn the full engineering deck into a makeshift airlock. Close the hatch to the rest of the ship, force the access panel into the space between hulls. She budgeted two minutes to locate something useful—a power repeater she could sabotage to force the drive to shut down, the wiring for the comm system, an unsecured console that was talking to the computers—then two minutes to get back out. Thirty seconds to close and seal the maintenance panel and pop the engineering hatch. She'd lose a roomful of air every time, but she'd only lose a roomful.

She put on the helmet and checked the seals, then opened the access panel. It fought her at first, then gave all at once. She thought she felt a rush of escaping air go past her, but it was probably her imagination. Twenty seconds already gone. She crawled into the vacuum between the hulls. The darkness was so complete, it was like closing her eyes. She tapped the suit's controls, but no beam of light came from them.

She backed out, closed the access panel, opened the hatch, and took off her helmet.

"Light," she said to the empty space. "Going to need some light."

The monitor hung from wires, asking for her password. It just fit past the lip of the access panel, and filled the space between the hulls with light so dim, she couldn't see colors in it. Shadows of struts and spars made deeper darkness all around, and shapes she couldn't make sense of. She had forty-five seconds before she had to head back. It was the fifth time she'd been down trying to scrape through the coating on the wires. In a real ship, it would all have been protected by conduit. On this piece of crap, the wiring had all been fixed directly to the hull with a layer of yellowed silicone epoxy. On the one hand, it was a blessing. On the other, she was horrified that she'd ever trusted her life to the ship. If she'd inspected between the hulls before they left Ceres, she'd have been sleeping in an environment suit the whole way to the *Pella*.

The coating peeled free. Thirty seconds. She took a bit of salvaged wire and shorted the circuit. A fat spark leaped out and the world lurched. Across the space, maybe four meters away, an indicator light went amber, and she was falling sideways. With the extra illumination, she could see the round, tree-thick body of the maneuvering thruster. She put out her arms, catching herself against a steel strut. When she pressed her helmet to it, the rumble of the drive drowned out the ghost-quiet radio. She reached for the wire, broke the connection, and the rumble stopped.

Out of time, she turned back, her head swimming. The ship was spinning, then. She had no way to know how quickly, but the Coriolis was enough to make her stumble on the way back.

With the panel closed, the hatch open, and her helmet off again, she sat still until her balance came close to returning. Then, moving carefully, drunkenly, she scratched the new information on the wall. She was developing a crude map of the ship's secret interior and keeping track of all she learned. She was tired enough not to trust her memory. From the count she'd started, she knew she'd been on thirty sorties. Now, for the first time, she'd done something. It was only one thruster, but the ship was spinning now, tumbling in circles instead of burning ahead in a line. All the acceleration would be bled into the changing angular momentum, and she wouldn't be going toward Jim as quickly. So maybe she'd bought a little time. It would make things harder for her, but she'd grown up in the Belt and on ships. Coriolis—and coping with the sick dizziness—was nothing new to her. She knew that the feeling of power and accomplishment she felt was out of scale with what she'd actually managed, but she grinned all the same.

Thirty sorties. Two and a half hours just of time spent in vacuum. That didn't count the minutes refreshing the air in her suit or planning out the next run. Maybe five hours total since she'd started this. She was exhausted. She felt it in her muscles and the pain in her joints. She hadn't eaten—couldn't eat. She was thirsty with the first strains of a dehydration headache coming on. There was no reason to think she would survive this. So she was surprised to notice that she was happy. Not the powerful, irrational, and dangerous joy of a euphoric attack, but a kind of pleasure and release all the same.

At first, she thought it was because there wasn't anyone there with her, guarding her, judging her. And that, she decided, was part of it. But more than that, she was simply doing what needed to be done without having to concern herself about what anyone else thought. Even Jim. And wasn't that odd? She wanted nothing in the world more than for Jim to be there—followed by Amos and Alex and a good meal and a bed at a humane gravity—but there was a part of her that was also expanding into the silence of simply being herself and utterly alone. There were no dark thoughts, no guilt, no self-doubt tapping at the back of her mind. Either she was too tired for that, or something else had happened to her while she'd been paying attention to other things.

This was the difference, she thought, between solitude and isolation. And now she knew something about herself she hadn't known before. It was an unexpected victory, and all the better for that.

She started getting ready for the thirty-first sortie.

She had almost a minute, because she'd figured out that coming up the comm array power supply took a lot longer than it did going back down. It was the sort of thing she'd have realized much more quickly if her mind hadn't been a little on the compromised side.

The comm system was held in place by more than epoxy. Long strips of metal tape lashed the transmitter in place, the welds still bright as if they'd been made yesterday. Three sorties ago—number forty-four—she'd thought there might be a diagnostic handset. Not that she could speak into it, but she might have been able to tap out a message. But despite the fact that handsets like that were standard and required, there wasn't one.

It had taken her some time to put together a backup plan.

For hours, the looped message had played in her ear, whispering on the back of residual charge. "This is Naomi Nagata of the *Rocinante*. If you get this message, please retransmit. Tell James Holden I am in distress. Comm is not responding. I have no nav control. Please retransmit…"

Thirteen seconds long, and barely louder than the sound of her breath, even with her head less than a meter from the transmitter. With the leads to the transmitter exposed, she was ready. She'd have four times through. It had to be enough that it wouldn't be mistaken for random interference. She pressed her head to the hull to distract from the whirling of her inner ear.

"This is Naomi Nagata," she said, matching the timing and cadence of her false self. "If you get this message, please retransmit. Tell James Holden I am in—" She slammed the wire onto the exposed leads. A shiver of electricity bit her fingertips even through the suit's gloves. The radio was silent, but she kept mouthing the words, replaying them like a song stuck in her head until the right moment, then yanked the wire free "—control. Please retransmit. This is Naomi Nagata of the *Rocinante*. If you get this message, please retransmit. Tell James Holden I am in—" Cut, pause. "—control. Please retransmit."

After the fourth time, she took the length of steel spring she'd been using as a knife and cut the transmitter. Her false voice went dead. She scrambled down, moving from strut to strut, watching her hands and feet with every movement so she wouldn't misjudge. The acceleration gravity made her ankles and wrists feel unstable. The air in her suit didn't feel stale or close; the carbon dioxide scrubbers worked well enough on passive that she wouldn't feel the panic of asphyxiation. She'd just gently pass out and die.

She ducked into the engineering deck, closed the access panel. On the way to the hatch, her knee buckled. She popped the hatch open, ripped off her helmet, and sank down, gasping. Her vision narrowed, bright sparkles filling in her peripheral vision. She dry heaved once, paused, did it again, and let her body's weight sink deep into the deck below her.

Tell James Holden I'm in control for some really broad definition of control, she thought and laughed. Then coughed until her ribs hurt even worse. Then laughed again.

At her seventy-first sortie, she hit the wall. It wasn't subtle. She had closed the hatch to the main body of the ship, closed the seals, and put her helmet onto the environment suit. Before she fixed it into place and started the next five-minute count, her hands dropped to her sides. She hadn't consciously intended to do that; it had just happened. Alarmed in a vague, distant kind of way, she sat on the deck with her back against the wall and tried moving them. If she'd just become paralyzed or something, that would change the situation. Give her permission to stop. But her hands still flexed; her shoulders still moved. She was just exhausted. Even the effort to swallow seemed heroic. She closed her eyes, wondering if she'd instantly fall asleep, but she was too weary for that. So she sat.

If the suit had a battery, it would probably be cataloging the failures of her body right now. The dehydration headache was worse now, and moving in toward nausea. Her skin felt raw where the unshielded sun had burned her. Though she wasn't producing as much, she was still coughing. And she figured her blood was probably about equal parts plasma and fatigue poisons by now.

Her two little victories—the thruster, the transmitter—had been the end. Since then, either her efforts had degraded or things had genuinely gotten more complicated, or both. The repeaters that would cause the core to shut down had either been omitted in the build or were tucked someplace that couldn't be reached from between the hulls. The sensor array that would trigger the bottle failure when a rescue ship got too close would have been a lovely thing to access, but it appeared to be mounted on the exterior where she couldn't get to it. There were half a dozen places she could have tried tapping into the computer system, but none of them had interfaces, and she didn't have any she could bring. Other plans and strategies flickered through her mind from time to time like fireflies. Some of them might have been good. She couldn't keep hold of them long enough to say.

She might have slept or the timeless skipping might just have been how her brain worked now. The voice she heard was just a whisper fainter than her own voice had been, but it snapped her back to herself.

"Hey there, *Chetzemoka.* This is Alex Kamal presently of the *Razorback.* Naomi? If you're there, I'd appreciate you giving me a sign. I'd sort of like to make sure it's you before we come over. Your ship's been acting a mite odd, and we're a little on the jumpy side. And, just in case it's not Naomi Nagata? I've got fifteen missiles locked on you right now, so whoever you are, you might want to talk with me."

"Don't," she said, knowing he couldn't hear her. "Stay away. Stay away."

Everything hurt. Everything whirled. Nothing was easy. When she got to her feet, her head swam. She was afraid she was going to pass out, but if she bent over, she wasn't sure she'd have the strength to stand back up. She had to find a way to wave him off. She had to keep him from getting close enough to be caught in the blast. Whether it saved her life or not didn't matter. She'd had her good day. It was more than she'd expected, and she was so deeply weary...

Breathing hard, she opened the engineering hatch for the last time and stumbled for the lift. And after the lift, the airlock.

Chapter Forty-Five: Amos

Even though it was strictly local, running off the *Zhang Guo*'s system, it was nice having working hand terminals again. Amos lay on a support wedged in the narrow space between the hulls. The rest of his work team was only the soft clanging of magnetic clamps and the gentle, soothing smell of a welding torch. The meter he had clipped to the power line was at zero.

"Now?" Peaches said.

"Nothing."

A couple seconds passed.

"Now?"

"Nothing."

Another second. The meter chirped, the indicator going from zero to eighty-nine. Amos grinned. "That's it, Peaches. I'm a little shy of ninety."

"Locking that in," she said, and even though the hand terminals were set for audio, he knew she was smiling. He plucked the meter free and sprayed sealant over the holes he'd made for the leads. "Erich? If you're there, we're ready for another run."

"Of course I'm here," Erich said. "Where would I go? Starting the diagnostics run now. You two go stretch your legs or something."

Amos whistled once between his teeth, the shrill echo making the sound seem larger. "I'm taking a break. You guys get that conduit open, just wait for me. Don't try to do something smart."

There was a rough clatter of agreement as he swung out and up, climbing to the access panel with the handholds and the structural supports. The B-team wasn't much by way of help, but they could do some of the time-consuming easy stuff while Amos and Peaches and Erich made the *Zhang Guo* skyworthy. So far, it had been as much cleaning up the servants' half-assed attempts to fix the ship as it had been finding why she'd been grounded in the first place. As showy as the ship was, her internal design was pretty nearly off-the-shelf. On the engineering deck, Amos dug up a cleaning rag and wiped the hardening shell of sealant off his fingers and wrist. Where it was thinnest, it was already solid, coming away from his skin like the shell off a shrimp.

Both doors of the airlock were open, and a portable stairway led down to the hangar floor. The windows were still dark, and a filthy, gritty rain tapped against the panes. The air smelled of ozone and cold, and Amos' breath ghosted. The overhead LEDs cast a harsh light, cutting shadows so distinct they looked fake. Stokes and the other household servants were clustered against one wall, clutching bags and hard cases and talking anxiously among themselves. Butch leaned against one wall, her hand to her ear in an attitude of concentration. Amos watched her as he came down the stairs. The woman radiated a sense of barely restrained violence. Amos had known a lot of people who had the same air about them. Some of them were criminals. Some were cops. She caught him staring and lifted her chin in something between a greeting and a challenge. He smiled amiably and waved.

He got to the hangar floor about the same time Peaches climbed out the airlock onto the stair. Stokes broke free of the huddled group and trotted over toward Amos, smiling anxiously. "Mr. Burton? Mr. Burton?"

"You can call me Amos."

"Yes, thank you. I wondered whether Natalia could perhaps go to the Silas house? Her husband is a janitor there, and she is afraid if she leaves without him, they will never see each other again. She's very worried, sir."

Peaches came down the stairs behind him with footsteps soft as a cat's. Her shadow spilled down the walkway in front of her. Amos scratched his arm. "Here's the thing. Pretty sure we're going to be able to start the final run-through in maybe forty-five minutes. Anyone who's here when we're done, they can bum a lift so long as there's room. Anybody not here should be far enough away they don't get burned down to their component atoms when we take off. Between those, I don't actually give a shit what any of you people do."

Stokes chuckled and made a short birdlike bob with his head. "Very good, Mr. Burton. Thank you." Amos watched him scamper away.

"Mr. Burton, is it?" Peaches said.

"Apparently," Amos said, then lifted a thumb to point after Stokes. "Did he think I was joking about something? 'Cause I was just telling him how the sun comes up in the east."

Peaches lifted a shoulder. "In his mind, we're the good guys. Everything we say, he interprets that way. If you say you don't care if he lives or dies, it must be your dry gallows humor."

"Seriously?"

"Yep."

"That's a really stupid way to go through life."

"It's how most people do."

"Then most people are really stupid."

"And yet we made it to the stars," Peaches said.

Amos stretched out his arms, the muscles across his shoulders hurting pleasantly. "You know, Peaches, it's nice how we got all this help and stuff, but I kind of liked it better when it was only you and me."

"You say the sweetest things. I'm going to track down some coffee or tea. Or amphetamines. You need anything?"

"Nope. I'm solid." He watched her walk away. She was still way too thin, but since he'd stepped into the room in the Pit at Bethlehem, she'd taken on a kind of confidence. He wondered, if she had to go back, whether she still wanted him to kill her. Probably something worth asking about. He stifled a yawn and tapped his hand terminal. "How's it looking up there?"

"Not throwing any errors yet," Erich said. "So this is what you do now?"

"This is what I've been doing for years."

"And you can make a living this way?"

"Sure, if you don't mind weird-ass aliens and corporate security assholes trying to kill you now and then."

"Never minded before," Erich said. "Okay, that's it. We're at the end of the run. I got that one hiccup from the water recycler, but everything else is good to go."

"If we're in this brick long enough to recycle the water, something will have gone badly wrong."

"That's what I was thinking too. You want me to start firing the reactor up? They've got scripts and a checklist."

"Yeah, why don't you let me take—"

The hand terminal squawked and a man's voice Amos didn't recognize came on. "Boss? I think we've got company."

"What're you seeing?" Erich snapped.

"Three trucks."

"Okay, fuck it," Erich said. "I'm starting up the reactor."

Amos trotted toward the front of the hangar. The lookouts at the windows were all standing and tense. They knew. The servants were still milling in their corner, out of the way. "Yeah,

I'd go ahead and run the check first," he said. "It'd be a shame to do all this just so we could give the folks in Vermont a nice light show."

The silence was harsh. Amos didn't understand what the problem was until Erich spoke again. "I don't take orders from you. *Burton.*"

Amos rolled his eyes. He shouldn't have said that on an open channel. So many years and so many catastrophes, and it was still all about not losing face. "I was thinking of it more as expert opinion," Amos said. And then, "Sir."

"Noted. While I take my time to do that, how about you go help hold the perimeter," Erich said, and Amos grinned. Like he wasn't already on his way to do that. Erich went on. "Walt, start getting the passengers in the ship. Clarissa can assist with the start-up."

"On my way," she said, and Amos saw her running across the hangar for the stairs. Stokes was watching her with alarm. Amos waved him over.

"Mr. Burton?" the man said.

"That girl going after her old man? Yeah, she might need to rethink that."

Stokes went pale and searchlights brighter than the sun flooded through the hangar windows. A voice echoed through bullhorns, barking syllables too muddled by the echo to be words. It didn't matter. They all got the gist. By the time Amos got to the front doors, there were figures in the lights. Men in riot gear approaching the hangar with assault rifles in their hands that looked a little more heavy-duty than crowd control demanded. The servants were lined up on the stairs to the ship's airlock, but they weren't moving fast. One of Erich's men—maybe twenty years old with a red scarf at his neck—handed Amos a rifle and grinned.

"Aim for the lights?"

"Any plan's better than no plan," Amos said, and broke the windowpane out with the butt of the rifle. The gunfire started before he could flip the barrel around to take aim. It roared like a storm, no gap between one report and the next. Somewhere people were screaming, but Erich and Peaches were in the ship and Holden and Alex and Naomi were somewhere off-planet and Lydia was safely dead. There was only so much to worry about. The guy next to him was screaming a wordless war cry. Amos took aim, breathed out, squeezed. The rifle kicked, and one of the glaring lights went out. Then someone else got another one. One of the Pinkwater soldiers pulled back an arm to throw something, and Amos shot them in the hip. A second after they went down, the grenade they dropped flashed and a plume of tear gas rose up through the falling rain.

Someone—Butch, it sounded like—yelled "Push 'em back!" and Amos crouched down, squinting back at the *Zhang Guo*. The civilians were almost all on, Stokes at the back waving his arms and yelling to hurry them. Something detonated, blowing the glass out of the remaining windows. The shock wave thudded through Amos' chest like the explosion had kicked him. He stood up, glanced through the window, and shot the nearest figure in the face. The deeper rattle came from outside, and stuttering muzzle flash brighter than the remaining lights. Holes appeared in the wall, beams of light shining through into the vast cathedral space of the hangar.

"We got to get out of here!" Scarf Boy shouted.

"Sounds good," Amos said, and started walking backward, firing through the window. A half second later, Scarf Boy was with him. The others either noticed them or had already reached the same conclusion. Two were already on the stairs, shooting as they climbed. At this point, no one was trying to hit anything; they were just keeping the others from advancing too fast for everyone to get on board. Amos' rifle went dry. He dropped it and jogged back to the stairs, holding his hand terminal to his ear as he went.

"How're we doing?" he shouted.

"You're very clever," Peaches yelled back. "We had a power hiccup on start-up. Would have lost maneuvering thrusters."

"We going to lose them now?"

"Don't think so."

"Good."

He stopped at the base of the stairs. Scarf Boy crouched behind him, reloading his assault rifle. When he had the new magazine in, Amos plucked it out of his hands and pointed at the stairway with his chin. Scarf Boy nodded thanks and scuttled up the steps, his head low. Shadows danced on the windows, and the side door burst in with a three-person team rushing in. Amos mowed them down. Half a dozen of Erich's people were on the stairs now, some still shooting as they climbed. One of them—Butch—stumbled as she got to the fourth step up. Blood soaked her arm and the side of her neck. Amos held the assault rifle up, spraying the walls, and knelt beside her.

"Come on," he said. "Time to go."

"Don't think that's happening," Butch said.

Amos sighed. He put his hand terminal in his pocket, took the woman's collar in one hand and the rifle's grip in the other, and ran up the steps to the rattle of his own gunfire. The woman screamed and bounced. Something exploded, but Amos didn't pause to figure out what. At the airlock, he hauled Butch through, fired one last burst down the stairway, and hit the controls to cycle the lock closed.

All around him, Erich's people and the house servants were huddled. Some were covered in blood. He was covered in blood. He was pretty sure it was all Butch's, but not a hundred percent. Sometimes, in the heat of the moment, he missed things like getting shot. He let Butch down to the deck and pulled out his hand terminal.

"Okay," he said. "Now would be good."

"The exhaust's going to kill everyone out there," Erich said.

"Are we caring about that?" Amos shouted.

"I guess not."

The drive roared to life. "Lay down!" Amos shouted. "We don't have time to get to couches. Everyone lay down. You want the thrust spread out over your whole body!"

He lay down beside Butch. Her eyes were on him with something that might have been pain or anger. She didn't speak, and neither did he. Erich's voice came over the ship's system, telling them to brace, and then Amos weighed a whole lot more than he had a few seconds before. A loud crunching sound rattled the deck—the *Zhang Guo* pushing through the hangar's roof on her way to the sky. The ship rattled, dropped, rose again. The deck pressed into Amos' back. If they had to make any hard turns, there were going to be at least a dozen people all mushed together in the corner where the deck met the wall.

The screen over the engineering controls flickered to life; clouds and rain falling down onto the forward cameras as the ship rose. Lightning flickered, the thunder rolling through the ship. He couldn't remember if a standard orbital escape called for three gs or four, but whatever it was would have been a whole hell of a lot more fun in a crash couch. His jaw ached, and he had to remember to clench his arms and legs to keep from passing out. All around him, the others weren't remembering that in time, or more likely never knew. Most of them, this was their first time up the well.

Over the course of long minutes, the rain and clouds on the screen faded. The lightning fell away behind them. Then, through the featureless gray, the first shining stars. Amos laughed and whooped, but no one joined him. Looking around, he seemed to be the only one still conscious, so instead, he lay back on the deck and waited for the thrust gravity to drop out when they hit orbit.

The stars slowly grew brighter, twinkling at first as the last gritty layers of atmosphere passed by them, and then growing steady. The Milky Way appeared like a dark cloud lit from behind. The thrust gravity began to ease and he got to his feet. Around him, other people were starting to come back to themselves. Scarf Boy and the others were hauling Butch out to the lift and the med bay, assuming the *Zhang Guo* had one of those. Stokes and the others were laughing or weeping or staring off in shock and disbelief. Amos checked himself for wounds and, apart from a series of four deep, gouging scrapes along his left thigh whose origins he couldn't recall, felt fine.

He turned his hand terminal to the open channel. "This is Amos Burton. You guys mind if I come up to ops?"

"You can do that, Burton," Erich said. There was maybe just a hint of smug in his voice. This saving face for Erich thing was going to get old fast, but right at the moment, he was feeling too high to care.

The ops deck was offensively lush. The anti-spalling had been made to look like red-velvet wallpaper and the light came from silver-and-gold sconces all along the walls. Erich sat in the captain's couch. His good hand was moving over the deck in his lap, his bad one holding on to the straps. Peaches was in the navigator's couch, her eyes closed and her smile beatific.

"Grab a couch," Erich said with a grin. His old friend and not the criminal boss who needed to keep Amos in his place. He switched to the ship system. "Brace for maneuvers. Repeat, brace for maneuvers."

"That's not how they really do that," Amos said, strapping in at communications. "That's just something they say in the movies."

"It's good enough for now," Erich said, and the couches shifted under them as the thrusters turned the ship. Slowly, the moon hove into view, and behind it, the sun. Silhouetted, Luna was a disk of black from here except for a thin limn of white along one edge and a webwork of city lights. Peaches chuckled like a brook, her eyes open now, her hands pressed to her lips. The tears welling up in her eyes glittered.

"Didn't think you'd see this again, did you Peaches?"

"It's beautiful," she said. "Everything's beautiful, and I didn't think anything ever would be again."

They were all silent for a moment, and then Erich switched the view, pulling it slowly down. Below them, Earth was a smear of white and of gray. Where the continents should have burned in the permanent fire of lights, there were only a scattering of dim, dull glowing points. The seas were hidden, and the land. A funeral shroud was over the planet, and they all knew what was happening beneath it.

"*Fuck*," Erich said, and it carried a weight of awe and despair.

"Yeah," Amos said. They were all quiet for a long moment. The birthplace of humanity, the cradle of life in the solar system, was beautiful in its death throes, but none of them had any doubt that was what they were seeing.

The comm controls interrupted them. Amos accepted the connection and a young woman in UN naval uniform appeared in a high-priority panel.

"*Zhang Guo*, this is Luna Base. We do not have an approved flight plan for you. Be advised this space is under military restriction. Identify yourselves immediately, or be fired upon."

Amos opened the channel. "Hey there, Luna Base. Name's Amos Burton. Didn't mean to step on anybody's toes. If you've got someone up there named Chrissie Avasarala, pretty sure she'll vouch for me."

Chapter Forty-Six: Alex

Hey there, *Chetzemoka.* This is Alex Kamal presently of the *Razorback.* Naomi? If you're there, I'd appreciate you giving me a sign. I'd sort of like to make sure it's you before we come over. Your ship's been acting a mite odd, and we're a little on the jumpy side. And, just in case it's not Naomi Nagata? I've got fifteen missiles locked on you right now, so whoever you are, you might want to talk with me."

Alex shut off the mic, and rubbed his cheek. They were on the float now, course matched with the mysterious ship only about fifty kilometers above them on the relative z-axis. The sun, larger by far than he'd ever seen it from Mars, glowed below them, heating the little pinnace almost to the limit of its ability to shed the energy. Behind him, Bobbie was watching the same feed he was.

"That doesn't look good," she said.

"Nope."

As a boy, back on Mars, there had been a little improvised firework that his friends would sometimes make for fun. All it took was a length of light-duty pipe, a mining spike, and a single-use rocket motor. The way it worked, they'd spike one end of the pipe to a flat section of wall, fix the motor to the other end with industrial tape or epoxy with the thrust pointing off to one side. Fire the motor, and the whole thing turned into a ring of smoke and fire, the pipe spinning around its axis faster than the eye could follow, the flare of the motor exhaust blinding and flickering. Sometimes the motor came loose and bounced along the corridor, posing a threat to everyone watching. Sometimes the spike came loose. Most times, it just left a circle of scrapes and scorch marks on the stone of the wall that pissed off the maintenance crews. They called them fire weasels. He didn't know why.

Above them, the *Chetzemoka* was spinning like a fire weasel. She wasn't quite tumbling, but the circle she was burning in was tight. All the acceleration she'd been using to burn hard out toward the Belt and Holden was getting eaten now, each point on her pathway canceling out the point a hundred and eighty degrees off from it. Her exhaust plume was a jet of flame and plasma that would glass anything that tried to approach her unless it came from above or below. And if they did that…

"What do you think happened?" Bobbie asked.

"Maneuvering thruster fired off, never got balanced."

"Can you match course with that? I mean even if we decided we wanted to?"

Alex pressed the tip of his tongue to the back of his teeth and willed Naomi to call him. To give him a sign that she was still alive. That he wasn't about to risk his ship and his life and the lives of the people with him to rescue a corpse. "Might have to come up with something clever."

He pulled up the tactical display. The *Razorback* and her cloud of missiles with no one left to shoot at. The *Chetzemoka* chasing its tail like a terrier that had gulped down its own body weight in uppers. Then, far distant, the UN escort decelerating in from the sun toward a matching course, and the *Roci* doing the same from the Belt. Everything was coming together right here—the head of the OPA, the prime minister of Mars, Avasarala's best cavalry—because it was where Naomi Nagata was, and as long as Alex and Holden were drawing breath, they'd be looking out for their own.

The screen lit up with an incoming message, but not from the *Chetzemoka.* Alex accepted it, and Holden appeared on the screen. For about four seconds, the captain didn't do anything but look into the camera and scratch his nose. He looked tired and thin. Alex felt the same way himself. Then a smile bloomed on Holden's face, and he seemed more like himself again. "Alex! Good. Tell me what we're looking at."

"Well, we haven't had any new messages since their radio cut out, but if that was an intentional message, this looks like about the worst definition of 'in control' I've seen in a while. This mystery ship's not quite on the tumble, but she's damned close. The way she's chasing her tail, it's not going to be easy making an approach, but I'm working on an idea. The *Razorback* wasn't built for airlock to airlock. This here's the kind of ride you land in a hangar. But we've got EVA suits for me and Nate. That's the prime minister. I call him Nate now. Don't be jealous. Anyway, I figure we put the *Razorback* at the center of the circle Naomi's making with our nose up and our ass down, then match roll to the circle she's making. Then as long as no one pukes in their helmet, we can send someone over to the airlock. Not sure it'll work, but it's the best idea I've got so far."

He leaned forward while the tightbeam laser flew the four light-seconds out to the *Rocinante*, then the four light-seconds back. To judge from the shape of Holden's face, he was probably at more than one g. Even if the *Chetzemoka* hadn't gone into its surprise spin, the *Razorback* would have been the first to reach it. Holden's temporary pilot was going to be buying Alex a beer, provided nothing new and unexpected blew up on them. Not that he'd have given good odds on that.

Five seconds in, he remembered that he'd wanted to mention that Bobbie had power armor. He didn't say it, though, since it would just interrupt whatever Holden was saying right then that wouldn't be back to Alex for a few more seconds. Light-delay conversations were all about etiquette and taking turns.

"Why don't we try that as proof of concept?" Holden said. "If it looks like something we can do, I can have the *Roci* take your place when we get there. Then if we need to cut in through the hull, we can. Have you had any sign from Naomi?"

"Not yet—" Alex began, but it turned out Holden hadn't been finished, just pausing for breath.

"Because that whole 'Tell James Holden I'm in control' thing was weird on a lot of levels. I checked the vocal profile of the message coming off the *Chetzemoka*—well, actually Fred did. It wouldn't have occurred to me. Anyway, the way she said James Holden in the first warning message about the bad bottle drivers and the way it was in this new one? Exactly the same. Fred thinks the new message may have been faked. Only then the way it got modified before it shut off... I'm seeing something here, Alex. But I don't know what it is."

This time Alex waited until he was sure Holden was done before he started talking. "We haven't had any sign at all, but it seems to me that someone on the ship's been trying to raise a flag. And this flying in circles bit makes it seem a lot less like a Trojan horse. Nothing to gain by doing it, other than make everyone inside feel powerfully like throwing up. Honestly, I don't know what we're looking at here either, Cap'n, and I don't think we're going to know until we get someone inside."

Eight long seconds there and back again. "I'm just worried that if she is in there and the ship's out of control, we're going to be sitting out here dithering while she needs us. I can't stand the idea that we've come this close, and now we're going to lose her. I know it's a little crazy, but I'm a little crazy right now. I keep thinking of her being smashed up against the wall by the spin, and me out here where I can't do anything."

"Yeah, thruster misfires don't work like that," Alex said. "You don't get any sideways impulse unless the thruster's actually going. After that, you've got a little spin station action pushing the folks behind the center of spin down and the folks forward of it up, but all that is gonna be in line with the thrust from the drive, so all you actually get is—"

"Alex!" Bobbie said. "We've got something."

He twisted on his couch, then turned it to face her. Bobbie's eyes were on the wall screen. A panel was there, opened to the view from the upper camera. The *Chetzemoka* was still in its mad spin, but something had come off, floating now across the clear, empty void, stars behind it like the glittering pupil of a vast eye. The eye of the storm. Bobbie tried to zoom in on it the same moment Alex did, and the system made a confused, upset chime, the focus fluctuating wildly before coming to rest. A figure in an EVA suit. There were no lights on the suit, and its back was turned to them, the intense sunlight making the gray material shine almost too brightly to make out details.

"Is she alive?" Alex said.

"She's moving."

"How long ago did she come out?"

"Not long," Bobbie said. "Seconds."

The figure in the EVA suit lifted her arms, crossing them over her head. The Belter signal for danger. Alex felt his heart speed up.

"Alex!" Holden said, from four seconds ago. "What's going on?"

"Someone came out of the ship. Let me figure this out, and I'll be back with a report," Alex said, then cut the connection. On Bobbie's screen, the figure had shifted to a time signal. *Five minutes.*

"What have we got?" Alex said.

"She's making the same signs," Bobbie said. "Here we go. 'Danger. Do not approach. Explosion hazard.' But then here's 'Low air,' and 'five'...shit, 'four minutes.'"

"Is it her?" Alex said, knowing there wasn't an answer for that. Even if the figure turned its face to them, Alex wasn't certain between glare and the suit's helmet if he'd have been able to identify Naomi. It was just a person in an EVA suit, running out of air and warning them over and over again that it was a trap.

But Alex thought that whoever it was, they sure moved like Naomi. And they'd both been calling the figure "she." They might not know, but they were both pretty certain. The body of the *Razorback* felt suddenly claustrophobic. Like the appearance of Naomi right there where he could see her required more room to move. Enough space to reach her. Alex set the pinnace's system to the diamond-bright suit and started it calculating.

"Where's she going to go?" Bobbie asked.

"Looks like she's set to drift across into the path of the ship again," Alex said. "If it don't hit her, maybe she gets past and the drive plume gets her."

"Or we watch her suffocate?" Bobbie said.

"I can take the ship in," Alex said.

"And crisp her decelerating?"

"Well...yeah."

"Get your helmets on," Bobbie yelled loud enough to carry into the back cabin. "I'm going in."

"That suit's got enough thrust to do a fifty-klick flip-and-burn in under four minutes?" Alex asked, but he was already sealing his suit as he said it.

"Nope," Bobbie said, reaching for her helmet with one hand and a spare bottle of air with the other. "But it's got really good mag boots and gloves."

Alex checked his seals and got ready to open the *Razorback* to the void. "Don't see how that's going to help."

The prime minister's cabin showed it was sealed. On the monitor, the figure—Naomi—signaled *Danger. Do not approach. Explosion hazard.* Bobbie yelped, took a deep shuddering breath.

Her voice was coming through the EVA suit's radio now. "God damn, it's been a long time since I was on the juice. This is some powerfully unpleasant shit."

"Bobbie, we're running out of time here. How are mag boots going to get you to Naomi?"

Behind her helmet's visor, Bobbie grinned. "How good's your control on those missiles?" she asked.

Chapter Forty-Seven: Naomi

Leaving the airlock this one last time was the most peaceful thing Naomi could imagine doing. As soon as she'd cleared the outer door, the sun and stars had stopped their gut-sickening whirl. She had taken her tangent from the whirling circle of life, and now her path was a line. Well, not a tangent, really. A secant, and doomed to cross paths with the ship again, only maybe not in her lifetime.

For a moment, she let herself enjoy drifting. The sun pressed against her back, the light radiating past her as she cast a shadow on whole stars, galaxies. The sense of whirling faded a little, and she wondered where Alex was, out among all these stars. She remembered to start counting. One thousand and…how long had she already been out? Seven? Eight? Well, she might as well think the worst. One thousand and thirty. Why not? She lifted her hands over her head. *Danger.* Then *Do not approach.* Then *Explosion hazard.* She felt like she was trying to warn the stars.

The Milky Way. *Don't come here. Stay away. There are humans here, and you can't trust them.*

She stretched with every motion, letting it all go. She should have been scared, but she wasn't. She was going to her death, and that sucked. She would have liked to live longer. To see Jim again. And Alex. And Amos. She would have liked to tell Jim all the things she'd been so careful for so long not to say. One thousand and sixty. Time to change her signs. Four minutes left. Four minutes and a lifetime.

Somewhere out there, Filip was with his father, the way he had been for years. Since he was a baby. And Cyn, poor Cyn, already as dead as she was going to be because he'd seen her in the airlock and thought stopping her would have been saving her. Thought the life she had with Marco was worth having. She wondered what would have happened if she'd stayed. If the *Chetzemoka* had flown without her. Would Jim have set off the bomb? She had to think he would have. He wasn't a man who reined in his curiosity well. The stars shuddered, blurred. She was weeping. *Danger. Do not approach. Explosion hazard.*

If the suit had been powered, it would have been screaming alerts at her. She was almost glad now that it wasn't. She wasn't even light-headed yet. She'd seen people pass out. As long as her CO_2 scrubbers kept working, it would be a peaceful way to go. No choking, no panic. Just a moment's disorientation and then, softly, out. Here she was, after so many years, throwing herself out another airlock. She could still remember that first one, back on Ceres. It had been set in the floor, of course, but she could still conjure up the feeling of pressure on her fingers when she'd told it to cycle open, still believing that it meant her own death. And even then, she hadn't wanted to die. She'd just wanted it to be over. To be free of it all. For the pain and guilt to be over. And the feeling of being trapped. She might have been able to stand all the rest of it, but not the sense of being caught.

This death wasn't at all like that. This was throwing herself in front of a bullet so that it wouldn't hit her friends. Her family. The family she'd chosen. The one built from people who had risked their lives for her. She wished Cyn could have met Jim. Could have understood how far she'd come from the girl he'd known on Ceres, back in the day. How much she wasn't just Knuckles anymore.

She wasn't religious, but she'd known any number of people who were. *Explosion hazard. Low air. Three minutes.* She wondered whether they would have thought what she was doing now was sinful. Giving herself over to the void in hopes that Alex would see her, would understand, would save himself.

And her. It would be nice if somehow he found a way to save her back. Or if Jim suddenly swept down from the stars to gather her up. She chuckled. God knew he'd try. Always blundering into being the hero, her Jim. Now he'd know what it had felt like for her all those times he'd squared his jaw and run off into near-certain death because it was the right thing. Pity she wouldn't be there to point it out to him. He might not connect those dots himself. Or he might. He'd changed over the years, and he wouldn't change back.

Danger. Do not approach. Explosive hazard. She'd lost count again. Two minutes? One? She didn't know. She found herself humming a melody she'd heard as a child. She didn't know the words to it. They might not have even been in a language she knew. It didn't matter. She was glad for the song's company. Grateful. More than that, she was grateful that she wasn't going to die nauseated. *Okay, fine. If this is what I get, this is what I get. Not a life without regrets, but none I can't live with. None I can't die with.*

Still, she thought to the universe, *if it isn't a problem, I wouldn't say no to a little more.*

Something moved off to her left, streaking out from behind her. Huge and metal and shining brightly in the sun. It looked like a missile, pointing back toward the sun as it retreated. Its drive wasn't firing. That seemed weird and kind of random. She wondered if—

The impact came in the center of her back, hard as an assault.

An arm wrapped around her shoulder and a leg around her waist locking her immobile. She squirmed by reflex, trying to escape the attack, but whoever it was had her cold. She couldn't escape. She felt the other person's free hand fumbling at her suit. Something hard and metal pressed against her thigh where the air bottles would go.

Her ears popped as the pressure in the suit suddenly changed. A clean, vaguely astringent smell filled her nose. A fresh bottle. She almost laughed. She was being held in a rescue hold. The newcomer did something else she couldn't quite figure, and then locked a tether to her waist and released her. When they rotated together, face-to-face, the newcomer grabbed Naomi's helmet and pressed her own against it.

"Bobbie?" Naomi said.

"Hey," the Martian ex-marine shouted, grinning. The sound carried from suit to suit by the conduction, and it made her sound terribly distant for someone who was holding Naomi in her arms. "Imagine meeting you here, right?"

"I'd say it's really good to see you," Naomi shouted back, "but that seems weirdly understated. The ship! It's rigged to lose bottle containment if another ship sets off its proximity alert."

Bobbie scowled and nodded. Naomi saw the woman's mouth moving as she relayed the information to someone. To Alex. She watched Bobbie listen to something she couldn't hear. She looked older than the last time Naomi had seen her. She looked beautiful. Bobbie said something else into her mic, then pressed their face-plates together again.

"I'm going to start moving us around," Bobbie shouted. "We need to point our feet toward the sun. Low profile. Suck up less heat, okay?"

Naomi buzzed with questions that didn't need answers. "Okay," she shouted back.

"Are you in immediate medical distress?"

"Probably. It's been a really hard day."

"That's funny," Bobbie shouted in a voice that meant it wasn't funny. "Are you in immediate medical distress?"

"No. I don't think so."

"All right. Put your arms over my shoulders and lock your forearms." Bobbie pulled back a few centimeters and demonstrated the forearm lock. Naomi made the Belter sign that meant roughly *Acknowledged and understood.* A few seconds later, Bobbie's armor fired thrusters, and Naomi's weight came back. She was being lifted up, carried into the stars. The sun-bright drive plume of the *Chetzemoka* passed them, dwarfing the small, dark box of the ship itself. It fell away toward the sun and slowly, over the course of long, eternal minutes, vanished below them.

They didn't fit in the pinnace. Not really. It was made for one, maybe two, and it had four with one of them in powered armor. The air was hot and thick, and the recyclers were starting to throw alerts and errors. Alex had shut down the reactor and switched to batteries so they wouldn't be generating as much heat.

"I mean, we could make a burn for it," Alex said, "but we got people coming from both directions and half as many crash couches as we've got folks."

He was in the one actual couch at the front of the pinnace. Bobbie sat curled near the mutilated deck where another couch had once been. The door to the cabin was open, and the prime minister of Mars floated there in a sweat-stained undershirt. He made the place seem dreamlike. For herself, Naomi floated near the ceiling. Alex had set the wall screens to show the outside, but it was all so much less vivid than the real thing. It didn't fool her.

The *Chetzemoka* was below them, a spinning black dot against the overwhelming white sun. She caught glimpses of it at the edges of the floor where the screen stopped. Alex had also had the *Razorback*'s system highlight the incoming UN escort ships and, in blue, the *Rocinante.*

"So," Alex said. "XO. You're...ah. Out here. That was kind of unexpected."

"Wasn't thinking to see you either, Alex," Naomi said. Her blood felt strange in her veins. Sluggish and bright at the same time. And she was having trouble focusing her eyes. Her hands had lost the worst of the swelling, though. The hours of work between the hulls had probably worked all the extra fluid back in where it belonged. Something like that. Her entire body hurt, and she was still discovering how profound her nausea had been as layers of it she hadn't recognized resolved. Her twenty-second sunburn from the jump off the *Pella* was swollen and tender to the touch, but not blistered. It would peel once it had healed enough. When she'd gotten into the *Razorback*, and the ship had been sealed, she'd drunk a liter of water from a bulb and she hadn't had to pee yet. The dehydration headache was starting to lose its hold. Bobbie had offered her painkillers, but something in Naomi resisted the idea of doing anything else to her body until she'd seen the inside of a medical bay.

She realized that her consciousness had flickered out when it came back. Bobbie and the prime minister were talking about good noodle restaurants in the major neighborhoods of Londres Nova. The air was thick and close and stank of bodies. She was sweating in her crappy EVA suit. The blue dot that was the *Rocinante* had grown a halo, the drive pointing toward them as it slowed to match their course.

In the corner of her eye a blackness flickered and was gone.

"Alex," she said, and then coughed so long and hard Bobbie had to brace her. When her lungs were clearer, she tried again. "Alex. Can you spare a couple of those missiles?"

"Depends, XO," Alex said. "What did you want me to do with them?"

"Kill that ship," Naomi said.

"It's all right," Alex said. "We warned everyone about how it's booby-trapped. No one's going to—"

"Not because of that. Just because it's time for it to go."

Because I tried to give it to my son instead of a childhood. Because I spent my own money to get it, and it turned into a trap for me and the people I love. Because everything about that ship was a mistake.

"Ah. Looks like it's registered to an Edward Slight Risk Abatement Cooperative. They going to be okay with us knocking their bird into the sun?"

"It'll be fine," Naomi said.

The prime minister lifted his finger. "It seems to me that—"

"Missiles away," Alex said, then smiled an apology. "You're the head of my government, Nate, but she's my XO."

"Nate?" Naomi said. "You're on a first-name basis now?"

"Don't be jealous," Alex said and pulled up a panel. Against the sun, the ship was nothing. A tiny darkness spinning below them like a fly. And then it was gone.

I'm sorry, Filip, she thought.

She turned her head toward the approaching *Rocinante*. It was closer.

Chapter Forty-Eight: Holden

If the medical bay could have raised its eyebrows and made judgmental little tsk-tsk sounds, it would have. Instead, the readout threw a list of amber-colored alerts so long that the first few scrolled off the screen before Holden could read them. Naomi grunted when the needle poked into her vein and the medical expert system's custom cocktail started flowing into her. Holden sat beside her, holding her other hand.

The transfer from the *Razorback* had been easy enough. Once they'd matched course, Alex snugged the pinnace up against the airlock, and all four of them had come over together. Holden had been waiting on the other side of the lock, not quite willing to believe that they were really back. Fred Johnson was there too in his greeting-a-political-grandee outfit. It was strange to see Fred visibly change roles, holding his body differently, his expression changing so subtly and profoundly it seemed like the shape of his skull had shifted. It left Holden a little curious about how much the old man presented to him was also tailored to the situation. Chances were, he'd never know.

When the inner door cycled open, he'd forgotten about Fred and the prime minister of Mars and the destruction of Earth and pretty much everything that wasn't Naomi. Her skin was ashen where it didn't look slick and swollen from radiation burns. Her eyes were bloodshot and bleary with a profound exhaustion. Moving into the room, she was careful, like any unexpected bump would hurt. She was the most beautiful thing he'd seen in years. He felt like he was the one returning home now that she was here. When she saw him, she smiled, and he grinned back. Somewhere a few feet away or a few miles, Fred Johnson and Nathan Smith were making some kind of formal greeting. It didn't matter at all.

"Hey," he'd said.

"Hey. You take care of the place while I was out?"

"Had some trouble with the contractor, but I think we got it straightened out," Holden said. Then Bobbie had put a wide, strong hand on his shoulder, shaken him slightly, and said, "Med bay." And then Naomi headed for the lift, leaning against Alex for support. She looked wounded, exhausted, halfway to dead. But she'd seen him, and she'd smiled, and it had dropped the bottom out of his heart.

The alert sounded, counted down, and gravity came back. Naomi coughed. It was a wet, painful sound, but the medical bay didn't seem concerned. The machine had a shitty bedside manner.

"Do you think we should get a medic?" Holden said. "Maybe we should get a medic."

"Right now?" Naomi asked.

"Or later. For your birthday. Whenever." The words tumbled out of his mouth without stopping by his brain once, and he didn't care enough to rein them in. Naomi was back. She was here. A vast fear he'd been carefully not noticing washed over him and started to dissipate.

This was how she felt, he thought. With the *Agatha King* and when he'd headed off to the station in the slow zone. When he'd gone down to the surface of Ilus. All the times he'd thought he was protecting her from his risks, this was what he'd been doing to her. "Wow," he said. "I'm kind of an asshole."

She opened her eyes in two bright slits and made a small smile. "Did I miss something?"

"Sort of. I just went someplace for a minute, and I'm back now. And so are you, which is really, really good."

"Nice to be home."

"But while you were... I mean while we were... Look, when I was back on Tycho, I was talking with Monica. And Fred. I mean I was talking to Fred about you and us and what I was entitled to know and why I thought all that. And Monica was talking about why I lied and whether what she did had any power and how it was ethical and responsible to use it. And I was thinking—"

Naomi raised her hand, palm out. Her forehead creased. "If you're about to tell me you had an affair with Monica Stuart, this may not be the best time."

"What? No. Of course not."

"Good."

"It's just I've been thinking. About a lot of different things, really. And I wanted you to know that whatever you were doing and going through that you didn't want me to be a part of? You don't have to tell me if you don't want to. I'm really curious, and I want to know. But whatever it was, it's only my business if you want it to be my business."

"All right," she said, and closed her eyes again.

Holden stroked her hand. The knuckles were raw, and there was a bruise on her wrist.

"So when you say 'all right'—"

"I mean I missed you too, and I'm glad I'm back, and could you go get me a bulb of green tea or something?"

"Yes," Holden said. "Yes, I can."

"Don't hurry," she said. "I may just take a little nap."

Holden paused at the hatch, looking back. Naomi was watching him go. Her eyes were tired, her body stilled by exhaustion, but she was smiling a little. It helped to see that she was glad to be back.

In the galley, a half-dozen voices were in competition, gabbling one above the other toward a kind of symphonic shared excitement. It sounded like he felt. Holden ducked in. Alex was sitting on one of the tables with his feet on the bench, talking to Chava Lombaugh and Sun-yi Steinberg, describing something about fast-cycling targeting stutter and acceleration. Chava was talking at the same time, her hands in motion, presenting some physical description of whatever they were on about. Sun-yi was just looking from one to the other, amused. At the next table over, Bobbie Draper was sitting down, but still looming over Sandra Ip and Maura Patel. Bobbie had swapped her powered armor for a slightly-too-small jumpsuit with TACHI stenciled on the back. She caught his eye, smiled, and waved. He waved back, but Sandra Ip had already recaptured her attention, and Bobbie was shaking her head and answering a question he hadn't heard.

Holden had the sudden, visceral memory of being at home with his family, eight parents sitting down to dinner together with their one son, having half a dozen conversations with and past each other. Even though he recognized he was already primed for it, the sense of peace and well-being that washed over him was profound. This was what family looked like, sounded like, how they acted. Even the new crew who he'd been trying not to resent felt more like distant cousins who'd come for a long visit than interlopers.

Alex hopped down and came over to him, grinning. They stood for a long, awkward moment before they gave in and embraced, clapping each other on the back and laughing.

"No more leave," Holden said.

"Holy shit. Right?" Alex said. "I take off for a few weeks, and everything turns into chaos."

"It really, really does." Holden went to the coffee maker and

Alex followed at his elbow. "I think this has to qualify for the worst vacation ever."

"How's Naomi doing?"

Holden picked out the tea that Naomi liked best. The machine chimed calmly. "Getting hydrated mostly. She sent me off to get her a drink, but I think she actually wanted me to stop hovering over her, trying to start a conversation."

"She may take a little time getting back to full power."

"Intellectually, I know that," Holden said, picking up the bulb of tea. It smelled of lemongrass and mint even though there was nothing anywhere on the ship that was remotely like either one. Holden grinned. "Chemistry is amazing, you know? It's really, really amazing."

"Any word from Amos?" Alex said, and his smile dimmed at the answer in Holden's eyes. He tried to force the carefree tone back into his voice when he spoke, but Holden wasn't fooled. "Well, that doesn't mean much. It won't be the first time a planet's blown up on him."

"They're starting to get confirmed death lists," Holden said. "It's still early. A lot of things still falling apart down there, and there's going to be a lot more bad before it sees better. But he's not on the list yet."

"So that's good. And c'mon. It's Amos. Everyone on Earth dies, and he'll probably stack the bodies and climb up to Luna."

"Last man standing," Holden said, but he headed back to the medical bay with his heart a little less buoyant. Naomi was gone, the needle that had been in her arm resting on the gel of the bed and the expert system gently prompting someone to intervene. Holden, the bulb of tea in his hand, checked the head and the galley before he thought to go back to the crew quarters.

She was on their bed, her knees curled up toward her chest, her eyes closed, her hair spilling over the gel. She snored a little, soft animal sounds of peace and contentment. Holden put the tea on the desk beside her so that it would be there waiting when she woke.

The ops deck was quiet, relatively speaking. Gor Droga, one of the weapons techs, was at a workstation, monitoring the ship and listening to something that had a beat on headphones. All Holden could hear of it was a slightly shifting bass line and an occasional phrase or two when Gor was moved to sing along. The lyrics were in something close to French without actually being French.

The lights were low, most of the illumination coming from the monitors. Holden didn't have a pair of headphones close to hand, so he just kept the volume low and watched Monica Stuart being interviewed. The man she was talking to was based on an L5 station, but the transmission gaps had all been edited out to make it seem like they were in the same room.

"No, it doesn't surprise me at all that the OPA would assist in escorting Prime Minister Smith. Fred Johnson has been vocal and active for years in bringing the OPA into the diplomatic discussion, often against resistance from the inner planets. If anything, I think there's a real irony in the fact that this series of attacks by the Free Navy have been the catalyst to cementing the OPA's legitimacy with Earth and Mars."

The camera cut to the interviewer. "So you don't see the Free Navy as a part of the OPA?"

And back to Monica. Holden chuckled. She'd changed her blouse between questions. He wondered what the lag had been like before it got edited down for the feed. "Not at all. The Free Navy is interesting in part because it gives the radical fringe of the OPA a different banner to raise. It represents a sort of self-selected culling of the elements that have kept the Belt from being better respected by the inner planets. And keep in mind, Mars and Earth weren't the only targets of the Free Navy's coup. Tycho Station is as big a success story as Ceres for Belters, and it was attacked too."

"Other pundits are calling that a changing of the guard within the OPA, though. Why do you see it as something external?"

Monica nodded sagely. It was a well-practiced motion, and it worked to make her seem intelligent and thoughtful but still approachable. There was an artistry in what she did.

"Well, Michael, sometimes when we make these distinctions, we're really creating them more than describing anything that's already there. We're seeing a very broad realignment on more than one side. It seems clear that elements in the Martian military have been involved with supplying the Free Navy, and also that Prime Minister Smith was their target. So would we call that a rogue element on Mars, or an internal power struggle? In fact, I think the best description we can probably make at this point isn't in terms of UN and Martian Republic and OPA, but the traditional system being brought together in the face of this new threat. This situation grows out of a deep history of conflict, but there are new lines being drawn here."

Fred chuckled. Holden hadn't heard him come up, but there he was, looking over Holden's shoulder. Holden paused the feed as Fred took a couch across from him.

"You can always tell your media relations team is doing their job when the journalists are down to interviewing each other," Fred said.

"I think she's doing good work," Holden said. "She's at least trying to put this all in a context where it makes sense."

"She's also rebranding herself as an expert on me personally. And you, for that matter."

"Okay, that is a little weird. Any other news I should know about?"

Fred glanced over at Gor, scowled, then leaned over and tapped the man's shoulder. Gor took off the headphones.

"Take a break," Fred said. "We'll make sure she's solid."

"Yes, sir," Gor said. "Be aware that this close to the corona, we're building up a little heat."

"We'll keep an eye on it."

Gor unstrapped and slid down the ladder. Fred watched him go with a wistful smile. "I remember when I could take a ladder that way. Been a few years, though."

"I don't anymore either."

"Thus does age make cowards of us all. Or maybe that's conscience," Fred said, and heaved a sigh. "Inaros and his ships haven't made it as far as Saturn's orbit yet, and piracy in the outer planets is spiking. The colony ships are well supplied, under-armed, and there are a lot of them."

"They weren't expecting a civil war."

"Is that what this is?"

"Isn't it?"

"Well. Maybe. I've been talking to Smith. I don't suppose Alex and Bobbie overheard much of what he was doing on the *Razorback*?"

Holden leaned forward. "I don't think they were spying on him, no. Were you thinking they would?"

"I was hoping your man might have. This Draper woman's too much the patriot. So, without outside confirmation, Smith's story is that there's a breakdown in the naval command. Might just be that someone's been selling a great chunk of their ordnance to Inaros. Might be there was another actor who was willing to swap out."

"For the protomolecule," Holden said. "That was the price of all this, wasn't it?"

"No one knows it's missing aside from you, me, Drummer's men, and whoever took it. I'll keep it quiet as long as I can, but when we get to Luna, I think I have to tell Smith and Avasarala."

"Of course you do," Holden said. "Why wouldn't you tell them?"

Fred blinked. His laugh, when it came, was deep and rolling. It came up from his belly and filled the air. "Just when I think you've changed, you come out with something that is uniquely James Holden. I don't know what to think about you. I really don't."

"Thanks?"

"Welcome," Fred said. And a moment later, "There are ships

burning for the gates. Martian military ships. It would help me a great deal to know if they answered to Inaros or to someone else."

"Like the one who got the protomolecule sample?"

"Anyone, really. I want to talk to Nagata."

The atmosphere between them went cool. "You want to interrogate her."

"I do."

"And you're asking my permission?"

"It seemed polite."

"I'll talk to her about it when she's recovered a little more," Holden said.

"Couldn't ask for anything more," Fred said, heaving himself to his feet. At the edge of the ladder, he paused. Holden watched him consider sliding down the sides the way Gor had. He watched Fred decide not to. Rung by rung, Fred climbed down out of the ops deck, shutting the hatch behind him. Holden turned the feed back on, and then off again. His head felt filled with cotton.

He'd been so focused for so long on distracting himself from Naomi's absence, now she was back, he felt almost overwhelmed. Monica was right. Things had changed, and he didn't know anymore what his place was in them. Even if he turned away from Fred and Avasarala and the politics of his own minor celebrity, what could an independent ship do in this new, remade solar system? Were there banks that would be able to pay him if he took a job flying cargo to the Jovian moons? And the colonists that had already gone through the rings to new, alien worlds? Would the Free Navy really stop resupply from getting out to them, and the raw materials and discoveries they made from getting back?

More than anything, the attacks seemed inevitable and petty. If the inner planets hadn't spent generations showing the Belters that they were disposable, there might have been some way... some way to adapt their skills and lifestyles into this larger human expansion. A way to draw all humanity forward, and not just part of it.

And how long would Inaros and people like him really be able to keep the flood of colonists out? Or maybe there was still something more, some layer of the plan that they hadn't seen yet? The idea filled him with something he decided to call dread because that was a better name than fear.

The monitor chimed. Alex, requesting a connection. Holden accepted it gratefully.

"Hey there, Cap'n," Alex said through a grin. "How're you doing?"

"Fine, I think. Just killing some time away from the cabin so I don't wake Naomi up. I figure she'll be asleep for twelve, fourteen hours."

"You're a good man," Alex said.

"You?"

"I've been showin' your temporary pilot all the ways he could have beaten me to the *Chetzemoka* if he'd thought of them."

"Be nice," Holden said, but he didn't really mean it. "Where are you? I'll come join you."

"Engineering," Alex said. "Which was part of why I wanted to talk to you. I just got some good news from Luna."

Chapter Forty-Nine: Amos

Loading mechs moved pallets of gray or white plastic crates along the length of the Aldrin docks and drowned out the jabber of human voices with the clanks and whirring of machines. Stokes and the other refugees from Rattlesnake Island were in a huddle along one gray wall, trying to only block the cart traffic a little bit while a civil servant with an oversized terminal processed them one at a time. The security force in black armor stood arrayed before the lock to the *Zhang Guo*, scowling. The wall screen was set to look outside at that truck-tire gray moonscape.

Chrisjen Avasarala's red sari stood out, a vibrant spot of color, and her voice cut through the clamor like it wasn't there.

"What the fuck do you mean we can't go on the ship?" she said.

"No warrant," Amos said. "Nobody's getting on my boat here without a warrant."

Avasarala tilted her head, then looked at the woman in charge of the security squad.

"Seeing that you and he seemed to have an understanding, ma'am," the security chief said, "I didn't want to press the point."

Avasarala waved her hand impatiently like she was fanning away smoke. "Burton, for one thing, that's not your fucking ship."

"Sure it is," Amos said. "Salvage."

"No. When you break into someone's private hangar and drive out in their ship, it's not salvage. That's still theft."

"You sure about that? Because it was looking awfully busted up down there. I'm pretty sure that was salvage."

"For another thing, we're under martial law, so I can do very nearly whatever the fuck I want. Including march through your precious little ship there towing you along behind in a ball gag and lacy underwear. So your warrant bullshit? You can roll that up and fuck it. Now tell me why I'm here."

"You know just 'cause you can do something, it doesn't mean you should. I don't look great in frills."

She crossed her arms. "Why am I here, Amos?"

Amos scratched his cheek and looked back at the *Zhang Guo*. Stokes and the servants were all out, but Erich and Peaches and the crew from Baltimore were all still inside. Some of them, including Erich, were either living under fake identities or weren't in the system at all.

"Here's the thing," Amos said. "If you did go in there, you might feel like you had to do something. And then I might feel like I had to do something. And then we'd all be doing things, and we'd all wind up having a worse day, just in general."

Avasarala's face went calm, her eyes focused a few centimeters to Amos' left. The security chief started to say something, but Avasarala put out a palm to stop her. After a few seconds, Avasarala grunted, shook her head, and turned to the security force. "You can skip this one. Go get a beer instead or something. It's all right."

"Yes, ma'am," the security chief said.

"Burton? You make goddamned sure there isn't any trouble from this, and you get her the fuck off my moon without anyone seeing her."

"You got it, Chrissie."

"Don't fucking call me that. I'm the acting secretary-general of the United Nations, not your favorite stripper."

Amos spread his hands. "Could be room for both."

Avasarala's laughter rang out through the dock. The security force broke up, moved on. The loading mechs repositioned. The carts continued on their various paths, busy as a kicked anthill. "I'm glad you made it," she said when she regained herself. "The universe would be less interesting without you."

"Likewise. How's the recovery going?"

"It sucks donkey balls," she said, shaking her head. "We're still losing thousands of people every day. Maybe tens of thousands. The food's running out down there, and even if I had enough rice to feed them all, the infrastructure's so fucked there's no good way to distribute it. Not to mention that there could still be more of those fucking rocks dropping anytime."

"Your kid okay?"

"Ashanti and her family are fine. They're here on Luna already. Thank you for asking."

"And your guy? Arjun?"

Avasarala smiled, and it didn't reach her eyes. "I remain optimistic," she said. "The *Rocinante* is on its way. You'll have something to ride on that doesn't make your cock look as small as that gaudy turd."

"That's good to hear. This boat's not my style anyway."

Avasarala turned away, shuffling awkwardly into the crowd. The low gravity didn't seem natural to her. He figured she probably hadn't spent all that much of her life up the well. Space was an acquired skill. Amos stretched, rolled on the balls of his feet, and waited until the last of the security force was out of sight. Chances were pretty slim they were going to press the issue once they'd been slapped down, but he still felt better watching them get gone.

While he was waiting, two Belters in Aldrin dockworker uniforms scurried by staying close together, their heads bowed. Luna was going to be a shitty, shitty place to be a Belter for a while, Amos thought. Still, it probably hadn't been that great before. He headed back to the *Zhang Guo*, and the entry lock opened as he got close to it, welcoming him back in.

The ship's interior was ugly as hell. The anti-spalling in the corridors was deep red and fake-velvet fuzzy with gold fleur-de-lis scattered over them in a weird, non-repeating pattern. The hatchways were enameled in royal blue and gold. Oversized crash couches were all over the place—in the corners of rooms, in niches in the hallways. The air recyclers added the stink of sandalwood incense without the smoke. All told, the ship was the embodiment of a stereotypical whorehouse done by a designer who'd never been to a real one. The security station was perfunctory, poorly designed, and barely stocked, but Erich's people were placed around it as well as they could manage. Even Butch, still in pressure bandages, had a rifle with fresh rounds trained down the hallway.

"Hey," Amos said. "We're cool. They're not coming in."

The release of tension was like a soft breeze, if soft breezes came with the sounds of magazines getting pulled from assault rifles.

"Okay," Erich said, lifting a pistol in his good hand. "Tyce. Police up all the guns. Joe and Kin, put a watch on the lock. I don't want to be surprised if anyone shows up unexpected."

"They won't," Amos said. "But hey, knock yourselves out."

"You got a minute?" Erich said, handing the pistol to a thick-necked man who Amos figured was Tyce.

"Sure," Amos said. They fell into step, ambling toward the lift.

"That was really the woman who's running Earth now?"

"Until she lets 'em have an election, I guess. I never really paid much attention to how that whole thing works."

Erich made a soft, noncommittal grunt. His bad arm was

curled up against his chest, the tiny fist tight. His good hand was stuffed deep in his pocket. Both made him look like something was eating him.

"And you... You know her. Like asking-favors know her."

"Yup."

At the lift, Erich punched for the ops deck. It wasn't where Amos meant to go, but it seemed like the conversation was leading toward something, so he went with it. The lift made a stuttering start, then rose gently past the high-ceilinged decks.

"I can't tell if this thing's a ship or a fucking throw pillow," Amos said.

"Wouldn't know," Erich said. "It's the first one I've been in."

"Seriously?"

"Never been out of atmosphere before. The low-gravity thing. That's weird."

Amos bounced gently on his toes. It was only about a sixth of a g. He hadn't really thought about it much. "You get used to it."

"You did, anyway," Erich said. "So how did you meet her?"

"We got in over our heads on some shit, and some folks she was against were trying to kill us. She came in and tried to keep us alive."

"So now you're friends."

"Friendly acquaintances," Amos said. "I don't have all that many what you'd call friends."

The lift stopped with a small lurch that it really shouldn't have had. The ops deck was all dark surfaces, the decking a deep chocolate brown, the walls an artificial wood grain, the consoles and couches lined in fake leather. Or hell, maybe real leather. It wasn't like he knew the difference to look at. Erich lowered himself into one of the couches and ran his good hand over his scalp.

"You know," he said. "You couldn't have done this without us. Me and your prisoner friend. And now the head of the fucking government, which excuse me if that still breaks my head a little."

"Well, I—"

"No, I know you would have done something. Just not this.

You couldn't have done this exact thing. This plan? For it, you needed to have us. All of us. And the only thing we had in common was you."

Amos sat across from him. Erich wouldn't meet his eyes straight on.

"*Plan*'s kind of a strong word for it," he said. "I was just grabbing whatever I could."

"Yeah, the thing is you had things to grab. I spent a lot of years in Baltimore. Know it like the back of my hand. Knew it. Now, I've got all my best people here and no fucking clue what here looks like, you know? Who controls the drugs around here? How do you fake an ID? I mean, I figure that underlying logic's the same anywhere, but..."

Erich stared at the wall like there was something to see there. Amos craned his neck to look, just to be sure.

"I don't know what we do from here. I don't know what I do from here. I've got people counting on me to get them through the queen of all churns, and I don't know where to take them or what we're gonna do."

"Yeah, that sucks."

"You do," Erich said.

"I suck?"

"You *know*. You've been out here. This? All this? It's your neighborhood. You know people. You know how things work. You know how to keep people alive."

"You may be overestimating the amount of time I've put into analyzing stuff," Amos said. "I got one ship and three people. That's been kind of a handful. All the rest of this just happened along the way."

"But it got us here." Erich shifted his gaze. His eyes were hard. "I've got enough cash squirreled away that if I get access to it, I might be able to buy a small ship. Not a good one, but something. Or relocate the team somewhere. One of the Lagrange stations or Pallas or... wherever. Start over. Make a new niche. If you want to take the lead, I'll give it up."

"Oh," Amos said. "Yeah, no."

"They'd be better off with you leading than with me."

"Yeah, but I don't know them enough to give a shit. I've got my own thing going. I'm sticking with it."

He couldn't tell if the release in Erich's eyes was relief or disappointment. Maybe both. Lydia would have known. Or Naomi. Or Holden. Alex, probably. For him, it was just a little change in muscle tension. Could have meant anything.

"I'll find my own way then," Erich said. "We'll be out of here in a couple days, if I can manage it."

"Okay, then," Amos said. It felt like there should be something more. He'd known Erich as long as he'd known anyone alive. Even if they saw each other again a time or two, the conversation they'd just had was the mark of the end. Both of their lives could have looked a lot different if Amos had said a few different words. It seemed like there should have been something to say about that. But since he couldn't come up with anything, he went back to the lift and headed down for the machine shop.

Going to the technical end of the *Zhang Guo*—the places where the owners and their guests wouldn't spend their time—was like stepping into a different ship. All the glitter and beauty gave way to a clean utilitarian design that wasn't as good as the *Roci*, but better than any other ship Amos had worked. All the corners were curved and softened in expectation of impacts. All the handholds were double-bolted. The drawers and cabinets in the machine shop were latched in two planes. The air smelled like fresh filters and lubricant. Someone had kept the place clean and in better order than a glorified orbital shuttle really deserved. Amos wondered if whoever that had been was still alive. It wasn't a question he could answer, though, so he didn't spend a lot of energy on it.

Peaches was sitting at a workbench. The outfit they'd gotten during their bike trip to Baltimore looked pretty sketchy in the clean and tidy surroundings. Torn at the shoulder and still too big for her. She looked like she was swimming in it. Her hair was pulled back into a ponytail with a zip tie and her hands were moving quickly and carefully over an open case of modular electronics. Her movements were as precise and flowing as an old recording of a piano player at the keys. She didn't look up as he came in, but she smiled.

"Got something for you. Salvaged a hand terminal. Nice one. Even got it talking to the local network. Finish the configuration, and you're good to go."

Amos pulled the seat next to her out from the body of the ship. She handed him the terminal, but still didn't meet his eyes.

"According to Chrissie, it ain't salvage."

"I liberated one, then. I was going to get one myself, but I can't. I've got nothing to connect to."

"Could use it like a disposable," Amos said, starting to key his configuration information. "Get you access to feeds anyway."

"Does it matter?"

"Well, if you don't think it does, then maybe not."

She sighed. There were tears in her eyes and a smile on her face. "We did it. We made it safely to Luna. Just like we hoped."

"Yeah."

"You know what I really missed when I was in the Pit? Anything that actually meant anything. They fed me, and they kept me alive, and we had this kind of support group thing where we could talk about our childhood traumas and shit. But I couldn't do anything that mattered. I couldn't work. I couldn't talk to people outside the prison. I was just being and being and being until sooner or later, I'd die and they'd put someone else in my cell."

She leaned forward, her elbows on the workbench. She'd burned the side of her thumb on something—a soldering iron, the barrel of a gun, something—and the skin was smooth and pink and painful-looking. "I won't go back there."

"Peaches, there's no there to go back to. And anyway, I'm pretty sure Chrissie knows you're on board here. She's not pushing the issue, so as long as we stay cool and act casual—"

Her laugh was short and bitter. "Then what? You can't take me with you anymore, Amos. I can't go on the *Rocinante.* I tried to kill Holden. I tried to kill all of you. And I did kill people. Innocent people. That's never going away."

"In my shop, that's just fitting in," Amos said. "I appreciate that seeing the crew again could leave you feeling a little antsy, but we all know what you are. What you did. Including all the shit you did to us. This isn't new territory. We'll talk it through. Work something out."

"I'm just afraid that if he doesn't back your play, they'll send me back, and—"

Amos lifted a hand. "You're missing some shit here, Peaches. Lot of folks seem to be. Let me lay this out again. There's no back, and it ain't just the real estate. The government that put you in prison only sort of exists anymore. The planet that put you in prison is going to be having billions of people die in the next little bit. Making sure you serve your whole term doesn't mean shit to them. There's a new Navy between us and the Ring, and there's still a thousand solar systems out there to fuck up the way we fucked up this one. Because what you're doing right now? Yeah, you're worrying about how it would go for you if none of that happened. And I'm thinking that you're doing it because you're not looking at the facts."

"What facts?"

"It ain't like that anymore."

"What isn't?"

"Any of it," Amos said. "With Earth puking itself to death and Mars a ghost town, everything's up for grabs. Who owns what. Who *decides* who owns what. How money works. Who gets to send people to prison. Erich just called it the queen of all churns, and he ain't wrong about that. It's a new game, and—"

His hand terminal chimed. Amos looked at it. The design was nicer than his old one, but the interface was a little different. It took him a few seconds to figure out what the alert meant. He whistled between his teeth.

"What is it?" Peaches asked.

He turned the screen toward her. "Seventy messages and twenty-three connection requests. Going back to before the rock dropped."

"Who from?"

Amos looked at the list. "Alex, mostly. A few from the captain. Fuck. I got six hours of stored video with just Alex trying to talk to me."

Peaches' smile was thin, but it was a smile. "At least you have people."

Chapter Fifty: Alex

"A bicycle?"

Amos leaned on the breakfast bar. "Sure. They don't need fuel, they don't get sick. Most of the repairs, you can handle on your own. You're looking for post-apocalyptic transportation, bikes are the way to go."

Alex sipped his beer. It was a local brew from a pub just down the corridor with a rich hoppy flavor and a reddish color. "I guess I never thought about it that way."

The suite on Luna was bigger than their rooms on Tycho Station had been, but of the same species. Four bedrooms opened onto a wide, recessed common area. A wall screen bent around the curve of the room, set to an idealized lunar landscape that was more photogenic than the real one. Every now and then, an animated "alien" girl would pop out from behind a rock, look surprised, and dart away again. It was cute, he supposed, but he would have preferred the real moonscape.

"So anyway, I didn't want to go through Washington. Too many people there, and if the pumps stopped working, I didn't want to be pedaling through knee-high sludge, right?"

"Right," Alex said.

Holden was on the *Rocinante*. Naomi was asleep in her room. She'd been sleeping a lot since the *Rocinante* had plucked them all out of the vacuum. The medical system said she was getting better and that the rest was good. It worried Alex, though. Not because she needed the sleep, but because maybe she didn't actually need it and was pretending to. Being here with Holden and Amos and Naomi was a bone-deep relief. He wanted it to be the end of their separation, everything come back into its right place like nothing had ever happened.

But it wasn't. Even talking to Amos, Alex thought he could feel little differences in the man. A kind of abstraction, like he was thinking of something else all the time and only pretending to give Alex his undivided attention. Naomi had been in medical debriefing since they'd arrived, and the physicians hadn't allowed anyone in to see her except Holden. If Naomi was finding excuses to stay isolated from them, that could be a very bad sign. They still didn't know all of what she'd been through that she'd wound up with the Free Navy and then escaped from it, but that it had been a trauma seemed obvious. And so he tried to enjoy the peace and pleasure of having his crew again and ignore the anxiety growing in the back of his mind, the sense that—just like with the governments and planets and system of the solar system—things here had changed.

Amos' hand terminal chirped. He sucked down half a glass of beer then bared his teeth. "I gotta go do a thing."

"All right," Alex said, pouring the rest of his beer into the sink. "Where are we going?"

Amos hesitated, but only for a fraction of a second. "Dock. Got something I need to move into my shop."

"Great," Alex said. "Let's go."

The stations on Luna were the oldest non-terrestrial habitation humanity had. They sprawled across the face of the moon and sank below its surface. The lights set into the walls glowed with a warm yellow and splashed across vaulted ceilings. The gravity—even lighter here than on Mars or Ceres or Tycho—felt strange and pleasant, like a ship ambling on without being in a rush to get anywhere. It was almost possible to forget the tragedy still playing out a little under four hundred thousand klicks over their heads. Almost, but not quite.

Amos went on about everything that had happened while he was down the well, and Alex listened with half his attention. The details of the story would be grist for a hundred conversations once they were back in the ship and going somewhere. It didn't matter that he get all of it now, and the familiar cadences of Amos' voice were like hearing a song he liked and hadn't listened to in a long time.

At the dock, Amos looked up and down the halls until he saw someone he knew sitting on a plastic storage crate. The crate was blue with white curls of scrapes along the side like a painting of waves. The woman was thickly built with black cornrows, dark brown skin, and an arm in a cast.

"Hey, Butch," Amos said.

"Big man," the woman said. She didn't acknowledge Alex at all. "This is this."

"Thanks, then."

The woman nodded and walked off, her low-g shuffle a little stiffer than the people around her. Amos rented a loading mech, grabbed the crate, and started for the *Roci*, Alex trotting along beside him.

"Should I ask what's in that?" Alex said.

"Probably not," Amos said. "So anyway, there we are on this island where all the rich people used to be before they fucked off up the well, right? And the ships are pretty much not there..."

The *Rocinante* had an actual hangar bay complete with atmosphere, not just a space on a pad and a tube to her airlocks. The new outer hull was titanium alloy and ceramic, the polished metal and flat black paint of the hull studded with PDCs and sensor arrays. The maw of the keel-mounted rail gun was like a little surprised *o* at her bow. In the artificial light of the hangar, she looked less dramatic than she had in the unfiltered light of the sun, but no less beautiful. Her scars were gone now, but it didn't make the ship seem less herself. Amos drove the mech to the aft airlock and cycled it open without breaking the slow, easy lope of his story. Inside, Amos lowered the crate to the deck, but didn't turn on the electromagnetic clamps that would hold it there. Instead, he slipped out of the mech and went into the ship itself. Engineering, cargo bay, the machine shop. The stern had always been Amos' domain.

"So those others," Amos said. "Johnson's people? They're done messing with my shit now, right?"

"Yeah," Alex said. "She's ours again. Just ours."

"Good." Amos shuffled into the cargo bay.

"So the servants, the maids and chauffeurs and whatever," Alex said. "They called security and then they just changed sides? Or... I mean how did that work?"

"Well," Amos said, popping the latches on the crate. "We had an introduction, see?"

The folds of the crate's lid rose of their own accord. Alex jumped back, misjudged the gravity, stumbled. A dark-haired head came up over the crate's edge, a thin ghost-pale face with ink-black eyes. Alex's heart started going triple time. Clarissa Mao, psychopath and murderer, smiled at him tentatively.

"Hey," she said.

Alex took a long, shuddering breath. "Ah. Hey?"

"See?" Amos said, clapping the girl's shoulder. "Told you it wouldn't be a problem."

"You have to tell him," Alex said, keeping his voice low. Bobbie was telling Holden about the work she'd been doing with veterans' affairs in Londres Nova, so he wasn't paying attention to them.

"I'm gonna," Amos said.

"You have to tell him now. She's on our ship."

Amos shrugged. "She was on our ship for months when we were coming back from the slow zone."

"She was a prisoner. Because of all the people she killed. And now she's on our ship by herself."

"I'll give you that does make this situation a little different," Amos said.

"Is there a problem?" Holden asked. "What are we talking about?"

"Little something I wanted to run past you," Amos said. "It'll wait until after the dog and pony show."

The meeting room in the security compound was built in an outdated architectural fashion: open archways and wide, sky-blue ceilings with indirect light and subtle geometric patterning. Everything about it was pointedly artificial, like the idea of an afternoon courtyard without the afternoon or the courtyard. Avasarala's voice came before she did, staccato and impatient. When she stepped through one of the archways, a young, seriously dressed man at her side, Bobbie stood up. Holden followed her lead.

"—if they want a voice in the decision. We're not going to fuck around bullshit electoral posturing."

"Yes, ma'am," the young man said.

Avasarala waved that they should sit back down as she took her own seat even as she kept talking to her assistant. "Take it to Kleinmann first. Once he's behind me, Castro and Najjar will have the cover they need."

"If you say so, ma'am."

"If I say so?"

The assistant inclined his head. "With permission, Chung is in a stronger position than Kleinmann."

"Are you second-guessing me, Martinez?"

"Yes, ma'am."

Avasarala shrugged. "Chung, then. Now go." As the young man left, she turned her attention to them. "Thank you all for— Where's Nagata?"

"Medical bay," Holden said. "The doctors are still deciding whether she's stable enough to release."

Avasarala hoisted an eyebrow and tapped a message onto her hand terminal. "They can make a fucking exception. I want her here. Thank most of you for coming. I'd beat around the bush and make everyone feel at home, but I've been in meetings for the last thirty-six hours, and I'm cranky. We're all clear that Earth is fucked, yes?"

"Hell yeah," Amos said.

"Good," Avasarala said. "Then I won't belabor the point. Along with that, the Martian Navy just shattered into tiny little pieces and Smith's too scared to call it treason."

"Can I ask," Bobbie said, sitting forward. Her hands, splayed on the table, seemed like she was trying to brace herself against a blow. "How bad does that look?"

"We're not making any official statements, especially when James Holden's in the room. No offense, but your track record for blurting information at inopportune moments is the stuff of legend."

"I'm getting better about that," Holden said. "But yeah. I understand."

"There's a thing that happens," Avasarala said, "when unthinkable things become thinkable. We're in a moment of chaos. Everything's up for grabs. Legitimacy itself is up for grabs. That's where we are now. This turd biscuit Inaros? He's out tooling around the Jovian moons where we can watch him play pirate. He's made his play to set the narrative. The Belt has risen up after generations of oppression, and is now taking its rightful wah, wah, wah. The position I'm in—"

"He's not wrong, though," Holden said, and Avasarala's eyes hardened. If looks could kill, Holden would have left in a bag, but he shook his head. "If the Belters fall in line with this Free Navy thing, it's going to be because they're all out of any other kind of hope. The new systems and colonies—"

"Have erased their niche," Avasarala said. "And that's shitty, and maybe we could have found a way to support them. Put them on some kind of cooperative basic, but they put a cherry bomb up the ass of the largest functioning ecosphere in the system, and it's going to be a while before handing them free food's going to be an option for me, practically or politically."

"They're never going to shut up and take handouts," Amos said. "Those bastards are three, four generations out there because they weren't looking to live on basic. I'm against eugenics same as the next guy, but the Belt hasn't been breeding for the kind of people who just kick back and see how much they can fuck and watch entertainment feeds before they die."

"I'm aware of the cultural problem," Avasarala said. "And as I said, it doesn't fucking matter anyway. If they'd be willing to take it, I still couldn't give it to them. So I have to find another way to cut the Free Navy off at the knees. But since Earth's navy is going to be busy making sure we don't have any more radar-invisible rocks dropping on us and Mars is in the process of ignoring that it's suffered a minor coup, it's going to be tricky. Tomorrow, I'm going to make an announcement. You get a preview. Lucky you.

"The United Nations, with assistance from the Mars Republic and cooperation from the OPA, is going to field a task force to address the criminal conspiracy of pirates and terrorists going under the Free Navy name. Not a war. A policing task force. And that's where you all come into play."

"You want me to lead it," Holden said.

"Yes," Avasarala said, "because literally every UN naval officer who wasn't dishonorably discharged is suddenly unavailable. For fuck's sake, Holden, I have crates of anti-herpes drugs that are more legitimately UN Navy than you are."

The old woman shook her head in disbelief and disgust. Holden's scowl was matched by a rising blush. Bobbie tried to hide her laughter, but Alex had to admit it was a little funny. Even if just to himself. Bobbie was the one to step in.

"What exactly are you looking for from us?"

"I want your presence and cooperation at the debriefing, for one thing. But more importantly, I need to know what you know. What you've found. We have to figure out how a third-rate gang leader managed to beat us at every turn—"

"He didn't," Naomi said, stepping in from under the spreading arches, a security escort at her side. In the shadowless light, she looked weirdly delicate. Her skin was peeling and she moved with the careful shifting of someone prepared for pain to come at any moment. But her sclera had faded from the blood-and-bone color to an ivory yellow that actually looked healthier, and her voice had lost the slushiness at its edges. A weight lifted from Alex's heart.

"The prisoner, ma'am," the security escort said.

"Yes, thank you, I noticed that," Avasarala said, then turned her attention to Naomi. "What do you mean he didn't?"

"Look at everything he tried to do and failed. He didn't kill Fred Johnson. He didn't kill Prime Minister Smith. He didn't take Tycho Station or destroy it. The *Rocinante*'s in one piece. He didn't keep hold of me. It's how he works. If he wins, it was the important thing. If he loses, it just disappears."

"And the protomolecule sample that he stole?"

Naomi blinked, seemed to lose focus for a moment, and shook her head. "He never said anything about that."

"Would he have?"

Naomi sat in the chair beside Holden. He took her hand, and she allowed it, but her attention was on Avasarala. Alex wasn't sure why that bothered him so much. The meeting wasn't an invitation for the two of them to work out their relationship status. And still, if she'd been just a little less guarded with him...

"Yes," Naomi said. "He would have. He likes to brag." The intimacy of that one piece of information filled Alex's chest with a sense of deep foreboding. Holden's face was calm. Unreadable.

"Good," Avasarala said, a sharpness in her voice. "That's very good to know." She considered Naomi silently. "You look like you're feeling better. You heard some of what I was saying?"

"Enough of it," Naomi said.

"Are you going to be able to help us?"

The question hung in the air, rich with nuance and complicated importance. Not *Why were you on his ship*. Not *How do you know him*. Not *Who are you to him that he brags about his plans to you*. Just, *Are you going to be able to help?*

"You okay?" Amos murmured.

"What? I'm fine," she replied.

"Because you're kinda fidgeting," Amos said at the same time Naomi said, "I want immunity from prosecution."

The air seemed to go out of the room. It wasn't a confession, but it painted a picture that none of them had wanted to admit might be possible. To ask for immunity was an admission of guilt, even if they didn't know what she was guilty of.

Avasarala's smile was indulgent and friendly and, he was almost certain, deceptive. "Blanket immunity?"

"For all of us."

"Who is 'all of us'?" Avasarala said, forming the words carefully as she said them. "Your friends in the Free Navy?"

"The crew of the *Rocinante*," Naomi said, and then stuttered. Paused. "And maybe one other person."

Alex shot a look at Amos. Did she know about Clarissa? Was that who she meant? Amos' smile was amiable and empty. Avasarala tapped her fingernails against the table.

"Not for Earth," Avasarala said. "Dropping the rocks? No one gets immunity for that."

Alex saw it hit. Tears appeared in Naomi's eyes, brimming silver and bright. "The crew of the *Rocinante*," she said. "The other one...I may ask for clemency and consideration later on. If the occasion arises."

"For Inaros?"

"No," Naomi said. "Him, you can fucking burn."

"I need to understand this fully," Avasarala said. "You, as a former member of Inaros' group, are willing to exchange complete and accurate information about his activities both before and after the bombardment of Earth in exchange for blanket immunity for the crew of the *Rocinante* on any matter not related to the present attacks?" That there had been no profanity in the statement gave it a solidity that unnerved Alex.

"Yes," Naomi said. "That's right."

The relief on Avasarala's face was hard as flint. "Glad to hear you say that, dear. I was worried I'd misjudged you." She rose to her feet, then grabbed at the table, cursing under her breath. "I miss weighing something. Half the time, I feel like I'm on a fucking trampoline. I'm going to go lie down and take a sleeping pill before I have a psychotic break, but the debriefing? It starts in the morning."

"We'll be wherever you want us to be," Holden said. "We're not going to hide anything." He was still holding Naomi's hand, and her fingers had curled around his. So maybe that was hopeful after all. As to not hiding anything... Well, Amos still didn't say anything.

The meeting broke up, except that it also didn't. Avasarala left, but the rest of them, including Bobbie, went to the security lobby, through the checkpoint, and out to the public lobby together. The sober silence gave way slowly to more mundane conversation: whether there was anyplace with food better than the mess on the *Roci*. Or if not better, at least different. Whether Naomi was up to drinking alcohol, because there was a little pub on one of the lower levels that was supposed to have some pretty good beers on offer. No one asked whether Bobbie was joining them. It was just assumed. As they shuffled and bounced in the thin gravity, Naomi and Holden kept hold of each other's hands. Amos and Bobbie traded dirty jokes. It was the powerfully ordinary talk that gave Alex hope. For everything that had happened, that was happening, that was still looming in the unseen and uncertain future, there were still moments like these. And so maybe it would be all right despite it all.

At the wide slope of Chandrayaan Plaza, where the traffic of carts and mechs and half-skipping people turned down a wide ramp deeper into the body of the moon, Amos cleared his throat.

"So that immunity for the crew thing?"

"It wasn't just for you," Naomi said, making it a joke, and also not one.

"Yeah, figured," Amos said. "But here's the thing. I was thinking about maybe taking on an apprentice. You know, help flesh out the crew. Get some skill redundancy."

"That's a good idea," Holden said. "Did you have someone in mind?"

Chapter Fifty-One: Naomi

Hell no," Jim said when they were alone in the suite. "Absolutely no. No fucking way, no. There have got to be a billion different ways to say no, and I'd still have to cycle through them a couple times to really express the depth of no on this one. Clarissa Mao? On the *Roci*? How is that anything but a massive load of let's-not-do-that?"

"And yet," she said, letting herself drift down to the bed, "you told Amos you'd think about it."

Jim tried pacing, but the slight lunar gravity made it difficult for him. He gave up and sat at the foot of the bed.

"We just got the crew back together. And Bobbie was there. I didn't want to spoil the moment."

"Ah. The moment."

She closed her eyes. Everything hurt. Her skin hurt. Her eyes felt gritty and swollen. The joints in her hands and feet ached. Her knees hurt. Her fingertips felt raw and oversensitive. She had the kind of headache that expressed as a sense of profound fragility until she moved too fast, and then it throbbed. It was better now than it had been, though. And it would get better. Slowly, over the course of at least days and maybe weeks, she'd come back to herself. Or some version of herself. But even if some of the damage was permanent, she'd feel better than she did now. Not yet, but soon.

Alex, Amos, and Bobbie were gone. Out to get beer and food. Their food. Pizza or falafel or sashimi. Earth food. There wasn't any good red kibble on Luna, or if there was, it wouldn't be served at the kinds of places they'd go. Part of her wished she'd had the energy to go with them. Part of her wished Jim had decided to join them instead of her. Part of her was euphoric and on the edge of tears that she was here, that she'd escaped, that it was over. She felt like her soul was a handful of dice that were still rolling, and what came up would decide the shape that the rest of her life took.

"I mean...Clarissa Mao?" Jim said. "How does anyone think that's a good idea?"

"Amos isn't afraid of monsters," she said. The words tasted bitter, but not completely so. Or no, not bitter. Complex, though.

"She is responsible for a lot of dead people," Jim said. "She blew up the *Seung Un*. Took out a quarter of the crew. And that one body they found? The one she was carrying around in a toolbox? Do you remember that?"

"I do."

"That guy was a friend of hers. She wasn't just killing faceless enemies. She was right down, look-them-in-the-eyes killing people that she knew. That she *liked*. How do you go from that to 'I know, let's ship out with her'?"

She knew she should stop him. He wasn't talking about her or the *Augustín Gamarra* or any of the other ships that had been sabotaged since using the code she wrote. He wasn't talking about Cyn, or the way he'd tried to intervene in her half-staged suicide. If he had been, there would have been more. How could she abandon her son? How could she let Filip think that she'd killed herself? How could she have kept something that important hidden from the people she said she cared about? All the sins she carried that even Clarissa Mao didn't.

She knew she should stop him, but she didn't. His voice was like tearing back scabs. It hurt to hear, and it left her exposed and raw and painful to the touch, and the pain felt good. Worse, it felt right.

"I'm not saying she should be killed. That whole thing about how if she's ever going back to prison, Amos is going to shoot her? I understand that he's joking—"

"He's not."

"Okay, I'm pretending that he's joking, but I'm not advocating killing her. I don't want her to die. I don't even want her locked up in inhumane, shitty prisons. But that's not what we're talking about. Shipping with someone means literally trusting them with your life all the time. And, okay, I was on the *Canterbury*, and we had some people there who were deeply, deeply sketchy. But even Byers only killed her husband. Clarissa Mao set out to destroy me in particular. Me. I just...I don't...How does anyone think this is a good idea? Someone who does the things she did doesn't just change."

She took a deep breath, pulling air into her bruised lungs. They still gurgled a little, but she was on enough reflex inhibitors that she wasn't coughing herself light-headed anymore. She didn't want to open her eyes, didn't want to talk. She opened her eyes, sat up, her back against the headboard, her arms wrapped around her knees. Holden went quiet, feeling the weight of what was about to come. Naomi plucked at her hair, pulling it over her eyes like a veil, then almost angrily, she smoothed it back so her eyes were clear.

"So," she said. "We need to talk."

"Captain to XO?" he asked, carefully.

She shook her head. "Naomi to Jim."

The dread that bloomed in his eyes hurt to see, but she'd

also been expecting it. She felt its echo in her own chest. It was strange that after all she'd done—all the demons she'd faced and escaped—this should still be so hard. Holden's hand terminal chimed, and he didn't even look at the screen. The lines around his mouth deepened the way they did when he'd tasted something he didn't like. His hands folded together, strong, controlled, calm. She remembered the first time they'd met, lifetimes ago back on the *Canterbury*. How he'd radiated charm and certainty and how much she'd hated it at first. How much she'd hated him for being too much like Marco. And then how much she'd come to love him for not being like him at all.

And now, she would break her rule of silence, and the thing they had between them would either survive or it wouldn't. It was a terrible thought. Marco might still be able to empty her, and he wouldn't even have to spend the effort of being aware of it. Existing was enough.

"I don't," Jim said, then stopped. He looked up at her through his eyebrows, like he was the one feeling guilty for it all. "We all have pasts. We all have secrets. When you took off, I felt...lost. Confused. Like part of my brain was gone. And now that you're here, I am just profoundly happy to see you. This right here? It's enough."

"Are you saying you don't want to know?"

"Oh lord, no. No, I'd pretty much cut off a toe. I'm pretty much made of ragingly deep curiosity and floating jealousy. But I can deal with those. I don't have any more right to make you tell me anything you don't want to than I ever did. If there's anything you don't want to say—"

"I don't want to say any of this," Naomi said. "But I want you to know. And so we have to get through this part, no?"

Jim shifted, pulling his legs up under him, kneeling at the foot of the bed, his face to hers. His hair was the color of coffee with just a little cream. His eyes were blue as deep water. As evening sky was supposed to be.

"Then we'll get through it," he said with a simple, boundless optimism that caught her by surprise and drew out laughter, even here.

"Well," she said. "When I was in my middle teens, I was living with a woman we called Tia Margolis and burning through the engineering courses on the networks as fast as I could, and there were ships that came through dock. Belter ships. Hard-core."

Jim nodded, and then—to her surprise—it was easy. In her mind, the idea of unpacking her past to Jim—to anyone—was a thing of anger and disgust and recriminations. Or worse, of pity. Jim, who for all his faults was sometimes capable of perfection, listened carefully and completely. She had been Marco Inaros' lover. She'd gotten pregnant young. She'd been involved—at first without knowing it—in the sabotage of inner planets ships. She had a son named Filip who had been taken from her as a way to control her. She described the dark thoughts, and realized it was very nearly the first time she'd talked about them openly, without a veil of ironic humor. *I tried to kill myself, but it didn't work.* Just saying the words out loud felt like being in a dream. Or waking up from one.

And then, somehow in the depth of her confession, the baring of her blighted soul that was always supposed to be a trauma and a terror, it was just her and Jim having a conversation. She'd found a way to get a message out to him during the battle, and he told her about getting it, and the conversation he'd been having with Monica Stuart, and why he'd felt betrayed by her. And then backtracked to how she'd been kidnapped, and then before that to her plan to use the protomolecule sample as a Ouija board to investigate the missing ships. And then they went back to the *Chetzemoka* and Marco's fallback plan, which brought up the way he always nested one scheme inside another, and before she got back around to Cyn, Alex and Amos and Bobbie were back, their voices burbling over each other like birdsong. Jim closed the bedroom door against them and, when he came back, settled beside her, his back to the headboard too.

When she did talk about killing Cyn during her jump, Jim

took her hand. They were silent for a moment while she examined her grief. It was real, and it was deep, but it was also complicated with anger at her old friend and captor. She hadn't let herself be aware of that at the time, but looking back, her whole stretch on the *Pella* seemed like an exercise in retracting into herself. Except when she'd defied Marco. She remembered saying that Jim was all the things he only pretended to be, wondered whether she should tell that part of the story, and then did. Jim looked horrified and then laughed. They lost track of their stories and spent ten minutes getting the timeline back: the *Chetzemoka* left the *Pella* after Jim and Fred had already departed from Tycho, or before? He'd told Alex to go investigate the *Pau Kant* before the rocks dropped on Earth? Oh right. Okay. She got it now.

They got sleepy together, her arm curled in his. The pauses grew longer, and softer. She thought *Oh, we should really talk about Amos and Clarissa Mao*, but then she was dreaming that she was on a ship that was burning at a full g for everyone else while she was on the float. All the other people in the crew, pressed to the deck while she moved through the air, reaching the tools and ducts they couldn't get to. In the dream, Alex was explaining that it was because she had so much built-up inertia that the rest of them would take a while catching up. In context, it seemed to make sense.

She woke up. She didn't know how much later it was, but there were no more voices from the main room. Jim was curled on his side, his back against her. His breath was deep and slow. She stretched slowly, careful not to disturb him. The aches in her muscles and skin and joints felt a little better, and there was a warmth in her chest. A looseness.

For years, she'd kept her secrets. Held them like she was keeping the pin in a hand grenade. The fear and the shame and the guilt had built up without her even noticing. The things she had done wrong—and there were so many—had grown in power. Not having them gnawing at her ribs from the inside felt strange. Empty, in a way, but a peaceful kind of empty.

Not that she was suddenly made of light and happiness. Cyn was still dead because of her. Filip was still abandoned. Abandoned again. Marco was still as much a pool of anger and hatred. Nothing about that had changed, and everything had. An old picture made into something new by replacing the frame. Jim shifted in his sleep. The thin, dark hairs on the back of his neck had a couple paler ones among them. The first touches of gray.

Something had changed between them. Not just during her sabbatical in hell, but now that she was back from her own personal underworld. She wasn't sure exactly who they were to each other, she and Jim, except that things would be different now. Because she was different, and her changing wasn't going to break him. He wouldn't try to make her stay the Naomi he'd imagined.

Things changed, and they didn't change back. But sometimes they got better.

She got out of bed slowly, shuffling to the little desk in the corner of the room. Their hand terminals were there, and the little bottle of Jim's anticancer drugs, since he wasn't on the *Roci.* She reached for her terminal, paused, and picked up his. She should ask first, but he was asleep, and she didn't want to wake him, and she didn't think he'd mind.

Monica Stuart's footage of the *Rabia Balkhi* passing through the ring gate was unexceptional. Nothing in it seemed at all strange, except for the story around it. What had Marco done with it, she wondered. Why had he started his piracy so long before the actual coup that would permit it to go large-scale? Just the effort of doctoring all the logs from Medina would be a risk he didn't need to take. Maybe it was something to do with the system the *Balkhi* was heading into...?

She shifted to her own terminal, connecting to the *Roci*'s system and putting out a series of simple pattern matching requests. It wasn't hard to do. Most of the information Stuart had been working with was public record. And optical telescopes around the system had been trained on the Free Navy since the moment Marco had started his assault on the Martian convoy. The list of systems where ships had gone missing wasn't long, but the pattern in it wasn't obvious either. She tried to remember if anyone on the *Pella* had talked about any of them: Tasnim, Jerusalem, New Kashmir. Of course, the naming conventions were also a mess. New Kashmir also got called Sandalphon, High Texas, and LM-422. She pulled up alternate names for the other systems. Now that Jim had learned the worst of her past, she was almost eager to start the debriefing with Avasarala's team, and if there was some clue she could bring from her time on the *Pella*…

She scowled. Ran the matching schema again with different tolerances. Behind her, Jim yawned. When he sat up, the sheets made a hushing sound. The *Roci* came back with a list of possibles, and she spooled through them. The *Ankara Slough* was an approximate match for the *Rabia Balkhi*, but looking through the differences she saw the drive signatures were wrong. It would have cost less to make a new ship than to swap a whole drive complex out of an existing one. In the front room, Alex said something and Amos answered. And then—to her brief surprise—Bobbie. Jim's hand touched her shoulder.

"Hey. You all right?"

"Yeah," Naomi said. "Fine."

"How long have you been up?"

She checked the time and groaned. "Three and a half hours."

"Breakfast?"

"God, yes."

Her back protested when she stood, but only a little. Her mind felt focused and alive and wholly her own for the first time in weeks. Maybe since the first, toxic message from Marcos had come in. She wasn't at war with herself, and it felt good. But…

Jim's hair was in wild disarray, but he looked handsome in it. She took his arm. "Is something wrong?" he asked.

"Don't know," she said.

"Would coffee improve whatever it is?"

"Couldn't hurt," she said.

In the main room of the suite, Amos and Bobbie were talking

about methods of unpowered travel, each of them subtly outdoing the other and both clearly aware of it and having fun. Alex grinned to her and Jim when they sat at the breakfast bar, and then poured them both demitasses of slow-pouring espresso with thick brown crème at the top. Naomi sipped, enjoying the heat and the rich complexity hidden inside the bitterness.

"You're looking better," Alex said.

"Feeling better. Thanks. Bobbie, the missing ships you were looking for. They were all MCRN, right? Navy?"

"Ships. Weapons. Supplies. The whole thing," Bobbie said. "I guess we know what happened to them now."

"No colony ships, though?"

The big woman frowned. "I wasn't looking for any."

"What's up?" Jim asked.

Naomi swirled the espresso in her little bone-colored cup, watching the whorls form and vanish in the low gravity. "The missing ships come in two flavors. Military vessels from Mars that the Free Navy have now, and then colony ships that went missing on their way out to new systems. And I make sixty, maybe seventy percent matches with the Free Navy ships to old military records. I can't find one match with the missing colony ships. I can't see a pattern in what systems they were going to or what they were carrying. And I don't know what hijacking them could have gained for Marco."

Amos made a low grunting sound in the back of his throat.

"Yeah," Naomi said, as if the sound had been words. "Something in the ring gates is eating ships."

Epilogue: Sauveterre

"I have a tracking number," the captain of the little freight ship said for what had to be the sixth or seventh time. "I have landing papers and a tracking number straight from Amatix Pharmaceuticals. I know the shipment arrived on Medina six months ago. I have a *tracking number.*"

Sauveterre sipped smoked tea from a bulb as he listened. He would have preferred whiskey from a glass, but he was on duty and the *Barkeith* was on the float. The first did for the whiskey, the second for the glass. Granted, the captain's office was private and he could have done whatever he pleased. And, he supposed, he did. Keeping to his duty was a more pleasing thing for him than whiskey, which was as it should be.

"Sabez you got a tracking number, *Toreador*," the voice from Medina Station said. "Amatix, though? Esa es Earth-based. No Earth-based companies on Medina."

The *Barkeith* was a *Donnager*-class battleship. A small city in space, run with machined precision and capable of turning not only the little freighter but Medina Station to particles smaller than grains of sand. But it and the rest of Duarte's fleet were waiting for permission from traffic control on Medina to proceed through the next ring gate and begin the second, stranger leg of their journey. It was an overabundance of etiquette on the fleet's part, but there were reasons for that. Not the least being the general reluctance to use heavy weapons too near the alien station that hung inert in the vast non-space between the rings. They weren't ready for that to awaken again. Not yet.

A light knock came at the door. Sauveterre straightened his tunic. "Come." Lieutenant Babbage opened the door, bracing with a handhold on its frame. She looked anxious as she saluted. Sauveterre let her hold the position for a moment before answering her salute and allowing her to enter.

"I have been en route for ten months!" the captain of the *Toreador* shouted. "If the colony doesn't get this shipment, they're fucked."

"Have you been listening to this?" Sauveterre asked, nodding toward the speakers.

"No, sir," Babbage said. Her skin was ashen under the brown. Her lips pressed thin.

"Üzgün, *Toreador*," Medina Station said. "You need to dock for medical, wir koennen—"

"I don't need to dock for medical! I need my fucking supplies! I have a tracking number that puts them on your station, and I will not—"

Sauveterre cut them off and took another sip of tea. "They've been going more or less like that for the better part of an hour. It's embarrassing on their behalf."

"Yes, sir."

"Do you know why I wanted *you* to hear it?"

She swallowed her fear, which was good, and her voice didn't tremble when she spoke, which was better. "To demonstrate what happens when there is a breakdown in discipline, sir."

"The end point of it, anyway. Yes. I've heard you violated dress code. Is that true?"

"It was a bracelet, sir. It belonged to my mother, and I thought..." Her voice trailed off. "Yes, sir. That report is true, sir."

"Thank you, Lieutenant. I appreciate your candor."

"Permission to speak freely, sir?"

Sauveterre smiled. "Granted."

"With respect, sir, the dress code was MCRN regulation. If we are going to enumerate transgressions against code, there are some larger ones that might also be worthy of examination. Sir."

"You mean like being here at all."

Her expression was hard. She'd overplayed her hand, and she knew it. It happened. Embarrassment and the childish need to stamp her feet and say it wasn't fair. He wouldn't have gone there in her place. But since it was on the table, it was on the table. No way but forward.

"We are in a time of flux, that's true. With the elected government failing its obligations, Admiral Duarte has taken authority and responsibility for the fleet on himself. I, following the chain of command, am carrying out his orders. You, also following the chain of command, are expected to follow mine. This is an independent initiative of the fleet. It's not a free-for-all."

"Sir," she said. She meant *Yes, sir*, but she hadn't said the *yes* part.

"Do you know what happens if I write you up for your failure to follow fleet discipline?"

"I could be demoted, sir."

"You could. If things continued, you could be drummed out. Removed from duty. Dishonorably discharged. Not over this, of course. This is small, but if it became large. You understand?"

"I do, sir."

"If you were discharged, what do you think would happen?"

She looked at him, confused. He gestured with his free hand, a sweep that gave her permission to speak.

"I... don't..." she stammered.

"I don't know either," he said. "Back at Mars, you'd have been released to civilian life. But where we're going, there is no civilian life. No human life at all. Do I turn you out to fend for yourself in the local food chain? Do I spend the time and resources it would take to send you back, and then back where? The forces that have taken control on Mars would see you as a traitor just the same as they would me. They'd throw you in the brig for life unless you cooperated with them. And if you were going to cooperate with them, then it wouldn't make sense for me to send you back in the first place. Would it?"

"No, sir." He could see understanding beginning to dawn in her eyes. Only beginning to, though. Humanity was so flawed. Not just her, but everyone. Half the population was below average intelligence. Half below average dedication. Average adherence to duty. The cruel law of statistics. It was astounding that as a race they'd managed as much as they had.

"Now that we are taking initiative," he said, "it is more important than ever that we maintain strict discipline. We're like the first long-haul missions back before anyone had an Epstein drive. Months, maybe years, as a community of warriors and explorers. There's not room for outsiders when there is no outside. I know you're upset that—"

"No, sir, I'm not—"

"I know you're upset that I'm coming down on you for something as minor as a bracelet. It seems trivial, and it is. But if I wait until it's not trivial, we come to matters of life and death very, very quickly. I don't have the latitude to take a cavalier position."

"I understand, sir."

"I'm glad to hear you say that."

He held out his hand, palm up. Babbage wiped away a tear with the back of her hand, and then dug in her pocket for a moment. When she put the bracelet in his hand, she paused, holding it for just a second longer. Whatever it meant to her, giving it over was a sacrifice. He closed his hand on the thin silver chain with its tiny sparrow-shaped pendant. He tried to make his smile gentle as he spoke.

"Dismissed."

When she had closed the door behind her, he turned back to his system. A new message had come in from Cortázar. His flesh crawled a little. Duarte's pet scientist had been sending more and more messages since the Belters had pulled the trigger. The man's enthusiasm unnerved Sauveterre. The man's personality was firmly in the uncanny valley, and his pleasure in the project they were undertaking at the new Laconia Station had a feeling of anticipation that was almost sexual.

Duty, however, was duty. He put Babbage's jewelry in the recycler and opened the message. Cortázar was too close to the camera or else had chosen for reasons of his own to be slightly out of focus. His wide chin and thin, black hair should have been unremarkable. Sauveterre rubbed his hands like he was trying half-consciously to wash them.

"Captain Sauveterre," the strange little man said. "I'm pleased to report that the sample arrived intact. Thank you very much for taking custody of it after its liberation. I am, however, distressed to hear that the fleet is running behind schedule."

"It's a few days over the course of months," Sauveterre said to himself and the screen. "We'll make it up."

"I know you are aware that both supplies and time are in short supply until the artifact has been brought to heel. In order to help make up for this shortfall, the research group has put together some plans and specifications for some of the modifications the *Barkeith* will need in order to dock with the artifact. Several of them can be started by your engineering teams en route. And of course, if you have any questions, I am at your disposal. Cortázar out."

The screen flipped to a series of technical drawings. There was more than enough about those to disturb him as well. They called all the alien technology by the name protomolecule, but of course, that far-traveled set of life-hijacking microparticles was only one object in a much grander toolbox. And if Cortázar had interpreted the top-clearance data from the MCRN probes correctly, what they had found would be much easier for humanity to tame and make use of.

Still, the changes Cortázar wanted for the *Barkeith* were unpleasantly organic. Less like they were fitting a new model of airlock on the ship, and more like they were carving it into some kind of colossal prosthesis.

It's the beginning of something very new and very powerful, and if good people don't step in to accept the power, bad ones will. It was what Admiral Duarte had told him the night he'd brought Sauveterre into the fold. It had been true then, and it was true now. He switched on the camera, adjusted his hair, and began recording.

"Message received. I will take the plans to my engineers at once. If they have any concerns, we will be in touch." Short, to the point, minimalist without being rude. Efficient. He hoped it would come across as efficient. He rewatched it to be sure and considered rerecording it and changing *concerns* to *questions*, but decided he was overanalyzing it. As he sent it off, his system chimed.

"Captain, we have clearance from Medina."

"Do we now, Mister Kogoma? Kind of them. What was the resolution of their tracking number situation?"

"The freighter is moving in to dock with the station, sir."

Well, there was another ship for the skinnies to commandeer. If the *Toreador* had known which way the wind was blowing, they'd have hightailed it back to whatever hardscrabble planet they'd come from and tried to make do without whatever they had lost anyway. As it was, the Free Navy would just keep gobbling up the ships that came through, starving out the colonies. Weakening them. By the time the Belters figured out they were fighting a rearguard action against history, Duarte would be in position.

War, Sauveterre thought as he pulled himself to the command

deck, had long since ceased to be about controlling territory. The job of a military was to disrupt its enemies. Generations of low-scale war in the Belt hadn't been an attempt to hold Vesta Station or Ceres or any of the dozens of little floating supply hubs in the vast emptiness. It had always and only been about keeping the OPA or any other Belt force from coalescing into an organized force. Until the rules changed, and that organized force became useful. The Free Navy would have made itself decades before if men like Duarte had let it. Now that the Belt finally had it, they would find just how useless it was.

As long as it kept Earth and what was left of Mars busy for a few years. After that... The reward of audacity was the chance to steer history.

The command deck was in trim. Everyone in their couches, the displays freshly cleaned, the controls polished. The *Barkeith* would arrive at Laconia Station as smart and sharp as she had left Mars. And they wouldn't be wearing bracelets. He drew himself down to his command station and strapped himself in.

"Mister Taylor, sound the acceleration alert. Mister Kogoma, inform the fleet and Medina Station that we are proceeding."

"Sir," the tactical officer said, "permission to open weapon ports."

"Are we expecting action, Mister Kuhn?"

"Not expecting, sir. An abundance of caution."

Kuhn didn't trust the skinnies either. That was fair. They were a bunch of thugs and cowboys who thought that because they had guns, they had power. Sauveterre thought it was early for the Free Navy to start double-crossing Duarte, but they were stupid and impulsive. It didn't do to assume an amateur force would make the same decisions as a professional. "Permission granted. And warm up the PDCs while you're at it. Mister Kogoma, please advise the fleet to do likewise."

"Yes, sir," Kogoma said.

The Klaxon sounded and Sauveterre settled into his couch, the sensation of weight returning over the course of seconds. The transit to the Laconia ring was short. The space between the rings was almost claustrophobic compared with the vastness of real, open vacuum. And dark. Starless. The physics wonks said that there wasn't any space on the other side of the rings. That whatever bubble they all existed in ended not in a barrier, but in some more profound manner that he couldn't picture. He didn't need to.

The Laconia gate drew closer, a handful of stars burning solid and clear on the other side of it, and growing as they came near. The exhaust plumes of the fleet vanguard glowed brighter as they passed through. There would be new constellations there. A different angle on the galaxy, like a whole new sky.

"Approaching the ring, sir," Keller said from the navigation controls. "Passing through in three. Two..."

Keller fell apart. No, that wasn't right. Keller was where she had been, sitting as she had been sitting. But she was a cloud now. All of them were clouds. Sauveterre held up his hands. He could see them so perfectly: the ridges of his fingertips, the spaces between the molecules, the swirl and flow of his blood beneath them. He could see the molecules in the air—nitrogen, oxygen, carbon dioxide all bouncing madly against each other, obscuring some more profound space between them. A vacuum that penetrated them all.

I'm having a stroke, he thought. And then, *No. Something else is wrong.*

"Kill the drive!" he shouted. "Turn about!" And the waves of his words passed through the visible but invisible air in an expanding sphere, bouncing against the walls, shuddering where they intersected with the cries of fear and a blaring Klaxon. It was beautiful. The cloud that was Mister Keller moved her hands and miraculously didn't slip through the vast emptiness of her control deck.

He saw the sound coming in the rush of molecules before it reached him and he heard the words. "What's going on? What's happening?"

He couldn't see the image on the screens to know if the stars were there. All he could sense were atoms and photons of the thing itself, not the pattern they made. Someone was screaming. Then someone else.

He turned and saw something move. Something *else*, not another cloud like himself, like the others, like matter. Something solid but obscured by the emptiness of material like a shape in the fog. Many shapes, neither light nor dark, but some other thing, some third side of that coin, passing through the spaces between the spaces. Rushing toward them. Toward him.

Sauveterre did not notice his death.

Acknowledgments

While the creation of any book is less a solitary act than it seems, the past couple of years have seen a huge increase in the people involved with The Expanse in all its incarnations, including this one. This book would not exist without the hard work and dedication of Danny and Heather Baror, Will Hinton, Tim Holman, Anne Clarke, Ellen Wright, Alex Lencicki, and the whole brilliant crew at Orbit. Special thanks are also due to DongWon Song and Carrie Vaughn for their services as beta readers, Ben Jones and Jordin Kare for their help figuring out what happens when a thruster misfires, and also to the gang from Sakeriver: Tom, Sake Mike, Non-Sake Mike, Porter, Scott, Raja, Jeff, Mark, Dan, Joe, and Erik Slaine, who got the ball rolling.

The support team for The Expanse has also grown to include Sharon Hall and Ben Roberts, Bill McGoldrick, Mark Fergus, Hawk Ostby, and Naren Shankar among many, many others at

Alcon Television, the Sean Daniel Company, and Syfy. Especially Alan for the Boom Coffee and Kenneth for essentially everything else.

And, as always, none of this would have happened without the support and company of Jayné, Kat, and Scarlet.

extras

meet the author

James S. A. Corey is the pen name of fantasy author Daniel Abraham and Ty Franck. They both live in Albuquerque, New Mexico.

introducing

If you enjoyed
NEMESIS GAMES,
look out for

ANCESTRAL MACHINES

by Michael Cobley

No world is safe.

The Warcage: two hundred worlds harnessed to an artificial sun in a feat of unprecedented stellar engineering. Built to travel through space as a monument to peace between alien species, now its voracious rulers have turned it into a nightmarish wasteland, capturing new planets for slaves and resources, then discarding the old.

Now, when a verdant agri-world is pulled out of its orbit, the captain of a smuggler ship must journey into the Warcage to rescue his crew.

PROLOGUE

The drone Rensik Estemil was in the middle of an intelligence-gathering mission down on Tier 104 when the peremptory summons reached him. It took him forty-three hours to stealth-exfiltrate Problematic Area 3 and ascend through hyperspace to Tier 49, home of the *Garden of the Machines*. Even so, on arrival he insisted on being recased in one of the new Iterant-9 varidroid shells before complying with the summons and going in search of the Construct.

He left the faceted blue reshell chamber and glided out along one of the hundreds of black-mesh walkways that coiled, curved and intertwined around the new and heavily armoured *Garden of the Machines*. From a distance, the Construct's stronghold had resembled a dark webby cloud through which a thousand tiny pin-points crawled between the bright clusters of test and trial bowers. Up close, there was a sense of the jungle about it.

Rensik found the Construct's command proximal in a gazebo positioned among the outermost walkways. A pale gauze-canopied archway afforded a generous view of the Slegronag Interval, an askew expanse on hyperspace Tier 49, a cavernous opening half a million miles wide and about three million long, its floor a vast plain littered with the split, cracked and smashed ruins of entire worlds, gargantuan heaps of planetary wreckage strewn in all directions. A dead, airless and abandoned graveyard over which the *Garden of the Machines* drifted on a course that zigzagged slowly along the length of the Slegronag.

"You took your time. A lack of promptness is scarcely a quality one expects from an Aggression field supervisor."

The Construct's new proximal was a hovering nine-sided unit from which a variety of tentacles and articulated arms sprouted. Before it, on a long low cradle, there sat what at first glance looked like a large black and green drone of unfamiliar design. It had a blunt-nosed blimp configuration with a number of what were probably weapon blisters dotted around its battered hull. Blackened, twisted thrust nozzles jutted at the stern. A dozen or more sections lay open while the Construct's tentacular tip-tools prodded at the innards. Twinkly gleams from the shadowy interior indicated the presence of remotiles, scanning hard-to-reach niches, sending back rich datastreams.

Rensik Estemil's newly acquired varidroid was a marvel of nano-compression and multi-function shield technology, and was comfortingly well armed. Yet he was dwarfed by this bulky, inert mass. The aura of lapsed millennia was almost tangible to his sensors.

A segmented tentacle tipped with a cluster of purple lenses snaked towards him.

"I've seen the reports of the Julurx operation," said the Construct. "Risky strategy, allowing the second-stage colony to develop unhindered, yet your engineering of a counter-horde turned out to be highly effective. Most creative. All the local legacy civilisations will be greatly relieved."

For the Construct this was the equivalent of a triumphal welcome-home parade, but then Rensik had been faced with a predicament freighted with the potential for ghastly consequences. A flotilla of Hodralog nomads had been scavenging through an eroded tiltway on the periphery of Tier 103, when they disturbed the hibernating mekspores of a replicating machine horde called the Julurx. The Hodralog, and their ships and AIs, were swiftly overwhelmed by the spores, which wasted no time in switching over to building the stage-two horde, using their newly acquired stores of organic and refined materials. Rensik and his wing of battle-hardened Aggression destructors, responding to panicky alerts from Tier 103's spire-city civilisation, reached the tiltway several hours after the last Hodralog was slain. But comm despatches from the ill-fated nomads had been relayed earlier to the Construct drones and by the time they arrived Rensik Estemil had a plan.

"Replicating machine hordes don't place much value on retaining nuanced data from previous outbreaks," Rensik said. "Otherwise they would have known how to counter my brilliant strategy of capturing unactivated stage-one spores and using them to engineer an anti-horde dedicated to eradicating the Julurx."

"How long?"

"Thirty-one-point-four hours."

"The Julurx must have reached one of the later stages after that space of time."

"Stage six," Rensik said. "Its first gigatropolis was partially complete when our anti-horde launched its main attack wave. Afterwards we repeatedly beam-scorched the vicinity, and a network of scanner-probes were left on-station."

"Good," said the Construct proximal. "Well summarised, if a little self-satisfied. And how would you describe the progress in Problematic Area 3?"

"Progressing satisfactorily."

"Droll. And I notice that you've changed your name again."

"I thought that minor individuations were permissible," Rensik said. "Has that changed?"

"Not at all. It is merely noteworthy to observe that since your involvement in the Darien Conflict you have changed your name nine times. Did you know that certain Human leisure-class subcultures pursue similar alterations in designation? They vie with one another to come up with the most outlandish forms of nomenclature."

"Fascinating," Rensik said. "When I arrived I was sure that you were going to explain why you were investigating this rusting relic – I had no idea that my name would prove to be of such interest."

"Perceptive," said the Construct. "Pithy and ironic." The lens-tipped tentacle swung in a bit closer. "We here in the tiers of hyperspace exist in a kind of sediment of relics, the debris of past universes compacted upon one another. Yet even up there, in the prime continuum, you cannot escape the undying fragments of the immemorial past, lingering gracenotes of vast symphonies of destruction, the heirlooms of bygone insanities." Another tool-tentacle tapped on the hull of the ancient drone. "This war machine is indeed, as you say, a relic. Until very recently it was preserved in the deep permafrost of a world on the spinward boundary of the Sendrukan Hegemony. Possibly the only intact example of a Zarl Imperium combat drone known to exist..."

"The Zarl Empire," mused Rensik. "Collapsed about a million years ago?"

"Indeed, although this device dates from the tyranny's high-point a little further back. Most of the materials used in its construction were anti-entropic, otherwise it would have crumbled to dust by now. But this is not the reason I asked you to see me. Have you ever heard of an exotic megastructure known as the Great Harbour of Benevolent Harmony?"

"Yes, I have," said Rensik. "Began as some lofty altruistic collaborative project over in the Greater Shining Galaxy about a hundred thousand years ago. Ended as the lair of several psychotic species hell-bent on slaughter, and was hunted down and destroyed by the Just Reprisal Alliance or something similar."

"It was more like fifty thousand years ago," the Construct said. "Archive documentation about the Greater Shining Galaxy's deep history is fragmentary with few details, except that it was apparently a massive macro-engineering achievement. And now it seems that it was never destroyed. Despite concerted massive attacks it survived and escaped."

A moment or two of silence followed, which from past experience Rensik knew was to be filled by a leap of understanding from the listener. There was really only one possible extrapolation to all this and it was a disturbing one.

"Has this thing arrived in our galaxy?" he said.

"Well done! Guess what emerged from hyperspace several hours ago near the border between Earthsphere and the Indroma Solidarity? On the Indroma side, no less, hiding in one of those huge starless gulfs that diplomats have been wrangling over for decades."

In one of his dynamic memory niches Rensik ran a swift scenario model, pitting the regional powers against the potential of something like the Great Harbour. The outcomes were not encouraging.

"We will need a serious magnitude of firepower to stop this thing," Rensik said. "An assault fleet of five, no, six thousand Aggression units, plus support tenders, would provide the necessary deployable force, especially if I were in command."

"We would not be able to assemble such a fleet in the very short term," said the Construct. "Based on third-hand reports from our galaxy's outlier stellar clusters, this intruder can be expected to move in the very short term against any isolated worlds in the area. Therefore I am sending you, and I'm even letting you use one of the upgraded shimmerships."

"I see, a solo mission," Rensik said. "Covert observance, monitoring comms, gauging capabilities and weaknesses, sending regular reports—"

"No, not solo – you'll be accompanied by a Human operative from Earthsphere's military intelligence."

Rensik groaned. "Humans—"

"Your experience in that field should be of considerable utility." The Construct paused as one of its tentacles snaked into some cranny within the ancient Zarl drone and a bright light stuttered for a moment. "While the assignment includes covert observation and intel gathering, your first task is to find out who commands and what their purpose and strategy are. I suspect that the regime, or regimes, will be despotic or tyrannical to some degree so the existence of resistance groups is practically a given. Your main task, you and your Human coagent, is to seek out the most effective of these rebel movements and offer what assistance you can. Feel free to be creative."

"How creative can I be while babysitting a..."

A priority data object pinged into Rensik's entry buffer. Decoiled, it turned out to be sparse background details on the Great Harbour and the personnel file for one Lt Commander Samantha Brock.

"I don't imagine that she'll require much in the way of babysitting," said the Construct.

"It seems that she might be useful," Rensik conceded after flash-reading the Lt Commander's file. "Although in my experience Humans usually find a way to complicate matters."

"And while the pair of you attempt to foment revolution among the downtrodden, I shall be working to keep both Earth sphere and the Indroma Solidarity from sending in their fleets. The imponderables of the Great Harbour are too great and some of the surviving accounts are too horribly suggestive to take the risk of triggering full-scale hostilities. The complications would be..."

The Construct paused as clusters of symbols began to pulse and slow all over the Zarl drone's battered hull. Cold blue flashes of light were visible inside the crowded interior. The Construct retracted its questing tentacles with alacrity just before most of the gaping panels slid or flipped shut. A strident bellow, half deep brazen roar, half rasping howl, blasted out at shattering volume. The Zarl drone tore free of the cradle's perfunctory restraints, rose up and whipped round to bear down on Rensik Estemil.

Rensik's defences surged into battle-readiness. With all tac-combatives ramped up to optimal, the initial moves and countermoves of sensor probes, feint targetings and shield shifts were taking place in fractions of a second. Rensik's sensors were also picking up a cascade of energy-state changes from within the Zarl machine which revealed previously undetected arrays of hideously powerful weaponry. Sections of its carapace were bulging to permit the extrusion of barrel snouts and to create launcher apertures while Rensik readied his own defences, starkly aware of how outgunned he had suddenly become but unwilling to back down...

And just when a convulsion of destruction seemed inevitable, the cryptic symbols glowing all over the Zarl drone's hull faded and died away. There was a chorus of muffled clunks, the war machine wobbled in mid-air for an instant then fell to the floor with a loud, sharp thud, rocked back and forth a couple of times and was still.

Rensik scanned it, found no energy sources, no datastream activity, nothing apart from vestigial ionisation around four points on the hull.

"Excellent!" said the Construct, drifting in closer. "Most informative."

It took Rensik no time at all to figure it out.

"I see. So you decided to unleash this grisly old killing machine, knowing that it would go for the most threatening target present – me. But all the time you had a cut-out of some kind rigged and ready..."

"A specifically exotic ultrafield, generated between four nodes previously attached to the drone carapace," the Construct said. "It scrambles coherent energy patterns, which effectively deactivated our antiquated friend here. Sometimes only a live trial can reveal the subject's essential nature."

"So glad to be of help."

"You have and will be again, I have no doubt. You should leave now. The shimmership is prepped and ready for you in Bay 14 – taking into account the ascent through hyperspace to the prime continuum, you should reach the vicinity of the Human home system in under nineteen hours. High-level approval has been granted so Brock's commanders will have received notice of her secondment to the joint mission by the time you arrive."

Even as the Construct finished the sentence a trio of caltrop-like lifter modules glided into the gazebo, fixed themselves to the Zarl drone, which then rose from the floor and in one smooth movement returned to the cradle.

"Safe journey," the Construct said as it resumed its study, flexing tentacle tips tugging open panels and hatches.

It certainly seems more talkative than before, Rensik thought as he left the gazebo and headed for the vehicle bays. *Still just as maddeningly eccentric, but definitely chattier...*

introducing

If you enjoyed
NEMESIS GAMES,
look out for

FORSAKEN SKIES

by D. Nolan Clark

Sometimes the few must stand against the many.

From the dark, cold void came an unknown force.

Their target: a remote moon, the quiet enclave of a religious sect intent on distancing themselves from mankind and pursuing a path of piety and peace.

If they have any chance at survival they must bring together a ragtag group of pilots any way they can. But the best they can get might not be good enough.

Part One: Hot Jupiter

1.

Flying down a wormhole was like throwing yourself into the center of a tornado, one where if you even brushed the walls you would be obliterated down to subatomic particles before you even knew it happened.

Racing through a wormhole at this speed was suicide. But the kid wouldn't slow down.

Lanoe thumbed a control pad and painted the yacht's backside with a communications laser. A green pearl appeared in the corner of his vision, with data on signal strength rolling across its surface. "Thom," he called. "Thom, you've got to stop this. I know you're scared, I know—"

"I killed him! I can't go back now!"

Lanoe muted the connection and focused for a second on not getting himself killed. The wormhole twisted and bent up ahead, warped where it passed under some massive gravity source, probably a star. Side passages opened in every direction, split by the curvature of space-time. Lanoe had lost track of where, exactly, they were—they'd started back at Xibalba but they could be a hundred light-years away by now. They could theoretically be on the wrong end of the universe.

The yacht up ahead was still accelerating. It was a sleek spindle of darkness against the unreal light of the tunnel walls, all black carbon fiber broken only by a set of airfoils like flat wings spaced around its thruster. At his school Thom had a reputation as some kind of hotshot racer—he was slated to compete in next year's Earth Cup—and Lanoe had seen how good a pilot the kid was as he chased him down. He was still surprised when Thom twisted around on his axis of flight and kicked in his maneuvering jets, nearly reversing his course and sending the yacht careening down one of the side tunnels.

Maybe he'd thought he could escape that way. Shake his tail.

For all the kid's talent, though, Lanoe was Navy trained. He knew a couple tricks they never taught to civilians. Like the fact that inside a wormhole, in seventeen dimensional space, you could turn yourself inside out and pull a turn tighter than a Poly's purse. He squeezed his eyes shut as all his panels lit up red but when he looked again he was right back on the yacht's tail. He thumbed for the comms laser again and when the green pearl popped up he said, "Thom, you can't outfly me. We need to talk about this. Your dad is dead, yes. We need to think about what comes next. Maybe you could tell me why you did it—"

But the green pearl was gone. Thom had burned for another course change and surged ahead. He'd pulled out of the maze of wormspace and back into the real universe, up ahead at another dip in the space-time curve.

Lanoe goosed his engine and followed. He burst out of the wormhole throat and into searing red light that burned his eyes.

Centrocor freight hauler 4519 approaching on vector 7,4,-32.

Wilscon dismantler ship Angie B, *you are deviating from course by .02. Advise.*

Traffic control, this is Angie B, *we copy. Burning to correct.*

The whispering voices of the autonomic port monitors passed across Valk's consciousness without making much of an impression.

Orbital traffic control wasn't an exacting job. It didn't pay well, either. Valk didn't mind so much. There were fringe benefits. For one, as the only person allowed inside the cramped work space, he was perfectly alone. He valued his privacy. Moreover, at the vertex between two limbs of the Hexus there was no gravity. It helped with the pain, a little. Ever since the accident, even the slightest weight on his flesh was too much.

His arms floated before him, his fingers twitching at keyboards that weren't really there. Lasers tracked his fingertip movements and converted them to data. Screens all around him pushed information in through his eyes, endless columns of numbers and tiny graphical displays he could largely ignore.

The Hexus sat at the bottom of a deep gravity well, a place where dozens of wormhole tunnels came together, connecting all twenty-three worlds of the local sector. A thousand vessels came through the Hexus every day, to offload cargo, to undertake repairs, just so the crews could stretch their legs for a minute on the way to their destinations. Keeping all those ships from colliding with each other, making sure they landed at the right docking berths, was the kind of job computers were built for, and the Hexus's autonomics were very, very good at it. Valk's job was to simply be there in case something happened that needed a human decision. If a freighter demanded priority mooring, for instance, because it was hauling hazardous cargo. Or if somebody important wanted the kid-glove treatment. It didn't happen all that often.

Traffic, this is Angie B. *We're on our way to Niraya. Thanks for your help.*

Civilian drone entering protected space. Redirecting.

Centrocor freight hauler 4519 at two thousand km, approaching Vairside docks.

Vairside docks report full. Redirect incoming traffic until 18:22.

Baffin Island docks report can take six more. Accepting until 18:49.

Unidentified vehicle exiting throat. No response to ping.

Unidentified vehicle exiting throat. No response to ping.

Maybe it was the repetition that made Valk swivel around in his work space. He called up a new display with imaging of the wormhole throat, thirty million kilometers away. The throat itself looked like a sphere of perfect glass, distorting the stars behind it. Monitoring buoys with banks of floodlights and sensors swarmed around it, keeping well clear of the opening to wormspace. The newcomers were so small it took a second for Valk to even see them.

But there—the one in front was a dark blip, barely visible except when it occluded a light. A civilian craft, built for speed by the look of it. Expensive as hell. And right behind it—there—

"Huh," Valk said, a little grunt of surprise. It was an FA.2 fighter, cataphract class. A cigar-shaped body, one end covered in segmented carbonglas viewports, the other housing a massive thruster. A double row of airfoils on its flanks.

Valk had been a fighter pilot himself, back before his accident. He knew the silhouette of every cataphract and carrier scout that had even flown. There had been a time when he saw FA.2s everywhere, when they were the Navy's favorite theater fighter. But that had been decades ago. Who was flying such an antique?

Valk tapped for a closer view—and only then did he see the red lights flashing all over his primary display. The two newcomers were moving *fast*, a considerable chunk of the speed of light.

And they were headed straight towards the Hexus.

He called up a communications panel and started desperately pinging them, wanting to know what the hell they thought they were doing.

Light and heat burst into Lanoe's cockpit. Sweat burst out all over his skin. His suit automatically wicked it away but it couldn't catch all the beads of sweat popping out on his forehead. He swiped a virtual panel near his elbow and his viewports polarized, switching down to near opaque blackness. It still wasn't enough.

There was a very good reason you didn't shoot out of a wormhole throat at this kind of speed. Wormhole throats tended to be very close to very big stars.

He could barely see—afterimages flickered in his vision, blocking out all the displays on his boards. He had a sense of a massive planet dead ahead but he couldn't make out any details. He tapped at display after display, trying to get some telemetry data, desperate for any information about where he was.

Then he saw the Hexus floating right in front of him. Fifty kilometers across, a vast hexagonal structure of concrete and foamsteel, like a giant dirty snowflake. Geryon, he thought. The Hexus orbited the planet Geryon, a bloated gas giant that circled a red giant star. That explained all the light and heat, at least. Damn. The kid had brought him to Geryon.

He tried to raise Thom again with his comms laser but the green pearl wouldn't show up in his peripheral vision. Little flashes of green came from his other eye and he realized he was being pinged by the Hexus. He thumbed a panel to send them his identifying codes but didn't waste any time talking to them directly.

The Hexus was getting bigger, growing at an alarming rate. "Thom," he called, whether the kid could hear him or not, "you need to break off. You can't fly through that thing. Thom! Don't do it!"

His vision had cleared enough that he could just see the yacht, a dark spot visible against the brighter skin of the station. It looked like Thom was going to fly straight through the Hexus. At first glance it looked like there was plenty of room—the hexagon was wide open in its middle—but that space was full of freighters and liners and countless drones, a bewilderingly complex interchange of ships jockeying for position, heading to or away from docking facilities, ships being refueled by tenders, drones checking heat shields or scraping carbon out of thruster cones. If Thom went through there it would be like firing a pistol into a crowd.

Lanoe cursed under his breath and brought up his weapon controls.

Centrocor freight hauler 4519 requesting berth at Vairside docks.

Vairside docks report full. Redirect incoming traffic until 18:22.

In twenty-nine seconds the two unidentified craft were going to streak right through the center of the Hexus, moving fast enough to obliterate anything in their way. If there was a collision, the resulting debris would have enough energy to tear the entire station apart. Hundreds of thousands of people would die.

Valk worked fast, moving from one virtual panel to the next, dismissing displays and opening new ones. His biggest display showed the trajectory of the two newcomers superimposed on a diagram of every moving thing inside the Hexus. Tags on each object showed relative velocities, mass and inertia quantities, collision probabilities.

Those last showed up in burning red. Valk had to find a way to get each of them to turn amber or green before the newcomers blazed right through the Hexus. That meant moving every ship, every tiny drone, one by one—computing a new flight path for each craft that wouldn't intersect with any of the others.

If he moved this liner here—redirected this drone swarm to the far side of the Hexus—if he ordered this freighter to make a correction burn of fourteen milliseconds—he rotated this dismantler ship on its long axis—

One of the assholes finally responded to his identification requests, but he didn't have time to look. He swiped that display away even while he used his other hand to order a freighter to fire its positioning jets.

Civilian drone entering protected space. Redirecting.

Centrocor freight hauler 4519 requesting berth at Vairside docks.

The synthetic voices were like flies buzzing around inside Valk's skull. That freight hauler was a serious pain in the ass—it was by far the largest object still inside the ring of the Hexus, the craft most likely to get in the way of the incoming yacht.

Valk would gladly have sent the thing burning hard for a distant parking orbit. It was a purely autonomic vessel, without even a pilot onboard, basically a giant drone. Who cared if a little cargo didn't make it to its destination in time? But for some reason its onboard computers refused to obey his commands. It kept demanding to be routed to a set of docks that weren't even classified for freight craft.

He pulled open a new control pad and started sending override codes.

The freighter responded instantly.

Instructed course will result in distress to passengers. Advise?

Passengers?

Up ahead the traffic inside the ring of the Hexus scattered like pigeons from a cat, but still there were just too many ships and drones in there, too many chances for a collision. Thom hadn't deviated even a fraction of a degree from his course. In a second or two it would be too late for him to break off—at this speed he wouldn't be able to burn hard enough to get away.

On Lanoe's weapons screen a firing solution popped up. He could hit the yacht with a disruptor. One hit and the yacht would be reduced to tiny debris, too small to do much damage when it rained down on the Hexus. His thumb hovered over the firing key—but even as he steeled himself to do it, a second firing solution popped up.

A ponderous freighter hung there, right in the middle of the ring. Right in the middle of Thom's course.

It was an ugly ship, just a bunch of cargo containers clamped to a central boom like grapes on a vine. It had thruster packages on either end but nothing even resembling a crew capsule.

Lanoe had enough weaponry to take that thing to pieces.

He opened a new communications panel and pinged the Hexus. "Traffic control, you need to move that freighter right now."

The reply came back instantly. At least somebody was talking to him. "FA.2, this is Hexus Control. Can't be done. Are you in contact with the unidentified yacht? Tell that idiot to change his trajectory."

"He's not listening," Lanoe called back. Damn it. Thom was maybe five seconds from splattering himself all over that ugly ship. "Control, move that freighter—or I'll move it for you."

"Negative! Negative, FA.2—there are people on that thing!"

What? That made no sense. A freight hauler like that would be controlled purely by autonomics. But in Lanoe's head the moral calculus was already working itself out. People—meaning more than one.

If he killed Thom, who he knew was a murderer, it would save multiple innocent lives.

He reached again for the firing key.

There had to be an answer. There had to be.

Instructed course would result in distress to passengers. Advise?

Valk could see six different ways to move the freighter. Every single one of them meant firing its main thrusters for a hard burn. Accelerating it at multiple gees.

If he did that, anybody inside the freighter would be reduced to red jelly. Unlike passenger ships, the cargo ship didn't carry an inertial sink. The people in it would have no protection from the sudden acceleration.

Centrocor freight hauler 4519 requesting berth at Vairside docks.

The ship was too stupid to know it was about to be smashed to pieces. Not for the first time he wished he could switch off the synthetic voices that reeled off pointless information all around him. He opened a new screen and studied the freighter's schematics. There were maneuvering thrusters here, and positioning jets near the nose, but they wouldn't be able to move the ship fast enough, there were emergency retros in six different locations, and explosive bolts on the cargo containers—

Yes! He had it. "FA.2," he called, even as he opened a new control pad. "FA.2, do not fire!" He tapped away at the pad, his fingers aching as he moved them so quickly.

Instructed action may cause damage to Centrocor property. Advise?

"I advise you to shut up and do what I say," Valk told the freighter. That wasn't what it was looking for, though. He looked down, saw a green virtual key hovering in front of him, and stabbed at it.

Out in the middle of the ring, the freight hauler triggered the explosive bolts on all of its port side cargo containers at once. The long boxes went tumbling away with aching slowness, blue and yellow and red oblongs dancing outward on their own trajectories. Some smashed into passing drones, creating whole new clouds of debris. Some bounced off the arms of the Hexus, obliterating against its concrete, the goods inside thrown free in multicolored sprays.

On Valk's screens a visual display popped up showing him the chaos. The yacht was a tiny dark needle lost in the welter of colorful boxes and smashed goods, moving so fast Valk could barely track it. But this was going to work, a gap was opening where the yacht could pass through safely, this was going to—

There was no sound but Valk could almost feel the crunch as one of the cargo containers just clipped one of the yacht's airfoils. The cargo container tore open, its steel skin splitting like it was a piece of overripe fruit. Barrels spilled out in a broad cloud of wild trajectories. The yacht was thrown into a violent spin as it shot through the Hexus and out the other side.

A split second later the FA.2 jinked around a flying barrel and burned hard to follow the yacht on its new course, straight down toward Geryon.

2.

Lanoe had to lean over hard into a tight bank to avoid the swirl of cargo in the Hexus but he almost laughed as he worked his controls, throwing his stick to the left and then the right. Whoever was running traffic control back there was a genius.

He sobered up again almost instantly, when he saw where he was headed next. Thom had been thrown for a loop by a grazing collision and now he was falling out of the sky. Up ahead lay the broad disk of Geryon, a boiling hell-cauldron of a planet. Out of control and spinning, Thom couldn't fight the pull of its gravity. He was going to fall right into that mess.

Geryon was a gas giant, a world with no surface, just a near endless atmosphere. From a distance it looked like it was tearing itself apart from the inside out. It was banded with dark storms, nearly black, that hid an inner layer of incandescent neon. The buzzing red light streaked outward through every crack and gap in the cloud layer, rays of baleful effulgence spearing outward at the void.

Lanoe barely had time to get a look at the planet before the yacht pitched nose-first into its atmosphere. He burned after it, down into the topmost clouds. He tried to paint the kid again with the communications laser, not expecting a result. He didn't get one.

As he tore through the dark haze of the clouds he lost track of

Thom altogether. Then suddenly the fighter burst through the bottom of a wisp of cirrus and Lanoe wasn't in space anymore.

On every side, tortured clouds piled up around him in enormous thunderheads, whole towers and fortresses of cloud with ramparts and battlements that melted away into mist every time he tried to make out details. Rivers of dark blue methane coiled and bent around waves of atmospheric pressure.

The sheer scale of it was lost on him until he saw the yacht, a tiny dot well ahead of him. It shot through a streamer of mist that arched high overhead, but the streamer was just one tiny arm of a vast storm as big as an ocean on Earth. And that was just what Lanoe could see from inside the fighter, a minuscule valley of this world of clouds, a tiny fragment of a colossal gas giant.

The yacht was out of place in that vast cloudspace. A mote of dust on the storm. It was still tumbling, end over end—the kid hadn't regained control. Damn it.

At least atmospheric resistance had slowed them right down—maybe Lanoe could actually catch the kid now.

The green pearl in Lanoe's vision blinked back into existence, surprising him. The comms laser had reestablished contact.

"Thom," Lanoe called. "Thom, are you there? Are you okay?"

The kid sounded terrified when he replied. "I'm... I'm still alive."

"Damn it, Thom," Lanoe said. "What were you thinking back there? There were people on that freighter. You could have killed them."

It took a long while for Thom to reply. Maybe he was just struggling to pull out of his spin. Lanoe could see his attitude thrusters firing, jets of vapor that were lost instantly in the dark cloudscape.

When Thom did come back on the line he sounded calmer, but chastened. "I didn't know that."

Lanoe couldn't help but feel for Thom. When the kid had run for it, when he'd stolen the yacht and headed for the nearest wormhole, Lanoe had followed because he thought maybe, somehow, he could help. To the kid it must have looked like there was a fury on his tail. "Get control of your ship," Lanoe told him. Though honestly it looked like Thom had already done just that. The yacht had stabilized its flight, even with one damaged airfoil. The kid had skill, Lanoe thought. He had the makings of a legendary pilot. If he didn't die right here. "You all right?"

"I'm fine."

"Then let's think about how to keep you that way. Slow down and let's talk about this. Okay? First things first, we need to get out of this atmosphere. Let's head back to the Hexus. I can't promise people there will be happy to see you, but—"

"I'm not going back," Thom replied. "I'm never going back."

It should have been over by now.

It should have been quick and painless. He should have hit that freighter dead-on and that would have been that.

Thom realized his eyes were closed. That was stupid. You never closed your eyes when you were flying—you needed to be constantly aware of everything around you. He opened his eyes and laughed.

There was nothing to see out there. Black mist writhed across his viewports. His displays were all turning red, but who cared? That was kind of the point, wasn't it?

Just fade to black.

If only Lanoe would shut up and let him get on with it.

"There's no way forward here, Thom. If I have to shoot you to stop this idiotic chase, I will. Turn back now."

"Why would I do that?" Thom asked.

"Because right now I'm the only friend you have."

"You were my father's puppet. I know you'll take me back if I give you the chance."

"You're wrong, Thom. I just want to help."

Thom leaned back in his crash seat and tried to just breathe.

He was surrounded by expensive wooden fittings. His seat was upholstered in real leather. He couldn't help thinking the yacht would make a luxurious coffin.

Thom was—had been—the son of the planetary governor of Xibalba. He was used to a certain degree of luxury. He understood now how much of that he'd taken for granted. Nothing had ever been denied to him his whole life.

No one had ever bullied him in school—his father's bodyguards had seen to that. No one had ever said no to him as long as he could remember. But now Lanoe wouldn't just give up. Wouldn't just let him go.

It was infuriating.

Thom wondered why he didn't just switch off his comms panel. Block Lanoe's transmission. Maybe, he thought, he just wanted to hear another human voice before he ended this.

Even if he didn't want to hear what Lanoe had to say.

"I was just your father's escort pilot, Thom. I'm not here to avenge him. The Navy assigned me to work for him, but it was just a job. I never even liked him."

"I hated him," Thom replied, unable to resist. Maybe he wanted to justify what he'd done. "I always hated him."

"Well, that's in the past now," Lanoe said. "As is my job—I don't owe him anything now that he's dead. I came after you because believe it or not, I do like *you*. That's all. Please believe me."

"I can't," Thom said. "Lanoe, I'm sorry, but I can't trust anyone right now."

Over the line he could hear Lanoe sigh in frustration. "Why'd you even do it? Why kill him? In a year you would have been away at university. Away from him."

"You think so?" Thom said. "You don't know shit, Lanoe."

"So enlighten me."

Thom smiled at the black mist that surrounded him. He couldn't think of a good reason to lie, not now. "I wasn't going to uni. I wasn't going anywhere. He was sick. All that stress of his high-powered job just ate away at his heart. You know what they do, when your body gives out like that? They give you a new one."

"So he would have lived a little longer—"

"You still don't understand, do you? I wasn't born to be his heir."

When you were rich and powerful, you didn't have to worry about getting sick. You didn't have to make do with an artificial pump ticking away in your chest, or taking immunosuppressive drugs for the rest of your life. You didn't even have to worry about getting old.

No, not if you had a little forethought. Not if you could afford to have children. Kids whose neurology was a perfect match for your own.

The old man—Thom couldn't bear to call him "father" anymore—could have arranged for Thom to have an accident that left him brain-dead. Then he could have his own consciousness transferred into Thom's young, healthy body. It happened all the time in the halls of power. The legality was questionable but a lot of rules didn't apply to planetary governors.

"I was designed," Thom said. "Built to be his next body."

There was a long pause on the line, until Thom wondered if Lanoe had finally given up. No such luck. "I didn't know," Lanoe said finally.

"He had to die," Thom said. In his mind's eye he saw it all over again. Saw himself pick up the ancient dueling pistol. Felt it jump in his hand. The old man hadn't even had a chance to look surprised. "Do you understand now? I'm only twenty years old, and he was going to just throw away my consciousness. Kill me. I had to kill him if I wanted to live. And now I have to keep moving. For another thirty-six hours."

"Thirty-six hours?"

"His doctors will have stabilized his brain, even if the rest of him is dead. They can keep his consciousness viable that long. If they catch me before his brain really dies, they can still go ahead with the switch."

"Let me help, then," Lanoe said.

Thom closed his eyes again. Nobody could help him now.

He leaned forward on his stick. Brought the yacht's nose down until it was pointed right at the core of the planet. Opened his throttle all the way.

The yacht dove into a dark cloudbank, a wall of smoke thick enough to block Lanoe's transmission.

This would be over soon.

A rain of fine soot smashed against Lanoe's canopy as he dove straight down into the pressure and heat of Geryon's atmosphere. The clouds whipped past him and then they were gone and he stared down into the red glare of the neon layer.

He couldn't see the yacht—it was hidden behind that shimmering wall of fire. He spared a moment to check some of his instruments and saw just how bad it was out there. Over 2,000 degrees Kelvin. Atmospheric pressure hard enough to crush the fighter in microseconds. The FA.2 possessed enough vector field strength to hold that killing air back, according to its technical specifications. Even so, he was sure he could hear his carbonglas canopy crackle under the stress, feel the entire ship closing in on him as the pressure warped its hull. His inertial sink held him tight in his seat as the ship rocked and trembled in the turbulent air.

If the fighter was in that much distress, could the kid hold up at all? Lanoe had no idea what kind of defensive fields the yacht carried. It was possible that the next time he saw Thom the kid would be a crumpled ball of carbon fiber, tumbling slowly as it fell toward the center of the planet.

Yet when his airfoils carried him rattling and hissing through the floor of the neon layer, he saw the yacht dead ahead, still intact, still hurtling downwards on a course that went nowhere good. There was nothing but murk down there, pure hydrogen under so much pressure it stopped acting like a gas and turned into liquid metal. No ship ever built could handle that kind of strain for more than a few minutes.

Lanoe didn't know if even comms lasers could cut through the dark, swirling mess, but then the green pearl in the corner of his vision appeared he opened the transmission immediately. "Thom," he said. "Thom—is this what you want? Did we just come here so you could commit suicide?"

There was no reply.

All over Lanoe's panels, red lights danced and flickered. Lanoe couldn't do this much longer, not if he hoped to get back to space in one piece.

He set his teeth and sped after the yacht.

Everything shook and strained and groaned. The wooden veneer on the console in front of Thom creaked and then split down the middle, a jagged crack running across his instrument displays. So close now.

The carbon fiber hull of the yacht couldn't take this pressure or this heat. The ship's vector fields were the only thing keeping Thom alive. If they failed—or if he switched them off—it would be over before he even knew what had happened. The ship would collapse around him, crushing his flesh, his bones. His blood would boil and then vaporize. His eyes would—

A sudden loud pop behind him made Thom yelp in surprise and terror. Broken glass splattered across his viewports and yellow liquid dripped down the front of his helmet. Dear God, was this how it happened? Was that cerebrospinal fluid? Was his head caving in?

No. No—the fizzy liquid running across his vision was champagne.

Behind the pilot's seat was a tiny cargo cabinet. There had been a bottle of champagne back there, put there by the old man's servants for when Thom won his next race. Wine made from grapes actually grown in the soil of Earth. That bottle had been almost as expensive as the yacht itself.

The bottle had been under pressure already—the added strain of Geryon's crushing grip had been too much for it.

An uncontrollable laugh ripped its way up through Thom's throat. He shook and bent over his controls and tears pooled in his eyes until his suit carefully wicked them away. He had been scared by a champagne bottle going off. That hadn't happened since he was a child.

Scared.

Fear—now that was funny. He hadn't expected to be afraid at this point. Thom was no coward. But now he was shivering. His heart raced—he could feel adrenaline throbbing through his veins.

He hadn't expected to be scared. He'd never been a coward before.

He looked out through his viewports at the dark haze ahead, at the center of the planet, and it was so huge. So big beyond anything he could comprehend.

Suddenly he couldn't breathe.

"Lanoe?" the kid said. "Lanoe, I think I made a mistake."

Lanoe clamped his eyes shut. There was nothing to see, anyway, except the tail of the yacht. "Yeah? You're just getting that now?"

"I'm sorry I dragged you into this," Thom said. The transmission was full of noise, words compressed down until the kid's voice sounded like a machine talking. "Something's gone wrong. Lanoe—I thought I could do this. But now—"

"That's your survival instinct kicking in. Self-preservation, right? Don't fight that urge, Thom. It's there for a reason."

"I think maybe it's too late. Oh, God."

Lanoe shook his head. The kid had some guts to have gotten this far, but what a goddamned idiot he was. "Pull up. Come on, Thom, just pull up and get out of here."

"I can't see anything—I don't even know which way is up!"

"The Hexus. Look for the Hexus. Its beacons should be all over your nav display—latch on to them. Pull up, Thom. Come on! Don't go any lower."

"I'm trying... my controls are so sluggish. Lanoe... I."

The green pearl kept rotating, numbers streaming across its surface. The connection hadn't been cut off. The kid had just stopped talking.

"Shit," Lanoe said. He started easing back on his control stick. Fed fuel to all of his retros and positioning rockets, intending to swing around and punch for escape velocity.

But then the kid spoke again.

"I don't want to die," Thom said.

Lanoe opened his eyes. He saw the yacht ahead of him. Its nose had come around, a little. The kid was doing his best. All of his jets were firing in quick stuttering bursts as he tried to check his downward velocity. If he could get his tail pointed down he could fire his main thruster and head back toward space.

But the nose was swinging around way too slow.

Lanoe saw why right away—it was that broken airfoil, the one he'd smashed against a cargo container. Airfoils were deadweight in space, but in an atmosphere like this they were vital, and Thom was running one short. That was going to kill him.

No. Lanoe wouldn't accept that.

"Listen," he said. "You can do this. Take it easy, don't waste any burns."

"I'm trying," the kid told him.

"Get your nose up, that's the main thing."

"I know what to do!"

"I'm going to tell you anyway. Get your nose up. Come on, kid!"

The yacht had fallen so far down Lanoe could barely see it. How much longer would the kid's fields hold out? They must be eating up all his power just to keep the yacht from being crushed. That extra energy could make a real difference, though.

"Thom—transfer some power from your vector field to your thrusters."

"I'll be splattered," the kid pointed out.

He was probably right. But if he didn't get his nose up, he was going to die anyway.

"Do it," Lanoe shouted. "Transfer five percent—"

One whole side of the yacht caved in. Lanoe felt sick as he watched the carbon fiber hull crumple and distort.

But in the same moment the yacht swung around all at once, and had its nose pointed straight up. Its main thruster engaged in a burst of fire and it shot past Lanoe's fighter, moving goddamned fast.

Lanoe's own fields were complaining. He was used to the fighter's alarms, its chimes and whistles and screaming klaxons. He ignored them all. He sent the FA.2 into a tight spin until his own nose was pointing up, then punched for full burn.

Ahead of him the wall of buzzing red neon came and went. The clouds of soot and dark blue methane. For a split second he saw blue sky overhead, pure, thin air, and then it turned black and the stars came out.

Ahead of him the yacht burned straight out into the night, standing on its tail.

In the distance, past the kid's nose, Lanoe could see the Hexus. If they could just make it there, maybe this chase could end. Maybe they could both come out of this okay.

"Thom," he called. "Thom, come in."

There was no green pearl in the corner of his vision. Lanoe came up alongside the yacht and saw just how much of it had collapsed. The whole forward compartment had imploded, all of the viewports shattered down to empty frames.

"Oh, hellfire, Thom," Lanoe whispered. "I'm sorry. I'm so goddamned sorry."